MAGNIFICENT PASSAGE

Desire's Masquerade

"Do you really fancy yourself in love with this Jason fellow?" Hawk asked her.

Mandy thought she saw a quick flash of regret, as if he wanted to call back the question. She wished he could.

Taking a deep breath, she closed her eyes for a moment, trying to compose herself. She was forced to continue the lie. If he suspected—even for a moment—that she was not really the governor's daughter, neither she nor her cousin would have the chance for a new life . . .

"Why, of course I love Jason—"

"Love . . ." he snarled. "You wouldn't know the meaning of the word." And then he hauled her roughly against him and bent over her, crushing his mouth against her lips . . .

❈❈❈

"Kat Martin is the best young historical writer I've read in a decade. Bravo!"
—Fern Michaels

MAGNIFICENT PASSAGE

KAT MARTIN

PAGEANT BOOKS

Publisher's Note: This is a work of fiction. The characters, incidents, and dialogues are products of the author's imagination and are not to be construed as real. Any resemblance to actual events or persons, living or dead, is entirely coincidental.

PAGEANT BOOKS
225 Park Avenue South
New York, New York   10003

PAGEANT and colophon are trademarks of the publisher

Cover artwork by Franco Accornero

Printed in the U.S.A.

First Pageant Books printing: September, 1988

10 9 8 7 6 5 4 3 2 1

To my husband, Larry, who got me started and helped me with the research. To my best friend, Diana Kerr, who convinced me I could do it. And to my agent, Sherry Robb, and the wonderful people at Pageant Books who made it happen.

MAGNIFICENT PASSAGE

Prologue

✦✦✦✦

SHE WASN'T SUPPOSED to be here—in front of the parade field near the soldiers' barracks. Truth to tell, she wasn't even allowed this far from the cottage. But she'd wanted a little fresh air, and when the wagon rolled in, the jangle of harness, the rumble of wheels, and the tall, sandy-haired man at the reins had captured her attention.

The man halted the team of horses some distance from Commander Russel's headquarters, set the brake, and tied the reins. He climbed from the seat, his broad shoulders squared determinedly. When the soldiers approached, he spoke to them only briefly, gesturing to the rear of the wagon, then strode purposefully into the low adobe building.

1

Samantha Ashton watched as the soldiers clustered around the wagon and a burly corporal lifted the tarpaulin thrown over something in the back. His face looked pale as he walked away. Two more soldiers lifted the canvas, stood momentarily transfixed, then hastily dropped the tarp. They cautioned several approaching women, who hurried away, whispering, without a backward glance.

More and more, Mandy—for that was what her friends called her—became curious about the wagon.

The day was blustery and cloudy and carried a bitter chill. Like thin knives, it sliced the air. Mandy pulled her serviceable gray wool cloak tighter about her navy blue homespun dress, but the wind continued to tug at the heavy fabric. She'd tucked her chestnut hair into the broad-billed bonnet she wore, so only a small portion of her face was exposed to the biting cold. Standing beside a post in front of Johnson's General Mercantile, she was close enough to watch the activity but far enough away to remain unnoticed. Few people traveled the dirt street, and fewer still paid her any heed.

A second group of men neared the wagon, having been summoned by the first, and again they seemed unable to resist the urge to look. One man walked quickly around the side of the building, his face a decided shade of green. More soldiers looked in the wagon, but they all left quickly. In minutes the cluster of men had disappeared, leaving only the wagon—and its contents—to beckon her forward.

Mandy had always been curious—a trait she was certain she'd picked up from her grandmother. Grandma Ashton always said curiosity never killed the cat, it just made him smarter. Now Mandy's curiosity was so overwhelming it felt like an itch.

She straightened her shoulders and marched to where the wagon sat forlornly near the edge of the field, nibbling her lower lip nervously. If her father found out, he'd be mad as a hornet. But, she reasoned, he was mad at her half the time anyway.

As she neared the wagon, tiny beads of perspiration dampened the hair at her temples. She caught a faint whiff of something foul, though the wind blew most of the odor away. She could see the rough-hewn sides of the wagon, the edge of the canvas hanging out the back. Just a few more steps and she'd be there.

A wide, firm hand grabbed her arm and pulled her up short, turning her toward him at the same time.

"I wouldn't do that if I were you, miss." The sandy-haired man gripped her arm tightly. His jaw was set, his face grim beneath his broad-brimmed hat. He was dressed ruggedly in a fringed buckskin shirt, snug-fitting buckskin breeches, and moccasins instead of boots. His proper use of English surprised her.

"Why not?" she asked stiffly, annoyed at being caught. He continued to hold her arm, his grip unyielding. He seemed a hard sort, even though he spoke well, and a sudden tremor of apprehension snaked up her spine.

As if sensing her fear, he let go of her.

"It's not a sight for a lady," he said flatly, his dark eyes cold.

The words sent sparks flying in her head. *Not a sight for a lady.* Mandy was so sick of being "a lady" she could spit. It was all she'd heard from her father for the past three years—ever since her mother died.

She eyed the stranger curiously. "And tell me, sir, just what would you know about being *a lady?*"

He smiled in spite of himself, and Mandy glimpsed even, white teeth. He was a big man, muscular, with powerful arms and a thick neck. But his waist was lean and his hips were narrow. His tanned face told of hours of work in the sun.

"As you say, miss, not a whole lot. But I'm telling you for your own good, go home where you belong."

Home where you belong. To Mandy, those were fighting words. Her father had kept her all but locked in the house for the past three years. "Stay home, Mandy. You'll be safe there. A woman's place is in the home." She wanted to ride horses, be out-of-doors, maybe even go fishing like she used to before her mother died. Of course she'd only been a child then—a tomboy, her mother had said. Now that she was older, she wasn't supposed to enjoy those things anymore. But she did.

Yesterday she'd turned sixteen. Now she wanted to go to dances and wear pretty clothes, but even that was forbidden. Looking in the back of that wagon became the most important thing in Mandy's life. It was a gesture of freedom, a step toward womanhood.

"I think that's my business, sir, not yours." She stared at him determinedly. "Unless, of course, whatever's in the wagon belongs to you?"

"Not hardly. I just happened to be in the wrong place at the right time."

"Then unless you're going to stop me, I'm going to look."

"I've got no right to stop you," he said. "But I'm telling you, there's a dead man in that wagon, and a dead man's no sight for a woman."

Now Mandy was determined. She lifted her chin defiantly and brushed past him, heading toward the wagon.

He didn't move.

She turned to look at him just before she lifted the tarp, and saw something unreadable in his eyes. Then she turned back and, with a bravado she suddenly didn't feel, lifted the canvas.

She swallowed the bile that rose in her throat. Her hand clutched the canvas so hard her knuckles turned white. The color drained from her face, leaving her cold and clammy, but she couldn't let go. Lying on the floor of the wagon, a once-blond soldier grinned through a slash where his mouth had been. Most of his scalp was gone, leaving only a fringe of hair along each side of his head. Dark empty holes stared up at her instead of eyes. His body was nude, but she wasn't offended by his sex—no male organs remained. Every inch of his thin, bloodless body was spiked with tiny wooden splinters, which had been set on fire and burned down into his flesh. His ankles and wrists were gouged so deeply from the leather thongs binding him that portions of bone were exposed.

The world spun before her. She dropped the canvas and turned toward the big man, who was walking rapidly in her direction. He cursed beneath his breath, but she couldn't make out the words. Her stomach rolled, and it was all she could do not to be sick. Her vision was growing narrower by the minute. She looked up at the man and swayed against him.

"It was Davey," she whispered. "My friend, Davey Wil . . ." The last syllable refused to leave her throat as she slumped into blackness.

Travis Langley cursed himself for the fool he was. He scooped the young girl into his arms and carried her toward the surgeon's distant quarters. She was light as a feather, a mere slip of a girl. *Why hadn't he stopped her?* He knew what would happen; even a battle-hardened soldier had been known to pass out cold from a sight like that. Truth was he hadn't really expected her to do it. Most women would have run, just from the smell. And he certainly hadn't expected her to know the soldier. The boy wasn't even stationed at Fort Laramie, or so Colonel Russel had told him.

He gritted his teeth, cursing himself again as he headed along the dirt street, carrying the tiny girl against his chest. Several soldiers eyed him curiously as he walked toward the surgeon's quarters, though no one attempted to interfere. He seemed to have a knack for keeping people at arm's length. Both his clothes and the years he spent with the Cheyenne set him apart from most folks. They never quite felt comfortable in his presence.

He glanced down at the girl in his arms. He couldn't see much of her face beneath the bonnet, and her thick chestnut hair covered a goodly portion of what did show. It did little to enhance her looks. He had the feeling she might be pretty if she were dressed in the right clothes, her face uncovered, and her hair worn loose instead of hidden in her bonnet.

The surgeon's door stood open a crack, so Langley pushed it wide with a moccasined foot.

"Oh, dear me!" The short, round-faced doctor dropped his pencil and rose from his desk, scurrying toward the girl like a flustered mouse.

"She's not hurt. She's just fainted. She had the misfortune to see that dead soldier in the back of my wagon. Seems it turned out to be someone she knew."

"Bring her over here. I'll see that she's taken care of." The surgeon eyed the man's rugged clothes with a hint of disdain. "She's Captain Ashton's daughter. He'll be mighty upset when he finds out what she's been up to. He's a real tyrant when it comes to Samantha."

Travis smiled to himself. He could just imagine how the good captain would take to his daughter being carried around the fort in the arms of a man like him.

"Thank you for your help," the doctor said, dismissing him curtly.

Travis touched the brim of his wide felt hat. "I'm sure she's in capable hands, but I'll stop by before I leave just to be sure she's all right." He backed through the door, closing it softly behind him. He felt more than a little guilty. He should have stopped her, and he damn well knew it. But she'd challenged him— something few men ever did—and she was barely more than a child. He regretted his behavior, but there was little he could do about it now.

He walked purposefully back toward the wagon. He'd be glad when Fort Laramie was just a speck in the distance, a landmark over his shoulder. He was eager to be on his way back to California—and home.

The room swirled around her, fading in and out, but her mind lingered in the past. She had been thirteen when she'd last seen Davey. Towheaded, freckle-faced Davey Williams had been her best friend before his family had moved away.

Mandy wrinkled her nose at the acrid smell filling her nostrils. She bolted upright, trying to get her bearings and avoid the loathsome odor.

"Where am I?"

"Just relax, Miss Ashton. I'm afraid you've had a bit of a shock."

She recognized Doc Milliken's squeaky, high-pitched voice as he capped the ammonia smelling salts. She leaned back against the pillow. The narrow cot felt solid beneath her, and she welcomed its firm support.

"Yes, I . . . I remember now." She shuddered, closed her eyes, and felt a wave of nausea.

"Try not to think about it, Miss Ashton. It's all over now."

Large tears rolled down her cheeks. "It was Davey," she told him. "Davey Williams. You should have seen what the Indians did to him." She turned her face away and sobbed softly into the pillow.

The sound of the door opening distracted her. With an effort, she sniffed back fresh tears.

The tall, sandy-haired man walked to her bedside. "Are you all right?" he asked, kneeling by the cot, his voice a little husky.

She nodded and wiped at her tears. He handed her a kerchief.

"I'm afraid I owe you an apology, Miss Ashton. I should have stopped you." His brown eyes filled with concern. "I just didn't think you'd really do it."

She smiled at him tremulously, surprised he had the courage to admit he was wrong.

"It wasn't your fault, Mr. . . .?"

"Langley. Travis Langley."

"It wasn't your fault, Mr. Langley. I should have listened to you. I don't know why I didn't. I guess I just wanted to prove something to myself."

"Did you?"

"Not really. But I guess it doesn't matter." She looked away.

"Maybe you'll have another chance one day," he said, drawing himself back up to his full height. His soft bedside manner disappeared, his brown eyes once more inscrutable. She felt a sudden chill as she watched him.

"Maybe," she agreed weakly. "Did you bring me here?"

He nodded absently, his mind, it seemed, already somewhere else now that he was certain of her safety.

"Thank you, Mr. Langley, for all you've done."

"You're welcome, Miss Ashton. Good luck with whatever it is you're trying to prove."

She smiled self-consciously and sat up, adjusting her bonnet, which was slightly askew but still firmly tied beneath her chin.

"Good-bye, Mr. Langley."

He touched the brim of his hat, backed through the door, and closed it softly behind him. He was a hard man, that one. Maybe even a dangerous one. He seemed to be the kind of man her father often warned her about.

Still, for the next few days she couldn't get him out of her mind. She wondered who he was, where he was from, and where he was going. She thought about him while her father railed at her and forbade her to leave the house for a week. She thought about him as she worked in her garden, trying unsuccessfully to blot the terrible image of Davey Williams from her mind. She thought about him at night before she fell asleep, though for the life of her she couldn't understand why.

Travis Langley, she discovered, was a man not easy to forget.

Chapter One

✦ ✦ ✦ ✦

JULY 20, 1868
FORT LARAMIE, DAKOTA TERRITORIES

SAMANTHA ASHTON TUCKED a stray tendril of chestnut hair into the prim bun at the back of her head and wished fervently there were something she could say to console her younger cousin.

It was the tenth day of frying temperatures, though a few puffs of clouds over the mountains hinted at relief. She'd left the window open to capture fortune's breeze, but the stifling heat left her perspiring beneath her high-necked brown muslin dress. She fanned herself futilely with an embroidered hankie and leaned against her straight-backed chair.

She and her cousin, Julia, were discussing Julia's future—for the tenth time that day—and Mandy was having trouble concentrating

13

on her cousin's heated words. Unconsciously, her glance strayed out the window.

As always this time of year, the bustling dirt streets were crowded with myriad people: emigrant families, complete with wagons, oxen, horses, children, and dogs; soldiers in dusty blue uniforms; and traders, some with squaws in tow.

In the fields beyond, the tall grass waving in the too-gentle breeze had long ago turned golden. A few deep gulleys that held the last precious drops of a recent summer shower were all that remained green. Three buff-colored antelope grazed peacefully. Only their black horns and white rumps against the golden hills betrayed their location.

Sighing wistfully and wishing she were outside somewhere instead of confined in her room, Mandy returned her attention to her cousin. Julia Ashton was petite and full-busted with wide green eyes and a teasing, ruby-lipped smile. Raised with wealth and position, she was spoiled and selfish but good-hearted, and she'd always valued Mandy's friendship.

Though she lived with her father in California, Julia had spent the year in Boston. She'd left her finishing school and come on the train to visit Mandy for the summer. They'd shared the small room that had been spartan before Julia's arrival and now was filled to overflowing with lacy underwear, bottles of perfume, dresses, hats, traveling suits, even a riding habit. Julia never traveled light. There was almost no space left between the rough-hewn walls of the cabin and Mandy's narrow, slatted bed with its trundle beneath, but Julia made use of every inch. She paced the room like a caged cat.

"Father's been trying to run my life for years," Julia said hotly, her slim arms akimbo. "But he's never succeeded, and he's not going to this time."

If Julia hadn't been so distraught, Mandy might have smiled. *She's every bit the governor's daughter*, Mandy thought. It was the way she always pictured her cousin—haughty and arrogant, wild, reckless, and passionately headstrong when convinced she was right. Storming about the room, Julia alternated between biting her bottom lip uncertainly and pressing both together in a determined line.

"I know how you must feel, Julia," Mandy said, getting caught up in Julia's indignation. "I know how much you love Jason. I wish there were something we could do."

"You can't know how I feel! You've never been in love. You've never even had a beau!"

The words stung like a slap. Mandy glanced away. More than a year older than her cousin, Mandy had never done more than dance with some of the local boys, and that had been at best a tolerable experience. A few young men, mostly soldiers, had attempted to court her, but her father always discouraged them. Of course that would all change one day, she told herself. She'd leave Fort Laramie and experience life, be her own person again—the way she used to be, before her mother died and her father became so strict and forbidding.

Julia stopped pacing and turned, her expression softer. "I'm sorry, Mandy. That was a rotten thing to say. I guess I'm just a little upset."

Mandy thought "upset" was a bit of an understatement.

Julia lifted a ruffled petticoat strewn across the bed and fingered the lace absently. "I wish I'd never written that letter to my father."

"Your father would have found out about Jason sooner or later. And when you didn't return to Boston, he'd have been worried sick. He'd probably have called out the cavalry and then you'd really have been in trouble."

Julia flashed a quick, uncertain smile. "I guess you're right," she said. She walked to Mandy's chair, sighing. "Someday, when you fall in love, you'll understand why I can't let Jason go. He's the most wonderful man I've ever met. He isn't like the others—and believe me, I ought to know! Jason's kind and considerate. He's charming—and handsome. He loves me and I love him!" She clenched her small fists and whirled away. "Damn it, Mandy, I won't go to California and leave him behind!"

Mandy wished things could be different. Uncle William had always been a good man, but an ambitious one. He'd had no time for his daughter, yet he'd always tried to do what was best for her. But Julia was stubborn and wild, her reputation notorious. Her escapades had made headlines all over the country. She was considered "a woman of legendary beauty," and men everywhere fell at her feet. Jason Michaels hadn't. Maybe that was why Julia had fallen in love with him.

"What about the way you're used to living?" Mandy asked, broaching a problem she was sure Uncle William had considered. "You've always had everything you want. How are you going to handle being an Army wife?"

"In a year I'll have my own money. Mama left me part of Grampa Whittington's estate. It's mine when I turn eighteen. Jason and I will want for nothing. And he's already put in for a transfer to the East. With his record, sooner or later he'll get it. Once Father accepts our marriage, he might even help Jason's career."

Julia threw back her shoulders and resumed her pacing. Her petticoats swirled widely with every turn. The floorboards creaked beneath her tiny feet as she marched impatiently back and forth.

"Why won't Father be reasonable? He and Mother were already married at my age."

"Your father is too much like mine," Mandy said. "He always thinks he knows what's best. He'll send men to bring you back and—"

"I won't go with them!"

Mandy studied her cousin's deepening scowl, Julia's fiery temper barely held in check. *She's so self-assured, so all-fired determined. Never afraid of anything or anyone.* Mandy felt a twinge of envy for her cousin's courage. She had spunk, spirit. She faced life head-on, took what she wanted. Never gave up.

As children they'd been best friends. Both their families had lived in Highland Falls, a small town in New York state, until Uncle William had moved his family to California and the Army had moved George Ashton and his family to the frontier.

Now she and Julia lived in two different worlds. Uncle William had become rich and powerful, had been elected governor of California. Mandy's father was content just being a soldier. He looked forward to achieving the rank of major one day, but that was the extent of his ambition.

"We've gone over every possibility, Julia. Even if you and Jason ran away they'd surely find you. Your father is powerful, and he's still your legal guardian."

"I don't care what Father is! He's not going to make me give Jason up." Julia's green eyes narrowed. Tiny gold flecks leaped like sparks, as if threatening to ignite the splintery log cabin. Her chin jutted forward at a familiar willful angle. She marched to the window, threw aside the crisp chintz curtains, and peered obstinately out onto the parade ground.

Mandy had seen that determined profile before, and it usually boded ill for someone. She wondered fleetingly just who would suffer this time and shrugged off a tiny warning voice.

"You have to think of Jason. If you do run away, your father might *never* accept the marriage. Instead of helping, he could ruin Jason's career."

Julia clenched her teeth. Tears of rage and frustration filled her green eyes, but she didn't speak.

Though Mandy had never been in love, she could easily imagine the heartbreak her cousin was suffering. She'd often fantasized about finding just the right man: Her father and mother had been terribly in love. Her father still hadn't recovered from her mother's death.

She stood up, wishing she could think of something comforting to say. Outside the window, two blue-capped Indian scouts sat stoically on their haunches, waiting for C troop to finish a close-order drill. Several ravens screeched loudly atop the chimney of Major Murphy's cabin, then flew away to inspect the roof of the whitewashed cabin next door.

Mandy thought of Julia's determination, her willingness to stand up to a man like the governor. How she wished she had the courage to stand up to her own father like that. But one stern look from her father's hard gray eyes and she withered.

The sound of clanging iron disrupted the stillness in the room. A blacksmith hammered a wheel back onto the axle of a worn covered wagon, the noise of his anvil piercing the air. Mandy's head began to throb in unison with the clanging iron.

Julia sniffed back tears with a bit more drama than necessary. "Jason says he's going to take a leave of absence. No one here at the fort will marry us, but we can cross the territorial line. I'll marry Jason under an assumed name. The marriage won't be legal, but if we can get some time alone together, maybe Father will worry about the scandal and let the marriage stand. I'm sure if he ever gets to know Jason, he'll give us his approval. Time, Mandy. Time is what we need."

Mandy hugged Julia protectively, trying to act as mature as her eighteen years would allow. She wondered enviously if she would ever be fortunate enough to love as her cousin did.

The sound of a man's heavy boots crunching against the gravel beside the house attracted their attention.

"Jason!" Julia flew to the sill and leaned out, taking the hand of the handsome Army officer who stood outside. His dark blue uniform was spotless, the brass buttons polished to a fine sheen.

"I'm on duty until eight," Jason Michaels said to Julia. "Maybe when I get off we could go for a walk." He smiled at her lovingly. The pleasure he felt in seeing her glittered in his blue eyes.

Mandy felt a lump in her throat. They looked so happy together. Such a perfect match. It just didn't seem right for Uncle William to keep them apart. Mandy was sure Uncle William didn't believe Julia really loved Jason, but Mandy believed it. She'd never seen her cousin so happy.

Though Julia had always been the life of every party, inside she had been lonely. If she lost Jason, she might be lonely forever. Mandy's heart felt leaden.

"Uncle George left this morning for a tour of duty at Fort Sedgewick," Julia told Jason. "Mrs. Evans, our next-door neighbor, is supposed to be our chaperone. She's been watching us like a jailer, but I'm sure a walk won't be considered a jailbreak." She smiled up at the tall lieutenant.

"I'll see you tonight, then," Jason said.

She nodded, leaned out, and kissed his cheek. She watched his receding figure until he disappeared from sight, then she turned her attention to Mandy.

"Mandy, there's something I need to discuss with you." She took a deep breath as if readying herself for a contest of wills, and Mandy shifted her weight nervously from one foot to the other. "Since I met Jason, I've discovered what I really want in life—a home, a real home, and a family. I want to marry Jason more than anything in the world. Please, Mandy. You've got to help me."

Mandy felt a tightness in her chest. "I wish I could, Julia, I truly do. If there were anything —anything at all, you know I would."

"I hoped it wouldn't come to this," Julia said, wringing her hands. She seemed a little nervous, her gaze a little hesitant. "There *is* something you could do. I've been thinking about it ever since I got Father's wire." She squared her shoulders in a gesture of determination.

"I didn't mention it before because I was certain we'd think of another way. Now time's running out, and we're all out of ideas."

"I can't imagine any possibility we've overlooked," Mandy said, sure there was very little chance of outwitting the governor. "But of course, if there is something . . ."

"You know I wouldn't ask you if there were any other way. I'm desperate, Mandy. Please, say you'll do it."

Mandy eyed her cousin suspiciously. Julia had always been able to talk anyone into anything. "What is it, Julia? What do you want me to do?" She watched her cousin's face carefully. Green eyes gleamed with mischief, leaving Mandy with an odd queasiness in the pit of her stomach.

"I want you to take my place," Julia announced. "I want you to pretend you are me."

"What?" Mandy clutched at the sill. One

hand crept to the base of her throat where she felt a rapid, fluttery pulse. "You can't possibly be serious! How can you even suggest such a thing? That's absolutely the craziest idea you've ever had."

"You can do it! I can teach you! We have the same color hair and eyes." Julia spun Mandy around to view her from every angle. "You're a little shorter, but they won't notice. Father hasn't seen you in years. He won't realize how much alike we've grown to look. It'll never cross his mind we could trade places."

"But I don't look like you—do I?" Mandy was more than a little flattered by the comparison. She had certainly never noticed the similarity. Now that she thought about it, both she and Julia did have similar facial features: well-defined cheekbones, full lips, a slightly upturned nose, and a clear complexion, though Julia's was a little darker. If she changed her appearance completely, changed her hair and clothes, they probably could look enough alike to fool a complete stranger—even one with a daguerreotype.

"But, Julia," Mandy argued, still unconvinced, "even if we do look alike, we certainly don't act alike. These men will have been told to expect a . . . a . . . ."

"Hellion?" her cousin suggested.

"Well, yes. . . . Not someone's who's . . . who's . . ."

"Quiet, reserved—and afraid of men."

"I'm not afraid of men! At least I don't think

I am. I guess I really haven't had much of a chance to find out. And you know I'm not really all that quiet—or reserved. I just act that way to humor Father."

"Then you'll do it!" Julia said, grinning broadly, pleased with herself.

"Of course not! I couldn't begin to fool those men."

"But that's the part I'll teach you! You're a good actress. You've been fooling your father for years—you just said so. Besides, I'll show you exactly what to do."

"Oh, Julia, I may not be as reserved as Father would like to believe, but I've never acted like you. I mean . . ."

"When we were younger, we weren't so different," Julia said. "You used to have plans, dreams. You used to let you hair hang loose and wear pretty clothes. You were even a little wild if I remember correctly—you used to ride like the wind, and build mud castles—and fish! Wouldn't you like to do those things again?"

Mandy fell silent. How many times had she sworn she'd leave Fort Laramie one day, leave her father's harsh rules, go out on her own, enjoy life the way she had before her mother died. She felt a stirring, an excitement she hadn't felt in years. The men would be returning Julia to California. California—the golden land. Anything could happen. People made new lives there, found the end of the rainbow.

Julia put her hands on Mandy's shoulders.

"You might actually learn to enjoy yourself again, have some fun for a change."

Mandy walked over to her narrow bed and sank down. How could she possibly do anything as insane as her cousin proposed? And yet, how could she pass up the opportunity of a lifetime? Her lifetime. Maybe the only opportunity she would ever have to change her life.

"Do you really think it would work?"

"Of course it'll work. We've got weeks before the men arrive, plenty of time for me to teach you everything you'll need to know. Besides, a lot of it will come back to you. All the social graces your mama taught you, you've just forgotten. As soon as you feel comfortable pretending to be me, Jason and I can leave."

Mandy's heart pounded. It couldn't possibly work, but maybe, just maybe. . . . She wanted to try, and not just for Julia's sake. At last, she would be free of her father's restraints!

She smiled up at her cousin and excitement surged through her veins. "Julia, I'll do it! Tell me exactly what you want me to do—and pray God is on our side."

Chapter Two

✦✦✦✦

"ANYBODY HERE NAME a' Langley? Travis Langley?"

A gray-whiskered old man pushed through the swinging doors. The saloon was noisy, crowded, and dark, even in the middle of the day. Smoke hovered in patches above dimly lit tables and the room smelled of beer and sweaty men.

Langley turned toward the door. "Who wants to know?" His deep voice carried easily above the clamor in the room. He straightened in his chair, rubbing an ache in the back of his neck.

He'd been playing poker for hours, winning a little, but mostly just unwinding from his last assignment. He and his partner, James Long, had delivered a payroll shipment for Jack Murdock's company and the delivery had been nothing but trouble. They'd shot two highwaymen, wounded both, then had to contend with getting the prisoners to the sheriff as well as delivering the money. He was damn glad it was over.

"Got a wire here from the Capitol. From the gov'nor hissef," the little man said. He looked wiry and spry, but ancient as the oaks, as if age had gnarled him like an old tree trunk, then left him to weather the years.

Langley slid his chair back, carefully laid his cards face down on the table, then moved toward the door and the grizzled old man. "I'm Langley."

"This here's fer a Mr. Long, too," the old man informed him, craning his leathery neck to meet Langley's gaze.

"Thanks." Langley flipped the old man a coin for his trouble. He opened the thin ivory envelope, scanned the message with a bit of curiosity, then started back to his table.

A buxom barmaid stepped in front of him, the long black ostrich plume in her hair brushing suggestively against the side of his face.

"Where you goin', handsome?" she asked. Her full bosom pressed tantalizingly against his chest. Reluctantly he pulled his gaze from the tantalizing swells and smiled into her pretty face. Her knee-length black and red lace dress left little to the imagination.

"You just get into town?" he asked. "I haven't seen you around." He took in the curve of her hip and the shapely leg propped on the chair to block his path.

She smiled up at him. "You'll be my first customer."

He grinned, gave her a baleful, appraising look, and shook his head. "Sorry, Red, maybe next time."

"You sure, handsome?" She twisted a slim finger in the fringe of his buckskin shirt.

"Business before pleasure," he told her. He stuffed a greenback into her cleavage.

She ran a hand seductively along the inside of his thigh.

A little reluctantly, he pulled away. "I'll be back," he promised.

She licked red lips, then turned away from him, smiling over her shoulder. Her blue eyes deepened in a disappointed pout.

With a teasing smile, he gave her shapely bottom a smack and sent her away, more than a little regretfully. She looked like she'd make a fiery bed partner—just the kind he liked. He wondered where she came from. Women were still at a premium out West, even her kind. She looked too young to have been in business long—but then, this was tough country. Men—and women—were forced to grow up fast.

He shook his head at life's cruel little jests and padded back to his table in the center of the room.

"Looks like we're gonna have to cut the game short, gentlemen." Still standing, he threw his hand in, then waited for his partner, James Long, to finish playing his cards. Tall, lean, and fine-featured, James appeared almost boyish at times. He was quick to grin and always looked to the bright side of life.

"What's up?" James scooted his chair closer to the table. His black eyes sparkled mischievously as he turned over his final card.

Langley smiled to himself—ace of diamonds. You could always count on James when the chips were down. And that went for more than just poker.

James grinned, raked in his winnings, then spoke to the other men at the table: two miners straight from the hard-rock diggings up north, a Texas cowhand looking to change his luck, and a merchant who made more money than the lot of them, but was easy pickings at the table.

"Better luck next time, boys," James said. The men grumbled but made no move to stop him collecting his due.

"Governor Ashton says we're needed urgently," Langley said. " 'Bout time we headed home anyway."

James unwound his lanky frame and stood up, careful to brush a telltale piece of lint from his black custom-tailored suit.

Langley picked up his well-worn broad-brimmed hat resting on the edge of the table and moved toward the front door, James close behind.

"Hey, Langley, where in hell you think you're goin'? You an' me got a score to settle!" From a table near the back of the saloon, Bull Miller's voice, thick with whiskey, rang across the bar.

Langley stiffened. Miller always was a fool. Now it appeared cheap liquor had dissolved the last of the man's common sense.

"I've got no fight with you, Bull," Langley said as he turned to face the big, bearded man.

"The hell you say! You cost me a damn good job!" Miller's face reddened; he clenched his fist and shook it, then noisily shoved aside two rickety wooden chairs blocking his path.

Langley bristled, his muscles tensing instinctively. He didn't want a fight with the brawny ex-guard, but he wouldn't run from one either. "You shouldn't have gotten drunk, Miller. That gold shipment was your responsibility."

James Long allowed himself an amused smile as he surveyed first his tall muscular partner, then the giant Bull Miller, then the dark oak mirrors and fancy leaded glass behind the bar. Though the men were unevenly matched in weight, James had no doubt about the outcome. Miller was far from the first man, the Gold Nugget far from the first saloon, to suffer his friend's wrath.

"This could get expensive, Hawk," he whispered, using the Indian name his friend preferred. Stepping back, he moved from between the two men.

Miller spat a stream of tobacco, missing the spittoon beneath the bar. Enraged, the giant man thundered across the room toward his opponent. A ham-sized fist whistled through the air. Hawk ducked easily, then drove a fist to Miller's middle, doubling him over. Miller sucked in a breath, bellowed in fury, and came up swinging. Tables were pushed aside to make room for the two men, and the crowd formed a surging, shouting circle around them. Bets were laid down, and several smaller fights broke out. The din of screaming, jostling men was deafening.

Hawk circled his opponent warily. As the man swung wildly, unable to aim his blow, Hawk stepped aside and delivered a powerful punch to Miller's jaw, sending the bearded giant sprawling atop two wooden chairs, which splintered beneath his weight. With a heavy thud, he crashed to the floor.

Hawk shook his bruised knuckles and glowered at the man at his feet. Groaning and wincing with pain, Bull raised his massive head, tried to push himself up, faltered, then sank into unconsciousness.

James grinned broadly. Being sober and more agile had given his partner an edge. Hawk brushed off his buckskin shirt and breeches, though they didn't need it, and ran a hand through his sandy brown hair. His moccasin-clad feet padded silently back across the barroom floor.

"Here." James gave him the dusty hat, and Hawk pulled it low—its usual place on his forehead. He glanced at the unconscious ex-guard.

"He'll be all right," he said to no one in particular. Then he added, "We'd better get started for Sacramento City." For the first time, he grinned. White teeth contrasted with his sun-browned skin. "I'd hate like hell to have to fight him when he's sober."

James chuckled out loud. "You have a point there, but as hard as you hit him, we'll be

halfway to Sacramento before he wakes up."
He turned serious. "What do you think the
governor wants with us this time?"

Hawk clapped his friend on the back. "Hard
to tell. Guess we'll find out when we get
there." He left a gold coin on the bar for the
broken chairs, winked promisingly at the red-
head, and pushed through the swinging double doors.

He swung into the saddle of his big bay
stallion; his friend mounted his black, and
they threaded their way through the busy
streets of Mokelumne Hill. Chinese laborers,
Mexican *vaqueros*, reed-and-rabbitskin-clad Indians, buggies, and heavily laden buckboards
all conspired to block their way.

The pair headed toward Sacramento City.
Though it was late in the day, by pressing
hard they could make Jackson by nightfall.

The ride was easy, but the heat of the day
made it uncomfortable. Merchants were clanking their heavy iron shutters closed by the
time the horses plodded up the narrow, dusty
streets of Jackson at the end of the day. A
small, dark-skinned Mexican youth raced up
beside the horses, his head barely reaching
Hawk's stirrup.

"Mister, Chapo see to your horses," he told
Hawk. "Work cheap. Take good care."

They rounded a corner and reined up in
front of the National Hotel, the small boy still
jogging beside them.

Hawk flipped him a coin. "Take 'em 'round

back and make sure they each get a can of oats." The boy nodded happily, grabbed both sets of reins, and headed toward the rear of the hotel.

The National was a three-story structure with wide porches off the bottom and second stories. It had been known as the Louisiana House before the Civil War. Northern sentiments dictated the name change. Hawk followed James into the cool interior.

"James! And Hawk! 'Bout time you two showed your faces 'round these parts." Letty Neal stepped from behind the counter.

Hawk bent and scooped the short, broad-hipped woman into a bear hug. "Good to see you, Letty." Both men had known Letty for some time. Hawk liked staying at the National. Letty ran the place with an iron hand, and both the food and her company were well worth the stop.

James removed his hat and leaned over to plant a chaste kiss on the old woman's cheek. "Got a couple rooms for us, Letty?"

"Always got a room for you boys. Where ya headin' this time?"

"Home. Governor wants to see us," Hawk answered.

"Well, you both look tired," she said. "Plannin' on turnin' in early, or can I buy you a drink?" She glanced at Hawk. "Laurel's been askin' after you."

Hawk smiled. "Think I'll take you up on that drink."

"Me too." James winked at Letty. "Think Sarah might be a bit thirsty tonight?"

Letty grinned. "You boys got some kinda appetite. Let's get that drink."

Hawk followed the two into the bar.

The drink and dinner satisfied part of Hawk's appetite; the rest Laurel took care of up in his room. Relaxed at last, he closed his eyes and drifted off. Thoughts of the governor's urgent message troubled his sleep.

"Travis . . . James. Come in, come in." Governor Ashton welcomed them expansively, guiding them into his dark, walnut-paneled, book-lined study. Shaking hands, he indicated two deep, red leather chairs.

"I trust your journey was not overly tiring," he said, seating himself behind a massive carved mahogany desk.

"No more than usual for this time of year," James responded formally.

"And you, Travis; you're looking well."

"Thank you, sir," Hawk replied.

"I'll come directly to the point, gentlemen." A big-boned, graying man who exuded power and authority, the governor had eyes that missed little and betrayed even less, but today he seemed anxious and distracted.

"I've called you here on an errand of utmost importance—to myself and my family." He was conscientious in his duties to the point of obsession, but he rarely spoke of family.

Hawk watched the governor's gray eyes curiously. They reflected determination, yet a bit of hesitancy. It wasn't like him.

"I assume neither of you has met my daughter," the governor said, shuffling the papers lying on his desk. He glanced around the room as if to hide his embarrassment.

"No, sir," James responded for both.

"Well, I'm certain you've at least read stories of her many escapades."

Hawk smiled and noticed James did the same. Julia Ashton had made the headlines of every social column in every newspaper in the West. She was glamorous and daring, and her exploits made great copy. Hawk distinctly remembered an incident a little over a year ago when Miss Ashton reportedly threw off most of her clothes and ended up in a fountain in the garden of the Sanford estate. The papers had spared no detail of the event, much to the governor's chagrin.

Rumor had it she'd slept with half the dandies in Sacramento, though she was still little more than a child. Julia Ashton was whispered about, written about, and snickered about. But she was a woman desired by every man she met. The governor rarely mentioned her. In fact, she'd been a constant source of embarrassment to him ever since he took office.

"I see that you have," the governor confirmed. He drummed his fingers against the leather pad on the top of the desk. "After her last fiasco, I sent her East, to a Boston finishing school. Since she stayed out of trouble in Boston, I allowed her to spend the summer with my brother and his daughter in the Dakota Territory. I presumed, quite wrongly, that in that wilderness there would be little chance for her to get into trouble. However . . . she has become involved with a young cavalry officer from Fort Laramie. I'm certain it's just a whim of hers, as usual, but she claims she's in love and wants to marry the man. Of course I cannot allow it."

"Maybe she really is in love," said James.

Hawk wondered if this could possibly be the "matter of utmost importance" the governor spoke of in his wire.

"Julia is extremely spoiled," the governor said. "I'm afraid I've indulged her far too often. She's willful, selfish. . . . She's never loved anyone except herself, and even if she really were in love, what kind of life would she have? She's always been pampered and cared for. She couldn't survive as a frontier wife. No, I must save her from herself. And that, gentlemen, is why you are here."

"But Governor Ashton, what could we possibly have to do with all this?" Hawk spoke for the first time.

"You, my friends, are going to bring the little darling home."

"What!" Hawk exclaimed.

"But Governor—" James protested.

"I'll make it well worth your while. I guar-

antee by the time you return to Sacramento
City, she'll have forgotten the boy's name and
will be ready for the social season." He smiled.
"A few long weeks on horseback, or a
crowded stage, should make her more than
ready for the luxuries of her home."

"But Governor," Hawk began, rising from
his chair to glower at the man across the desk,
"we're not nursemaids. We can't drag a female child across a thousand miles of hostile
country against her will. It's just not in our
line of work."

The governor seemed undaunted. "I assure
you, gentlemen, no one else *but* you could
drag her here. You've read the papers. You
know a little about what you're dealing with.
When Julia wants something, she'll do anything in her power to get it.

"I've asked your help because there is no
one else I can trust. She may be hot-headed,
but she is still my daughter. We haven't been
close since her mother died, but she's my responsibility, and it's high time I did something about it. I'll pay you six months' wages
to bring her home."

Hawk raised a brow at the sum. At most, it
would take two months to complete the job—
half a year's pay for a couple months' work
wasn't bad. Along with the savings he already
had, it would be more than enough to make
the final payment on the ranch he was buying
near Placerville. He'd be able to close the sale
earlier than anticipated. The sooner he made

the final payment, the sooner he'd be able to take possession of the property. He could hardly wait.

He glanced to his partner. James nodded his agreement.

"Well, Governor, looks like you win." Hawk sank slowly back into his chair, glad for the money, but unhappy about the nature of the assignment. The last thing he wanted was to drag an unwilling woman halfway across the country—especially a spoiled one like Julia Ashton. He'd already formed a dislike for the girl, just from the stories he'd heard.

"There's only one more thing I ask," the governor added. He scratched at his graying temple. "Your solemn word, as gentlemen and as my friends, that you will not"—he searched for the right words—"take . . . *liberties* with my daughter. I know how enticing she can be, but I want your word you will not in any way . . ."

Hawk looked the governor squarely in the eye. "You have my word."

"And mine, sir," James added.

"It's settled, then." The governor looked relieved. "Here is a daguerreotype of my daughter. It's a little old, but I prefer it to the engravings in the papers. My secretary, Isaac, will give you the rest of the information you'll need before you leave.

"This must be kept strictly confidential. Julia's reputation would be sullied worse than it is already if it were discovered she traveled here without a female chaperone. But, against my wishes, she left Mrs. Riden back in Boston. Besides, you'll need all your wits about you just to get *her* here. She'll try to make your life miserable on that trip. Don't be afraid to use whatever force you need, within reason, to keep her in line. Now, get a good night's sleep, and I wish you a safe and successful journey."

The governor shook hands with the two men. "Good luck, gentlemen. Now, if you'll excuse me, I have a meeting at the Capitol." With his shoulders a little straighter than when he arrived, he departed.

A servant brought the two men a whiskey and Isaac brought the needed information. Hawk drained his glass in one quick motion. James followed suit, and they left the study.

They crossed the formal entry and the wide front porch, and walked into the bright sunlight. Great expanses of manicured lawn surrounded the mansion and red, pink, and yellow roses flowered beside the house. The two men headed up the curving carriageway to where their horses were tied.

"Well, Hawk, what do you think we've let ourselves in for?" James asked.

"God only knows. Guess we'll find out in Fort Laramie—if she's still there."

Chapter Three

✦✦✦✦✦

AUGUST 12, 1868
FORT LARAMIE, DAKOTA TERRITORIES

JULIA FOLDED ANOTHER blouse and laid it atop the other articles in the trunk.

She and Mandy were trying to select only the items Julia would need for her elopement—to Julia, "necessity" meant at least one steamer trunk.

"Jason's so nervous he can hardly eat," Julia said. "I think he would have moved his leave forward if the fort weren't so darned short-handed. He's had that wagon he borrowed packed for three days." Her clothes were strewn all over Mandy's bedroom.

"Well, he only has to wait one more day." Mandy handed her cousin a red plaid dress, one of the few practical dresses Julia owned. "Then as soon as you two get far enough away, you can get married. You'll be Mrs. Jason Michaels."

"Has a nice ring to it, doesn't it? Mrs. Jason Michaels. Oh, Mandy, I can't wait." Julia's face glowed happily, like a little girl whose secret wish was about to come true.

Mandy wondered if her cousin's bright cheeks reflected her enthusiasm for getting married—or her anticipation of the honeymoon ahead. She felt her own cheeks redden at the thought.

"I really think we've done a good job of planning so far," Julia said. "If my calculations are correct, my father's men probably won't even get here for another week. With our head start, your three-week trip, and the weeks it will take the men to return and re-start the search, Jason and I ought to have plenty of time to get married—and enough time alone for Father to worry I might be pregnant."

"Julia!"

Julia smiled as if Mandy were a naive child, and shook her head. "Sometimes, Mandy, I just don't know about you."

Mandy refused to be ruffled.

Julia packed a lacy chemise, then sniffed a bar of honeysuckle soap Mandy had given her as a present and packed it away. Suddenly Julia giggled.

"Do you remember the time we put the Chinese firecrackers in old Mrs. Finch's stove?"

Mandy laughed. " 'We' didn't put the fire-crackers in the stove—you did! But it certainly was funny. Mrs. Finch kept saying, 'What did I put in those pies?' She actually thought she'd made the stove explode!"

Mandy sank down on the bed and wiped tears of laughter from her eyes. She looked over at the younger girl.

"I'm going to miss you, cousin."

She and Julia hugged, knowing it would be months, maybe even longer, before they would see each other again. But there was no turning back now. Mandy wondered briefly at the path each had chosen.

She glanced over Julia's shoulder, her gaze drawn to the street outside the bedroom window. A man in buckskins and another in a dusty black suit were being pointed toward the house. Their horses, well lathered, looked as though they'd been ridden hard.

"When you get to—"

"Julia!" Mandy interrupted. "Look at those two men over there." She pointed down the street. "They're coming toward the house. You don't suppose . . . ? Surely your father's men couldn't be here yet!" Mandy peered back out the window.

"Oh, my Lord!" Julia shrieked, quickly counting on her fingers the weeks since she'd first written her father. "If he wasted no time, if he was determined from the start—it might be them!"

The words sent Mandy into a panic. She ran to the window, wringing her hands. Beads of perspiration gathered at her temples. *What had she gotten herself into?* How could she have ever agreed to Julia's plan? She closed her eyes and slowly opened them again. The men were still coming toward the house—and getting closer.

"We have to be calm, Mandy," Julia kept saying. "We've played this scene twenty times. We just hoped to have a little more warning, that's all."

Mandy could barely comprehend her cousin's words. She couldn't move or speak. Her eyes were glazing over. The "posse," as she had laughingly nicknamed them, looked even more dreadful than she'd imagined.

"Mandy, please. Just keep calm," Julia said, as if Mandy were going to a ball instead of embarking on a thousand-mile journey across the toughest country on the continent.

"Everything's going to be fine. You go put on your 'Julia' clothes, just in case. I'll keep an eye on the men." They'd altered several of Julia's dresses—a rose batiste, a soft pink muslin, a riding habit—by shortening them a few inches and taking in the waists until the dresses fit perfectly. Mandy hadn't worn such pretty clothes in years.

"It probably isn't even the right men," Julia was saying, but she didn't sound convinced. "I'll hide in your father's room just to be on the safe side. If it is them, you'll have to start acting now. You get them away from here. I'll leave a note for Mrs. Evans saying you had to leave urgently to visit your sick Aunt Adelaide over at Fort Casper, just as we planned. I'll be sure to tell them an aide from the fort came to take you back. Mrs. Evans is expecting me to leave, so there's no problem there. When I'm finished, I'll go to Jason. We can leave as soon as it's dark."

Mandy just stared out the window, unable to accept any of this as real. It had all seemed like a game up until now. Learning to flirt, learning to swoon. Julia even gave Mandy lessons on how to cry on cue, although she wasn't able to master the art. Julia's slim hands on Mandy's shoulders spun her around.

"Please, Mandy," Julia pleaded, "if you care about my happiness, you'll do as we planned. You've got to keep those men away from Sacramento City as long as possible. Jason and I need time!"

Still Mandy stared blankly, trying to register her cousin's words.

Julia closed her eyes. Her bottom lip trembled, and large tears rolled down her cheeks. It was a good act, and it always worked. But this time Mandy was sure the tears were real.

She shook her head as if to clear it, embraced her cousin quickly, determined not to let her down, and hurried to her narrow upright chest beside the window. She pulled out Julia's rose batiste dress and tugged at the pins holding back her hair. She stepped into the low-cut dress, designed to display Julia's ample bosom, as were all her dresses, and worked the buttons that closed up the front. Feeling warm air on parts of her skin rarely exposed caused Mandy's cheeks to flame. God, how would she ever be able to carry off such a deception?

She straightened the bodice of the dress and powdered her nose. Julia grabbed a brush and fluffed Mandy's hair, now cut shorter to curl just above her waist. Several wispy tendrils curled near her ears.

Mandy checked the mirror, adding a little rouge to highlight her cheekbones and a bit of

color to her lips. The thick swatch of hair she
had worn across her face was brushed back,
exposing more of her creamy complexion.
Gold flecks, much like her cousin's, glittered
in her green eyes.

With her chestnut hair brushed out and
curling loosely, her décolletage showing for
the first time, and the tight-waisted dress en-
hancing the figure she usually took such care
to hide, she looked beautiful. Though she'd
always known she was attractive beneath her
plain facade, it felt wonderful now to look like
a woman—a beautiful woman, just like her
cousin. If it weren't for the circumstances,
Mandy would have been thrilled.

They finished in minutes. Mandy summoned her courage. She knew she looked like
Julia, but she certainly didn't feel like her. Her
whole body felt numb, and there was a distinct buzzing in her ears.

The men were dismounting in front of the
house.

"You know, Mandy," Julia whispered as
she headed toward the bedroom door, "going
to California might turn out to be the best
thing that's ever happened to you."

Mandy sighed. "Maybe—if your father
doesn't kill me when I get there."

Julia laughed. "I wish I could be there to see
his face."

Mandy grimaced at the thought and a sinking feeling gnawed at the pit of her stomach.
God, she must be out of her mind!

Three loud raps on the door put the plan into motion. It was now or never. Mandy checked to be sure her father's bedroom door was tightly closed, Julia well hidden within, as the pounding became more insistent. She squared her shoulders, tossed back her hair, and marched resolutely to the front door. She opened the door only slightly.

"Miss Julia Ashton?" A tall, dark-haired man peered at her through the narrow crack. The man was dressed in a well-tailored black suit so covered with dust it appeared almost gray. From his unkempt hair and unshaven appearance, it was obvious he'd ridden long and hard.

Giving him a look of disdain, as she was certain Julia would have, she stared haughtily back at the man. "What do you want?"

He seemed aware of her regard and began almost apologetically, "I'm sorry my friend and I did not have time to dress properly for the occasion, Miss Ashton. My name is James Long, and this is Travis Langley. We've been sent by your father to bring you home."

Travis Langley! The name sent chills down her spine. She could barely make out a second shape behind the door, but she remembered the big man well. Now their plan was doomed to fail before it ever got off the ground. She stood in the doorway trying to decide what to do. More than two years. *Would he remember her? Would he recognize her?* She hardly recognized herself.

"Noooo!" she cried, slamming the door in their faces and throwing the bolt. She could hear their voices through the planking.

"Damn! We should have known better," said Long.

"Now we'll have to break in," grumbled Langley.

Mandy dashed for the window, lifted the sash, climbed over the sill, and slid to the ground, running out through her tiny garden and off toward the stables. She knew they would catch up with her, but she needed to give Julia time to get to Jason. Her heart beat wildly. She couldn't believe she was actually doing this. And now she had Travis Langley to contend with. Of all the bad luck! *How could fate have sent someone she'd met before?*

Hawk wedged a steel-hard shoulder against the pine boards of the door. The wooden latch snapped easily, propelling him into the room. James followed close behind. Chintz curtains billowed through an open window, making it clear the lady had escaped.

"You follow her. I'll circle around and cut her off," Hawk directed. James nodded and ran for the window as Hawk made his way back out the front door. It would be easy for him to overtake her small stride. Hawk's temper flared as he pictured the disheveled young woman with the ample bosom, chestnut hair, and wide green eyes he'd glimpsed through the crack in the door. She was definitely not the child-woman he'd expected. Her breath-taking appearance had caught them both off guard. He wouldn't let it happen again.

As soon as the men departed, Julia slipped out the back door, behind the shed, and off toward Jason's quarters. She stopped only once—to leave a note on Mrs. Evans's door. No one seemed to be around as she hurried to tell Jason of their dilemma. It would be dark in a few hours. If they could get to their wagon and out of town by cover of night—and if Mandy played her part well—they might have a chance.

Mandy ran pell-mell up the dusty path, the full skirts of the dress scattering dirt and pebbles. *She had to do it. She had to. Had to.* She chanted the words in rhythm to her running feet. She had to do it for Julia. She had to do it for herself.

She passed a flowering bougainvillea and glimpsed the whitewashed walls of the stable. Where in heaven will I go from here? she thought. Running as fast as her tiny feet would carry her, she glanced over her shoulder to see if she was being followed. She rounded the corner of the stables at a break-neck pace and slammed headlong into a solid object. The sudden stop left her breathless and dazed. She was breathing hard from her effort, her legs shaky, her body trembling. She knew she should have fallen, but something was holding her up. She couldn't seem to get her bearings. She steadied herself, closed her eyes, and waited for the spinning to stop.

When she opened her eyes again, her heart raced even harder than before. Her gaze traveled from a wide, muscular chest to the hard lines and tanned features of the man who imprisoned her in his arms. Travis Langley! She'd know that face anywhere.

She remembered his hard, cold eyes, and her instincts warned her to free herself, run away, forget the whole crazy scheme. Hysteria threatened to overwhelm her. She had to get away. God only knew what punishment Langley would mete out when he discovered what she and Julia had planned. She struggled against him, but he held her easily, his gaze steady, mesmerizing her with its intensity.

She swallowed hard, beginning to feel faint again. Should she tell him who she was, forget their plan? Instead she straightened in his arms and tried to control her trembling. He hadn't said a word; he just held her immobile. He seemed to be enjoying her discomfort. A slow, lazy smile curved one corner of his mouth.

"Let me introduce myself, Miss Ashton. I'm Travis Langley. Your father sent me to deliver you to California, safe and sound. I intend to do just that."

The more she calmed herself, the more she realized he hadn't the faintest idea of their former meeting. He really thought she was Julia. He'd never given Samantha Ashton the slightest thought in the last few years, while she'd wondered about him often. The realization raised her hackles and sent a surge of spirit through her veins.

He really thinks I'm Julia! she fumed. Well, fine, Mr. Langley. You want Julia, you've got her. She threw herself into her role and tried to think what Julia would do, her success giving her courage.

Taking a deep breath, she clenched her teeth and kicked the big man hard in the shins. He didn't flinch, but his smile faded and his grip tightened even more. She knew the kick hurt her more than it did him, with his tough rawhide leggings, but he shook her just the same.

"You little hellcat," he said, his voice low and menacing. "Do that again and I'll kick you back." The tightness around his mouth confirmed his threat.

Mandy could feel the blood drain from her face. *How could she travel all the way to California with this cruel, overbearing man?* All the ugly memories of Davey Williams and the tough man in buckskins resurfaced, haunting her. He was hard and uncaring, and if she didn't admit the truth about her identity, she'd be forced to spend weeks on the trail with him. God only knew of what the man was capable.

She opened her mouth to speak, then thought of Julia and Jason. She'd given her word, promised to help them elope. She had to go through with it.

He smiled down at her mirthlessly. "You'd better learn to behave like a lady, Miss Ashton . . . or I might forget I'm a gentleman. We've got a long trip ahead of us. You'll do yourself a favor if you start doing exactly what I say. You'll find I'm not as easily pushed around as your Sacramento dandies."

Of all the gall! The man had to be the biggest bully she'd ever met. She wanted to stand up to him, tell him exactly what she thought of him, but her instincts warned her against it. She could feel his hard thighs even through the thick folds of her skirt and shuddered involuntarily in the circle of his arms, suddenly afraid to move a muscle. Swallowing hard, she stared woodenly at the unyielding features of the big, broad-shouldered man. She felt completely helpless for the first time in her life.

"Whatever you say, Mr. Langley," she choked out, trying to continue her facade but uncertain whether she'd succeeded. Now it was even more imperative to act the part of her cousin. Travis Langley might have a sudden return of memory.

Hawk eased his hold but kept her securely entrapped in his arms.

"Now that's a whole lot more like it. You just settle down, and we'll head back up to the house. You can pack a few things, and we'll get on the trail before the whole fort comes out to defend you."

He'd been lucky so far. Few people had observed their scuffle, and those few didn't seem to be too interested in getting involved with someone his size. He chuckled as he thought of the buckskins he wore, and the gleaming bowie knife strapped to his leg. Most folks would rather not tangle with someone they were certain was a renegade half-breed.

"You'd better be careful, sir," Mandy heard herself say, not believing the words were her own. "You'd best remember who you're dealing with." Now that her captor had eased his hold, some of her acting lessons returned. She decided she'd better continue before her courage lagged again.

"You'll have to answer to my father if you lay one hand on me."

Hawk glanced down at the tiny girl pressing her slim hands defiantly against his chest. Her bosom heaved above the low-cut neckline of her dress, and her chestnut hair tumbled wildly about her shoulders.

"Your father gave explicit instructions to use whatever force necessary to get you back to Sacramento City, including trussing you up like a sack of potatoes, if necessary." He couldn't resist embellishing the governor's words a little. He hadn't wanted to take this assignment in the first place. The idea of wrangling the governor's spoiled and selfish daughter all the way to California provoked him sorely—even more now that he discovered how attractive she was.

"But he couldn't have . . . he wouldn't . . ." Mandy sputtered. She couldn't believe she'd heard correctly. Surely Governor Ashton would never allow these men to harm his own daughter. It was the one thing she'd taken comfort in.

"Oh, but he did. Now let's get moving." He grabbed her arm and tugged her unceremoniously back toward the house.

Mandy grabbed her skirts with her free hand and followed the tall, brawny man up the path. God, how could she ever have agreed to Julia's scheme? As she stared at the muscular back of the man ahead of her, she wondered whether she had the courage to go through with it—and whether Julia's happiness would be worth it. Then she thought of her dismal muslin dress stuffed in the bureau drawer, thought of the last five miserable years she'd spent at the fort. *California.* She could make a life of her own there. She had to remember that.

As the couple neared the cottage, Mandy could see Sergeant Dickerson on the porch, inspecting the splintered latch. A pulse in her temple sounded the alarm. Someone must have heard the commotion and summoned the sergeant. Now what was she supposed to do? He would surely recognize her and ruin their plans!

The tall man in the dusty suit had already reached the porch, confident, it seemed, in his partner's ability to drag their charge, however reluctantly, back to the house.

Mandy's only hope was to brazen it out. She pulled free of the big man's grip and marched right past the sergeant. She moved to the window and presented her back to the room. Glancing over her shoulder, she could see the man in black pulling an official-looking document from his breast pocket. He began explaining his mission and appeared to be showing the sergeant the governor's signature and official seal. Mandy kept her back to the sergeant as much as possible and prayed he wouldn't notice how short "Julia" had become in the last few hours.

Agonizing minutes passed. At last the sergeant seemed satisfied. He tipped his hat, drew up his large frame, and headed toward the door. With a simple "Ma'am," he was gone.

Relief washed over her like a warm spring rain. That was the second time she'd succeeded in her role. A little more confident, she threw back her shoulders, headed into the bedroom, and began throwing one thing after another violently into a satchel. Playing a spoiled child certainly took a lot of energy.

James and Hawk had hoped to spend a couple of days at the fort, cleaning up, buying supplies, and resting a bit before heading back to Sacramento City. Now, with the sergeant having his doubts, and after having a taste of what was in store for them from their charge, they decided the best course of action was for James to get the needed supplies and meet Hawk and the girl at a point outside the fort. Then they could ride for three or four hours before making camp. The farther they could get away from the fort, the better.

"Hurry up in there. We haven't got all night," Hawk commanded. He watched her carefully from the parlor. The little minx had made a fool of him once; he wasn't about to let it happen again.

"Well?" Mandy questioned haughtily. She stood with her chin high, her hands on her hips as she'd often seen her cousin do. Loftily she waited for him to close the door.

"Well, what?" he answered coldly. "Would you like me to come in and help you pack?" His smug look said he knew full well the extent of her problem.

"I have to change my clothes. Aren't you going to give me some privacy?"

"Why? So you can go out the window again? Not a chance."

"But surely you can't expect me to change in front of you?" Mandy suddenly felt sick. This trip was going to be even worse than she expected.

He looked at her hard, paused, and at last relented. "We'll turn our backs, but if I hear anything but the rustle of petticoats, I assure you I'll be in there before you can turn around."

The ominous tone of the big man's voice

made Mandy cringe. Quickly she donned the dark green, high-fashion riding habit, though she refused to wear the hot and confining trousers beneath the skirt. Instead she wore her lightweight cotton pantalets. She pulled on her boots and adjusted her cravat. She knew she looked more like an English countess riding to the hounds than a young woman about to embark on an arduous cross-country journey, but the men expected to be escorting a governor's daughter—and that was exactly what she intended to be.

She strolled into the parlor, holding her head high and trying to appear nonchalant. "I'm ready when you are," was all she could manage.

The man in black took one look at her and sighed. "Have you nothing more suitable? It's going to be a long, hard trip." He looked as though he were just beginning to grasp exactly how long.

"Take me as I am or not at all!" Mandy snapped back, tossing her head as she'd seen her cousin do. She didn't trust these strangers, but if she withered now she'd not be able to take another step. She was terrified inside and knew she was running on pure force of will.

As she crossed the room she caught a glimpse of herself in the mirror. She still had trouble recognizing the lovely girl who stared back. She'd never really realized how pretty she was, yet for one brief moment she thought, Oh, what I'd give to slip into my unobtrusive facade.

"It's your neck," the big man growled. He grabbed her wrist and jerked her across the room. "Do you want to leave word for your cousin and your uncle before we leave?" It seemed almost an afterthought.

"I'm sure Sergeant Dickerson will take care of telling everyone at the fort how you abducted me, leaving him powerless to help because of some silly paper!"

"You catch the door, Hawk. I'll take her bag." The man in black picked up the small tapestry satchel, which was all they'd allowed her to bring, and headed for the door. Travis Langley grumbled beneath his breath and tugged her along behind.

Mandy wondered fleetingly why Langley's friend called him Hawk, but as she looked at his slightly Indian appearance, she decided it was a fitting name for the big bully. She was surprised he wasn't named *Bear!*

As they crossed the porch she snapped into character. "I hope I'm not supposed to ride behind one of you all the way to California."

"We were hoping Lady Ann might meet with your approval," James Long told her congenially. "Your father sent her to you as a gift."

Mandy's gaze traveled to a dainty sorrel mare with four white-stockinged feet. The horse pranced nervously beneath its saddle, awaiting her arrival. Moving toward the mare,

Mandy ran her hand down the horse's sleek neck. She'd never owned anything so beautiful. Being a governor's daughter, it appeared, did have some advantages.

With James's assistance, Mandy climbed aboard somewhat awkwardly. "Why can't I ride sidesaddle?" she inquired, tucking her skirts up so she could ride astride as she secretly preferred.

"Because the country's too rough," Hawk answered. "We're supposed to get you to California in one piece."

Mandy sat rigidly in the saddle. With little confidence, she was ready to begin her journey.

From where Hawk sat, he could see a bit of well-turned calf above the girl's booted ankle, but his face remained a mask of stone. Showing no emotion was a way of life among the Cheyenne. He was even able to control the twinge he suddenly felt in his breeches as he continued to admire the attractive bit of baggage he would be transporting. Inwardly he groaned, wondering if the money would be worth it.

Watching from behind lace curtains in Jason's quarters some distance away, Julia sighed with relief. She watched the threesome ride out of the fort with no further mishaps. Jason had left to fetch the wagon and complete the final preparations for their trip. Soon

they would be setting out in the opposite direction, and both were eager to put their part
of the plan in motion.

Julia shuddered with a momentary pang of
guilt. The men who'd taken her cousin looked
even more ominous than she'd expected. But
she knew her father must have great confidence in them or he would never have en-
trusted her to their care. He might be angry,
but she knew he loved her, though he never
showed it. She breathed a little easier. It
would do Mandy good to get away from her
father and her life at the fort, if only for a
while. Smiling, she decided it would all work
out for the best in the long run, and headed
back to finish her last-minute preparations.

Chapter Four

+ + + + +

TRAVIS LANGLEY PUSHED relentlessly till just before dark, trying to get as far from the fort as
possible.

Sparsely covered rolling plains followed the
broad, shallow Platte. They'd passed a num-
ber of trading posts just outside the fort, but
had seen no sign of life, save a few wild pigs,
for the past hour. Leaving the main trail, they

headed for the rendezvous point: a grove of trees near a tributary stream the men had passed on the way to the fort.

By the time they halted their exhausted animals, well past sundown, Mandy was ready to collapse. Her nerves were taut and her muscles ached from hours in the saddle without pause. Only the cool breeze whistling through the pines revived her lagging spirits as she sat atop her mount, her riding habit covered with a fine layer of dust.

She sighed wearily, trying to gather her strength. She grabbed the horn and was just about to heave herself down when she felt two strong hands around her waist lifting her effortlessly from the saddle. Though secretly grateful for the assistance, she didn't admit it. For the plan to work it was imperative she be convincing. She knew what Julia would do.

"Put me down this instant and keep your hands off me!" she demanded, the first words she'd uttered since she left her home. She pushed against the big man's muscular chest and looked indignantly up at the tanned face glaring at her from beneath a broad-brimmed hat.

He tightened his hold, his large hands almost spanning her waist. He seemed determined not to let go now that she had challenged him. Watching the set of his jaw, she felt a tiny prickle of alarm, but quickly subdued it.

"You try my patience, Miss Ashton," he said. "We're going to be together on the trail for some time. If you persist in this attitude, you'll only make it tough on yourself."

"I can take care of myself just fine without any help from you. And I'll thank you to keep your hands to yourself." She held Langley's penetrating, dark-eyed gaze for as long as her courage would allow, then her bravado withered. She could feel the heat of his hands around her waist and shivered, the nervousness in her stomach replaced by an odd, tingling sensation.

"I'm sorry," she conceded stiffly, now eager to be left alone. "Thank you for helping me down. Now, if you would be kind enough to unhand me. I'm very tired."

"That's more like it," Langley replied smugly, his mouth curving in a lazy smile. "A little more of that attitude and you and I'll get along just fine."

She could see he was pleased with himself for gaining the upper hand, and her anger flared. "We're never going to *get along just fine*, Mr. Langley, and you're never going to get me to California, so you might as well give up now."

"I wouldn't bet on that if I were you." His gaze turned dark, his temper flaring again. Too abruptly, he released his hold, causing her to lose her balance. She stumbled against him, then regained her footing, her own temper barely under control.

Without another word he turned and stalked in the opposite direction. She watched his imposing figure move toward his horse, silently cursing herself for letting him get under her skin. He was obviously a ruffian and somewhat of a heathen. She vowed to be more careful in the future.

In James's absence, Hawk made camp. He tethered the horses and started a fire. Soon he had a venison stew, meat left over from last night's supper along with a few prairie turnips, simmering over the coals. The hearty aroma wafted through the camp, and he felt his stomach rumble. By the time the stew was done, the sound of a horse's hooves clattered over the rocky ground. Hawk recognized James's familiar figure even from a distance.

"No more trouble at the fort?" Hawk asked, noting James's easy smile as he entered the camp.

"Not a hint. Her lieutenant must be out on patrol. Besides, not many military men are willing to jeopardize their careers by going up against the orders of a governor." He stepped down gingerly from the horse and began to unsaddle him. Hawk busied himself with the pack animal, untying the tarpaulin and removing the rack.

"How did you and Miss Ashton get along?" James inquired as he buckled his horse's halter.

Hawk could see the mischievous gleam in James's eyes, and it rankled him more than a little.

"Why don't you ask her?" he said sourly as he finished rubbing down the mule.

James watched Hawk pad noiselessly back

to the slowly burning fire. Even though they would travel part of the way by stage, they'd already decided to head west for a distance on horseback, just to be on the safe side. They could board the stage at Fort Bridger or, better yet, Great Salt Lake City.

James tethered the horse and mule beside the other horses, then searched out the girl. He spotted her at the edge of camp. His curiosity piqued, he sauntered up beside her, trying to appear nonchalant.

"Good evening, Miss Ashton." She made no move to acknowledge the greeting. He tried again. "I hope you're not overly tired after today's ride." Still unable to draw her into conversation, he tried another tactic.

"Look, Miss Ashton, we don't want any trouble, and we won't give you any if you'll just cooperate. This journey is going to be long and hard at best. We have nothing against you personally; for us this is just a job. We'll try to make it as pleasant for you as possible, if you'll only let us." He was beginning to understand what Hawk had been dealing with.

Mandy just wanted to be left alone. Right now she couldn't possibly imagine how she let her cousin talk her into such a crazy scheme. She'd given her word, and she'd abide by it, but the question remained unanswered. Again she tried to think how Julia might handle this.

"Mr., ah . . ."

"Long. James Long," he said.

"Mr. Long," she continued haughtily, trying to imagine her cousin at her most overbearing. "When my fiancé finds out you have abducted me, he is going to come after me, and he'll kill you." She spoke softly, ominously, as if the threat were real. She hoped she sounded convincing.

"That, Miss Ashton, is exactly what we're trying to avoid. Now, why don't you come have something to eat. Tomorrow's going to be even harder on you than today."

The soft tone of the man's voice lulled Mandy into a sense of confidence. This man was obviously a gentleman; both his speech and mannerisms confirmed it. Before his return to camp, he had shaved and donned clean clothing. He looked refreshingly refined in his well-tailored suit. Maybe he would become her ally on this journey. Considering his uncouth partner, she could very likely wind up needing one.

Walking toward the fire and the aroma of the stew, Mandy realized she was ravenous. She accepted the tin plate from the man in buckskins. Then, honoring him with just the briefest of glances while turning up her nose in feigned revulsion, she ate every bite on her plate.

Once her hunger was sated, all she could think of was getting some rest. "Where am I supposed to sleep?" she inquired somewhat regally, determined to keep up her pretense.

"Anywhere you please," came Langley's brusque reply. "Your bedroll is over there."

He pointed toward three blankets laid out to-gether, and Mandy's eyes grew wide. Straight-backed, she marched over to the blankets, dragged hers as far as possible away from the other two, and lay down to sleep.

She didn't miss the men's amused smiles at her action. Apparently they enjoyed making her feel uncomfortable. Shaking their heads, they stretched out on their bedrolls beside the fire.

Mandy lay tossing and turning. The still-ness overwhelmed her. She knew the men were sleeping; she could hear James Long's occasional snore. The night was clear and crisp. Every star in the heavens was brightly visible, and they were so close to the horizon they seemed to surround her. Tall pines spread their branches like deep green gables, but they were no comfort. She listened anx-iously, hearing first one frightening sound, then another. When a coyote howled, she shrieked and ran toward the fire.

Both men jumped to their feet. "What's the matter?" James asked worriedly. "Hawk, did you see anything?" James scanned the camp for any sign of trouble.

"I heard a noise," Mandy told them sheep-ishly. "I . . . I . . . guess I got a little fright-ened." She knew she was being silly, but her heart pounded just the same. She'd heard a thousand coyotes, but never when she was alone, miles from home, with two men she didn't know.

"It's only a coyote," James said, rubbing his eyes sleepily. "Go back to sleep."

"Not so brave now, eh, city girl?" Langley grumbled, heading back to his place by the fire.

"I was just surprised, that's all." Mandy wished she hadn't let them know she was afraid. She'd be lucky to get any sleep at all. She was far more worried about the two-legged coyotes near the fire than the four-legged ones on the hill.

As she returned to her bedroll, she reflected on the coming ordeal. She hoped being raised in a military family would give her some advantage. She recalled her early years when she rode constantly, climbed trees, hiked, and fished with the boys. She used to be able to sit a horse better than most men. She could also shoot a rifle and a sidearm and do a little tracking. She'd ridden some with her father these past few years, but not as much as she would have liked.

Her thoughts turned to the man who'd raised her, to the last five miserable years she'd spent with him. He'd become completely unreachable. She guessed something inside him must have snapped after her mother died. It was one of the reasons she understood her younger cousin so well—they both had experienced great loss at an early age, and both were raised by men unable to show their love.

She was thankful it had toughened her in

some ways. But she wished she could be a little tougher when it came to men. She had so little experience, and her father had painted such a dismal picture of what men were like, that her heart beat wildly every time she thought of spending more than three weeks alone on the trail with these two. It had all seemed so easy, almost unreal, when she and Julia had been making plans. Now that she was here—alone with them—it was a whole different story. *What could Uncle William have been thinking—sending men after Julia with no chaperone?*

Hawk returned to sleep somewhat fitfully. He always kept an ear cocked for intruders; it was something he'd taught himself years ago. Now, as he slept, he tossed and turned and, against his will, the dream came.

He was a small boy again huddled on a pallet of threadbare woolens in the back of a canvas-covered wagon. His body looked shrunken and frail; his sandy hair lay dull and matted across his forehead. Beads of perspiration ran down the hollows of his cheeks.

"Papa . . . Papa . . . ? Where . . . are you, Papa?" He tossed and turned, moaning as he slept. He felt a hand on his forehead and bolted upright.

"It's all right, boy." His uncle Martin leaned

over him. "Gonna take us both a while to git used to your pa and ma bein' gone."

Travis straightened, fighting the sting behind his eyes. His father would have wanted him to be strong. "It ain't fair, Uncle Marty. Why'd it have to happen to them?" His cheeks burned with heat. He always got angry when he thought of the accident, though he knew it was nobody's fault.

"Don't seem like life ever is fair, boy. Your Aunt Beulah and me worked hard all our lives. We ain't never cheated no one. Always tried to do what's right, but our boy was taken from us just like your ma and pa. Who can understand the ways of the Almighty?" Uncle Marty scratched his beard-stubbled chin. "Maybe the three of us gittin' together makes up fer some of it." His uncle smiled.

The dream flashed backward to another place, another time. At first hazy, then sharply focused.

He was talking with his father—a "man-to-man talk." They were riding in the shiny open carriage, moving along the shaded streets of St. Louis. They stopped in front of the family's two-story colonial home and his father laid a hand on Travis's shoulder.

"I'm going to be doing some traveling for a while, son," his father said. "Things are getting a little tight financially, and it's time I did something about it. I want you to watch out for your mother. You're the man of the family when I'm away, and I expect you to be in charge." His father gave him a big bear hug. "I'm proud of you, son."

The dream clouded, then cleared.

Thomas Rutherford, dressed in a somber black suit, sat next to him on the settee in the parlor of his home.

"I'm sorry, son," he was saying, "they're gone. Wheel sheared off the carriage while they were crossing Potter's stream. Your father and mother drowned beneath the wreckage." Mr. Rutherford's arm went around Travis's shoulder. "I'm sorry."

Travis didn't move or say a word.

"I'm afraid there won't be much money left after the bills are paid. I'd like to take you in, but your uncle Martin thinks you belong with family. He's headin' west. Looks like you'll be going with him."

The dream came full circle.

He was back in the wagon, the sun just beginning to creep over the horizon to outline the rugged mountains in the east. He could see the stiff mesquite scrub bending slightly in the brisk morning breeze, the dark sky fading to a rose-hued gold. He caught the first stirring of activity in the other two camps just a few yards away. As they'd had no money for the protection offered by a wagon train, they were traveling west with just two other families.

Travis watched the brightening sky, pulled on his shirt and trousers, and waited for a little warmth to seep into the nightly desert chill.

He saw them just before their piercing screams echoed across the camp. The eerie sounds chilled him worse than his fever. He stood motionless, so still he could feel the hair rise at the back of his neck.

Uncle Marty leaped over the wagon tongue, grabbed a rifle, and stuffed a long-bladed skinning knife into the top of his drawers.

Aunt Beulah sobbed hysterically. She scanned the hordes of painted attackers; her calloused hands twisted the apron tied over her calico dress. The ground thundered with the sounds of running horses, their hooves jarring the hard dry earth.

Travis jumped down and ran toward his uncle, just as his aunt ducked beneath the wagon.

"Uncle Marty," Travis cried out, "there's so many of 'em! What are we gonna do?" They were already so close he could see their naked brown flesh, painted and glistening with sweat.

"Get under the wagon, boy—and pray!" was all his uncle had time to say before stumbling off to join the other two men running across the clearing.

Shrieks and screams filled the air. Travis turned just in time to see a warrior, his face a mask of red glowing with hideous, white-circled eyes, thrust a hand beneath the wagon.

"Aunt Beulah!" Travis watched her scramble away frantically, tripping over the hem of her skirt as she tried to escape. She fell to her knees, sobbing, pleading. The warrior didn't hesitate. He plunged the shaft of his knife between her breasts, and she crumpled to the dusty earth.

"Nooo!" Travis screamed, tears of rage and frustration running down his cheeks. People he loved were dying. He couldn't let it happen again!

He rushed forward and leapt onto the Indian's back just as old Mrs. Murphy aimed her husband's worn musket and fired. The warrior made a strangled noise, ran forward, and fell dead at the woman's feet.

"There's one I'll take with me," she cackled. She kicked the dead Indian and started reloading.

Travis heard the whistle, then the sickening thud of the arrow as it entered her spine.

He pulled himself to his feet. Racing forward, he dodged several attackers. A tomahawk blow sent a man spinning into the dust. Travis ran on. Nothing mattered now except reaching his uncle's side. Just a few more feet. He saw the big painted brave hurl a lance. The lance whistled by, a blur of feathers and paint. The shaft impaled his uncle to the wagon. Uncle Marty's blood oozed into the desert sand.

Covered with blood and sick with the sight of death around him, Travis raised his eyes to a thickset, dog-faced warrior glistening with sweat and blood and paint. Travis could hear his own heart pounding. He glanced from the

Indian to his uncle's lifeless body, then back to the warrior, who whooped victoriously.

Travis clenched his teeth and attacked. He pummeled the Indian's chest, scratched, and clawed, but the squat warrior knocked him aside, a quick, sharp blow hurling him into the dirt at the Indian's feet.

The man bent over Travis before he could rise, pulling his hands behind his back and binding them with a rawhide thong, then tying his flailing feet. With a loud hoot, the warrior lifted him easily. He dragged him toward a spotted horse and carelessly flung him across the animal's withers. He could feel the animal's sweaty coat, the bony back pressed into his middle. The Indian swung up behind him.

Travis struggled against the leather that bound his hands, felt it cut into his flesh, but couldn't make it budge. He could see painted warriors stripping the wagons, hear their gruesome shouts of triumph with every new discovery. Then they began scalping and mutilating the bodies of the dead.

The wagons were burned to blackened skeletons, and vultures circled the last wispy black tendrils of smoke that rose into a lighted sky before the brave who had captured him crossed the first ridge.

A noise pierced the haze of his dream. His bowie flashed. Travis grabbed the intruder's foot, jerked him heavily to the ground, rolled on top, and shoved the blade beneath the man's chin.

The intruder's high-pitched gasp and weak struggle brought Hawk fully awake. He stared into huge green eyes, luminous with fear. Silky strands of chestnut hair cushioned his hands.

"Damn you, woman! Are you trying to get yourself killed? Don't ever do that again. Not to me or any other man worth his salt!" He could feel the girl tremble beneath him, her bosom rapidly rising and falling against his chest.

"I . . . I . . . You looked like you were having a bad dream. I just wanted to . . . I was just trying to help."

Hawk could barely concentrate on the girl's words. God, she was a beauty. Her face glowed softly in the yellow rays of dawn. Full red lips, slightly parted in surprise, exposed her delicate pink tongue.

Beginning to feel the stirrings of arousal, he rolled away. He pulled the girl to her feet. Her face looked pale, and her riding habit was covered with dust and twigs. He took a deep breath, a little unsettled at what had happened.

"I'm sorry. All right? Just don't do me any more favors. You might wind up dead. I'd have a helluva time explaining that to your father."

She brushed herself off, her fear receding and anger flaring in its place. "You try to kill me, and you're worried about my father?"

Hawk ignored her. The sky was pinkening with first light. It was time they were away. "Look, lady, you'd better get your bedding rolled up. We'll be leaving as soon as we eat."

Mandy set her jaw and marched back to her sleeping pallet. How dare he treat me this way, she thought. Visions of the big man, his dark eyes flashing, his hard body pressing against hers, intruded on her anger. He was an odd man, that one. She wondered what his nightmare was about. He seemed to be struggling with some unknown enemy, fighting for his very life. She'd only meant to help him, the ungrateful lout. Well, she wouldn't make that mistake again.

Hawk watched as the girl knelt and straightened her bedroll. He smiled and shook his head, remembering the rush of warmth he'd felt with her pinned beneath him. The scent of lavender still clung to his buckskin shirt. He pulled a single long strand of chestnut hair from where it curled deliciously against his chest. No matter how he looked at it, this was going to be one hell of a long trip!

Chapter Five

❖❖❖❖❖

THEY FINISHED A simple breakfast of hard tinned biscuits and jerked venison.

James packed up the camp and Hawk saddled the horses. They were headed into the Laramie Mountains, not following the usual route along the Platte traveled by stagecoach and wagon. It was a tough trail, but Hawk seemed to know exactly where he was headed. Mandy already thought of him as Hawk. He seemed so much a part of the land, so much a part of nature, just the way the Indians did. In fact, most of the time he seemed more Indian than white.

Mandy's little mare stumbled, then perked up her ears as the men picked up the pace. Mandy gave Lady Ann her head. She was trailwise and surefooted, comfortable to sit. Mandy had owned a horse only once in her life. Schooner, her big sorrel gelding. She'd loved that horse. Loved the freedom that riding the big horse gave her. Now, as she rode along on Lady Ann, she thought of Schooner and, as always, felt a sharp stab of guilt.

She had been racing Schooner over the prairie, defying her father, running him faster than ever before. She hadn't been watching the terrain and suddenly he stumbled. His head went down and Mandy pitched forward; she could feel the stiff strands of his mane against her cheek as she flew over his head. Great clouds of dust billowed around them, blotting out the light as she and the animal thundered to the earth. She felt a shattering pain in her arm when she hit the ground, and heard Schooner's shriek of agony. Then the horse began neighing shrilly as he tried to lift himself up from the dirt.

Oh, God, what had she done? She rolled over. The pain in her arm shot through her, throbbing with every movement, but the pitiful sounds Schooner was making drove her on. Her mouth tasted gritty, her cheeks were scratched and smeared with dirt. She crawled toward the sorrel and watched helplessly as he tossed his russet mane wildly and thrashed his hooves in the air.

"Schooner, oh, God, Schooner. Please, boy. Please lay quiet." She stroked his sleek neck, crooned softly in his ear. She looked about wildly for her father. He'd been riding behind her, mad at her for being too far from the fort. When she spotted him at the bottom of the hill, he was headed toward her at a gallop. He dismounted before his horse came to a full stop and ran to her side.

"Are you hurt?"

She nodded. "I think I broke my arm, but it's Schooner. See what's wrong with Schooner." She closed her eyes and prayed the big sorrel would be all right.

Her father moved along the horse's withers, along his back, and down his flanks, stroking, soothing, probing, and examining. When he finished, he returned to her side. He untied the yellow bandanna from around his neck and lashed her arm across her breast as best he could. Then he helped her to her feet.

"But what about Schooner?" Her heart pounded. She felt light-headed. She knew the answer but prayed she was wrong. Her father didn't speak. Instead, he lifted her carefully atop his sparse military saddle, then pulled his carbine from its scabbard behind the cantle.

"No!" Mandy shrieked. She grabbed the barrel of the weapon and refused to release her hold, even though each movement caused needles of pain to shoot through her arm. "You can't shoot Schooner! It was my fault. My fault we fell, not his." Fresh tears ran down her cheeks.

"Please, Papa," she whispered. "I'll do anything you ask, but please, please don't shoot Schooner."

"Schooner has a broken leg," he said gently. "It isn't fair to make him suffer."

"Please, Papa. Please. It's my fault."

"Yes, it is your fault! Now do you understand where your recklessness leads?"

Mandy looked helplessly at Schooner. For years the horse had been her friend—her one ally. Now his soft brown eyes were wild with pain.

"He's asking us to do what's right," her father said.

She nodded, then looked away. Her father's footsteps crunched on the dry earth and pebbles as he walked toward Schooner. She heard the hammer on the Springfield cock, and closed her eyes tightly.

The wind whistled beside her ear. Then the gunshot echoed its grim message, and the labored sound of Schooner's breathing ceased.

"Miss Ashton?" Hawk's deep voice broke her reverie. "The trail gets a might steep through here. I'd advise you to start paying attention instead of daydreaming about your beau." His tone annoyed her and she couldn't resist answering in kind.

"What's the matter, Mr. Langley, afraid I'll fall off a cliff, and you won't be able to collect your reward? That is what you're after, isn't it? The reward. Just like in the posters: Wanted dead or alive, Julia Ashton, for unspeakable crimes of the heart."

Hawk dropped back beside her and scowled fiercely. "I don't think that's funny. Your father believes what he's doing is in your best interest. From what I've seen so far, I think he's probably right."

"And just what's that supposed to mean?"

"It means, Miss Ashton, it's time you grew up and started thinking about someone besides yourself."

"And what about you, Mr. Langley? Just who do you think about besides yourself?"

He scowled even harder, his mouth a hard grim line. She was smiling at her slight victory when Lady Ann stumbled again and nearly went down.

"Pull up," he commanded, his tone gruff.

Mandy did as she was told. Hawk dismounted and picked up Lady's right front foot. The mare whinnied and shook her head, her bit jingling with the movement.

"She's picked up a stone." He shoved back his hat, then turned to Mandy, his mouth curving in a smug, satisfied smile. "Looks like you'll have to ride with me."

"I will not! I'll walk first." She dismounted, straightened her skirts, and started along the narrow trail.

Hawk caught her in two long strides.

"I said you're riding with me. Your horse will be fine by tomorrow, but now is not the time for your games, Miss Ashton." Before she could open her mouth to protest, he scooped her up and deposited her roughly astride his saddle, then swung himself up behind. She tried not to lean against his broad chest, but there was little room between them.

James followed on his gelding, intent on navigating the tough trail.

By the end of the first hour the effort not to touch the big man had tired her greatly. She could feel his hard gaze boring into her back, and knew he was enjoying her discomfort.

"Tell me, Mr. Langley," she began, deciding maybe a little conversation would take her mind off the feel of his hard torso, uncomfortably warm and close. "How is it my father trusts you to bring me home?"

"Why shouldn't he? Do you think he expects me to tear off your clothes and ravish you somewhere along the trail?"

Bright heat rushed to her cheeks. *How could he say such a thing?*

He seemed to study her reaction, as if measuring her in some way. She kept her back to him, but her hand trembled slightly, and she knew he'd seen it.

"Don't tell me I've shocked you," he said, turning her face toward him and noting her high color. "I had no idea you were a woman of such delicate sensibilities." He was having a hell of a time figuring the woman out. He could usually read women like a book, fit them into just the right mold, but not this one. The last thing he expected from Julia Ashton was the blushing virgin act. How big a fool did she think he was? Half the dandies in Sacramento City told stories of her lusty appetites, yet she made him feel guilty for a simple, honest remark.

She finally stopped fighting the saddle and rested her back hesitantly against his chest. Her head fit well beneath his chin. He was having a devil of a time concentrating on the trail and a tougher time controlling the swell in his breeches. He wished he'd let her walk after all.

"Your father and I met four years ago," he

told her finally, hoping to divert the train of his thoughts. "Your aunt Maude introduced us. I'm surprised she never told you the story."

He felt the girl stiffen slightly. Then she shrugged her shoulders.

"Well, you know how Maude is," she said simply.

He smiled. The image of the feisty, gray-haired Irish woman came clearly to mind. "I like your aunt Maude. She's a real lady. But she's not meek. She's got plenty of fire left in her boiler."

He heard the girl laugh softly at his description, the clear lilting sound giving him another twinge. He cleared his throat and continued.

"Anyway, she and a friend were attacked by highwaymen on a back road between San Francisco and Sacramento City. James and I happened onto the scene and foiled the robber's plans. We're good at that—foiling plans, I mean. Don't you agree, Miss Ashton?"

"There seems to be very little on which we agree, Mr. Langley."

He chuckled softly. Mandy could feel the vibrations in his chest. The feeling sent shivers the length of her.

"Maude introduced us to your father. We did some work for him, some of it highly confidential. Over the course of time, we became friends as well as business associates. Your father's a good man—but then I'm sure you've known a lot of good men, haven't you, Miss Ashton?''

She paused. ''I'm not sure what you're implying, but if you're referring to Jason Michaels, you're quite right. He is a good man.''

She knew damn good and well that was not what he meant. The woman was really incredible, he thought. Not only spoiled and selfish, but an unbelievable actress as well.

Mandy tried to concentrate on the big man's conversation, but all she could think about were the muscles rubbing against her back. She flushed continually, the heat of his body making the day seem hotter than ever. By the time the ride ended, all conversation had ceased and Hawk's dour mood had returned. He was grumpy and couldn't seem to be rid of her fast enough.

He paid little attention to her the rest of the evening and she was glad for the time to herself. She turned in as soon as she'd eaten dinner and, exhausted, fell asleep even before the sun went down.

Hawk looked over at the tiny figure, deeply asleep on the opposite side of the camp. He was glad she was getting some rest—she was going to need every ounce of her strength. He intended to push her hard again tomorrow, just in case her *Jason* had any plans of retrieving her. He didn't trust the little minx. Not one bit. So far things had been too easy. Something was just not right. He could feel it in his bones.

The long afternoon shadows gave way to darkness. He checked the horses once more, then sprawled beside the campfire on his bedroll, propping his back against the puzzle-bark of a fallen log. He stared into the night sky.

Towering pines surrounded the clearing like straight-backed guardian soldiers. The pungent smell of smoke, pitch, and grease—remnants of a roasted venison supper—tinged the air. He'd had a hard day, thanks to the closeness of the green-eyed girl, but the weather had been tolerable, and the hearty meal left him quietly satisfied. James was also propped against the log, his black leather boots strewn casually beside him.

James chuckled softly, his gaze resting on the sleeping figure. "Well, Hawk, what do you think of her so far?" he asked, breaking the silence. Absently, James poked a naked branch into the exhausted fire, sending a shower of sparks into the clear night sky.

Hawk watched the flickering lights disappear among the stars. He furrowed his brow and groaned aloud, forcing himself to face the inevitable question.

"I do my best not to think about her at all, but if you insist . . ." He paused a moment, trying to find the words. "I guess she's just about like her father said—spoiled and selfish. Every so often I think maybe he's wrong; so far it's hard to tell. She's a good-lookin' woman, I'll tell you that." He shoved his hands behind his head and continued to watch the sky. "You've known a lot more of these little rich girls than I have; what do you think?"

James smiled into the darkness. He unfastened another button on his now-dusty white shirt and scratched a mosquito bite on his neck. He thought of the wealthy Chicago family he'd left behind. He'd wanted no part of the life his domineering father had planned for him. Working in an office, taking over the family business, living in the city. He left home at eighteen, went west to seek his fortune.

He smiled again at the memory. He'd done well enough, but it was a tumbleweed existence, with little future. After he'd tagged up with Travis Langley, he'd been able to save some money. For the first time he had plans for the future, and this assignment was a big step in that direction.

He turned his attention back to his friend. "Well, most of the rich girls I've known were conniving little misses used to getting everything they asked for." He thought of the many debutante balls he'd been forced to attend. "I guess in that way she seems the same, but in other ways she doesn't quite fit the picture. I'll tell you one thing," he said ruefully. "If she's half as stubborn as she appears, we'll have our work cut out for us. I've got a hunch she's trying to lull us into making some sort of mistake."

Hawk grumbled and peered hard into the darkness. Though he didn't relish it, he was determined to make the best of the assignment.

"I've got a feeling you're right, but I've got some ideas of my own on that score. A few weeks out here without her nursemaids ought to calm her down a little. I plan to run her ragged for the first week or so. Take some of the fire out of her. Besides, the sooner we get her home, the sooner we get paid."

James chuckled. "Maybe she'll go the rest of the way like a little pussycat, and we won't have any problem at all."

"Not likely. The governor's not payin' us that kind of money for nothing."

"I suppose you're right," James admitted. "Look, Hawk, I know you're not thrilled about this little adventure, but that money will sure come in handy."

It was Hawk's turn to laugh. "Already got yours spent on that saloon you've been wantin' to buy?"

"Well, I won't have quite enough yet, but I'm getting closer all the time." James poked the fire again. "What about you? Will you have enough to close the deal on your ranch?"

Hawk didn't answer. He was on his feet and moving silently toward the edge of camp. His big knife flashed in the moonlight. He moved stealthily, his moccasins muffling the sound as he stepped atop a giant boulder and climbed high enough to gain the advantage over the man who was trying to sneak into their camp.

Hawk scanned each rockfall and ravine, his eyes quickly adjusting to the darker light away from the fire. A dry twig snapped, and his body tensed. His knife flashed again as he stood poised and alert for the attack. His quarry's shadow moved among the rubble below, and Hawk crouched, ready to spring. Just as his muscles bunched for the move, he pulled himself up short, releasing his breath slowly, trying to control the tension pumping through his veins.

He broke into a wide grin as he spoke in Cheyenne to the man below. "Running Wolf, you have grown soft in your last few years." He jumped down beside his Indian friend. "There was a time when I would have only known you were here by the blade at my throat."

The younger man laughed good-naturedly. "I was just being courteous to your advanced years by allowing you to hear me," he answered, also grinning broadly.

The two men grasped forearms in greeting, then Hawk threw his arm across the slimmer man's shoulders. "It is good to see you, my friend." They walked back toward camp, and Hawk noticed James holster his revolver as they entered. "James, this is Running Wolf."

The lean Indian made a greeting in sign language, and James signed a greeting in return. Then Hawk and Running Wolf sat cross-legged beside the fire and began to speak in earnest. Unable to understand Cheyenne, James leaned back against the log, lit a cheroot, and silently offered one to Running Wolf, who accepted.

"How did you know where to find me?" Hawk asked.

"Black Hawk, a man like you is not hard to find. Wherever you go, your people watch. They have not forgotten you."

"Nor I them."

"It has been too many moons since you have come to us. Your mother and father long for your presence in their lodge."

A shadow passed over Hawk's heart. He nodded his head in agreement. "You're right, my brother. And still I cannot come. But soon. Soon."

Running Wolf lit the cheroot with an ember and inhaled deeply, drawing his lean muscles taut. Smoke curled lazily upward. "I did not come to speak of family, my friend. I came to tell you of the white man's trespass into the Black Hills. They search for the yellow stones. So far there are few white eyes. But soon there will be many. Our land will be torn beneath the heels of their boots."

It was not the first Hawk had heard of the white men crossing into the territories of the Cheyenne and Sioux nations. It was a subject that tore at his loyalties, tore at his heart.

"I have heard of this, Running Wolf. But there is little to be done. Greed is always a cruel opponent."

"Yes, my brother, but you know many of the white fathers. We urge you to speak with them, tell them of our troubles. You are one of us. You understand why we must have this land."

Hawk nodded. Since he'd left his village he'd done everything in his power to help his people find land they could call their home, but his efforts had done little for their cause. "I will do all I can." He wondered how helpful his words would be.

Running Wolf's lean countenance relaxed, his task accomplished to the best of his ability. He broke into a smile and nodded his approval. "It is all any man can ask of another."

The conversation continued for only a brief minute more, Running Wolf wary of being even this close to the soldiers at the fort. When all had been said, the two men rose.

"Good-bye, my brother." Running Wolf clasped Hawk in farewell, signed a farewell to James, and silently disappeared into the cover of the pines.

Hawk sat back down and recounted the conversation to James.

"It's a problem with no answer," James said.

"No, I suppose not." Hawk reclined full length on his bedroll, stretching the knotted muscles of his back.

"It'll probably mean more bloodshed," James said.

"I'm afraid so."

The night was warm, even at this high elevation. Hawk pulled his buckskin shirt over his head, determined to get some rest. His mind was plagued with thoughts of what appeared to be a disastrous course of events for the Indians—and for many whites as well. When he returned to Sacramento City, he'd try once more to help his people, but first he'd complete the job he was being paid for.

He tossed and turned a bit, but eventually his eyelids grew heavy. Finally he drifted to sleep. Worrisome thoughts of his Indian brothers conjured the dream.

He could see a boy, marching endlessly, his bare feet cracked and bleeding, the desert stretching out for miles ahead. Only the women's voices shepherding the children rose above the thudding of the horses' hooves in the deep powdery dust. A tug on the rawhide rope around his neck sent him sprawling for the tenth time. Every muscle ached.

The warrior on the spotted horse yelled something the boy didn't understand as he tried to scramble to his feet, only to be jerked down again. He didn't know how he would go on, but he had to try. His father would have wanted him to try. He rose again and struggled forward, planting one foot in front of the other. He felt the blisters rising on his arms and back where the Indians had ripped off his shirt, leaving his pale skin exposed to the desert sun. *I'll make it*, he promised himself. He'd take all they could dish out and still go on—for his father, for Uncle Marty and the others, for himself.

The dream wavered; the desert disappeared.

He was in a quiet, cool forest. He could hear the songs of birds, and the squirrels rustling in the trees. There were other Indians, different this time. The women wore clothes of soft white leather; the men were tall and fine-featured. None wore paint. A big Indian in full headdress moved toward him, stepping between him and the dog-faced Indian who had led him across the desert.

"You have come far, young one," the man said in broken English. "You have lived when most would have died."

He watched the man's eyes: keen eyes, able to read his thoughts, his character.

"I am Strong Arrow, of the Cheyenne," the man said.

Travis did not answer.

"We are not at war with your people," the man continued. "I am sorry for your pain . . . your loss."

Travis felt kindness in the man's words. It made him feel weak, feel like crying the tears he had not shed. But he knew he couldn't afford to show his weakness. He steeled himself for the consequences and spat into the dirt at the man's feet.

The man did nothing.

"My friends say I should not take you," the man said in his broken English. "I should leave you with the Comanche. But I have lost my own son. A boy . . . just about the same in years as you. I think you have no one. Maybe we will help each other." The man looked hard into Travis's eyes. The decision was made.

The rope was cut from around his neck, and he was led away. He was given food and water. At least he would survive.

Sounds of a distant coyote brought him fully awake and ended the dream. A fine sheen of perspiration covered his chest and arms and the night breeze chilled him a little. He unfurled a light blanket and lay back down to rest. This time he slept soundly. Only thoughts of the governor's daughter, sleeping not nearly far enough away, caused him a moment or two of discomfort.

Chapter Six

✦✦✦✦

It was not until several mornings later that Mandy was able to relax enough to enjoy the beauty of the mountains: the rocky red soil, the screech of the blue jays, the cool clean air.

They were crossing the Deer Creek Range, Hawk had told her, pointing to a doe and fawn grazing on the side of a ravine. A red-tailed hawk had circled above, and Mandy wondered if it could be an omen, as the Indians believed.

After tending to her needs, she returned to the camp and the rich aroma of fresh coffee as it boiled over and sputtered onto the hot rocks of the firepit. Hawk had apparently freshened up in the stream. Clean shaven, he wore a fresh buckskin shirt and breeches. The deep vee in the front exposed a good portion of his sandy-haired chest. His damp hair curled softly over his collar. As he knelt to pour her a cup of the steaming coffee, his muscled thighs were clearly outlined through the soft leather of his snug-fitting breeches.

Mandy suddenly felt self-conscious. She took a deep breath and turned her gaze in another direction. For the past few days, she'd begun to realize just how attractive this man was. She hoped it wasn't the reason her heart pounded every time he came near. Accepting the cup, she almost wished their second meeting could have been under different circumstances. Of course, if it had been he probably wouldn't have paid her any more attention than he did the first time. The thought irritated her more than a little.

"Can you cook?" Hawk inquired rather abruptly. "It's time you earned your keep."

"Of course I can cook," Mandy responded, his manner rankling her. Then, anticipating his next sentence, she added, "But not for the likes of either of you." She was starting to get back into her Julia role, and considering the train of her thoughts, it was probably a good thing.

"You'll cook or you won't eat," countered Hawk. "Nobody gets a free ride—not even the governor's daughter."

Mandy noticed James's sidelong glance, but Hawk paid no heed.

"Then I won't eat," she said defiantly, "and my father will kill you if Jason doesn't."

At the mention of her fiancé's name, Hawk bristled. If he had been about to weaken, he wouldn't now. "Fine," he said through clenched teeth. Then he started frying the bacon. Some remote part of him wondered why the sound of the man's name made him angry.

When breakfast was ready, he and James ate ravenously, Hawk exaggerating the slurping noises and licking his fingers. "Delicious! Too bad you weren't hungry," he taunted.

"I'm hungry, all right. I'm starving, but you two couldn't care less!"

"You cook and you can eat," Hawk repeated. He scraped the leftovers into the coals with a little more effort than necessary, then carefully covered the fire. He grabbed Mandy's saddle with one hand, his own with the other, and headed to the horses.

Mandy gritted her teeth and tried to ignore the rumble in her stomach. Julia would never know how lucky she was not to be on this trip. Grabbing her satchel, Mandy flounced off, disliking the men, and her role, more than ever.

They rode hard all day over rough ground. The sun beat down mercilessly. They crossed several meadows and passed beside a small lake nestled at the end of a valley. By late afternoon Mandy began to complain, as she was certain her cousin would, in an effort to slow them down.

"I'm tired. Can't we rest for a while?"

"Keep riding," was Hawk's response.

"But I'm thirsty."

"You've got a canteen."

"I want a *cold* drink—from the stream. And I don't see why we can't rest." Abruptly she pulled up her horse and dismounted. The hem of her riding skirt rustled pebbles as she walked toward the shallow stream beside the trail.

Hawk's eyes narrowed. Reining his horse up, he swung a leg above the saddle horn and jumped down. "Get back in the saddle," he commanded, his long strides swiftly overtaking her smaller ones.

"No! I need to rest awhile. It's much too hot to be traveling this time of day, anyway."

"I said get back in the saddle. You don't run this little expedition, and it's time you figured that out." His voice sounded low and menacing. Feet apart, he stood blocking her path to the stream.

"I will not!" Determined not to weaken, she straightened her shoulders, dodged the hulk in front of her, and again walked toward the stream.

"You're going back in the saddle one way or another." Hawk set his jaw, his resolve hardening with every passing moment. Well acquainted with the spoiled type of woman he imagined the governor's daughter to be, he was determined not to be run over by her, or any other woman.

Moving swiftly, again he reached a spot ahead of her on the narrow path. Glaring into her flashing eyes with a glowering pair of his own, and without further conversation, he leaned down, picked her up, and threw her over his broad shoulder. Grumbling, he stalked back up the hill.

Pounding the corded muscles of Hawk's back, kicking, and screaming did Mandy little good. She was furious, but Hawk was just too big for her to fight. He paid no heed to her struggles, as if the burden on his shoulder bothered him no more than a pesky insect. When he reached the horses, he held both her wrists in a wide hand, and with the other bound them together. He deposited her roughly, face down over the saddle. Then he grabbed a rope, reached under the horse, and caught her bound hands. Seething with indignation, Mandy found herself securely tied across her mount, barely able to move.

"You're a vicious, heartless . . . monster! You can't treat me like this and get away with it! My father's going to hear about this. Untie me!"

Without a word Hawk mounted his big roan and led the little mare, with Mandy protesting loudly across its back, off down the trail.

James, having already sensed the tension developing between the pair, watched the scene unfold from a distance. He'd already decided it would probably be best to let nature take its course where his friend and this lady were concerned, and he'd resolved to stay as much in the background as possible.

After the first few minutes of ranting and raving, Mandy realized it was just too tough to talk, or do just about anything, in her current position. As she lay bouncing up and down, wincing with every step, she silently cursed the man who had bested her once more and renewed her vow never to let it happen again.

Two hours later, just when Mandy was certain she would die of the pain, Hawk relented.

Untying her carefully, he lifted her from the mare, his gentleness a surprise as he held her while she tried to stand on her unsteady legs. Again she felt an unfamiliar tingle in the hollow of her stomach and a rush of warmth to her cheeks. Lifting her gaze to meet his, she could have sworn his look softened, turning his eyes velvet brown. He held her a little longer than necessary, and she wondered at his intentions. Then suddenly he let her go, almost pushing her away. Turning, he walked swiftly to his horse. She knew she should have been furious at him, but she was just too tired.

By evening, she'd decided that cooking was better than starving and was certain Julia would have agreed.

"I've decided I cook better than you do," she told him, trying to retain as much dignity as she could. "I might as well have decent food while we're together."

He eyed her tired expression. "Where'd you learn to cook? I thought a lady like you had servants for that sort of thing."

The way he said the word *lady* stiffened her spine, but she let the remark pass. "We weren't always rich, Mr. Langley," she said, telling as much truth as she could. It was not her nature to lie. "When I was a little girl I lived in Highland Falls, near the military academy at West Point. My cousin and I both lived there. Both of our fathers attended the academy."

"I've met your cousin," he told her, and her veins turned to ice.

"Oh, really? When was that?"

"A little over two years ago. I'm afraid it wasn't a very pleasant encounter."

"What a surprise," she said sarcastically. Then she couldn't resist asking, "What did you think of her?"

Hawk watched her intently. "She seemed nice enough. She's no better at following orders than you are—and not nearly as pretty." He grinned broadly. It was the first real smile she'd seen.

"What would you like for dinner?" she asked, moving the subject to safer ground. Her cheeks burned from his compliment—or insult—she wasn't sure which. Keeping her face averted, she stretched a little to try and work the kinks from her back.

"Come here."

Her head came up cautiously. "Why?"

"Because I said so. When are you going to start following orders?" His voice sounded stern, but his eyes were teasing. "I thought your father was a military man."

"Odds are, I'll never do exactly as you say, sir," she answered with a bit of arrogance. But she walked to where he sat on a fallen log beside the fire.

"Sit down."

She eyed him suspiciously. He grabbed her hand and pulled her onto the mossy grass at his feet.

"I'll cook tonight," he told her. "You've had enough fun already." His eyes danced with mischief, and she blushed again, thinking what a fool he'd made of her earlier. "You can start first thing in the morning," he finished.

Mandy sighed with relief. Every muscle in her body ached. As if he had read her thoughts, she felt warm, wide hands rubbing the pain in her shoulders. She stiffened slightly, but, as she realized he had no evil intentions, began to relax. He massaged her back, then lifted her hair and massaged the soreness in her neck a little. She thought she noticed a slight tremor in his hand as he touched her bare skin, but she couldn't be sure. She knew what he was doing wasn't quite proper, but her muscles were so sore, and his fingers so magical, she let him continue.

His voice sounded gruff when he spoke again. "I think I'd better get started on supper." He turned away abruptly. "Try and be a little more cooperative tomorrow, Miss Ashton. The sooner you start doing what I tell you, the better off you'll be." With that he walked away.

Mandy fumed at his arrogance. *What I tell you.* Just who did he think he was, anyway? Her father? She'd had enough of men like him to last a lifetime. She wasn't about to start taking orders from another man, just when she was about to break free.

Unbidden, her thoughts strayed to the gentle way he'd touched her, the strength and concern she'd felt from his hands. Hawk was a strange man indeed—but attractive, if you could ignore that vile temper. He did have an intriguing cleft in his chin . . . and a powerful jawline that tightened almost imperceptibly when—God! How could she be thinking such things? Especially about a man like him! What was happening to her out here in this wilderness? She shuddered to think she was becoming more like her cousin every day.

Chapter Seven

✦ ✦ ✦ ✦

THE END OF the week brought another day of hard riding.

The terrain changed from steep pine-forested hills to arid rolling plains. Miles of them. The landscape broken only by periodic flat-topped buttes. It was stark and lonely, but magnificent in its own brutal way.

Hawk remained distant, though courteous, and Mandy acted cool in response. She was beginning to like James Long. He was truly a gentleman, one with a great wit and sense of humor. He kept them entertained with stories of the two men's past adventures and, braving his friend's wrath, told her a little about Hawk's Indian background.

"He still isn't certain he wants to be associated with us *white eyes*," James said, grinning and ignoring Hawk's scowl. It was easy to see their mutual respect. Mandy longed to join in their friendly camaraderie, especially out in this desolate country.

By late afternoon, Mandy, bone-weary from such long days in the saddle, was almost too tired to cause her alotted amount of trouble for the day. But Hawk was relentless. Reminding herself of her promise to her cousin, and in protest to the grueling pace, she began to curse him under her breath, then finally aloud.

"Are you trying to return me to my home, or get me out of my father's hair for good?" she questioned waspishly. Then she wondered if there might be some truth to her words. He remained silent. "Have you no decency? How much am I supposed to suffer just because I happened to fall in love?"

Both men drew up their mounts at that remark. They looked as though they felt she might be somewhat justified in her thinking.

"I suppose we're far enough away. Our trail's too cold to follow by now, and the route we took should have lost him anyway. We'll make camp early," Hawk promised. His dark eyes scanned the countryside.

"Thank God." Mandy sighed. The pace so far would have strained even the most seasoned traveler.

They found a likely campsite on the north side of the Mormon trail, the route they would

now be following, at least as far as Great Salt
Lake City. The land was flat and grassy. Deep
wagon ruts marked the trail, worn by years of
determined *emigrants*, as they were known.
The pilgrims who traveled west thought of
themselves as migrating *from* their former
homeland instead of *to* a new home as most
immigrants did.

The trio tethered their animals beneath a
grove of cedars that lined a small inlet on the
winding Platte. Mandy couldn't wait to get the
week's worth of dust and grime off her body.

"I'm going to take a bath downstream," she
announced as soon as they were settled. "I'll
thank you to give me some privacy."

"You're not going anywhere," Hawk said.
"At least not until I have a chance to scout the
area." He turned his attention to James. "I saw
some fresh sign earlier, in that direction."
Hawk pointed downstream. "I'd better take a
look."

Mandy was certain Hawk was just being
contrary. There hadn't been any Indian problems recently, at least not in this area. Besides,
Red Cloud had already agreed to sign a peace
treaty. Who did Hawk think he was fooling? It
was just another ploy to keep her close to
camp. Deciding to confront him, she marched
resolutely in his direction.

"You take great pleasure in disagreeing with
me, don't you?" she told him. "You're just
trying to make my life as miserable as possible.
Is Father paying you extra to torture me all the
way to California?"

She was grimy and tired and yearned for a bath in the stream. She stamped her foot and pouted, just as her cousin had taught her. But she was beginning to have difficulty separating her "Julia" role from the real Samantha. Or was she really more like her cousin than she thought? This sandy-haired stranger had her frustrated and confused.

Hawk just glowered and stalked away.

"We'd better do as he says," James said, giving her a sympathetic glance. "The water looks inviting to me too, but I've come to respect Hawk's sixth sense when it comes to trouble. It's saved our necks on more than one occasion." He put his hand on her shoulder, meaning to console her, but she pushed his hand away.

She was in no mood to be placated. She just wanted a bath. She tossed back her head and plopped down on a big boulder without so much as a backward glance.

"Leave her be." Staring at the girl's stiff back, Hawk was all too aware of the fetching picture she made in the dust-covered riding habit. When she turned around, a ragged tear in the bodice revealed a little too much cleavage and a split seam a good bit of ivory skin. He saw a fleeting image of himself ripping the clothes off piece by piece, leaving only her mane of chestnut hair to cover her charms. He shook his head as if to clear the unwanted notion.

"I'll be back before dark," he informed James, heading toward the big roan. "Maybe our little minx will be in better spirits by the time I return.'' The knowing look on James's face said the odds were against it. Hawk smiled to himself as he rode from the camp. The governor certainly had raised a little spitfire.

James busied himself setting up the camp. Though the horses had been rubbed down and tethered by the stream, there was still the pack mule to tend and wood to gather for the fire—if Hawk felt it was safe. He'd give Julia a little time to herself; maybe it would put her in a better mood. Tomorrow they would slow the pace a bit. Maybe that would ease everyone's nerves.

While James was busy setting up camp, Mandy took a walk in the shade of the trees. No one had paid much attention to the cedar grove, except as a good location for an early camp. Now, as Mandy made her way through the cool mossy interior and out the opposite side, she spotted a small tributary stream babbling noisily over rounded rocks and swirling into a shallow pool beneath a hillside of yellow balsam. It was just too tempting to pass up a second time. She glanced around quickly to make certain no one was near—she could be in and out before they even missed her.

As fast as her nervous fingers would allow, she unfastened the dusty, restricting garments, stepped out of her slip, and stood in her chemise and pantalets. She meant to do no more than wade by the edge, but the cool stream rippling against her legs was irresistible. With only a moment's hesitation, she threw off her remaining garments and eased out into the stream. The water barely covering the swell of her hips, she sank into the cooling depths. Her tired muscles relaxed as she allowed the invigorating water to wash over her, carrying away the dust and dirt and some of her woes.

Feeling carefree for the first time in days, she ducked her head beneath the surface to wash as much of the grime from her hair as she could, then all too soon made her way resignedly to the edge of the stream.

Out of nowhere, a hand clamped over her mouth. She tried to scream, but the sound came out as a muffled sob. Pinned against a man's hard chest, she felt powerful arms beneath her knees lifting her from the stream. She made no move to fight, too terrified even to breathe.

Willing herself to be calm, she focused her eyes on the leather fringe on the man's shirt and the sandy hair on his chest. She glanced up, recognizing immediately the grim-set features of the one who caused her such distress. He motioned her to be silent as he carried her, drenched and dripping, behind an overgrown fallen log.

What could this madman be thinking? Had he been spying on her the entire time she was in the stream? Surely he only meant to punish her for not obeying his orders. She drew herself up, wanting to unleash a verbal tirade and hoping she could force him to release her so she could dash for her clothes.

He shook his head and silently pointed in the direction of the stream. Three Sioux braves, bare-chested, bare-legged, and scantily clad only in breechcloths, rode brazenly up to the opposite bank of the creek. Gleaming red, yellow, and black war paint in geometric designs was smeared across their glistening bodies. Intent upon watering their lathered ponies, they sat quietly talking only a few feet away from the log.

Mandy's senses reeled. She'd lived on the frontier most of her life. She'd seen firsthand the horrible torture Indians reserved for their captives. These three were part of a war party—out for scalps. The image of Davey Williams's mutilated body blocked all other thoughts from her mind. She clung to Hawk in terror, too afraid to remember her nakedness, her breathing shallow and weak.

Crouched behind the massive fallen log, Hawk held the trembling girl in his lap. Her eyes glittered with fear. Her arms clung to his neck. By now his buckskins were soaked through, allowing him to feel her slightest movement. He cursed the situation he was in and the sudden swelling in his breeches.

Finally the Indians finished watering their

horses. Hawk tensed as the braves glanced across the stream and pointed in his direction. He could feel the girl's heartbeat quicken against his chest. A raven flew from the branches overhead. The Indians laughed, apparently satisfied, turned, and, stirring up a cloud of dust, rode away.

Relieved, Hawk glanced down at the girl clinging to him in terror. Glistening beads of water trickled down perfectly shaped breasts tipped just slightly upward as if to catch the warmth of the sun. A rose-colored peak at each crest hardened against the breeze. He could feel smooth skin beneath his fingertips.

The wind ruffled her damp hair. Only now did Mandy remember her circumstances. Turning crimson from the top of her dampened locks to the bottom of her toes, she glanced briefly into Hawk's eyes. What she saw there paralyzed her a second time. The eyes that met hers weren't hooded with the indifference she usually saw, but seemed to smolder with heat. She could feel the pressure of his muscled thighs beneath her, the warmth of his strong arms, and her heartbeat quickened.

She struggled to her feet, sensing a new and different kind of threat, but he caught her arm and hauled her against him. His mouth covered hers, his lips strong and warm but unyielding. She pressed her hands against him in protest, and the muscles beneath his buckskin shirt bunched at her touch. She tried

again to push him away, but her struggles
were weak, useless—part of her didn't want
to be free.

The kiss deepened. Hawk tasted, sampled,
caressed her with his lips. His tongue found
its way into her mouth. He tasted musky and
masculine. The smell of leather and horses
filled her senses. He kissed her thoroughly,
passionately. One hand held her chin, another
pressed against the small of her back, forcing
her tightly against him. She trembled violently, and against her will her arms slipped
around his neck. She heard a tiny moan and
realized only dimly it had come from her. She
ran a hand along his neck, buried it in his
thick sandy hair, and pulled him closer. His
hard chest pressed against the peaks of her
breasts, and the chill she'd felt only moments
before was replaced by a shiver of anticipation.

He kissed the line of her neck, his lips warm
and moist, then returned to her mouth. The
current of desire moved swiftly, flooding her
with waves of pleasure. Her body felt cold
and hot at the same time, as if she were
drowning in a pool of liquid fire. With a moan
and a final surge of willpower she tore herself
free, trembling with a new kind of terror.

His eyes raked her. She swallowed hard,
trying to compose herself, trying to think
straight. "How . . . how dare you sneak up on
me!" she accused, hoping her voice didn't

sound as shaky to him as it did to her. "Just who do you think you are?" She was having trouble remembering her role, remembering even where she was. The world seemed blurred, fuzzy.

His voice rang harsh, husky. "You little idiot, you almost got yourself killed, or worse— a white woman with that mane of hair would make a nice prize for the whole tribe—after those braves had their fill of you." He hadn't meant to spy on her. He'd spotted her accidentally. He intended to stay hidden, give her the privacy she needed, yet keep an eye out for intruders. But the Sioux bucks set events in motion. He had to quiet her for all their sakes.

Mandy's stomach lurched. She closed her eyes, shuddered, and swayed against him. *He was right!* Thank God he'd come along when he did. She glanced down and for the first time remembered her nakedness. Feeling bright heat rush the length of her, she gasped, darted from behind the log, and ran to get her clothes. Hiding behind a rock, she put them on quickly, not wanting to tempt Hawk further. She felt as if her body were strung as tight as a bowstring. *What was happening to her?*

She buttoned her riding habit with trembling fingers, shocked at her scandalous behavior. In truth, once the real danger had passed and her fear subsided, she was glad he'd seen her naked. Glad she could have such an effect on him. She was sick and tired of his indifference. At least now he knew she was a woman—not just some object he was transporting.

She pulled on her riding boots and tugged weakly at the laces, but her thoughts dwelled on the warmth of his kiss. His lips had been demanding, but they'd held a touch of gentleness she hadn't expected. She'd been kissed once before, by a soldier at the fort who walked her home from a social. She had given him a resounding slap for his boldness. But not Hawk. Why had she responded to Hawk's kisses and not the soldier's? What was wrong with her? How could she even be thinking about a callous brute like him? She couldn't believe she was the same woman who, only weeks before, wore ill-fitting clothes to discourage men's attentions. She must be going mad!

More shaken from his encounter than he cared to admit, Hawk felt an ache in his breeches that wouldn't soon be soothed. He walked to where he'd tied the roan, some distance from the stream. Fortunately, James would have enough sense not to build a fire until he knew it was safe.

It would be a cold camp tonight.

He wondered which band the three Sioux were from. Red Cloud had a treaty in the works, and an uneasy peace was holding. Of course there were always a few hotheads who weren't satisfied with being cooped up on the reservation. After spending most of his youth with the Cheyenne, he didn't blame them. The whites, like an unending army of invaders, infiltrated and destroyed the Indian lands. If he hadn't left the tribe when he did, hadn't learned how useless their battle really was, he would very likely be one of those hotheads himself.

He untied the horse's reins and led the animal back to the creek. He couldn't say he was sorry he'd had to drag his reluctant charge from the stream. He grinned to himself. She was perhaps the most fetching piece of baggage he ever had the good fortune to behold. He remembered the way her green eyes flashed, her chestnut hair wrapping itself seductively around her most intimate charms. He was more than a little regretful of the promise he'd made her father. He hadn't meant to kiss her—the traitorous little witch, supposedly so in love with her *Jason*. He guessed her father was probably right. She really loved only herself.

Well, he was certainly never going to fall in love. That was strictly for fools.

Chapter Eight

✦ ✦ ✦ ✦ ✦

HAWK, JAMES, AND Mandy, bone tired and saddle weary, crossed the Big Sandy and the Green rivers and were traveling through particularly dusty terrain.

The trail stretched for miles ahead, the ground broken only by occasional patches of sagebrush. Mandy was doing her best to delay them as long as possible when a dust devil whipped around, choking off the already stifling air.

As the dust settled and her vision cleared, Mandy saw a tiny bobcat cub lying wounded, mewling softly, on the trail ahead. She rode her horse up and dismounted, approaching carefully so as not to frighten the animal. She stroked the cub's soft fur and crooned to it gently, examining a wound in its leg. The cub didn't fight her; it seemed to sense her concern. The ominous click of a revolver being cocked swung her around.

"Go back to your horse, I'll take care of the cub," Hawk told her, his eyes gentle.

"You're not going to shoot the poor little thing?"

"We can't let him suffer. I'll put him out of his misery." He set his jaw in a grim line, but his voice betrayed his concern. "Please, just do as I say."

Mandy was lost in the past. She could almost hear her father's voice, see Schooner's soft brown eyes looking up at her as he thrashed helplessly in the dry dusty earth.

"No!" She rose and faced Hawk squarely. "The leg's not broken; we've got to try and save him." Her voice sounded brittle in the hot afternoon air.

Hawk stared down at her, still gripping his Colt. "There's nothing we can do. Just get back on your horse."

Mandy didn't budge. "The only way I'm going to let you shoot him is if you shoot me first!"

Hawk glowered down at her. For a moment he seemed uncertain. Then he sighed and holstered his gun.

"Women!" He stalked heavily back to his horse.

Mandy had the strangest feeling he was glad she hadn't backed down. She gathered the cub in her arms and headed for a nearby creek. She cleansed the animal's wounds as best she could, tore some strips of cloth from her petticoat, and bound the torn leg.

She refused to budge for the rest of the day while she waited, praying the cub's infection would abate and the fever would break.

Hawk fumed, but Mandy suspected he grudgingly admired her determination, was proud of her concern for the wild creature. Grumbling, he made camp where they were, rationalizing aloud that for what they were being paid, one extra day wasn't worth worrying about. He even showed her how to make a salve for the wounded leg using some of the Indian herbs in his saddlebags mixed with a small amount of animal fat. Again, as she watched him with the cub, she sensed a gentleness in the big man she hadn't thought possible.

By morning the cub was definitely improved. He ate scraps from a supper of antelope that Hawk shot before dark, and he was able to hobble around on his three good legs.

"He'll be all right now," Hawk assured her. It was obvious he was pleased by her ministrations. "I have to tell you, Miss Ashton, you did a fine job on the little one. Where'd a city girl like you learn to doctor like that?"

"I . . . ah . . . ah . . . I used to have a governess who was a nurse," Mandy stammered, the question throwing her. She lowered her eyes and looked away, refusing to hold his intense gaze, hating to lie to him on one of the few occasions he'd shown her kindness. Mandy felt him watching her. He sensed her change of mood, and the moment was lost. Giving her an uncertain glance, he withdrew to his usual wary distance.

"Well, we've wasted too much time already. Let's get mounted and back on the trail. We wouldn't want to keep the governor waiting, now, would we?" He was back to his familiar taunting self.

And Mandy was infuriated as usual. How could he be so caring one moment and such a devil the next? Well, she'd been cooperating far too much lately, anyway. She'd promised to slow them down, and slow them down she would. Sooner or later she'd find the opportunity.

Days on the plains came and went, as endless as the prairie they were crossing. The three had fallen into a quiet routine. Mandy and James were becoming quite amiable, their friendship deepening with each passing day. James always seemed to have a cheerful word. Mandy and Hawk rarely spoke. Sometimes she would catch him looking at her when he thought she wouldn't notice, but he never allowed his gaze to linger. Mostly he treated her with indifference, always courteous, but with a hint of disdain, as if he knew something about her of which he disapproved.

One night after a meal of tough prairie chicken roasted over a sagebrush fire, Mandy strolled to the edge of camp to admire the night sky. On these limitless plains the stars were as plentiful as the clumps of sage and seemed to touch the very earth around them.

"Isn't it beautiful, James," she commented, hearing his now-familiar footsteps coming up behind her. Though she'd lived on the frontier most of her life, she'd never really appreciated the beauty of the vast landscape. Out here, it was impossible not to. The immense emptiness magnified each star, turning it into a perfect white diamond, a jewel gleaming in an onyx setting.

"Yes, it is. Very beautiful. Almost as beautiful as you."

"James, don't . . ." she whispered. For some time now, she'd been afraid of becoming too close, afraid he might misunderstand their rapidly developing friendship.

"Don't worry, Julia. As lovely as you are, and as much as I might wish it weren't so, I see the way you look at Hawk." His honest answer set those fears to rest and presented a new one.

"Don't be silly!" she countered, feeling the color rush to her cheeks. "Why, we hardly even speak. Besides, he obviously dislikes me." For some reason, the thought depressed her.

"He doesn't dislike you, Julia," James replied, trying to explain to her something even he didn't understand. He'd never seen his friend act so strangely in all their years together.

"It's just that . . . well, Hawk was raised by the Cheyenne, and they have a strong sense of morals. He just thinks you're, well, spoiled, and maybe a bit of a tease. Considering you're supposed to be in love and engaged, he may have a point."

"How dare he think such a thing!" Mandy sputtered. "Why, I've never teased that . . . that . . . He was the one who dragged me from the stream. I certainly didn't ask him to!"

Seeing the dismay on James's handsome face, Mandy realized too late that Hawk had never mentioned the episode at the creek. A small place in her heart thanked him, grudgingly, for his discretion.

"I mean, I can't imagine how he could think I was a tease. I never even talk to the man," she finished lamely.

"Simmer down," he soothed. "Hawk's no fool and neither am I. I just wish you looked at me that way."

"Well you are both wrong!" Mandy stormed. "I'm in love with Jason, and I'm going to marry him. I wouldn't give Hawk the time of day!" She hoped she sounded more convincing to James than she did to herself.

"Take some advice from a friend?" James asked.

Mandy was too mad to answer.

"Make sure you don't fall in love with Hawk."

"Men!" she stormed, wondering what the warning meant. "You're all alike!" Furiously, she turned and stomped back toward camp, throwing Hawk a sidelong glance, wanting to slap his conceited face. Oh, that man. Would she ever stop thinking about him?

"Whatever you say," James called out as she walked away. He watched her retreating figure, stiff and determined, and smiled to himself. Maybe she didn't know how beautiful she was, didn't realize the effect she had on the men around her. That image certainly didn't match the one in the newspapers, but he really didn't care. He was sure she thought of him only as a friend, unfortunate as that might be. Considering his promise to the governor, it was probably for the best. He could see the constant battle Hawk waged with himself just to keep his hands off the girl.

James glanced back to the fire. She stood beside it, her gaze fixed in the flames. He realized he'd grown fond of her, no matter who she loved. He hoped, for her sake, it was this mysterious *Jason*. He pitied any woman who fell for Hawk. Hawk believed there was only one good place for a woman—and that was in bed!

But there was definitely something different about this particular woman, the governor's daughter. He sensed it, and so did Hawk. Aside from being one of the prettiest women James had ever seen, it was almost as if she were two different people. Most of the time she was willful, spoiled, and just generally a handful of trouble. But other times, like when she'd fought Hawk for the cub, she could show amazing concern and tenderness.

A half day's ride put them just shy of Fort Bridger. Mandy knew the fort had been settled originally by a mountain man named Jim Bridger and at one time was home to Kit Carson, the famous scout and explorer. It had been a landmark on the trail for decades. Over

the years the fort had fallen into disrepair, but
with the Indian troubles of the last few years
the Army had decided to revitalize it.

Mandy had never traveled this far west and
was looking forward to visiting a place she'd
heard about since her childhood. Hawk swiftly
put an end to that idea. Instead they stopped
some distance from the fort and James was
sent in with the pack mule for the necessary
supplies.

"Why can't we all go to the fort?" Mandy
asked wistfully as she watched James ride
away. She longed for a bath in a real tub and
a night in a real bed.

"You know very well *why*, little one," Hawk
told her flatly. "Because neither James nor I
wish to fight the entire U.S. Cavalry just to
make your father happy."

He'd begun to use the nickname "little one"
after her adventure with the cub. Mandy liked
the sound of it spoken with just a hint of a
Cheyenne accent.

"Couldn't we go if I gave you my word of
honor not to speak to anyone about our trip?"
They rested on a wide log. There was wood to
gather, bedding to unroll, and a meal to start,
but the short break felt good.

"You couldn't go if you swore on a stack of
Bibles and your mother's grave," Hawk finished, ending the discussion.

A twinge of sorrow at the mention of her
mother creased her brow. It did not go unnoticed by the big man.

"I'm sorry," he apologized, looking as if he felt a little ashamed. "What was she like?"

"She was a wonderful woman. We used to do everything together. She taught me to cook," she teased.

"Then she did a good job."

"She also taught me to sew and how to raise a garden, how to play the pianoforte—dozens of things. My father and I loved her more than anything." She twisted a strand of her hair, afraid to say more, but she thought wistfully of how happy her family used to be. The house had been warm and cozy, not barren and empty as it was now. After her mother died, her father had stripped the house of anything that reminded him of his wife.

When her mother was alive, there were fancy lace doilies, colorful hooked rugs, warm chintz curtains. Her mother had been proud of her home, as simple as it was. Born wealthy, she'd grown up with all the luxuries money could buy, but her love for a young Army officer had been more important.

The family moved to the frontier when Mandy was nine, but her mother still insisted she learn all the social niceties she firmly believed necessary to a young woman's education. As Mandy played the role of the governor's daughter, she was grateful for all the dismal hours she'd spent at the task.

"She was very beautiful," she whispered, her mind picturing her mother smiling up at her.

Hawk's gaze lingered on her face. "Looking at you," he said, "that's easy to believe."

Mandy felt a rush of heat to her cheeks. She glanced down shyly, reveling in the compliment.

Hawk watched her a minute more, then cleared his throat and turned away. "We'd better get to work."

She nodded and started scanning the ground for a place to make a pallet for her bedroll.

Later that night, after a supper of roasted rabbit and the last of the pan biscuits, they sat on a flat rock in front of the fire. James wouldn't be back until morning, and Hawk appeared to be in good spirits, having just come from a dip in the Black River. His hair was still damp and curling softly, and his snug-fitting breeches, a little moist in places, clung to his powerful thighs.

As much as possible Mandy kept her gaze from straying, but his nearness caused her heart to thud. She could feel his gaze caressing the line of her cheek. Recalling his tender attitude earlier in the day bolstered her courage.

"Beautiful country, isn't it?" she began.

"Yes it is."

"You know it well." It was a statement, not a question.

"I was raised northeast of here. That's where my tribe lives." He glanced off in the distance, his mind somewhere in the past.

She took it as a good sign. Maybe he would

share a little of himself with her. She would risk it.

"You still say 'your tribe.' Aren't the whites 'your tribe,' too?"

He looked down at her thoughtfully. "Yes, I guess they are. Sometimes, when I think of how they treat the Indians, I wish I didn't have to claim them. But most of the time, I'm just as proud of my white heritage as I am my Indian."

It was the most he'd ever revealed of himself, and it gave her the courage to go on.

"What are you really like, Mr. Travis Langley? But you prefer Hawk, don't you?" He didn't answer, but just stared into the flames. "Are you really the ogre you make yourself out to be, or the soft heart I sometimes suspect?" She thought of the cub, and the times he'd been gentle when she'd least expected it.

A small smile lifted one corner of his mouth. "Probably a little of both, like most folks. I think most of us have more than one side to our nature." The firelight flickered seductively and cast a warm bronze glow to his skin.

"And you, Miss Ashton? Or shall I call you Julia?"

"Please, call me . . . Julia," she answered, and then suddenly wished she could hear him call her Samantha. She could imagine how soft it would sound coming out with a deep throatiness, masculine and sensual.

"And you, Julia," he corrected. "Are you

really the reckless spitfire you would have me think, or the sensitive young lady I saw tending the cub?"

She smiled, intent on answering truthfully. "A little of both, I suspect." She reflected on her behavior at the stream, but quickly sent her thoughts in another direction.

She was enjoying the intimacy she felt growing between them, which had not existed before. But she wanted to move the conversation away from herself.

"James said you were raised by the Cheyenne. Was it terribly hard on you?" She knew Hawk rarely spoke of his past. His dark eyes held hers, as if deciding how much to reveal.

"At first it was tough. But once I accepted my new life, I liked it. The Cheyenne are the only family I have left. My real parents died in a carriage accident when I was young. I was traveling west with my aunt and uncle when the Comanche attacked our small band of wagons. I was the only one who survived." He glanced away, a quick flash of pain reflecting in his eyes.

"I'm sorry." Her heart went out to the small boy who had suffered such tragedy.

Hawk searched the girl's green eyes. She looked as though she wanted to reach out to him, to comfort him. It made his chest tighten.

"That was a long time ago. Fortunately for me, the Comanche didn't want to fool with a bad-tempered white boy, so they traded me to the Cheyenne. The Cheyenne call themselves 'the human beings.' It fits them somehow. They're warmhearted, generous people."

Without realizing, she touched his hand as if trying to absorb some of the hurtful memories.

"How did you happen to leave?" she asked.

"Something just seemed to call me. My curiosity wouldn't let me rest until I knew about my past. I went to St. Louis to find a friend of my father's—one of the few people I could remember. He received me as if I were his long-lost son. Gave me everything I needed to readjust to civilization—schooling, manners, speech. I'll never forget him. He died just a few months ago." He felt a second flicker of pain, then set his jaw and called his mask back into place.

"Enough about me," he added, a little too jovially. "Tell me about you. Do you really fancy yourself in love with this Jason fellow?"

Mandy thought she saw a quick flash of regret, as if he wanted to call back the question. She wished with all her heart he could.

Taking a deep breath, she closed her eyes for a moment, trying to compose herself. She was forced to continue the lie. If he suspected —even for a moment—that she was not really the governor's daughter, neither she nor her cousin would have the chance for a new life. She steeled herself for the feeling of guilt she knew would come and answered with as much sincerity as she could muster.

"Why, of course I love Jason. We're going

to be married, and there is nothing anyone can do about it.'' If she hadn't known better, she would have sworn she saw him flinch. Then a look of cold steel came into his eyes that only moments before had been brown velvet.

"Love . . ." he snarled. "You wouldn't know the meaning of the word." He hauled her roughly against him and bent over her, crushing his mouth cruelly against her lips.

Mandy struggled, trying to free herself. She pushed against his chest, but he grabbed her wrists and shoved them behind her. His lips assaulted her, leaving a fiery trail wherever they touched. She struggled harder, terrified her limbs would soon refuse to obey. He held her easily, controlling her, gentling her.

His kisses turned soft. He caressed her lips with his. She felt her arms, no longer restrained, go around his neck, her fingers slipping through the damp strands curling over his collar. His tongue sought the warmth of her mouth, probing its recesses tenderly, sending flames of sensation burning through her. Then he was kissing her cheeks, her neck, moving back to her mouth. His lips scorched her soul. She was weak and light-headed, helpless to resist. She felt him unbuttoning the front of her dress, burying his face in the soft cleft between her breasts. Her tormented mind knew what she was doing—what she was feeling—must be wrong, but the heat of her passion would not let her stop. His rough hands explored the taut peaks of her breasts, teasing them, causing new sparks to flicker through her. The warmth of the flame spread to her loins, igniting her with a strange, aching need.

Then suddenly, as quickly as he'd begun, he stopped, almost tearing himself away. "Love!" he taunted, his breath coming in ragged gasps. "That's your idea of love. Just a quick, meaningless toss." His voice, husky with passion, echoed his obvious disgust. "You'd better get some sleep before I forget any rash promises I may have made. Good night, Miss Ashton," he ended sarcastically, stalking heavily away.

Mandy was too stunned to move. She hated herself for what she'd allowed him to do. She hated him for what he made her feel. She didn't understand him or herself. What was happening to her? Ashamed and humiliated, she lay down on her bedroll. She was glad he couldn't see the tears streaming down her cheeks.

Chapter Nine

✦ — ✦ — ✦

MORNING BROUGHT A drizzling rain that soaked the prairie and drenched the travelers.

Somehow it seemed appropriate, matched her mood, and that of the big man. James arrived early with the supplies and handed her a poncho. She mounted Lady Ann, who was as soggy as she, and they departed.

Mandy took a deep breath and braced herself for the day ahead. She could smell the parched musky odor of the damp earth as it turned dark and soft, soaking up the needed wetness. If she were able, she thought, she would melt away, lose herself in the river of mud at her feet. If only she were back in the safety of her world at the fort. There she had no worries, no feelings to be crushed carelessly at a man's whim—at least not feelings like those she'd been experiencing of late. Of course it had been lonely, but wasn't loneliness better than this hollow empty feeling she carried around most of the time now?

She knew it was partly the lies. It was not her nature to be deceitful. Now that she cared about her two companions—in ways even she didn't understand—it was even harder. But she had no choice. She'd given her word, and she'd abide by it. Julia's happiness—as well as her own—depended on it.

She thought of the vast, beautiful country they'd crossed, the things she'd already learned and seen. Whatever happened, she'd done the right thing.

The day was wet and cloudy, and a little windy at times, but it was not cold. It did, however, cancel any plans Mandy might have had for delaying their journey. She would have to wait until the storm finally abated.

The scent of pine needles filled the air now; the morning was clear and clean. The mountains they were traveling through were the most rugged and beautiful Mandy had ever seen. The peaks remained tipped with snow, and fluffy white clouds floated just beneath the crests. Jagged buttes gave way to great gorges, forested hillsides, and tumbling streams. The scenery was so spectacular Mandy took courage from the beauty surrounding her. Maybe today she would find the opportunity she'd been seeking.

Dressed once more in the tattered riding habit, Mandy rose and made a breakfast of sourdough biscuits and bacon. The three were on the trail with little delay. They had proceeded only a short distance when Hawk spotted a plume of white smoke curling on the horizon.

"We're only a day's ride from Great Salt Lake City," he said, his manner brusque, "but it never pays to be careless. James, you stay with the girl. I'll go ahead and see what's up."

James nodded his understanding, and Hawk• urged his big roan forward. In seconds he was out of sight.

James glanced around briefly, then rode to the forward position to keep a sharper eye on the trail ahead. Engrossed in watching for any sign of trouble, he paid Mandy little heed.

A plan had been forming in Mandy's mind for several days. If ever the men relaxed their vigil—and she was certain they would, sooner or later—she would simply turn around and ride back in the opposite direction—as far and as fast as she could. James might try to catch up with her, but he was not the tracker Hawk was. If she left the trail on rocky ground, she was sure she could lose James. She wouldn't go far—just far enough to cost them another day. By late afternoon she'd let them find her. Besides, she was sick and tired of being bullied by that big white Indian.

Recognizing her opportunity, Mandy turned Lady Ann around on the path and cautiously picked her way back down the hill. As soon as she rounded the first bend, out of James's sight, she urged the mare into a gallop. Off she went, down the hill as fast as she could go.

The wind sang against her ears, and the little mare flew over the soft-packed earth. Mandy slowed, left the trail just as she had planned, and, finding an open area, again gave Lady Ann her head. She thought of Schooner and was careful to watch the ground

* in front of her—and little else. Finally slowing to a walk, she trotted down the hill through a cool pine forest and several hours later emerged in some high-meadow flatlands. She marveled at the magnificent scenery and continued on toward where she believed she'd rediscover the trail.

"She's gone, Hawk. It's all my fault." James waited at the base of the ridge, twisting his hat in his hands. "I rode ahead on the trail just as a precaution. I guess she's been so good lately, I let myself be lulled into trusting her. I followed her trail back down the hill a ways, but lost it in some rocks. I figured we'd have a better chance together."

Hawk's face went white with suppressed rage. "That woman! She's got the face of an angel and the heart of a witch."

"I was so worried about a possible attack, I let her slip off. I shouldn't have trusted her, Hawk. I'm sorry."

"Fortunately, it was only a group of friendly Utes. As for trusting that . . . that . . . baggage, we'll find her soon enough, and this time I'll teach her a lesson about trust."

"Now, Hawk," James cautioned, "remember, she *is* the governor's daughter."

Hawk didn't reply. Instead he set his jaw, wheeled his horse, and headed in the opposite direction, back down the hill.

James felt a chill go through him at the de-

termined look on his friend's face. This was
no longer just another job. Maybe Hawk cared
for the girl more than he knew—and caring
for a woman was not something a man like
Hawk wanted to do. James pitied her, but
whatever happened now, he knew she'd
brought it on herself.

As the sky turned pink and gold, Mandy
began to feel alarmed. Why hadn't the
men caught up with her? They should have
easily found her by now. Glancing at her surroundings, the reason for their delay became
apparent—she was lost.

She'd left the trail only to throw them off a
little. She certainly hadn't meant to get herself
lost in the process. Fighting down a moment
of panic, she told herself there was no reason
to be afraid. She'd camped every night for
weeks and was certainly able to take care of
herself. She wished she had a gun, but a fire
should be enough to keep away any predatory
animals. Maybe the men would even see it.
She chided herself for not having enough fore-
sight to stash a little food for her dinner.

She located a good campsite, made a fire—
thank God she had sulfurheads in her saddlebags—and unfurled her sleeping gear. Ignoring the gnawing in her stomach, she lay down
on her bedroll to try and sleep. Grudgingly, she
admitted she missed the comforting presence
of the moccasined man silently checking the

camp and keeping a protective eye in her direction. As it was, every tiny noise seemed
magnified a hundred times. How she wished
she'd been watching the trail instead of indulg-
ing herself in a race with the wind.

After what seemed hours, she fell asleep.
Velvet brown eyes and an even smile filled
her dreams.

Chapter Ten
✦ ✦ ✦ ✦

"WE'D BETTER MAKE camp and start again at first
light." Hawk reined up his big roan. "We
might miss her tracks and lose even more
time." Pitch dark and still no sign of her. Her
trail in the soft mud had disappeared when
she'd descended into a rocky ravine and had
ridden into an area of granite crowns on the
other side of the mountain. They'd searched
well into the night, looking for hoofprints
where her horse had left the rocks.

"I curse the day we took this job, and all
females from here to California."

"We'll find her, Hawk," James said.

Visions of the delicate and pampered governor's daughter alone in the Rockies filled
Hawk's mind. There were a hundred deadly

perils just waiting for the unwary. The girl had no experience with the mountains. She had no weapon; he wasn't even sure she had enough sense to make a fire. Damn! He should have been more careful. His stomach knotted as he thought of wolves, snakes, and mountain lions, to say nothing of the deadly hundred-foot crevasses she might accidentally stumble into. He pictured her scared, crying, alone in the night, but somehow the image didn't fit the woman he was seeking—a woman savvy enough to lose a Cheyenne brave in his homelands. He chided himself. There was no way she'd planned to camouflage her tracks. She'd just gotten herself lost.

"She'll be all right," James was saying. "She's learned a lot these past few weeks. If she just stays calm, she'll be fine."

Hawk hoped James was right. He had to admit she'd held up a lot better than he'd expected. She pulled her weight and, though she constantly tried to slow them down, she was handling the tough trip just fine.

In the distance he heard the lone, bitter howl of a wolf, echoed by several others. He lifted his hat and ran an anxious hand through his hair. Damn her! Damn her to hell for making him feel so lousy.

Mandy awoke with a start. Something rustled the leaves in the rocks beside her. She shivered and hoped they would find her soon.

She decided she would circle her campsite until she cut back across the trail, assuming she hadn't gone too far astray. Then she could either continue her ride back toward Fort Bridger, or, she prayed, be "recaptured" by her handsome companions.

The night had seemed endless. The distant howl of a wolfpack kept her nerves on edge, though she'd finally gotten a little sleep. The sun was just creeping over the mountain, beginning to warm the clearing. Ignoring the hunger gnawing her stomach, she lifted her gear and walked to the glistening sorrel dancing at the end of her rope. Mandy was already attached to the pretty little mare with the white-stockinged feet. She petted the velvet muzzle and placed the blanket, then the saddle on Lady Ann's back. Being near the little mare gave her some measure of confidence. She tightened the cinch and mounted, pulling her tattered riding habit up to its usual place on her calf.

She wished she'd brought more clothes, but the men's unexpected arrival and their demand she take only what she need had distracted her. The rest of her clothes, they said, could be sent west by stage. Now she was paying dearly; there were rips and tears in everything. The only clean thing she had left to wear was the pair of men's breeches Julia insisted she bring, and they were far too revealing.

She'd hoped to use some of Julia's money to

buy some new things along the way, but the men carefully avoided any place with people. Well, Great Salt Lake City was not far off. If they ever found her.

With that last disquieting thought she rode off, slowly circling, hoping to find her way. She'd ridden for about three hours when she pushed through some tall grass and came upon the main trail. Awash with relief, she relaxed a little in the saddle, content that at least she was no longer lost. Almost immediately she sighted horsemen on the trail behind her and recognized Hawk's rugged tanned features followed by James's more genteel ones. She felt her heart lurch with such joy it surprised her. Shrugging it off, she thanked God she didn't have to endure another miserable night alone, no matter how insufferable their company.

As Hawk crested the grassy ridge, he spotted the little mare and its pretty rider. His chest tightened at the sight of her. She had stopped in the middle of the trail and just sat there, bare calves exposed, head held high, her mane of thick dark hair falling around her shoulders. She looked almost regal, even in her torn riding clothes. She must have known it was useless to run farther. Instead, she just sat arrogantly awaiting her captors.

Seeing her safe and unharmed, Hawk's worry changed to blinding rage. How dare she sit there calmly when they'd been up half the night searching for her! He rode up beside her, reached an arm around her waist, and pulled her roughly off her saddle onto his.

"All this trouble for your wonderful Jason?" he sneered, his temper murderous. "Did you really think you could get away with this? Do you have any idea how much trouble you caused us, you spoiled little . . . ?" He clenched his teeth. "And for what? So you can prove something to your father! Well, I think he's right. The only person you'll ever love is yourself."

Mandy's excitement and relief at being found disappeared as she listened to Hawk's vicious tirade. The hurtful phrases made her wish she'd tried harder to escape. Though he was right about the trouble she'd caused, she'd only done what she had to. She'd hadn't meant to get lost. She wished she could tell him the truth.

"We should have left you out there alone for a few days. It might have taught you a lesson," he snapped.

Mandy couldn't take any more. Wasn't he the least bit concerned about her welfare? She could have been killed out there by herself!

"I love Jason, you cruel-hearted bastard," she retorted defensively. "At least he would be happy I'm safe. The only thing you care about is my father's money." Mandy didn't care what she as saying as long as it stopped Hawk's vicious remarks.

Hawk was like a man gone mad. He'd hardly slept all night for worrying about her, and here she was, calmly riding back to Fort Laramie and her lover. He longed, at that moment, to put his hands around her slender throat and choke some sense into her.

He let her down from the horse and dismounted. He moved toward her and she circled like a wild animal, wary yet ready to pounce at any moment.

"You don't care about this *Jason*," he taunted. "You just want something your father has forbidden. Well, this time you aren't going to get your way. Do you hear me?"

Every word was a challenge.

"I hear you. And I'm telling you I'll do exactly as I please. And nobody, especially an overgrown bully like you, is going to stop me." Tense and frustrated to the point of breaking, Mandy sprang at Hawk. She pounded his chest, clawed and scratched like a wildcat.

Hawk grabbed her hands and held her easily at bay, a cynical smile curving his lips. "Why you little she-cat, you really don't care about anyone but yourself, do you?"

How could he be so heartless? She was the one who'd suffered out in the dark all alone. She was the one who hadn't slept all night, who'd had no gun for protection, no food since yesterday.

With a huge effort, she broke free. Before she could stop herself, she drew back a hand and slapped Hawk across the face with all the force she could muster, the resounding crack so loud it echoed across the clearing. A fleeting look of surprise flickered across his handsome face. Panic-stricken, she widened her eyes with horror at what she'd done. In an instant Hawk captured her again, a look of grim determination turning his features almost demonic.

"I should beat you the way the Cheyenne do their women when they misbehave, but I doubt your father would approve. So instead . . ." As he talked, one arm grasped her wrists, the other tightened like an iron band around her waist. He was half carrying, half dragging her across the damp earth.

Before she realized what was happening, Hawk had reached a fallen cedar log, had draped her over his lap, and was raising her tattered skirts over her head.

"What are you doing?" she demanded, her voice shaky. "Are you out of your mind?"

"I'm doing what your father should have done years ago." His fingers tugged at the cord holding up her cotton pantalets. Frustrated, he growled and ripped them down to her knees, exposing her bare bottom.

Mandy flushed from head to foot. *How could he?* She squirmed and wriggled, trying to escape. "Let go of me!"

Hawk ignored her. His strong grip pinned her across his knees. Without hesitation, he began to spank her—fast and furiously, the flat of his wide hand smacking her bottom again and again.

"Let go of me—you monster! You're hurting me!" Tears of rage and frustration filled her eyes, and her voice cracked. But Hawk was relentless. The more she wiggled and squirmed, the harder he spanked her—the stinging, burning sensation worse every time his hand connected.

She began to cry in earnest. "Please, Hawk," she pleaded, her breath coming in ragged gasps. "I'll do whatever you ask. Anything . . . I promise."

As his hand began to hurt, Hawk's temper cooled and his senses returned. The girl lay unresisting across his lap, sobbing, her smooth round bottom pink with the imprint of his hand. Remorse inched its way into his thoughts. He pulled up her now worthless pantalets and her skirts down, and cursed himself for losing his temper.

Lifting her off his lap, he helped her to her feet. The tears on her cheeks tugged at his heart. Damn! If only she hadn't hit him. He couldn't believe how badly he'd lost control. What was it about this particular woman that infuriated him so?

Mandy refused to look at the big man. "I hate you! You're cruel and heartless," she swore between sobs. "I'll never forgive you for this. Never!" Shame and humiliation drove her to risk his anger again. Holding together the shredded clothing as best she could, she bolted for the woods.

"You shouldn't have been so tough on her,

Hawk," James said accusingly, returning to the clearing. He had walked away from the pair when he realized what was about to take place, not wanting the girl's humiliation to be worsened by his presence. He felt more than a little disconcerted by the whole episode; now, hearing her muffled crying, he wondered if he should have intervened.

"Leave me alone, James," Hawk told him bitterly.

James met his friend's brooding gaze and realized Hawk was more than a little disconcerted himself. James walked away, leaving his friend alone with his thoughts. He could hear the big man's moccasined feet padding stiffly back toward the horses.

After the morning's misadventures, Hawk determined there would be no further travel until the next day. Since the area they'd stopped in would make an acceptable campsite, he proceeded silently with his usual responsibilities, and James did the same.

With hours remaining before dark, Hawk set out to find fresh game for supper, a small peace offering. Walking quietly up and over a grassy knoll, he spotted a jackrabbit unfortunate enough to be outside its burrow. As it bolted for its hole beneath a clump of sage, Hawk dispatched it neatly with a throw of his knife. The knife was just one more precaution. The less noise they made in these mountains the better. They'd already been far too conspicuous.

When Hawk returned to camp, James volunteered to skin the rabbit. Then he skewered it on a green pine bough and placed it over the fire, the succulent drippings soon searing the hot rocks below.

The delicious aroma of the rabbit drifted through the forest. Mandy smelled it and her stomach growled, a reminder she hadn't eaten since yesterday. Knowing she must face her companions sooner or later, and in concession to her growing appetite, she threw back her shoulders, held her head high, and marched into camp with all the dignity she could muster.

She accepted the tin plate James offered and, throwing him a sidelong glance that accused him of abandoning her in her time of need, ate ravenously. Hawk turned away guiltily when he noticed she preferred to stand while eating the delicious rabbit.

After dinner she helped James with the few dishes they used, her silence almost tangible.

"We'd better turn in early," Hawk suggested with a scowl. "Tomorrow's going to be a long day." He wanted to travel hard to make up for lost time.

It was a silent camp as each of the men made his way to his sleeping place beside the fire. Mandy followed at a distance.

James had no trouble relaxing, his thoughts on Great Salt Lake City. There would be no gaming tables, but a bath and a real bed, and maybe a comely maid to eye if he got lucky.

He wished fervently they were closer to Virginia City. There he could find a little companionship of the sort to warm his bed and lessen the strain he was feeling from eyeing the governor's daughter as she worked around the camp.

James sighed and settled himself a little deeper. Fortunately or unfortunately, depending upon how you looked at it, he knew his petite charge thought of him only as a friend. It would have been easy for him to think otherwise if he let himself. He had rarely seen a more enticing woman.

But he was smart enough to know once a woman's mind was set there was little chance of changing it. He wondered who the girl really loved, this Jason fellow or Hawk—or maybe herself, as the governor suggested. He doubted the latter, but knew time would tell. He contented himself with thoughts of Great Salt Lake City and of Virginia City in the not-too-distant future and drifted into a peaceful slumber.

Hawk spent the night in an agony of confusion. Tossing and turning, he kept seeing over and over the luscious woman with the chestnut hair. He could still remember the fire in her eyes, like golden sparks leaping at him as she tried to claw his face. He hadn't meant to hurt her; in fact, he'd never been so relieved to see anyone in his life. She looked astonishingly beautiful sitting astride her little mare, skirts pulled to the middle of her calves, hair disheveled and falling around her shoulders like a glorious mane. Then he had remembered she was nonchalantly heading back toward her lover with no concern for what they were going through, no regard for their safety or her own, and he had completely lost his temper.

He chuckled to himself as he recalled her slap. His cheek still stung where her tiny palm connected. He wouldn't have believed someone her size could pack that much power in a single wallop. He had to admire her guts. Most *men* wouldn't have dared to do what she did. He couldn't really blame her, the way he'd taunted her. Besides, if he really admitted it, it was the worry she caused him, without the slightest remorse, that brought on the spanking.

That thought brought to mind a trim waist he could nearly span with his hands and a beautiful snow-white bottom. He knew he'd done no permanent damage, had just left his handprints—bright red on her ivory skin.

A persistent throbbing in his loins made him groan. Thank God they'd be in Virginia City before too long. He planned to find the most buxom wench in town and exorcise this ache he'd been suffering for weeks. He would cleanse these hellish thoughts of the woman from his mind one way or another.

Mandy lay on her stomach on her bedroll,

trying to sleep. She was still sore from the spanking, but by tomorrow she knew she'd be able to ride. It was her pride that smarted most. Damn that Black Hawk, or whatever his name was.

She thought of the way she'd slapped him. She must have been crazy to do what she did. It terrified her to think how much worse the consequences might have been. What could she have possibly been thinking? She knew she should hate the big brute, but even as she tried, she remembered the feel of his powerful arms around her waist, the warmth of his calloused hand. A hot blush spread over her as she thought of Hawk's outrageous actions. How dare he take such liberties! Grinding her teeth in frustration, she thought for the hundredth time how fortunate her cousin was in not making this journey, though the spanking might have done Julia some good.

Her mind returned to a pair of deep brown eyes and the feel of his muscular legs. If only there were some way to control her unruly thoughts. Scratching and slapping him hadn't helped a bit. She wondered what would. Getting rid of him in Sacramento City for starters. She'd promised Julia to delay as long as possible, but as far as Mandy was concerned, she'd done more than enough along those lines. Now she would just be glad when the whole charade was over.

Chapter Eleven

✦✦✦✦✦

JAMES MIGHT HAVE enjoyed the day, but Hawk's mood was black and the girl's even blacker.

The camp was like a battle line. No one said a word through breakfast. They ate hurriedly and resumed the journey.

The day was sunny and clear, the crispness in the air a testament to the last rays of summer, but they rode along in silence. The stiff breeze shook the towering pines, creating a lonely sound that reflected the bleakness of his friends' moods.

Night camp wasn't much better. The air was thick with hostility, sideways glances, and accusing stares. Tomorrow they would reach Great Salt Lake City and James was determined to end this feud between his two companions. He'd tried to talk to Hawk during the day, but received Hawk's usual "Mind your own business." James smiled to himself as he realized the extent of his friend's misery. This whole affair was becoming more amusing every day.

After the three finished a supper of fish stew prepared from his catch of rainbow trout and some plantain, James pondered the problem. He was determined to end this antagonism before they reached Great Salt Lake. He finished his chores and spotted the object of his intentions.

In a melancholy mood, the girl had wandered some distance from camp and was seated on a granite outcropping overlooking a tiny valley several hundred feet below. James could see her pretty silhouette across the clearing and the setting seemed perfect for the conversation he had in mind.

"Lovely night, isn't it?" he began cheerfully. "Mind if I sit awhile?" She shook her head. "How are you feeling this evening?" He noticed the blush rising to her cheeks and quickly amended, "I mean, are you too weary for a little conversation to cheer a friend?"

At James's reference to their friendship, Mandy brightened; in that instant it became clear she'd come to regard him as just that—a close and thoughtful friend. She decided whatever reason he had for not intervening on her behalf must have been a good one. She fleetingly wished this handsome stranger could be the object of her desires, instead of his black-hearted companion.

"No, of course not, James. Do you really need cheering?"

"Well, it does pain me to see two people I like not speaking to each other."

"I may never speak to him again after what he did to me," she said.

"Julia, Hawk was worried sick when he found you gone. It was a damn fool thing to do, and he was afraid you might get yourself hurt or killed out there in the dark. We tracked you into the night far later than we should

have. The horses were exhausted, and Hawk still wouldn't quit. I've never seen him in such a state. The only reason he stopped at all was for fear we'd miss your tracks in the dark and waste even more time."

"Hawk . . . worried about me? I find that hard to believe."

"Well, it's true. And when he finally did catch up with you, and you acted so indifferent, he just lost his temper. As a matter of fact," he added, "it's the only time I've ever seen him lose control.

"The Cheyenne are taught self-control from birth," he continued. "It's a quality highly prized among their people. You must really get under his skin." He chuckled. "Besides, if you don't mind my saying so, you really did deserve what you got."

Mandy flushed from head to toe and tried to change the direction of the conversation. She knew it would do no good to argue with either one of them on this subject. She was still not convinced Hawk had her best interests in mind. He was probably only worried about the money he would lose if he didn't bring her back to Sacramento City.

"How much money is the governor . . . I mean, my father paying you to bring me back?" she asked after a pause.

James hesitated only briefly. "A thousand dollars. . . . He must care a great deal about you, Julia."

"He cares a great deal about his reputation

and the family honor." Mandy spoke defensively as she felt her cousin would. She wasn't certain how much concern the governor really had for his daughter, but if he really wanted what was best for her, Mandy should be able to convince him that what she and Julia had done was in his daughter's best interest. She wondered briefly how the two men would react when they discovered they had transported the wrong woman all the way to California. She shuddered and pushed the awful thought away.

She tried again to find safer ground. "How did you and Hawk happen to meet?" Sarcastically she added, "That ought to be an interesting story."

James grinned openly. Seizing an opportunity to present some of Hawk's better qualities, he began to reminisce. "Well, we met back in 'sixty-two. I'd been running a poker game in Denver at the Red Dog Saloon. Been winning a lot—as usual." He winked. "I was beginning to worry that some of the gents in town might take it into their heads to get back their losses—one way or another. One man in particular worried me. Sergeant Max Gutterman. Ugly cuss. Only had one eye. Rumor was he'd lost the other fighting Indians. Some said his wife took up with a half-breed. The rest of the soldiers never let him live it down."

* * *

James had packed up late in the afternoon and had ridden out of Denver, headed toward Cheyenne. His saddlebags bulged with the money he'd won, and he was looking forward to seeing Millie Edwards, a lady friend of his. Ten miles northwest of Denver he made camp.

The air was cool. Autumn. His favorite time of year. He finished supper and stretched out on his bedroll, glad to be out in the fresh air again. He loved his life as a gambler—and the ladies who went along with it—but he still enjoyed the freedom of the trail.

He'd just started to stretch out when the sound of a snapping twig bolted him upright. He grabbed his revolver and stared into the silver-blue muzzle of a Colt .44.

"I wouldn't do that if I was you," Tom Jenkins said as he and Max Gutterman stepped into camp. Jenkins held his weapon steadily; Gutterman's fingers shook a little on the trigger of his gun. Three other riders covered them from their horses.

James slowly laid down his pistol and stood up, careful not to make any sudden moves.

"Okay, Long, where's the money?" Jenkins, a hard-faced man with a mustache and blond hair, spoke for the others.

"I won that money fair and square, Jenkins, and you know it."

The blond man chuckled mirthlessly, and his companions joined in. "Fair ain't got nothin' to do with it. Now, where's the money?"

James did not reply.

"Sergeant Gutterman, check his saddle-bags. Johnson, keep that gun leveled on him. He's craftier'n he looks."

"Money's here, all right," Gutterman called out. A bit of a German accent mingled with a western brogue. His barrel chest spread the button holes on the dirty shirt beneath his overalls. A patch covered one eye.

"Let's kill him and get this over with." Gutterman cocked his revolver and looked as though he was enjoying himself.

The others sat quietly atop their mounts.

"Well, friend," Jenkins said, a satisfied smile on his face, "sorry to disappoint you, but you win some, you lose some. Richie, take his horse—"

A graying rider nudged his mount toward the place where James's gelding was tethered.

James stood rigidly, trying to determine whether to make a move for the weapon at his feet, run for the trees, or play out his hand and hope the men would take the money and leave him alive. The latter seemed the least likely of the possibilities.

Time was running out. He'd have to make a move—and soon. Suddenly, from somewhere in the trees, a blood-curdling Indian war cry crystallized the night. Bullets bounced off rocks and whizzed into the dust, but he saw no one.

He hit the dirt and rolled behind a rock.

"Let's get goin'!" Jenkins commanded, forgetting James in his haste to escape.

Ignoring the danger, James leaped at Gutterman, punched him hard, grabbed the saddlebags, and dived again for the rocks.

Another chilling scream sent the barrel-chested sergeant running for his horse, Jenkins close behind. Gutterman mounted and glanced around, trying to locate James and the saddlebags, his face a mask of fury. Another barrage of bullets ended any further lingering.

Gutterman and Jenkins joined the others, and all five rode hell-bent for leather, a receding cloud of dust the only evidence of their trail.

Mandy sat on the boulder spellbound, her hands gripping the folds of her skirt. "You must have been terrified!"

James smiled ruefully, pleased with her concern. "That war cry scared me more than it did the gents. I can remember thinking, I've just missed dying by an outlaw's bullet; now I'm going to be scalped."

"What happened then?" Mandy prodded, eager to hear the rest.

"A huge Indian rode into camp, bold as you please." James chuckled as he recalled the image. "When he started speaking to me in English, you could have knocked me over with a feather."

" 'I am called Black Hawk by my friends,' " James said solemnly, doing a perfect imitation of his stoic companion. " 'Others call me Travis Langley.'

"I looked at him—and on the big Appaloosa he was riding, he looked eight feet tall. 'Then Black Hawk it shall be, my friend,' I said. And we've been just that ever since."

Mandy exhaled slowly. She'd become so engrossed in the story that she held her breath. "That's an amazing tale, James." She pictured the big man riding boldly into the camp.

"I wouldn't have believed Hawk capable of such a selfless act," she said, not really meaning it. The statement brought her swiftly back to the present.

"He's really not so bad, Julia, if you just get to know him a little."

Mandy set her jaw. "Get to know him!"

James sighed resignedly, and Mandy felt a momentary pang of guilt. She knew James had done his best to patch things up.

He rose and glanced back toward camp. "It's getting late. Think I'll check the horses before I turn in. Thanks for the company."

"Good night, James," she called after him, alone with her thoughts again.

Maybe James was right, she concluded, mulling the whole episode over in her mind once more. Maybe she'd gotten so immersed in her *Julia* role she'd let herself get mixed up. She knew there was something good and caring about Hawk. She could feel it. Surely she couldn't be completely wrong in her judgment of another human being—even one as hard to figure as Hawk.

She cringed a little as she thought of her actions—and his. She had known there would be some consequences to acting like Julia— she just hadn't figured on this one.

A few yards farther, deeper in the woods to her left, she could make out Hawk's strong profile against the backdrop of the rising moon. It was still a long way to California, and these last two days had not been pleasant. Now was as good a time as any. Taking a deep breath, she straightened her shoulders and headed toward the big man.

At the same instant, Hawk glanced up and started moving in her direction. They met halfway, both trying to speak at once.

"Hawk, I . . ."

"Julia, I . . ."

Each made an attempt to laugh. The sound came out tight and nervous.

"You go first," Hawk conceded, a look of contrition on his face.

Mandy stared at his square jaw just for a moment, her eyes moving upward to his straight nose, where she noticed a tiny crook that probably marked some past encounter. She grudgingly admitted it was just one more thing about him that attracted her.

"I just wanted to say I'm sorry for all the trouble I've caused you." Moonlight glistened on his thick sandy hair and lighted his dark eyes, allowing her to glimpse his concern.

"I'm the one who should apologize," Hawk countered. "I let my temper get the best of me. It's not something I do often."

"So I've been told," she agreed softly.

They faced each other only inches apart, she having to tip her head just to meet his gaze, unwilling to move or even breathe, for fear the spell would be broken.

Hawk stared into her gold-green eyes. The moonlight reflected the same golden highlights in her chestnut hair. She seemed innocent, vulnerable, and yet he knew it could not be. Before he could stop himself, he reached out to her, pulling her firmly against him, his mouth descending to claim her soft lips. She stiffened a little at his boldness. Then, as the kiss deepened, her lips parted, allowing his tongue access to the sweetness of her mouth. She relaxed against him, her arms going around his neck.

She felt so right in the circle of his arms, so small, yet she filled his senses, seemed more than enough woman to meet his needs. He groaned with desire. Slowly he began to explore the heady feel of her, his hands surrounding her tiny waist, then moving upward toward the swell of her upturned breasts. He could feel the rise and fall of her breathing, heightened by her excitement.

His mouth strayed from her lips to the smooth line of her neck, then moved upward again to nibble gently at the warm spot beneath her earlobe. His hands moved skillfully.

He could feel her tremble, even through the layers of her clothes. Unbuttoning the front of her dress, he cupped a firm, full breast, then caressed the rose-colored nipple and felt it harden against his palm.

Mandy heard her own tiny moan at the touch of his hand on so intimate a part of her body. She knew she should be stopping him, but instead felt herself relaxing in his arms, responding fully. She could feel him weaving her deeper into his spell as he began to trace a path of fire with his kisses, assaulting again the curve of her neck, exposed where he had pushed aside her hair. Moving down, his teeth nipped at her shoulders, then his mouth moved to capture the peak of her breast.

She couldn't believe what was happening. Though she'd been told the ways of a man and woman, never in her wildest imaginings could she have guessed what it would be like in reality. She felt powerless, completely under his control. The muscles of his back rippled beneath her fingers. She could feel his corded thighs, his male hardness pressed firmly against her. She couldn't move; it was all she could do to stand. She swayed against him and wave after wave of emotion surged through her. Her body responded to his every touch, and though she knew it must be wrong, she wished it could go on forever.

Hawk had lost all reason. He'd only meant to allow himself one chaste kiss, hoping it would stave off his desires until he reached

Virginia City. But her lips were honey, their softness leaving him aching with desire. He'd never wanted a woman as he did this one. Now he was lost. In another minute he'd have the girl on the ground and her clothes in shreds.

Steeling himself for the gut-wrenching reaction he knew would come, and with a power from he knew not where, he tore himself free, setting her away from him with an iron resolve.

Without a word he turned and strode away.

Mandy felt as if he'd poured ice water on her. Her head was spinning, and her heart beat so loudly she was certain he could hear it even as he walked away. What must he think of her? Why did she keep letting this happen? She just didn't understand. With trembling fingers she buttoned and straightened her clothes. A trail of tears scattered like rain upon the swell of her breasts.

Across the clearing, Hawk stood questioning his emotions. He'd never been so shaken in his life. Even when he'd awakened in the middle of a Comanche village as a child, he had not felt this unnerved. He was out of control, and he didn't like it. One more second alone with the girl and it would have been too late. His solemn word would have been broken—and for what? A two-faced vixen who'd probably bedded every rich dandy in Sacramento City. One who was right now cheating on her fiancé by kissing him.

He hated himself for what he allowed to happen and vowed not to weaken again. If only he could get over his nagging feeling the girl was an innocent. He knew in his heart it wasn't possible, and yet . . . Stalking back to camp, his mood blacker than ever, he lay down to another night of restless sleep.

Unbidden, the dream came.

Thin plumes of white smoke drifted up from tiny cooking fires beside teepees scattered across a wide green meadow. Dry pine needles carpeted the earth beneath the trees on the slopes of the hills—a shield from the warm summer sun.

The boy was older now, but the dream told him he had not yet reached his eighteenth year. He dressed hurriedly in loincloth and breeches, stepped into the bright morning light, and walked toward the edge of the camp. The moccasins beneath his rawhide leggings padded quietly across the dry grass; a bone-and-feather breastplate covered much of his chest, and his thick sandy hair hung well past his shoulders.

Even through the mist of the dream he could tell his skin, though darkened by the sun, remained lighter than that of the others. He moved with the stealth of a great cat, striding swiftly to the river. He bathed briefly in the icy mountain stream, dressed again, and headed toward his father's lodge, determined to make Strong Arrow understand his mission.

The dream wavered.

For an instant he was the little white boy, Travis, and all those remote memories filled his mind.

Then, just as quickly, he was Black Hawk again, son of a chief, a cunning hunter and fearsome warrior. A man who had put the past behind him and had come to love his Indian family as he once had the white mother and father of his foggy remembrance.

Across the meadow, he could see Running Wolf as a youth, with wide-set eyes and a teasing smile.

"My brother," Running Wolf called out, "you have missed most of the morning. You enjoyed yourself last night?" His wry smile made him look younger than his sixteen years. His black eyes twinkled mischievously, as he kicked a pebble in the dusty earth. "Maybe you especially enjoyed Dark Moon?"

"Dark Moon is a fair maid," Hawk answered. "Any man would be fortunate to enjoy her company." He made the statement flatly, betraying no emotion. Dark Moon had made her desire for him obvious, and he, too, felt the stirrings of passion, maybe even love, for the beautiful Indian girl. But he had not yet acknowledged her, though Strong Arrow pushed vigorously for the union.

They walked on toward Strong Arrow's teepee. Hawk could smell smoke from the cooking fires. The great chief met them at the entrance.

Hawk bid Running Wolf good-bye and stooped to enter the lodge, following behind his father. They took their places beside the fire, and the older man waited for his son to speak. Hawk could not find the words.

Finally, Strong Arrow spoke instead. "My son, I know why you have come."

Hawk stiffened. "You know? But how could you?"

"I have watched you with the others and with Dark Moon." His father's gaze held his. "Your white blood calls you."

"Father, I . . . I . . . wish there were something I could say." The pain of his leaving pierced Hawk's heart. There were not words enough in either language to make his father understand the gratitude and love he felt for all his father had done.

Strong Arrow laid a corded brown hand on Hawk's shoulder. "I know what is in your heart, my son. I know this is something you must do. When it is right, you will be able to walk in both worlds, but your heart will always remain here"—Strong Arrow placed a hand to his own heart—"with mine."

"Thank you, Father." Hawk was barely able to speak the words. A lump swelled in his throat, and his chest felt heavy. He swallowed hard. His father was right. He must go.

The dream changed.

Hawk lay in his teepee remembering the

white world. What few memories he had were sparse and disconnected. But he could remember the little things: the rustle of petticoats, the taste of ice cream, the softness of a deep feather mattress—and a man named Thomas Rutherford. Rutherford, his white father's best friend, had offered to take him into his home after his parents died. Hawk hoped the man would offer to help him again. The time was at hand for him to leave the security of his village. He must return to the white world to find out who he really was—Black Hawk or Travis Langley.

Hawk came awake with the first gray streaks of dawn. He blinked, trying to get his bearings, then sat up with a heavy sigh. He felt someone watching him before he turned his head. The girl stood ten feet away, looking at him.

"You were dreaming again," she told him. "I wanted to wake you, but after the last time . . ."

He smiled slightly and shook his head. "You're learning, Miss Ashton, you're learning. But I thank you for your concern."

She walked toward him as he got up from his bedroll. "Is it always the same dream?"

He stared hard at her, trying to assess her motives. "Parts of the same dream. Most of it's pretty unpleasant."

"So I gathered." She seemed genuinely concerned.

"Sometimes it's about the Comanche attack. Sometimes about leaving my village."

"Isn't there any way you can stop them?"

He released a deep breath. "Not that I've discovered so far. I'm used to them by now." He turned away and began to roll up his bedding. She watched him for a moment as if she wanted to say something more, then turned and walked away. He watched the gentle sway of her hips, and the memory of her kisses, the feel of her skin beneath his hand, set his blood to pounding. His hand trembled slightly as he tied a string around his bedroll. He struggled with his thoughts, determined to send them in another direction, and went to check on the horses.

Chapter Twelve

✦ ✦ ✦ ✦

FLEECY CLOUDS CROWNED the snow-capped pinnacles of the nearby Wasatch Mountains, the last range before their descent into the Great Salt Lake Basin.

As the trail wound over the crest of the ridge, Mandy could see a fertile valley below ringed by towering peaks, the tallest still powdered at its summit though the summer had been a warm one.

After interminable days on the prairie, where the landscape was broken only by endless clumps of sagebrush and an occasional trader's shack, the patchwork of farmland lying in the valley below was a welcome sight. It had been years since Mandy had seen farm country—not since her childhood, when she spent summer months visiting grandparents at their home in New York state. She blinked back a sudden wetness at the warm flood of memories; those times were some of her happiest.

But here the farms were laid out in regular rectangular parcels; no rolling hills or curving roadways broke up the terrain. A scattering of low-roofed farmhouses, each with a small garden behind, and cottonwoods, acacia, and a multitude of fruit trees—apple, peach—and vines dotted the landscape. It was easy for her to see why the Saints, the Mormons, were proud of their accomplishments.

Traveling a scant hour more, the group reached the outskirts of the city. Every twist in the road brought something new to look at and a smile to Mandy's face. What a lovely place to live, she reflected enviously. Compared to her stark surroundings at the fort, Salt Lake City seemed a paradise.

Guiding their horses past the jostling line of freight wagons, buggies, and a departing stagecoach, they finally reached the center of town. Mandy discovered most of the buildings were constructed of adobe that had turned a mottled gray in its battle with the elements, giving it the appearance of stone. There were also two-story granite block structures with ornately carved false fronts. The streets were wide, but dusty this time of year.

Mandy could see workmen carrying loads of brick or stirring tubs of mortar as wagons arrived with lumber and kegs of nails. James said the bustle of activity was construction work on the great temple.

A schoolmarm in a brown cotton dress, her hair pulled into a tight knot at the back of her head, and wearing a pair of wire-rimmed spectacles peered at the three weary travelers. Mandy thought how much the woman reminded her of herself just a few short weeks ago. She shuddered at the image. That was a part of her past she was glad to be leaving behind.

They checked into the Salt Lake House, a rambling structure much larger than it appeared from the street.

"What are the Mormons really like?" Mandy asked. "Will we get to meet one?" Every gentile, as all non-Mormons were known, had heard wild tales of the Mormon settlement. It was a forbidden subject in many households.

James chuckled. "There are few others in these parts, save traders and travelers like ourselves. But right now, I think the first order of business is a nice hot bath."

"A bath," she reflected wistfully. "A real bath."

Hawk watched as his lovely charge continued to smile for what seemed the first time in days, and was glad. "We'll get cleaned up, and I'll buy you both the best steak dinner in Great Salt Lake," he offered in an unusually expansive moment. When he saw the girl brighten even more, he felt a small stirring in the area of his heart.

James completed the arrangements with the innkeeper, Mandy accepted his arm, and accompanied him up the broad staircase.

"Not exactly the governor's mansion, but not too bad after sleeping on the ground for so long," James pointed out as he surveyed the tiny room with its narrow iron bed. "You know," he added somewhat thoughtfully, "I wouldn't have expected a governor's daughter to hold up so well on a difficult trip like this. You're a pretty fair traveling companion, Miss Julia Ashton." His easy grin and the sparkle in his black eyes indicated the sincerity of the compliment.

"Why, thank you, James." His compliment pleased her, but she wished she didn't have to accept it under false pretenses.

Just then a slight girl in her mid-teens, accompanied by a young boy, entered the room carrying pitchers of hot water. James checked the window, probably to be sure it was too far down for Mandy to jump, waited patiently until the pair completed their duties, then backed out into the hall. Mandy could hear the sound of the skeleton key turning in the lock, securing the door from the outside.

"Did you hear that, Max?" Jake Wiley whispered through yellowed teeth. "That little filly in there is the governor's daughter!" Wiley's bony finger pointed toward the locked door.

Sgt. Max Gutterman, with Wiley beside him, crouched around the corner and down the hall from the girl's room. Gutterman had seen James Long ride in and had followed him to the hotel, hoping to find a way to even an old score. He smiled to himself. This could be even better than he expected.

"What governor ya suppose it is?" Gutterman queried. He scratched his armpit through a hole in his red-checked shirt.

"How should I know? But any governor's bound to be willin' to pay plenty to get his daughter back." Wiley's dark eyes gleamed with thoughts of greenbacks so close at hand.

"For once, Wiley, you may have something," Gutterman concurred. He cocked his head at Wiley and adjusted the patch over his eye. "Besides, I got something to settle with that fellow she's with. You round up Pete and the Mex and bring 'em up the back stairs. Soon as you git back here, we'll pay the little lady a visit."

She was a pretty little thing, Max thought.

Reminded him of his wife, Myra. His mood blackened at the thought. Myra was no good. She'd taken up with a half-breed scout right under his nose. Made him a laughingstock in front of the whole outfit. His buddies had snickered behind his back for weeks before he'd caught her in bed with the man.

He'd loved Myra, would have done anything to please her. But nothing he did was ever enough. The best thing to come out of their marriage was Sarah. Sarah was a beautiful little girl, just like her mother, with bright green eyes and long brown hair. But that slut Myra let Sarah slip off one day when she should have been watching her. They searched for hours before they found her, face down in the pond. Two weeks later Max had found Myra in bed with the half-breed. He shot them both to death on the spot.

This girl looked a lot like Myra, all right, except smaller, and maybe even prettier. Fancy a man like himself meeting up with the governor's daughter.

Instead of being disheartened by James's lack of trust, Mandy viewed the locked door with a feeling of security. She stripped off her grimy garments, pinned her thick hair atop her head, and climbed into the tub. As she sank down, tiny lavender-scented soap bubbles floated up and tickled her nose. She relaxed a few minutes, then slipped beneath the surface to cleanse her hair. When she popped up, she felt refreshed from head to foot.

All too soon the water began to cool. Mandy sighed and resigned herself to getting out, wishing she didn't have to wear another ragged dress but thankful it was clean. She'd washed it yesterday in anticipation of their arrival.

Just as she finished combing out her damp hair, she heard a light knock at the door. Quickly she donned her faded dress and gave James permission to enter. The tall man sauntered in carrying a stack of boxes so high they almost blocked his view. With a smile, he dropped them on the bed, several lids falling off to expose lace and frills.

With a squeal of delight, Mandy dug into the pile. There were stockings, lacy drawers, petticoats, and dresses: lovely muslins, one of palest pink trimmed with yards of ivory lace, and another—a buttercup yellow with tiny embroidered flowers—that made her yearn to discard the tattered dress she wore. One box contained a traveling suit of navy linen, the jacket trimmed with a white collar and cuffs, and the skirt dipping stylishly to a point in both the front and back. The last box held a fashionably low-cut dinner gown of gleaming gold silk. Beads glittered on the bodice and were scattered like jewels about the skirt.

"James, they're all wonderful—the loveliest dresses I've ever seen—I mean . . ." She hoped he didn't catch her slip, then felt her cheeks redden as she held up a pair of dainty embroidered drawers.

"You shouldn't have, James." Leaning over, she kissed him shyly on the cheek, still unable to believe her good fortune.

"I didn't," he admitted somewhat regretfully. "Hawk did. It seems one of the shops had a special order from a woman about your size, but the lady left town in a bit of a hurry— without the clothes. Hawk thought you might enjoy them. But I appreciate the kiss, anyway," he added teasingly.

"Hawk?" she repeated, unable to comprehend the fact. "But he couldn't . . . He wouldn't . . ."

"But I'm afraid he did. I only wish I'd thought of it first." It was an honest reply, spoken with what sounded like a tinge of regret.

"Where is he? I'd like to thank him."

"He's gone to meet with Brigham Young. He'll be here in time for that dinner he promised. You just rest for a while. I'll be back after you change." Excusing himself, he headed for the door, once more securing it against her possible escape.

But escape was the furthest thing from Mandy's mind. Travis Langley had been thinking of her, seeing to her needs, caring about her. The thought made her head reel. If only she could stop pretending to be someone else and tell him the truth.

Thank God the charade would soon be over.

Tomorrow they would leave on the west-
bound stage for Virginia City, Hawk and
James apparently satisfied that her fiancé had
not followed this far. It would be a bumpy,
miserable five-day ride across a dry, dusty
desert, but still the fastest way to travel the
five hundred miles of desolate country ahead.
James had explained that Lady Ann would be
trailed behind a series of coaches at a much
slower pace until reaching Sacramento City.
James said he and Hawk each kept a horse in
Salt Lake as well as in California.

The trio would take a brief rest in Virginia
City, then travel on to Reno, a new settlement
founded at the farthermost easterly stop of the
Central Pacific Railroad. From there it would
be only a short half day's journey into Sacramento City. In less than a week, Mandy cal-
culated, she could shed her Julia role and be
herself again.

"Well . . . Travis Langley. How long has it
been? A year? Two?" Brigham Young, an imposing, mutton-chopped, gray-bearded figure
stood in the parlor of his two-story wood-
frame house. At sixty-seven, Young remained
a virile, well-spoken man of integrity and authority.

Brigham offered his hand, and Hawk
grasped it firmly.

"Been a while, Brigham."

"I appreciate your taking the time to stop

by. My man at the Salt Lake House informed me you were in town." He smiled, straightening his somberly cut black suit. "Not much goes on around here I don't get wind of. Man like you, word travels even faster. What brings you to our fair city?"

"I'm on an assignment." Hawk smiled as he thought of Julia. "Seems Governor Ashton was about to lose something he was partial to—"

"Like his daughter?" Brigham interrupted.

Hawk frowned. "News really does travel fast around here. Yes, sir. Like his daughter. But I'd appreciate it if you'd forget that, sir. Wouldn't do the pretty lady's reputation any good if folks found out she was traveling with us."

"Can't say I approve of her traveling without a chaperone, but I guess her father knows best."

"You might be better off worrying about the two of us." Hawk grinned broadly. "Miss Ashton seems more than capable of taking care of herself."

Brigham nodded. "I think I can understand that. When you have as many wives as I do, you grow rapidly to learn how capable the 'weaker sex' really is!" Both men laughed heartily.

"But enough of this small talk." Brigham motioned for Hawk to follow him into his study and pointed toward an overstuffed chair. Hawk seated himself as the thickset man called to one of his many wives. "Mary, bring Mr. Langley some refreshment. He and I have a few things to discuss."

The conversation grew serious as each spoke of what was going on in his particular part of the country. Hawk was interested in the progress of the railroad, scheduled to connect both sides of the continent sometime in the spring. The Union Pacific and the Central Pacific were pushing across the country at a breakneck pace, and it appeared as though they'd meet somewhere in the Utah Territory.

Brigham wanted to know about the Indian problems—something that affected him and his pilgrims time and time again. The conversation continued for well over an hour.

"Well, Travis," Brigham said, clapping him on the back as they headed to the door. "Express my regards to the governor."

"I'll be happy to, sir."

"And take good care of your . . . assignment."

Hawk smiled. "You can count on that, sir."

Mandy tried to force herself to rest, but the anticipation of an evening out was just too much. Finally conceding defeat, she changed into snowy-white lace and embroidered undergarments, and slipped into the beautiful bright yellow muslin. She ran her fingers across the soft clean fabric and twirled in front of the mirror, her petticoats rustling with the movement. Digging through the box, she discovered a pair of matching yellow ribbons, so she braided her freshly washed hair and plaited it gaily with the ribbons. How deliciously feminine she felt.

As she finished securing the second thick braid across the top of her head, a commotion outside her door caught her attention. She paused for a moment, wondering if Hawk might have returned early. When she stepped toward the locked door, the latch splintered and four men exploded into the room. Mandy jumped back, a small scream caught in her throat. Her heart pounded as fear pumped through her veins. The men reeked of whiskey and stale tobacco and leered at her drunkenly.

She fought to regain her composure. Some of her fear receded, replaced by fury at their intrusion.

"What do you think you are doing in here?" she stormed. "Get out this minute!"

"Simmer down, little lady, and you might not get hurt," said a stocky man with a patch over one eye.

She thought quickly and decided to play for time. "Don't you dare threaten me. I'll have you arrested. Leave immediately!" Hoping her bravado had momentarily distracted them, she bolted for the door.

A calloused hand clamped over her mouth, muffling her cry, and her feet were lifted from the floor. Kicking and squirming she tried to free herself, but the arms that held her only clamped tighter. Mandy's terror mounted with each passing moment. Trying a new tactic, she sank her teeth into the man's sweaty palm and twisted against his strong grip.

"Ouch! Why, you little wildcat! I oughta . . ." The stocky man balled his hairy hand into a fist and struck a hard blow to her jaw. The room spun briefly, then inky blackness engulfed her.

"Wrap her in that blanket and take her down the back stairs," Gutterman instructed. "Throw her over my horse, I'll be right behind you. Jus' wanna make sure no one follows us."

Jake Wiley did as he was told. Pete followed next, then the Mex.

"What the devil's . . . ?" James came up the main staircase just in time to see a stranger emerge from Julia's room and head toward the rear staircase. He flattened himself against the wall, pulled his revolver, and inched quietly along. Shoving the door open with a booted foot, he glanced around the room. A pulse throbbed at his temple. *Where was the girl?* Cautiously he eased farther into the room.

Gutterman held his breath. Waiting behind the door for the gambler to enter, he didn't move a muscle. As Long took another step, Max slipped silently behind him and smashed the barrel of his gun across the man's skull. Long slumped to the floor.

Max smiled crookedly. " 'Bout time we met

up again, gambler.'' Cocking the hammer on the heavy revolver, he pointed the weapon at Long's unconscious body. Then voices in the next room carried softly through the walls, reminding him of the danger.

He cursed his luck. Instead of pulling the trigger, he kicked the man squarely in the ribs, holstered his gun, and stepped out into the hall. *It was probably just as well. The gambler might come in handy.* Long could make sure their demands reached the governor when the time came.

Gutterman closed the door softly behind him. "That's twice you've been lucky, gambler," he mumbled beneath his breath. "Next time, I promise your luck will run out."

Chapter Thirteen

✦ ✦ ✦ ✦

SOUNDS OF DRUNKEN laughter and coarse male voices mingled behind the blurred glow of a campfire. Mandy touched the bruise on her jaw and began to take stock of her surroundings. Even through the darkness she could tell the country was rugged. They were somewhere in the mountains. Tall pines and the chill in the air told her they were at a fairly high elevation. The men had covered a lot of ground in the last few hours.

Her yellow dress was torn and dirty and every part of her body ached. Though her right hand was free, her left was bound securely with a rope surrounding the thick girth of a tree. *What could they possibly want with her?*

Then by catching brief snatches of conversation, Mandy realized they thought she was Julia Ashton, the governor's daughter. *They meant to hold her for ransom!* She felt the sting of tears, but refused to cry. She had to be strong. Hawk and James would find her. Besides, the men probably meant her no harm as long as they were paid the ransom money. Inching closer to the tree, she tried to make herself as inconspicuous as possible. All she had to do was wait.

A thousand hammers split his skull. "Ugh-hhh!" James moaned as Hawk laid a damp cloth over the angry, egg-sized lump at the back of his head.

"We haven't got time for this." James tried unsuccessfully to distract Hawk from the task. "We've got to find Julia!" Half rising from the bed, he felt a wave of nausea. Bright colored spots danced in front of his eyes.

"You're not going anywhere," Hawk told him flatly. "Looks like you've got a concussion. You'll be out of commission for at least a couple of days. The doc's on his way up. Don't you worry about a thing. I'll find the girl." A muscle bunched in his jaw, then he continued. "Our best chance is for me to go after her alone. They won't be expecting that."

James listened as his friend laid out his strategy.

"If I'm not back in three days, go to Brigham. Get a military escort if necessary." Hawk's expression seemed carefully guarded.

"Hawk, I . . . I'm sorry. Looks like I let you down again."

"You did your best. Now just stay quiet. Try to get some rest. I'll bring her back."

James felt a gentle hand on his shoulder just before Hawk strode from the room.

Walking to his horse, Hawk again thought of the task at hand. Cold hard anger worked the muscles in his jaw. He'd find the girl, all right. He just hoped he wouldn't be too late. He felt a flash of white-hot rage. If they harmed one strand of her shining hair, left one bruise on her flawless skin . . .

The smell of bacon and beans filled the air, reminding Mandy she hadn't eaten since breakfast.

"Better take this, girl," the one called Pete said, handing her a tin plate. "I think the boss has plans for you after supper. Wouldn't want you to lose your strength and take all the fun outa it, now, would we?" His laugh revealed a gaping hole in yellowed teeth where one front tooth was missing.

"What do you mean, 'plans for me'?" Mandy asked. She didn't like the look in the man's dark eyes.

"You'll find out soon enough, little missy," he replied. A lecherous smile curved his lips.

Leaving the plate, he shuffled back toward the fire.

Mandy tugged at the rope binding her wrist, but the knot was behind the tree, well out of her reach. What could the man have meant? Surely no one would dare harm a governor's daughter. But doubts and an icy dread crept into her mind. Please God, she prayed, let them find me soon.

Hawk checked the tracks again. Their trail was easy enough to follow, but the spore was cold, the men still some distance ahead. James must have been knocked out for several hours. Urging the big roan faster, he pushed into the night, driving himself mercilessly. The full moon rising over the craggy peaks lighted the rugged terrain, making his job easier. Faster and faster he moved the big roan over the landscape.

"Glad to see ya liked the grub, little lady." The stocky man in the dirty red-checked shirt appeared by her side. His unwashed smell caused her stomach to roll.

He adjusted the dirty black patch over his eye and ran a hand through his greasy brown hair.

"Yes, ma'am, you're gonna need all your strength for the little show you're gonna put on fer us." Cutting the rope that bound her wrist, he jerked her unceremoniously to her feet and shoved her toward the campfire. The other three men sat cross-legged on the opposite side of the fire. Each grinned knowingly.

"Now, start takin' them clothes off, little lady, real slow-like," Gutterman instructed, "one piece at a time." He said the last words slowly.

"I'll do no such thing!" she said, turning her attention toward the men seated on the ground. "You'd better leave me alone if you know what's good for you. My father is powerful. You do anything to hurt me, and he'll see you men are hunted down and killed. You'll never get your money then." Backing slowly away from them, she felt thick fingers bite into her shoulder, then spin her around.

Gutterman slapped her hard across the face, the crack resounding against the granite walls of the canyon as the blow hurled her into the dirt. She touched her fingers to her split lip, already swelling and throbbing angrily. The metallic taste of blood mingled with the salt of her tears.

"You'll do exactly what I say. Besides, what we got in mind ain't gonna hurt ya none. Ya might even enjoy it. Right, Jake?"

"Right you are, Max. I heerd you high society gals go 'round beggin' for what yer about
to get."

Mandy thought she might faint. Where
were Hawk and James? Maybe they found her
gone and thought she'd run away again.
Maybe this time they wouldn't come after her.
Oh, God, please help me. A gunshot sobered
her. A little puff of dust rose at her feet where
the bullet just missed, the terrible sound ring-
ing in her ears.

"Now, do as the hombre tells you, *señorita
hermosa*. Start with the shoes." The harsh Mexican accent brooked no argument. She could
barely make out a dark-skinned, thick-
mustached man behind the fire.

Ever so slowly, she removed first one dainty
slipper, then the other. Sick with fear, she felt
fresh tears stinging her eyes, but hadn't the
will to stop them.

"Now the dress, little missy," came Pete's
anxious nasal voice. She felt rough hands behind her, then heard a rending of the cloth.
The lovely yellow dress fell in a heap at her
feet.

Again a shove.

"Now the petticoats," came several voices,
their tones more insistent.

Through her tears, she mercifully saw the
men only as a blur. She could barely hear their
voices for the buzzing in her ears. She fum-
bled with the knotted ties, purposefully
clumsy, stalling for time. Finally, reluctantly,

she dropped the last petticoat, and another shove forced her to step from the fluffy folds.

She stood before them clad only in her corset and thin embroidered pantalets, which outlined every curve of her body. Standing in the flickering firelight, she could see something next to hunger on the men's faces. She knew it would only be moments before they would fall on her, pushing into her soft flesh like rutting animals.

Shivering, she felt the cold steel blade of Gutterman's knife slice through the strings of her corset, one by one.

Icy rage ran through Hawk's veins like water beneath a frozen stream. Only a small tic at the corner of his mouth betrayed his emotion. As he watched the scene below, three men sat in gleeful anticipation, awaiting the end of the lewd display, while a fourth man, his face all too familiar, forced the girl to remove her clothes. Hawk felt a tightening in his chest, but subdued it quickly. No matter what happened in the clearing below, he would have only one chance to save the girl. He must wait until exactly the right moment. If he failed, neither of them would survive.

Circling the camp, his moccasins treading soundlessly, he reached a position behind the horses. He sliced through the remuda lines, freeing the animals, then threw several stones against a limestone wall to create just enough disturbance to attract the men's attention.

"What was that?" a yellow-toothed man questioned without turning his head. His gaze remained riveted on the near-naked woman standing in front of the fire. Gutterman had unbraided her chestnut hair and draped it across her shoulders, where it gleamed compellingly in the flickering firelight.

"There . . . behind the horses, *mis amigos*, I also heard it."

"Pete, you and Juan go check it out. Jake an' me promise not ta start without ya." A wolfish gleam in the man's lone eye said it was a promise not likely to be kept.

"Shucks, Sergeant, we wanna watch." Pete's yellow teeth jutted forward, the hole in front making him lisp.

"Hurry back, boys," Max Gutterman taunted. "We ain't gonna wait long."

The two men headed toward the horses. One ranged left, while the other ventured into the rocks at the right. Pete Varley glanced back through the branches to assure himself he wasn't missing his share of the evening's pleasures. Damn! Just his luck. Some damned raccoon makes a noise, and he has to miss all the fun. Well, maybe this way he'd be able to take his time, savor every minute. Take the girl two or three times. He stumbled, looked up, and a shot of fear snaked through him. He tried to call out as a cold steel blade plunged deep between his ribs. His cry for help died with him.

"Pete . . . Pete! ¿ *Dónde está?*" came a hoarse Mexican whisper. Rounding a rocky outcropping, Juan Quintana passed below a narrow limestone ledge. The rowels of his spurs jingled, making him nervous as he carefully scanned the brush and boulders.

He felt the pressure of an arm around his neck, immobilizing him before he could turn to face his attacker. He could feel the stinging pressure of the blade as it sliced across his throat. His scream of terror was muffled by the blood oozing into his breathing passage.

Hawk moved on into the darkness, as silent as the shadows he used to his advantage.

Mandy cringed as Gutterman twisted his fingers in her tangled mass of hair.

"I'm tired of waiting for those two loafers," he said. "They was gonna git third's and fourth's, anyhow."

The lust in his good eye was growing every moment as he fingered the peak of Mandy's breast. He pulled her tighter against him, and bent to plant a sticky kiss on the curve of her neck. His lips felt thick and moist. With a quick movement he landed her heavily on the ground, his bulky frame suffocating her.

"You hold her arms, I'll go first, then you can have her," Gutterman instructed. "She sure is a beauty, ain't she? Don't believe I've ever seen a body more ripe fer the pickin' than this'n.''

Mandy felt her arms stretched roughly above her head and smelled the man's stale breath; the bile rose in her throat, and she prayed for blissful unconsciousness. Closing her eyes, she steeled herself for the ordeal ahead.

''What the . . . ?'' Gutterman felt a heavy weight slump atop his back.

''Jake, what the hell's . . .'' He pushed Wiley's body aside, letting the sentence die as he stared into the glassy eyes of his dead companion. He rolled off the girl and looked to a tall figure whose eerie shadow danced like a ghost in the flickering firelight.

Mandy fought to make sense of what was happening. She tried to sit up. Her mind reeled. She couldn't seem to focus, then her gaze fell on the body lying grotesquely twisted in the dust beside her. Blood dripped from a massive wound in Wiley's side, and his eyes stared straight ahead. Confused, she glanced up, trying to comprehend.

A sudden movement to her right, and she spotted the familiar brown eyes and sandy hair of the man she remembered so fondly. Standing with his moccasined feet apart, the muscles of his wide shoulders and corded arms tensed, and his huge curved blade gleaming silver and red in the firelight, Hawk had never looked more ominous.

For a moment she felt weak with relief.

Then she realized the danger wasn't over—for either of them. She looked at Gutterman. He moved about wildly, panic making him clumsy and disoriented. He seemed to be looking desperately for something.

Mandy inched away from the men. She spotted her chemise, torn and dirty, and slipped it over her head, but her eyes remained fixed on the men. She wished there were some way to help, but feared her interference might only make things worse.

"Juan! Pete! Get back here!" the stocky man screamed. His good eye shot around the camp in a furious search for his companions.

"They won't be coming back, Gutterman. But don't worry, you'll be joining them soon enough, wherever they are." Hawk's deep voice was little more than a whisper, but there was no mistaking its threat. He watched the man like a giant cat toying with its prey.

Turning, Gutterman spotted his revolver lying only a few feet away. He dove for it, landing heavily. He reached the pistol and fired just as Hawk hurled himself forward.

The two men rolled in the dust, fighting for control of the weapon. Scuffling inches from the fire, the searing flames a threat to both men, Gutterman broke free and struggled to his feet. Hawk stood up, punched Gutterman viciously, then lunged. Again both men sprawled in the dirt. Hawk's powerful shoulders and arms locked with another pair of equal strength, first one man on top, then the other.

Mandy pulled the pistol from Jake Wiley's dead body and aimed it at the thrashing men, but the chance of hitting Hawk was too great. She was forced to watch helplessly, waiting for a chance to shoot, her stomach knotted with fear. Gutterman's thick arms flexed as the men struggled to their feet, hands locked around the weapon. A quick flash of blue metal reflected in the firelight. A shot rang out. Hawk grimaced. Mandy gasped as the victim's body muffled the sound. Unsure which man had been shot, she watched in horror. Then Gutterman closed his eye. Hawk let the body slump to the ground. Blood pumped in bubbly spurts from the wound in Gutterman's chest. Mandy sank to her knees, still clutching the weapon, and tearfully thanked God for Hawk's safety.

Hawk strode quickly across the camp to kneel beside the weeping girl. Carefully he drew the weapon from her hands, then pulled her into his arms. She felt no more than a wisp as he carried her away from the bloody scene. He spoke soothing words of assurance and tightened his hold, wishing he had the power to erase the terrible memories. In the moonlight he could see tears glistening on her cheeks, and it tore at his heart.

"You're all right, little one. You don't have to be afraid. I'm with you," he soothed. "Everything's all right. You're safe now." He let her cry softly against his shoulder for a while, then lifted the hem of his buckskin shirt. "Here. Dry your tears. They can't hurt you anymore." He clenched his teeth and added beneath his breath, "No one's ever going to hurt you again."

Mandy clutched Hawk tighter, her arms circling his thick neck. She felt surrounded by his powerful presence—safe at last. She ran her hand down the length of his tanned arm just to assure herself he was really there and felt his muscles ripple at her touch.

"I knew you would come for me," she whispered, her trembling controlled by his nearness. "Somehow I just knew."

Hawk pressed his lips to the girl's forehead, then lightly kissed her tear-stained cheek. She knew he would come, he scoffed. Nothing, no one, could have kept him from coming. The magnitude of her power came swift and hard, appalling in its enormity. He thought of the stories he'd read, the hearts she'd broken, her fiancé back at the fort.

"I promised your father I'd bring you home," he said. "I couldn't disappoint him, could I?"

Mandy stiffened slightly. Of course he would come. She had never really doubted it—but not for her sake. For the money her uncle had promised. Fresh tears welled, this time for the loss she suddenly felt. Still, she clung to his muscular neck. She needed his comfort no matter how grudgingly he gave it.

Feeling a wet stickiness where her leg

touched his body, she noticed the blood for
the first time.

"You're hurt!" she cried, lightly touching
the wound in his side with her fingers.
"Please, put me down, Hawk. I can walk now.
Why didn't you tell me? Let me take a look at
it."

"I'll be all right. But I think we'd better find
a place to spend the night. I'm afraid I'm losing more blood than I thought." Reluctantly,
he released his hold. He noticed the worry
distorting her lovely features as she put her
own distress aside, slipped an arm under his
shoulder, and helped him onto his horse.
Then she dashed back to retrieve a torn petticoat to use for bandages.

She climbed up behind him in chemise and
pantalets, unrolled a blanket from behind the
saddle, and wrapped it around her shoulders.

"I rather liked you the way you were,"
he teased, reflecting on ivory calves and a
rounded, creamy bosom. Chiding himself for
his thoughts, he felt little better than the animals who'd tried to take her. A sudden swelling in his breeches as she wrapped her arms
around his waist to steady herself made him
groan. How could his body be reacting this
way at a time like this?

"There's a little cabin about half an hour's
ride up ahead," he told her. I passed it on the
way in. It's not much, but at least it's a place
to spend the night. I'm afraid the bullet's still
in there. You'll have to help me get it out." He

made the statement flatly, leaving no room for argument.

Mandy nodded, hoping the wound wasn't as bad as it appeared. She could feel the blood oozing through the makeshift bandages, dripping down onto her fingers where they pressed against his narrow waist. She prayed nothing would happen to the big man she cared so much about, even if he didn't feel the same way about her.

He swayed in the saddle, so she kept her arms wrapped protectively around him. He turned the roan and headed for the safety of the cabin.

Lying in the pool of blood beside the dying fire, Max Gutterman opened his one good eye. He could feel the blood seeping into his navel, congealing around the wound in his chest. Somehow, some way, he'd survive. If it was the last thing he ever did, he'd find the white Indian—and the woman—and make them pay.

Chapter Fourteen

✦ ✦ ✦ ✦ ✦

TOWARD THE END of the ride, Hawk rode slumped over the horn. Mandy struggled just to keep him in the saddle. She fought down her rising fears and kept her mind on guiding the roan in the direction Hawk had told her. When she came up on the cabin at last, she was relieved to see that, though abandoned, it appeared to have a sturdy roof and a chimney still intact. The evenings were becoming colder as autumn approached. Mandy could feel Hawk shiver from the chill and his loss of blood. Sliding to her feet, she helped him down, trying not to notice the feel of his muscular arms around her shoulders, or the heat of his body pressed so close.

Together they made their way into the cabin. The place looked as though it had been deserted for some time; dust and insects scattered as they opened the door. Mandy made a bed for Hawk on the earthen floor in front of the hearth and tried to see to his comfort. Then, searching the grounds nearby, she gathered some wood and made a fire. Soon the chill was gone from the room, though Hawk continued to shiver.

"It's time we took care of this bullet, little one. The sooner it's out, the better off we'll both be. Probe for it with your fingers, but if you can't reach it . . ." With an unsteady hand, he freed his knife from his belt.

"Stick the blade in the fire and get that pint of whiskey out of my saddlebag."

Silently, Mandy obeyed. When she returned with the whiskey, she used the knife to open his soft buckskin shirt, then stuck the blade into the flames. At first her gaze remained fixed on the wound. She'd helped tend a few injuries at the fort when the doctor was away, but never by herself, and never one as serious as this might be. She gently washed away as much of the blood as possible with water from Hawk's canteen, hoping to get a better look. Her hand trembled slightly as she moved the wet rag across his bare skin. She tried not to notice the corded muscles, tensed in anticipation, and the soft, sandy mat of hair that covered his wide chest.

Grimly, she waited while Hawk downed the whiskey, hoping it would dull the pain.

"Well, little one, are you ready?"

"Maybe I should try to make it back to town and bring help," she said, beginning to panic. "I've never done anything like this before. I might kill you."

"Just calm down. I doubt you could find your way back even if we had the time to spare, which we don't. I'll guide you through this." His eyes searched hers, trying to lend her some of the little strength he had left.

"Just trust me, okay?"

She knew he was right. She would have to

do it or he would probably die. Setting her fears aside and getting herself back in control, she dug her fingers into the wound, trying her best to locate the slug. The opening was too small. The bullet must have changed trajectory. Maybe it bounced off a rib after it entered Hawk's body. Unwillingly, she gripped the handle of the knife and pulled it from the cleansing heat of the fire.

"Open the wound enough to try again for the bullet," Hawk instructed. Beads of perspiration gathered on his forehead.

"Hand me that stick of wood by your foot."

Mandy obeyed. Hawk bit down hard on the soft piece of wood, and Mandy steadied herself. She touched the knife. It had cooled enough to begin. The sickening feel of the blade slicing through flesh made the bile rise in her throat.

Using two fingers this time, she probed deeper into the wound. Again and again she tried without success. Hawk bit harder on the wood and closed his eyes. Sweat trickled down his cheeks. Then, mercifully, he lost consciousness.

Mandy touched something solid at last. She reached into the wound and plucked the offending lead from its recess beneath a rib. She reheated the knife, cauterized the wound as best she could, then bandaged it with scraps from her torn petticoat.

She removed the stick, pulled the blanket up, then bathed the perspiration from Hawk's face with a little water from the canteen. Satisfied she'd done all she could, she lay down to rest, falling into an exhausted slumber by Hawk's side.

Several hours later, she woke to find him shaking with fever and mumbling incoherently.

"Wishana . . . Wishana," he called. He said the word with such yearning it soon became apparent this was a woman, and from the sound of it, not a mother or sister.

She remembered that first night away from the fort. He'd been dreaming of his past that night too. He'd mentioned the name Strong Arrow and someone called Running Wolf.

"Wishana," he whispered again, then began mumbling in Cheyenne.

Jealousy seared her like the white-hot knife she'd just used. How could she be jealous of a woman she'd never met, never even heard of before? But she was. It galled her that the name could affect her so and at the same time make her overwhelmingly curious.

"Wishana, my . . . lovely . . . one," he mumbled.

The words twisted like a dagger in her heart. Feeling him shiver again, she forced herself to move closer, molding her body to his and pulling the covers higher, trying to give him the extra warmth he needed.

Sensing her presence, Hawk moved, still calling the lyrical name. One hand sought the swell of Mandy's breast, and she felt her pulse quicken. Then exhaustion took its toll, and the hand dropped harmlessly to his side. Mandy relaxed, unsure whether to be offended at the intimate touch meant for another woman, or sorry he hadn't the strength to continue. Drifting off to a fitful sleep, she wondered again who the lovely woman could be who had stolen Hawk's heart.

Morning found him much improved. His fever had broken sometime before dawn, though he continued to sleep. Mandy rose and found coffee in his saddlebags. She also found the pair of men's breeches Julia had persuaded her to bring. Hawk must have found the clothing in her satchel and brought them just in case. She climbed into the breeches and donned a loose shirt, which she tied into a knot at her waist. Mandy felt the heat rise to her cheeks. The trousers were revealing in a manner she'd never experienced.

Dragging Hawk's heavy .44 caliber from its holster, Mandy headed for the door, determined to bring back fresh game to help speed his recovery. Once outside, some of her old confidence returned. It felt good to be outdoors again, free again. Her father had spent hours teaching her the fine art of shooting, though usually at targets. He'd been determined to see that she could defend herself.

After a few near-misses she bagged a small rabbit, skinned it, and found a few wild onions. The clothing heightened her sense of freedom, and she reveled in it. The breeze lifted her hair, left loose and falling to her waist, and, except for her worries about Hawk, Mandy had never felt better. She knew something was happening to her out here on her own. Her strength, her self-assurance, the wonderful sense of independence she used to have were all coming back to her. She felt like her old self again—only better. Now she felt like a woman. She thought of the big man lying on the floor of the cabin, the heat of his kisses, the touch of his hand on her breast. Well, maybe not fully a woman—yet.

Back at the cabin, she rummaged through the dusty cupboards until she discovered a kettle big enough to hold a stew. The smell of it simmering over the coals roused Hawk from his slumber.

"Ummm, that smells good," he commented groggily, his voice barely audible. "What is it?"

Relief swept through her at the sound of his voice. "Rabbit stew," she said, grinning proudly. She was inordinately pleased by her accomplishments—both the rabbit and Hawk's recovery. "I know you must be starved. She moved toward him and knelt by his side. "It's good to have you back," she said softly. "How are you feeling?" Her eyes searched for signs of pain.

"I've felt better, but it looks like I'm going to live, thanks to you." Making an attempt at lightheartedness, he winced with the effort.

"Don't try to sit up," she cautioned. "Just

rest your head in my lap, and I'll feed you."

"Can't remember when I've had a better offer." His wry smile pulled at her heart. Then she remembered an Indian woman named *Wishana*.

Filling a tin cup with tiny bits of meat and wild onions, she returned to his side and propped him up in her lap as gently as possible.

"Who is Wishana?" she asked, trying to appear nonchalant as she tipped the cup to his lips.

"Where did you hear that name?" he asked before taking a sip. A shadow passed over his features, masking his emotions.

"You called for her last night in your sleep. Is she a friend of yours?"

"Just a woman I know." Wincing a little, he moved to sip more of the broth from the cup she held in her hand. "Tell me about the rabbit. It's delicious. How did you get it?"

"I shot it," she replied proudly, wishing he hadn't changed the subject. "And furthermore, I'm planning to shoot something else for supper."

"Sometimes you amaze me, Miss Julia Ashton," he said with a shake of his head. The girl looked radiant, more alive than he had ever seen her. He felt a yearning to hold her, to capture some of her strength and energy. Shaking his head unbelievingly, he suddenly became aware of her snug-fitting breeches. His practiced eye slowly assessed the shapely calves and thighs, his gaze particularly attracted to the rounded bottom so clearly displayed as she rose from her place on the floor.

"I see you found the clothes I brought. You certainly do them justice." He allowed himself an amused grin, but was interrupted by a quick stab of pain. Even with the wound in his side, he had trouble resisting the urge to run a hand up her thigh to caress her shapely bottom.

Recognizing the heated look in his eyes, Mandy moved swiftly out of his reach.

"You'd better try to rest today. Maybe we can leave tomorrow if you're feeling better."

"We'd better leave tomorrow," he cautioned. "If we're not back by Monday, James will have the whole Seventh Cavalry out looking for us."

"Where *is* James? Why didn't he come with you?" With all that had happened, and her worry about Hawk, she'd forgotten about James. Almost guiltily, she hoped nothing was wrong with her friend.

"Gutterman and his cronies did a job on him, too. Gave him a hell of a lump on the head, but he should be okay by now."

She shivered at the memory of last night's events. "What a terrible man. He was the same man who tried to kill James before, wasn't he?"

"Yes. I'd have recognized that face anywhere." He looked away. "He won't be able to try it again."

"You killed them all, didn't you?" Her voice dropped to a whisper.

"I had no choice," he said gruffly. Closing his eyes, he shifted, trying to get comfortable on the hard floor. Fatigue began to drift over him again, and he slipped into a restless sleep.

Mandy pulled the covers beneath his chin and wondered, wistfully, if he ever dreamed of her.

Chapter Fifteen

✦ ✦ ✦ ✦

BY THE NEXT morning, a Sunday, Hawk felt well enough to ride. His wound was healing nicely, and his spirits were high. The only blemish on the day was the discomfort he suffered from the nearness of the dark-haired girl in the tight-fitting trousers.

"Hawk, are you sure you're all right?" she inquired worriedly, noticing the perspiration gathered on his brow. She shifted her position behind him on the horse and he groaned.

"I'm fine," he answered a little too gruffly, feeling her soft breasts pressed against his back, and the warmth of her breath on the nape of his neck. "I'll just be glad when we get to town."

*   *   *

They reached Salt Lake City by nightfall and encountered a relieved James.

"Thank God you're both all right. I've been worried sick." James looked at Hawk. "How bad are you hurt?"

"I'd be a whole lot worse if it weren't for this little minx of ours." Hawk inclined his head toward Mandy with pride in his eyes. "She took the bullet out and patched me up. Did quite a job, for a city girl." He winked and grinned in her direction.

She beamed with pride. "Hawk is the one who deserves the credit. He took on all four of those . . . those . . ." She shuddered at the thought of what might have happened if Hawk hadn't arrived in time.

"Well, it's all over now," James finished, noticing her tremor. "Hawk, do you think you're up to that dinner you promised before all this happened?"

"I could eat a mule, skin and all," Hawk teased, "though I doubt anything could taste as good as the rabbit stew this one cooked for me." The quick flash of even, white teeth again displayed his pride in her.

James noted the exchange and cocked an eyebrow. Turning his attention back to Mandy, he eyed her tight-fitting garb. "I've heard the Salt Lake House has the best steak in town. . . . That is, Miss Ashton, if you're not too fond of those breeches you're wearing to put on a dress."

Mandy flushed hotly at the mention of her all-too-revealing outfit. "Oh, Hawk," she gasped, "I never thanked you for the beautiful clothes!" Her mind momentarily raced back to the lovely yellow muslin lying in a ragged heap somewhere in the mountains.

"If I'd known what a fetching sight you'd be in those breeches," he teased, "I doubt I'd ever have bought those clothes. Now, you've got just enough time for one of those baths you're so fond of before dinner. Think I'll wash up and rest a little myself."

The journey down the mountain had taken more out of him than he cared to admit. Rising from the chair, he winced a little with the effort. "I'll meet you both back down here in an hour and a half."

The short rest brought Hawk renewed strength. He donned fresh buckskins and shaved. Mandy spotted him standing in the lobby, his hair still damp and curling thickly over his collar. He stood with his massive shoulders thrown back and a proud look in his eye—like a man whose racehorse just won the derby. Mandy reveled in their new bond of friendship. Hawk seemed to regard her in a completely different light—one bordering on respect, if she read him correctly, which he rarely felt for a man, much less a woman.

Hawk let his gaze roam over the high swell of upturned breasts and the tiny waist of the woman standing at the foot of the stairs.

"You look beautiful tonight, Miss Ashton," he said. The pink muslin dress was not in the least revealing. Yet seeing her lovely features framed by the gently scooped neckline made him harden with desire. How could any woman have such an effect on him? If he didn't get some female companionship soon, he'd have to avoid being in the same room with the girl.

"Thank you, Travis," she teased, wanting an excuse to try the sound of his name on her lips.

Hawk raised an eyebrow. "I usually prefer not to use that name unless I have to," he confessed. "But I think I like the way it sounds when you say it."

Mandy felt her pulse quicken as Hawk extended his arm. Entering the dining room of the Salt Lake House, a no-nonsense establishment that boasted fine linen and good food, she noticed several appreciative glances from some of the bolder men, and thought she caught the slightest hint of a scowl from Hawk as he apparently noticed them too.

Once seated between her two handsome companions, Mandy decided to try and satisfy some of her curiosity. A willowy young woman brought her a thick steak cooked just slightly less than done, as James suggested. Mandy took a small bite of the delicious meat, then a bite of potatoes, and broached the subject.

"James mentioned a meeting you had with Brigham Young. What's he like?" Young was a legend among westerners. Stories about him ranged from his daring search for the promised land to secretly whispered gossip about his dozens of wives.

"I guess a lot of people would like to know the answer to that," Hawk replied as he continued to enjoy the hearty meal. "Actually, he's about the same as any other man. Maybe a little more honest, a little more concerned with the welfare of others. I suppose you're curious about his wives?" His gaze lingered a bit too long on the swell of her breast.

She blushed beneath the heated look.

"Well, the truth is," he continued, "he's got more than his share, all right. At least twenty-five. But many of them aren't wives in the strictest sense of the word. That is to say," he paused, heightening her embarrassment, "they don't all share his bed. Some of them were widows, or just women with no man to look out for their interests." He threw her a look that made obvious exactly what he'd expect from a wife. "Not that Young doesn't have more than his share of real wives as well as the other kind."

Hawk smiled to himself as he watched the girl's expression. She seemed torn between embarrassment at the delicate nature of the subject and a desire to understand an alien world. Polygamy was not a life-style Hawk found attractive, although it was considered proper among the Cheyenne, and many of his brothers had more than one wife. He had no intention of marrying, at least not for years, but if he did, he was certain one wife would be more than ample.

Mandy could feel her blush deepening, making her certain she'd heard all that was necessary about the bedroom proclivities of Brigham Young. But she was still curious about Hawk's meeting.

"What did Mr. Young want to see you about?" The strains of soft music could be heard coming from another dining room, and Mandy glimpsed a willowy girl seated at a pianoforte.

"He wanted to speak with me about Red Cloud's treaty. Whether I thought it would hold or not, and what to do about it if it didn't. I told him Red Cloud would keep his word— but that he didn't speak for all of the Cheyenne or the Sioux. Just like that scouting party we ran into."

The look in his eyes said he well remembered the scene at the river and the feel of her naked body. She could no longer meet his gaze.

Hawk smiled lazily, enjoying the girl's discomfort and the obvious train of her thoughts.

"That bunch," he continued, will keep right on raiding and killing. Just like the white men who kidnapped you, there are renegades in every tribe and of every color." Hawk noticed the girl's rosy blush replaced by a distinct pallor at the mention of the outlaws and chided himself for his carelessness.

"I think that's enough of this kind of talk. We have a tough five days ahead of us, and I, for one, could use some rest. What say we finish eating and turn in?'' He received a nod from both James and the girl and they finished their meal in silence. Hawk's gaze took in the soft curls at the nape of the girl's neck. They'd escaped from the pins holding the gleaming mass atop her head and teased him unmercifully. When he'd finished his coffee, he heard himself offer to escort her upstairs, then cursed himself for the fool he was. The last thing he needed was another night of restless frustration.

Mandy graciously accepted the proffered arm and headed up the wide staircase. She moved with a lightness in her step from both the lovely supper and the attention she'd been receiving from her two handsome companions.

Reaching the door to her room, she felt Hawk's arm go around her and she raised on tiptoe to receive his good-night kiss. A part of her knew better, but the evening had progressed so pleasantly it seemed a fitting end. She accepted the gentle brush of his lips and inhaled his musky scent. Then, just as she was about to end the chaste contact, his mouth came down harder, wanting more, insistent, yet hesitant in some way. The kiss deepened, his tongue hot and probing, the taste of him turning her senses to flame.

He pulled her closer, surrounding her with his arms. She could feel his chest, his thighs pressed against her. She gasped as his strong hands began to roam over her, one cupping the swell of her breast, the other moving lower to caress the curve of her hip. She knew she had to stop him, but couldn't seem to find the strength. She felt his hand move more intimately over the material of her dress to grasp the roundness of her bottom, pulling her even more firmly against him.

"Hawk, please," she pleaded, tearing herself away. Her whispered words begged for understanding. "You don't know what you're doing to me."

Waging a war with himself, Hawk held the girl a moment more, then released her, feeling a hungry ache in his loins. His gaze searched her green eyes for the truth of her words, but his mind recalled stories of the wild and reckless governor's daughter, rumored to have bedded half the dandies in Sacramento City. He pictured the sensuous curves of her body being caressed by another, and the thought turned his stomach to ice. His mind could not reconcile those stories with this woman, and yet it must be so. He cursed the day he ever made that promise to her father.

He watched her step back into the room and close the door. Turning the key in the lock, he spun on his heel, and headed for his room. The wound in his side was paining him, but the real pain lay in the area of his heart. It would be a long night. In Great Salt Lake, one he couldn't ease even with the solace of a bottle.

Mandy lay on her bed pondering her responses. She'd wanted Hawk tonight. If he hadn't stopped, she might have let him enter her room. Let him do with her as he wished— as she wished. But the memory of a woman named Wishana danced at the edge of her mind. Would it be another woman he dreamed of as he caressed her? She couldn't bear the thought. She wouldn't allow her body to betray her again.

Chapter Sixteen

✦ ✦ ✦ ✦

HAVING JUST TRAVELED over hundreds of miles of rugged terrain on horseback, Mandy thought she'd be able to handle just about anything. She hadn't counted on the Overland Stage. That first day, her tiny frame was crushed between the massive body of an overweight mule skinner in smelly leather jerkins and the bony shoulders of a gangly young journalist wearing spectacles and a striped suit three inches too short for him. James sat across from them, next to a raw-boned, plainly dressed woman looking to marry a silver miner in Virginia City, while Hawk joined the driver on the top of the coach.

Six impressively matched sorrels dashed at full gallop out of the city, only to be replaced at the first way station by a scruffy team of second-rate animals. James informed her it was standard procedure to use the best stock where they would do the most good—in front of the ticket office.

The coach itself, the famous Concorde, was a fiery red contraption of the latest design. Though it had a top-heavy appearance, it was actually a sturdy vehicle whose most ingenious feature was the suspension of the carriage on two thoroughbraces, three-inch thick leather strips that served as shock absorbers—or so the makers said. Mandy found herself jostled from side to side until she thought her bones would crack. Her only consolation came when she discovered that as many as twenty-one people had been known to ride in one coach, counting the space on the top. Mandy felt cramped with just the five of them.

Sleeping arrangements were nonexistent. The coach never made more than the briefest of stops, just to change teams and provide a little food for its exhausted passengers. Sleeping was done sitting up.

The journey progressed uneventfully until about the halfway point, when the mule skinner was replaced by a tough-looking Spaniard wearing tight black pants trimmed with silver conchos up the sides and a short-waisted jacket. Two ivory-handled pistols hung low across his hips. Entering the coach, the man immediately took a seat next to Mandy, giving her an appreciative glance. He removed his colorful embroidered sombrero to reveal a thatch of wavy, black hair, and bowed slightly.

"Begging your pardon, señorita. Allow me to introduce myself. My name is Emilio Enriquez. I am pleased to make your acquaintance." He pronounced his name expansively with a clipped Spanish accent, drawing her hand to his lips in an exaggerated show of gallantry. She found the man slightly attractive, if you could overlook the feral gleam in his eye.

Supper found them at a low-roofed way station of adobe construction. It was obvious Shamus and Anabelle Dutton, a retired military man and his wife, ran the station with an iron hand, which made it one of the more pleasant stops the travelers had made. A tasty meal of tender chicken, some beans, and a bit of corn surprised everyone, and made Mandy feel like taking a breath of air after the meal.

Searching for Hawk or James, she decided they probably felt the same after being cooped up in the coach all day and went their separate ways. Giving it little further thought, she headed out the back door toward a small knoll overlooking the station.

Emilio Enriquez followed the woman with his eyes as he struck a match to the cheroot clamped tightly between his teeth. He took a long draw, the tip glowing orange in the darkness. With a slight smile, he started up the dusty path. His gaze rested on the gently swaying hips of the woman ahead of him. She stopped near the crest of a low hill.

"You enjoyed the meal, señorita?" he questioned, causing her to jump and turn at the sound of his voice.

"Señor Enriquez!" Mandy gasped at the unexpected presence. She glanced back toward the station. She'd drifted farther away than she intended.

"Yes, yes I did enjoy the meal," she answered nervously. "It was a pleasant change from most we've had." She could see the wolfish gleam in his black eyes even in the dim light. "I think I'd better be going back." She glanced away. "They're probably getting ready to leave."

"What's your hurry, señorita?" he cajoled, stepping in her path. His white teeth flashed in the moonlight, contrasting sharply with his smooth, olive skin. "One of the horses threw a shoe. They'll be a while longer. Why don't you stay and keep me company?" As he spoke he moved his hand to stroke the line of her jaw.

"I'd better be going," she repeated, sensing danger.

"No, señorita. I think you will stay with me." His mouth came down hard on hers, and she struggled against him.

He pushed her roughly against the sandstone outcropping. She tried to scream, but his mouth silenced her. She felt his hand fumbling with the buttons of her traveling suit. Rough fingers brushed the swell of her breast. She panicked and struggled even harder.

Suddenly she was free, the movement so quick she lost her balance and stumbled against the rock, her skirts swirling in the dust. She heard men scuffling, the sound of a blow, then Hawk's husky voice.

"What do we have here?" he said, his voice laced with sarcasm. The Spaniard sprawled in the dust several feet away. "Your beloved Jason didn't show up, so you decided to fill your bed with anyone who happened to be handy. You don't care what kind of scum you lie with, do you?"

"Stop it!" Mandy pleaded, covering her ears with her hands to blot out the hateful words. "I didn't even know he was out here."

The man on the ground hadn't moved. Hawk just stared at her, his jaws clenched, his hands balled into fists.

"How dare you say such things to me!" she fumed. "That man attacked me, and you suggest it was my idea!" Gathering her skirts, she tried to brush past him.

Hawk fought to control his temper, but the girl's pale skin gleamed through the open front of her traveling suit, fueling his jealous rage.

"You want another man to fill your bed?" he snarled. "Well, you better get one thing straight right now! No man—do you hear me? No man is going to bed you—unless it's me!"

He hauled her roughly against him. His lips covered hers, his mouth fierce in its possession. It was a kiss that branded her. Terrified her with the threat of it, yet made her yearn for more. Brutally he tore himself free, then left in long, heated strides.

Mandy stood trembling, forced to trail behind him down the hill or stay behind with the unconscious Enriquez. Reluctantly she opted to follow, somewhat uncertain which man posed the greater threat.

Chapter Seventeen

✦ ✦ ✦ ✦

THE FRAGILE TRUCE that had existed between Hawk and Mandy was broken. The balance of the journey was made in hostile silence, though James came through with a little of his good-natured camaraderie.

Mandy had never been happier than she was that Friday afternoon when the coach crested a ridge revealing a city outlined in the distance, rising just above the desert at the base of a barren range of mountains.

Her first impression of Virginia City was that it fairly glittered. The heat of the day created a shimmering haze that cloaked the city even at a distance, making it appear vaguely mystical. Basking in the desert sun, the city sprawled across miles of sand and sagebrush, and elegant residences, as well as tents and shanties, were dug into the hillside.

Everyone in the West knew about the fabulous Comstock lode. It had delivered unimaginable riches and created a city in the middle of a barren wasteland. When they pulled up in front of the stage depot, Mandy breathed a long sigh of relief to be at last free of the confining coach. She stretched her tired muscles, and turned to look at the town. There was only one way to describe Virginia City— it glittered. Silver decorated everything: silver coins, silver buckles, even silver-trimmed carriages pulled by high-stepping, perfectly matched teams in gleaming silver livery. The buildings were immaculately cared for and palatially appointed.

"Let's get checked into the hotel and get cleaned up," Hawk suggested. "Maybe we ought to turn in early and get a good night's sleep for a change." He winked at James and the tall man smiled. Hawk was certain neither he nor James had intentions of doing much sleeping that night. Hawk planned to spend the night in the arms of a warm, willing woman—one whose faithfulness was expected and paid for—and he guessed James would probably be doing the same.

"A bath and some sleep sounds wonderful to me," Mandy agreed, "but maybe we could go out for supper later? Virginia City looks so exciting." She looked up at Hawk wistfully, hoping he had come to his senses about the incident with the Spaniard.

Hawk groaned inwardly. Well, there wouldn't be much happening until later anyway, he rationalized. Maybe he could take her to an early supper, then head over to Sally's Place after that.

"Let's see how we feel after a rest. We'll talk about it then." He was stalling for time, trying to figure out how to keep the girl under control while he and James went out on the town.

Picking up their satchels, they headed toward the stately International Hotel. A row of freshly painted white columns held up the broad front porch, and they entered through carved mahogany doors. Oriental rugs covered inlaid wood floors; the walls were decorated with lovely paintings in the European tradition, and imported Italian marble sconces lit the interior. A uniformed bellman showed them up the sweeping staircase to their rooms.

"I'm sure your father would insist we spare no expense in seeing to your needs," Hawk commented dryly, opening the door to a beautifully appointed room.

"I'm certain he would," Mandy replied in kind. At least she could enjoy the lovely room he'd rented for her, the most elegant she'd ever seen. She walked over to the canopied bed that dominated the room and longingly caressed the beautifully carved headboard. Her hand sank into the soft down of the feather mattress. She could hardly wait to get bathed and beneath the fluffy covers.

"I've taken the liberty of ordering your bath," James informed her, "and of having a tray sent up. Think I'll take Hawk's advice and catch a nap myself." His eyes sparkled with mischief, and she wondered what plans he had made.

The food and the tub arrived at the same time. James backed out of the room, leaving Hawk to guard their precious cargo.

"I'll see you two in a few hours," James called through the door as he headed to his room.

With an exhausted sigh, Mandy turned toward Hawk. "Would you unfasten me before you leave?" She pulled aside her heavy mass of hair and presented Hawk her back so he could work the buttons.

"I'll unfasten you," he replied, "but I'm not leaving." A slight smile curved his lips, and she guessed he was punishing her, still angry about the Spaniard.

"What do you mean *not leaving?* You can't expect me to . . . to . . . I'm not going to take a bath in front of you!"

"You forget, little one, you already have." His brown eyes mocked her.

Mandy eyed the steaming tub and its mounds of snowy bubbles and looked beseechingly up at the big man. "Please, Hawk," she cajoled.

Relenting just a little, he turned his back. "I won't look while you get undressed, but I won't leave."

Mandy hesitated. The tub looked so inviting. She knew Hawk had conceded all he was willing. Either she got into the water now, or skipped the bath altogether. Hurriedly she undressed and slipped into the gleaming copper tub, piling her hair on top of her head.

"Would you toss me the comb in my satchel?" she asked. If he were going to remain, he might as well be of some help.

Smiling smugly, as if enjoying himself immensely, he moved closer, handing her the tortoiseshell comb, which she used discreetly to secure her unruly mane. Mandy already regretted her impulse to get into the tub. She should have gone to bed dirty.

"You're a mighty fetching sight, Miss Ashton," he teased.

"You said you wouldn't look."

"I said I wouldn't look while you got undressed," he corrected. "I wouldn't have missed this for the world." Hawk sat down on the bed and looked askance at the lovely girl. She'd moved as low as she could in the tub, and the bubbles protected her modesty, but

two dark spots colored the bubbles just beneath the surface. Beads of water glistened on
her shoulders, reminding him of rose petals
after a rain. Her graceful neck arched above
her shoulders, perfectly complimenting her
heart-shaped face. Hawk felt a sudden pain in
his chest and a tightening in his groin. He
clenched his jaw, resentful of the power she
held over him. He wished there were some
way he could make her suffer some of the pain
she gave him.

"Did your Jason get this privilege?" he
couldn't resist asking, knowing he had her at
his mercy.

"Jason was my fiancé, not my husband,"
she answered with a controlled calm, staying
in character. "You have seen far more of me
than he ever has." Mandy clothed the lie in a
truth. She found herself thinking of the word
husband for the first time in her life. By now
her cousin Julia would be happily married to a
wonderful loving husband. She felt a twinge
of envy for her once-black-sheep cousin in her
new role as wife.

Hawk's eyes raked her. "You aren't going
to pretend you're a virgin, are you?"

Mandy blushed to her toes. Surely he
couldn't think Julia a harlot? What had her
cousin done to deserve that? A niggling memory of stories she'd heard pushed its way to
the front of her mind. Maybe . . . or maybe it
was the way she had responded to his kisses.
A nice girl would have slapped him for the

liberties he'd taken. Look at what she was doing right now! Sitting naked in a tubful of water—even bubbly water—was against every rule of proper deportment. No wonder he thought she was a . . . a . . . oh, God, she couldn't even say the word.

She swallowed hard. "Hawk . . . I know what you must think of me after the way I acted when you kissed me . . . I mean I . . ." She tried to find the words. "I don't understand it myself. I've never done anything like that before."

A short laugh was his response.

"Who do you think you're kidding? You knew exactly what you were doing." Hawk's mind conjured unwanted images of the warm, pliant woman who responded to his every touch. "You weren't thinking of your precious Jason."

Tears of shame filled her eyes.

"Get out of here, you . . . you . . ." She wanted to slap his arrogant face again. "You're the most heartless man I've ever known. At least do me the courtesy of leaving while I finish my bath."

Rising from the bed, his mouth set in a hard line, Hawk left the room. He slammed the door behind him and turned the key in the lock. How did she always manage to make him lose his temper? He'd had no intention of fighting with her when he'd stayed in the room. He was just evening the score a little. Standing outside, he could hear her gentle

sobs and cursed himself for his rash behavior.
Now he'd have to take her to dinner, or his
conscience wouldn't allow him to enjoy himself later on.

His mind returned to the pretty picture she
made in the tub. He could see her silky skin,
her eyes snapping with fire. He smiled ruefully. Sally had better be ready for a long night
tonight.

Chapter Eighteen

✦ ✦ ✦ ✦

MANDY FINISHED CLEANSING the grime from her
body, washed her hair and her tear-stained
face, and rose from the tub. Lying exhausted
across the soft featherbed, she wondered how
fate could have been so cruel as to have
thrown her at the mercy of these two. Vaguely
she hoped her cousin's happiness would be
worth it.

She had to admit Julia had been right about
one thing. She'd grown to enjoy part of her
charade. Being reckless and carefree had its
advantages. The girl who had buried herself
behind a proper facade at the fort no longer
existed. She'd been replaced by an outspoken
young woman not so easily pushed around.

Clearing her mind of unpleasant thoughts, she finally fell into an exhausted sleep.

Several hours later, an incessant pounding at the door awakened her. "Who is it?" she called out timidly, wiping the sleep from her eyes. She'd learned in Great Salt Lake City that it paid to be cautious.

"Get dressed. We're going to dinner," came Hawk's brusque command from outside her door. "Wear the gold one."

Mandy had no time to answer before she heard his heavy steps recede down the hall. Unsure whether to be excited by the turn of events or wary of this new tactic, she hurriedly began to dress.

She swept her hair up off her neck, again using the comb she'd found among the clothes Hawk bought, and tried to create as sophisticated a style as possible. She slipped into a fresh chemise, donned corset and petticoats, struggled into the glittering beaded gold gown, then pulled the bell rope for a lady's maid to do up the buttons.

As the girl left the room, Mandy glanced in the mirror and felt the color rush to her cheeks. The gown was daringly low cut, showing more of her ample bosom than she ever would have dared. But Hawk said wear it, and wear it she would. Secretly she hoped it drove him wild with desire for her. It would serve him right for his arrogance this afternoon. She was bending over the bureau to retrieve the matching fan when she heard another knock at the door, this one a little more genteel than the last.

Mandy moved to the door nervously. "Come in," she almost whispered.

The key turned in the lock and a tall, broad-shouldered man dressed in well-fitting breeches and a black evening jacket over a crisp white shirt strode into the room.

"Hawk! Is it really you?" She eyed the handsome figure from top to bottom. He looked every inch the gentleman. She had been certain if he ever wore anything more formal than his buckskins, he would have looked foolish. But here he was, perfectly at ease. He moved as though he'd worn these clothes every day of his life. The notion galled her a little.

"You look very handsome," she admitted softly, feeling suddenly shy.

Hawk enjoyed the girl's confusion immensely. Secretly he thanked Thomas Rutherford for the ten-thousandth time. His gaze swept over her. She was elegantly gowned in the richly beaded gold satin dress he'd purchased. It fit perfectly, hugging her tiny waist and flaring in a sweeping line to the floor. He assessed the exquisite picture she made, savoring every detail. The gown exposed a great deal more of her bosom than he had expected—only the rose-colored peaks were hidden from his view.

He felt the blood pulse through his veins. If he'd known what affect the dress would have on him, he never would have bought it.

"And you, dear lady, look ravishing. But then I wouldn't have expected anything less from the governor's daughter." Hawk's eyes swept her again, and Mandy knew he meant the somewhat backhanded compliment. He offered her his arm, and she accepted it with a tiny tremor.

They left the room and headed down the broad hallway, the magnificent gilt sconces flickering a soft light over them as they moved gracefully into the salon.

The gaiety in the crystal-chandeliered room was contagious. James had declined to join them, so she and Hawk were dining alone. A black-clad, stiffly formal maître d'hôtel seated them at an intimate candlelit table. Gold-flecked walls and huge potted palms stylishly completed the room. Mandy was heady with delight. This was turning out to be the most wonderful night of her life.

Hawk ordered champagne, which Mandy had never tasted—though she couldn't admit it—and she loved it. The golden liquid caressed her tongue like sweet dew. The bubbles tickled her nose. She found herself constantly blushing and glancing away at the intensity of Hawk's gaze.

After dinner, a small group of musicians played.

"May I have this dance, Miss Ashton?" Hawk asked, standing and extending his arm.

Dazed, Mandy rose from her seat and stepped out onto the floor, surprised the rugged man knew how.

He guided her lightly, expertly, never missing a step. She floated gracefully with his every movement. She had danced with the soldiers at the fort, but the men were clumsy and she uncomfortable. This was like floating on an organdy cloud.

"How is it, Mr. Langley," she teased, "that you wear a suit and dance the waltz as easily as you sit a horse and hunt wild game?" She felt Hawk's strong hand surrounding her waist, and her heart thumped loudly. He drew her just a little closer than proper as he whirled her around the floor, and the smell of musk, tinged lightly with champagne, filled her senses.

Hawk smiled at the girl's unintentional compliment and, as the dance ended, escorted her from the floor. He seated her and himself, then began to answer her question, the alcohol easing his task.

"When I left the Cheyenne, I made my way to St. Louis to find Thomas Rutherford, the man I mentioned before. He welcomed me into his home as if I were his own son. I had a tough time of it at first. Nothing I did seemed to turn out right. Not long after I arrived, he gave a formal dinner party—something he'd already planned and couldn't avoid. He insisted I attend. Said I belonged there just as much as he did. He bought me the right clothes and helped me with my manners.

"By the time dinner was served, I was so nervous I could barely think. I forgot my lesson on the proper use of the company silver and picked up the meat with my fingers." He smiled ruefully at the memory. "The whole table gasped and Mrs. Haddington, one of Thomas's best clients, almost had apoplexy. But Thomas stood by me. He looked Mrs. Haddington straight in the eye and picked up his own meat with his fingers. I guess I loved him from that moment on."

Mandy's heart went out to the big man. He always seemed so confident, so self-assured. His eyes revealed the love he felt for the man who had taken him in. How she wished he looked at her with that same loving gaze.

"The man had infinite patience," he was saying. "He retaught me to speak proper English, hired private tutors to teach me everything from reading to the arts—even how to waltz," he added teasingly.

Mandy was having trouble concentrating on his words. She could feel his gaze caressing her. She longed to touch the line of his jaw. A memory of warm, firm lips lingering over hers played on her heart. Her eyes strayed to a corded muscle along his neck. She wanted to run her fingers through the soft hair curling against his collar.

"I worked hard on Rutherford's farm," he said. "But I never felt I belonged there any more than I did the Cheyenne village. I stayed a few years, then left to come west. I'll never have the chance to repay the debt I owe him."

She caught a flash of regret before his smile slipped into place, and felt another pang of sympathy for the man who moved easily in both the Indian and the white world, yet belonged to neither.

Another waltz began, and they rose to dance again. This time he held her even tighter. By the time the dance ended, she glistened with a light sheen of perspiration wherever Hawk touched her.

"You realize I'm the envy of every man in the room," he said, flashing her a boyish grin.

She smiled at his compliment. "And if looks could kill, I'd have died a thousand deaths," she responded, lowering her lashes. It galled her a little, the way women openly admired him. There wasn't a woman in the room who wouldn't gladly have traded her places.

Feeling suddenly playful, she giggled. "Can you imagine what they'd say if they knew I was traveling alone with you and James?" To herself she added: A gun-toting gambler and a white man dressed as an Indian. God, it really was shocking! At least if anyone found out, Julia would get the blame. She smiled at the thought.

"They'd probably say we were the luckiest two men west of the Mississippi," he said softly.

"Hawk . . . this has been the most wonderful night of my life." She lifted her champagne glass, which seemed always to be full, and smiled.

For the first time, Hawk noticed her dimple. Maybe he should make her smile more often.

She giggled again, and suddenly he understood she'd had too much champagne.

She hiccupped. "Excuse me," she said, spilling the champagne.

The whole scene brought to mind the newspaper article he'd read about her near-nude scene in the fountain. His mood blackened.

"I should have known a spoiled little girl like you couldn't behave herself. You're going up to bed right now."

"Hawk, please," she pleaded. "What did I do to displease you?" But as she rose from the chair, the room spun.

He steadied her. The smell of violets drifted up from her shoulders, and he sighed in defeat. He longed to pull the pins from her thick hair and bury his face in the silky strands. He could feel desire for her begin to swell again. Damn her for the little witch she was! Gritting his teeth, he decided they'd better leave before it began to show.

"You just drank a little too much champagne. Come on, it's time for you to turn in, anyway." In silence they reached the lobby, then moved up the stairs to her room.

"I had a wonderful time, Hawk." Her gaze drifted up to meet his, then she turned away. A heady rush began again as they stood in the doorway.

Without giving himself time to think, Hawk covered her lips with his, gently at first, then more insistently. His tongue touched every part of her mouth. Her breath tasted warm and sweet. He kissed her cheeks, her neck; then his lips moved to her shoulders, smooth satin above the shimmering dress. He eased her into the room and closed the door behind them. Pulling her against him again, he kissed her deeply.

Mandy's senses reeled. His lips were warm and demanding. The champagne made her head spin; now his kisses were melting away any resistance she might have left. His lips teased the line of her neck, nibbled at her ear.

A raging desire swept through her, draining the last of her will. His mouth moved to the swell of her breast and her pulse quickened further. Her breath came in tiny ragged gasps.

Hawk knew in that moment he could have her. All thoughts of her lover had fled. Her breath felt hot against his neck. She was warm and pliant in his arms, and her passion was evident in the rapid flutter of her heart. She would make no move to stop him, and he wanted her as he never wanted another.

Visions of young dandies caressing her body just as he did scorched his soul. Why shouldn't he have her? There were others before him who had! *I give you my word, sir.* The promise twisted like a knife. He wanted to lash out at her, make her suffer as he did. Lifting his head from her breast, he paused, then smiled menacingly and stepped away from her.

"Don't you even have the decency to try

and stop me? I'm sure your *Jason* would be very proud of you."

Mandy's eyes filled with tears. She covered her ears with her hands.

"Please don't, Hawk," she pleaded, her voice barely a whisper, "you don't understand."

"I wish he were here to see you now, wrapped in another man's arms," he taunted. "Did you kiss him the way you kiss me?"

With no regard for the consequences, Mandy drew back her hand, determined to slap the insolent smile from his face. Anything to stop the hurting remarks. Hawk caught her arm midway, restraining her easily. He stood motionless.

Suddenly he released her. She held his gaze for only a moment. Had she glimpsed a flicker of regret? She whirled and ran sobbing to the bed. She heard the door slam as he left the room.

Hawk turned the key in the lock, clenched his teeth, and stormed down the hall.

Mandy dissolved in tears. He was right. Why hadn't she tried to stop him? He could have taken her tonight. She would have let him. Oh God, what was wrong with her? She'd practically begged Hawk to take her to bed. No wonder he treated her with disdain. She deserved it.

Undressing, she set aside the lovely gown

and lay down in her chemise. Tonight had been the most wonderful night of her life. How could she have let it end so miserably?

Please, Lord, let this nightmare end.

Tomorrow they would leave by stage for Reno, then board the train for Sacramento City. By tomorrow night it would all be over. She wondered, not for the first time, if it would ever be over for her. Pulling up the quilt, and counting the ticks of the cherrywood clock, she drifted into a fitful sleep.

Chapter Nineteen

✦✦✦✦

HAWK MADE HIS way out through the carved mahogany doors and into the night. The fresh air felt good against his skin, cooling his temper but not his appetites. He shrugged off his jacket, removed his tie, and unbuttoned his collar. Once again he'd done and said things he regretted. He clenched his jaw and strode toward Sally's Place, the most infamous whorehouse in Virginia City.

His mind replayed the scene at the hotel. He hated the little wench for the way she made him feel. She was toying with him just as she was with the young lieutenant, so why was he having such a hard time convincing himself?

He shoved open the swinging doors with a little too much effort, and they slapped loudly behind him. The dimly lit interior was smoky and noisy. The red velvet walls and plush settees attempted to set the mood for its boisterous clientele. Hawk headed straight for the long, carved oak bar.

"Double whiskey," he ordered, scowling. He could already hear Sally's familiar laughter across the room. She spotted him almost immediately, ran to him, and threw her arms around his neck in a warm embrace.

"I heard you were in town," she said, her dark eyes sparkling. "I wondered how long you'd keep me waiting." Her husky voice sounded a little breathless.

Hawk's gaze took in the swell of her breasts and the curve of her hips. Sally Ginelli was not the first owner of the house, but she was the prettiest. In fact she looked much too young to run twenty girls and one of the wildest saloons in the West. But Sally was an exceptional woman.

The two had known each other for years, since before the place had been Sally's. Now Sally could afford to take to her bed only men friends she enjoyed.

Sally Ginelli sized up the tall, well-dressed man leaning against the bar. She'd rarely seen him in anything but buckskins—unless it was nothing at all—so the handsome figure he cut tonight set her blood to boiling. Of course he always had that affect on her.

She took another look at him. He'd been away too long this time. She could feel herself moisten just thinking about his muscular body thrusting into her. Her arms still circling his thick neck, she pulled his head down and covered his mouth with a hot, damp kiss.

For weeks Hawk had thought he wanted nothing more than to make love to Sally Ginelli. One night in her soft, yielding arms, he reasoned, and he would be rid of his yearning for the tiny, chestnut-haired girl he'd left across the street. Now, as he kissed the raven-haired woman, he noticed for the first time how thin her lips were and thought of another pair, full and yielding beneath his mouth.

"Let's go," he ordered gruffly, grabbing Sally's hand. He pulled her across the room and half carried, half dragged her up the stairs to her suite at the end of the hall.

"Get undressed," he grumbled, muttering to himself and pouring himself another whiskey from the crystal decanter on the black lacquer bar. The room was tastefully decorated—surprisingly so, considering the rest of the brothel. Fascinated by the Far East, Sally filled her suite with oriental tapestries, vases, and beautifully carved teak furniture.

Hawk tossed back the whiskey, poured himself another, threw it down, and quickly shed his clothes. He strode into the bedroom, his mouth set as if this were a task instead of the pleasure he'd envisioned.

Sally stood in front of a carved cinnabar mirror, clad in a skimpy lace chemise. Taking in her appearance with a sweeping glance, he pulled her into his arms. "I said get undressed," he whispered harshly. He grabbed a handful of her chemise and ripped it away, leaving her naked and trembling with desire. The glazed look in her black eyes told him she was enjoying his roughness. She had far too many men whimpering after her and enjoyed an occasional tussle with one not quite so gentle.

Hawk dragged the black-haired beauty down onto the soft mattress. He could feel her ample breasts spilling almost eagerly into his hands. He grasped them and, expecting to feel their firm roundness, felt only slack pleasantness. Pulling her closer, he pressed his lips to her thinner ones and reached around behind to cup a round, firm buttock. Instead he felt the same slack flesh as before.

In the inner recesses of his mind, he knew Sally felt no different than she ever had. Her skin was soft and yielding. Her kisses moist and warm. Why, then, did she not excite him? His mind kept filling with visions of firm, upturned breasts, rose-colored nipples, a smooth ivory bottom—and miles of chestnut hair. As he caressed Sally's heavy breasts, he battled the images in his mind.

At last, feeling his manhood soften, he

knew he'd lost. With a muttered curse, he pushed the disappointed girl away from him and rose from the bed.

"Did I do something wrong, honey?" she asked, her voice husky with passion.

"It's not your fault. I've got other things on my mind, that's all. I'll be back soon," he lied. Odds were he'd put this place behind him for good. He left the room and dressed quickly, then headed downstairs and out the swinging doors. There were a lot of bars in Virginia City, and he planned to hit them all.

"Another whiskey, bartender, and keep it coming," Hawk demanded for the tenth time. For three hours he'd done nothing but drink. Now the room was beginning to spin. He guessed he was probably drunk enough to sleep. Rising from the stool, he paid his bill and staggered from the bar. The cool air outside the Bucket of Blood roused him a little as he headed for the hotel.

Once upstairs, he brushed the wall several times on his way down the hall, then groped through his pockets for the key. He pulled it out and unlocked the door.

Mandy awakened with a start. She heard a soft click as a key turned the lock in her door. Alarm was replaced by surprise when she saw Hawk enter her room. Was he just coming in to check on her? Maybe he'd become confused and entered her room by mistake. Pretending to be asleep, she watched him covertly from beneath her lashes. She couldn't believe her eyes when she saw him begin to undress. What in the world did he think he was doing? Then, seeing him slip and lurch against a chair, she guessed his condition. Hawk was blind, staggering drunk. Now she was certain he'd come to her room by mistake. He didn't look sober enough to have evil intentions.

She decided to lay as still as possible. When he fell asleep, she would slip from the bed, dress, and sleep on the settee. She heard him stumble again, then saw him turn in her direction. She'd never seen a man naked before. Mesmerized by the sight, she watched, both shocked and fascinated. Even in the darkness she could make out his wide shoulders and thick chest, the sandy mat of hair covering it reflecting in the slice of moonlight peeking through the window. His waist was narrow and tapered gently to slim hips and powerful legs. The muscles in his stomach rippled as he eased himself down onto the bed. Her cheeks flamed as she glanced away from his most intimate parts.

Naked, Hawk climbed beneath the covers. The room stopped spinning, but he couldn't seem to get comfortable. He rolled onto his side. Even through the alcohol mist, he could feel someone in the bed beside him. Had he somehow gone back to Sally's room instead of his own? He felt the thin material of her chemise. He thought he'd taken care of that the first time. Grabbing a handful, he ripped the offending fabric away. He heard a tiny gasp of surprise before his mouth came down hard on hers. A small place in his mind remembered Sally's voice as passionate and husky, not timid and frightened, but he cast the thought aside.

His hand roamed the length of her. Her skin felt warm and supple, not soft and slack as before. His arousal strengthened. He plundered her sweet mouth with his tongue.

All the passions he'd withheld these past weeks surfaced. The liquor was wearing off, leaving him hardened with a steaming, insatiable desire. For weeks he'd been agonizing. Now he was a man with one single purpose— to impale the writhing, struggling body beneath his with all the power he could.

Mandy fought like a tigress. Terrified, she realized too late that this time Hawk was not going to stop. Maybe she'd brought it on herself by letting him take liberties before. She didn't know. Secretly, she admitted, she'd dreamed of Hawk making her a woman. But not like this. She tried to free her lips to plead with him. But he was relentless. He moved his body to cover hers, holding her hands effortlessly above her head. He didn't hurry, but kissed her deeply, passionately, and even through the whiskey she could taste the virile maleness

of him. A strong hand caressed her breasts,
urgently, forcefully, yet with practiced patience. He stroked her thighs, the line of her
hip, the smooth flat surface below her navel,
forcing her to respond. Her struggles weakened. She could hear a soft, mewling sound
and dimly discovered it was coming from
her. Her body was betraying her—even as
he forced himself on her, she wanted him.

Hawk released his hold on her hands, and
she slid them around his neck, pulling him
even closer. She returned his kisses and felt
his tongue hotly probing the depths of her
mouth. She writhed against him, a tiny part of
her wishing she could stop, but another part
wanting more. His mouth tortured the peaks
of her breasts, then the quivering flesh above
her navel. As he kissed her again, she felt his
fingers probe her most intimate recess. He
found her ready for him. Her shame was complete. With practiced ease, he positioned himself above her. She could feel his male
hardness pressed determinedly against her,
reaching the only obstacle that remained.

Hawk stopped. What the hell . . . ? He
pushed again. Once more he felt the barrier to
his desires. The excitement pumping through
his veins cleared the last of the alcohol mud-
dling his thoughts and, like an icy gust of
wind, realization dawned. Lifting his lips from
the warm, soft ones beneath, he found himself staring into the gold-flecked, green eyes
he knew so well. They were darkened with

passion, her lips crimson from the heat of his kisses.

Damn! He closed his eyes for a moment and took a deep breath to calm himself. What had he done?

"Forgive me, little one. . . ." A deep feeling of regret—and a terrible guilt—knifed through him. "I guess you were telling the truth," he whispered. But he'd gone too far to stop this time. "I promise it will hurt only for a moment." The best he could do for her was to make it as pleasant as possible, hoping he wouldn't leave her with a permanent hatred of men. Determined to be gentle with the innocent in his arms, Hawk forced himself to go slowly. He kissed her deeply, thoroughly. Then he moved his lips to the stiff buds of her full breasts. His body was on fire. The blood pounded in his ears. He covered her mouth again, used his tongue to distract her, then he thrust home.

Mandy gasped aloud and renewed her struggles against him. She felt a white-hot tearing in her loins. Tears gathered in her eyes and slipped down her cheeks. He held her firmly, patiently, speaking soothing words, trying to gentle her. Through the pain and terror, she felt his tenderness. It soothed her taut nerves and, trusting him a little more, she began to relax. He started moving again, at first slowly, carefully, then faster. The pain receded, replaced by a strange, building momentum she didn't understand. She closed

her eyes and gave herself up to the won-
drous swirling sensations.

The weeks of frustration had taken their
toll. Try as he might, Hawk could not contain
himself. He reached his release, tensed as a
thousand stars burst upon the horizon, then
relaxed against the warm flesh beneath him.
He held her close and kissed her brow.

"I'll not hurt you again," he promised. He
kissed her fully, rolled to his side, then pulled
her against him.

Dazed and confused, Mandy didn't understand what she was feeling. Part of her was
glad it was over, but another part yearned for
something more. Hearing Hawk's gentle
words, she assumed he was finished with her.
She brushed the tears from her eyes and tried
to roll away from him.

"Not so fast, little one." The tenderness in
his deep voice calmed her. He nuzzled her
ear. "My word is broken. There is nothing to
keep you from me now. This time it's your
turn," he whispered, and she groaned as she
felt his warm lips move to cover hers once
more.

Tenderly he kissed her lips, her eyes, her
cheeks, the tip of her nose, then moved back
to her lips. He used his tongue deliciously, to
explore every corner, every line of her mouth.
As bruised and battered as she felt, her body
began to respond. She allowed herself to enjoy his tender ministrations. He ran a finger
between her breasts, then cupped each one

fully. He bent his head to kiss the flesh above her nipple, then covered the peak with his mouth. His tongue sent shivers of delight through her body and a fresh surge of desire.

Mandy felt possessed. All the yearnings, all the forbidden delights were happening to her now. Her whole body ached with wanting this man. She could never have imagined the overwhelming need one human being could have for another.

Hawk sensed her desire for him, and it inflamed his passions even more. With a supreme effort he held himself back, willing himself to go slow. With aching control, he continued to teach her the pleasures of love. He kissed every part of her trembling flesh, then entered her slowly, lovingly, savoring the warm, silky feel of her. He'd been with many women in his life, but he'd never experienced the intensity of emotion and desire he felt with this one. The thought surprised and distressed him. He brushed it aside. Now was not the time for recriminations. Tomorrow would be soon enough for that.

Moving faster and faster within his silken cocoon, Hawk felt the girl stiffen and call out his name. She trembled with pleasure beneath him. Pleased, he gave himself up to his own passions.

Mandy was spiraling down from a cloud of ecstasy. Wave after wave of delight washed over her, rippling through her body, depleting her, yet filling her with a kind of awe. She felt the tension in Hawk's body, and her instincts told her his release, too, was near. In that moment, nothing mattered but her love for him. Love. She could admit it now. She loved him. It was all that mattered. She coiled her fingers in his thick soft hair and pulled him closer. His firm cheek nestled beside hers, his lips just brushing her shoulder.

"Wishana, my love," he whispered just before he relaxed against her, so softly she almost didn't hear it.

Her eyes closed in agony. Oh God, how she wished she hadn't. Her heart twisted in her breast, her anguish deeper than she thought she could bear.

Hawk pulled her closer, enfolding her in the circle of his strong arms. They lay together, spent and entwined.

Mandy shivered as an icy tentacle of despair wrapped around her heart. A single tear slipped from the corner of her eye.

Chapter Twenty

✦ ✦ ✦ ✦ ✦

LEMON-YELLOW RAYS, fresh and warm, peeked through the ruffled curtains and crept into Mandy's eyes. She awoke with a start, her eyes darting from the rosewood furniture to the arched canopy above her bed. Myriad emotions hit her hard and fast. She was in Virginia City, a thousand miles from home, in bed with a man—and no longer a virgin. A hot flush burned her cheeks as she recalled the night before, the strange and wonderful sensations, the warmth of Hawk's touch. Her thoughts darkened. What new epithets would he hurl at her today? She recalled the way her body had responded and her flush deepened. Her mind replayed the scene with crystal clarity, from the violent beginning, through the gentleness—to the rage of tingling, furiously pleasurable feelings at the end. He had taken something precious from her last night but had given her something in return. She admitted to herself she had no regrets, no matter what the consequences.

She felt a small stab of pain in her heart, remembering how he had called for Wishana. *Wishana.* Such a lovely name. Mandy wondered again who the woman could be, and another wave of pain assailed her. If only he'd been thinking of her instead.

She rolled onto her side and for the first

time sensed she was being watched. A feeling of dread gnawed at her. *What did he think of her? What cruel remarks would he make?*

Hawk could easily read the troubled expression in the lovely green eyes. He reached out a hand and lifted her exquisite chin, wishing he could reassure her, yet unwilling to risk the consequences, unwilling to give her a greater power over him than she already had. Instead, he kissed the side of her neck and nibbled the petal-like ear. A thousand comforting phrases came to mind, but he staunchly refused to utter them.

"Don't look so troubled, little one," he whispered instead. "It had to happen sometime. I'm sorry it happened as it did . . . but at least we both enjoyed it."

Mandy felt a tremor at his touch, but the words he spoke didn't match the gentleness of his hand. How could he sound so casual? She'd expected recriminations, derision, name-calling, but not indifference. It seemed, somehow, even more devastating.

"You certainly sound nonchalant for a man who just raped the governor's daughter," she threw at him, hoping to elicit some response. She suddenly felt used, betrayed.

"Raped! I admit I took some liberties in the beginning," he conceded, "but you certainly acted as if you enjoyed it." He was beginning to get angry. He already felt guilty for seducing the girl, to say nothing of breaking his word of honor. But one thing was certain—

she'd wanted him as much as he'd wanted her.

Mandy felt her fury building. *How dare he use her so cruelly, then try to put the blame on her!* She pulled the sheet up to cover her bare breasts, but Hawk was covered only to the waist, exposing his broad chest and muscular shoulders. Mandy felt a shiver of desire for him and hated herself for her weakness.

"I was a virgin," she taunted, determined to make him pay. "What am I supposed to tell my fiancé on our wedding night?" She could see him flinch, and she was glad she could hurt him. Glad she could make him feel some of the twisting, sickening pain she was feeling. He'd made love to her by mistake. She knew that now, though she'd tried to deny it before. He was thinking of another. *Wishana.* A name she would never forget—never forgive.

Anger seethed through Hawk like molten lava at the mention of the man she'd left behind.

"I'll give you something to remember on your wedding night!" He pushed her down into the soft featherbed. What a fool he'd been to think she cared about him last night. She was only using him for her pleasure, as she had the rest. She'd been a virgin, all right. But, the way she'd responded, if it hadn't been him it would have been another. Well, it was his turn to be the user.

With a muttered curse, he ripped away the sheet that lay between them. He savagely claimed her mouth with his and roughly caressed the swell of her breasts. He felt the taut peaks stiffen against his hand. *Her body betrays her*, he thought, *even when her mind says no*.

Mandy struggled against him. She couldn't allow herself to weaken again. But even as she struggled, she was lost. The lips that bruised hers turned soft and gentle, torturing her in their possession. His hands roamed the length of her, making her tremble. She knew she wanted him again and felt shame and the sting of tears. She was afraid to meet his gaze, dreading the disdain she knew she would find. A glimpse revealed only passion—or was there something more?

He was gentle with her now, softly spiraling her upward toward new heights of pleasure. He kissed her neck, her shoulders, then the swell of her breasts. Her shame was forgotten, replaced by a demanding heat. They made love slowly, fulfilling both their needs, until the sun was high in the morning sky. Then they napped for a time.

Hawk rose slowly from the bed where he'd found such pleasure, leaving the girl asleep. He wished they could stay forever, never have to face the realities of the world outside. He dressed and slipped quietly from the room, closing the door softly behind him.

Mandy awoke to find him gone. She knew she should feel ashamed of what she'd done, but all she felt was a warm, sensuous glow and an aching need to have the big

man back in her arms. She thought of the
day ahead. How would she endure it?
Would she look somehow different? Would
Hawk tell James what had taken place between them? Heat stained her cheeks at the
thought. She rose from the bed and donned
her silk wrapper.

By tonight they would be in Sacramento
City. The moment she'd longed for would
arrive. . . . If only she could delay it! A knock
at the door interrupted her thoughts. She
opened it to find two bellmen and a steaming
tub of water. Hawk must have sent up a bath.
She wished it could wash away this fearful
ache she felt inside.

"Hawk, where the hell have you been?"
James's face looked flushed and angry as he
marched across the lobby floor. "The stage left
an hour ago. Now we'll miss the train. The
governor's expecting us. He's going to be fit to
be tied." He shook his head and paced nervously.

"We're not leaving yet," Hawk grumbled,
his manner brusque. He had trouble meeting
James's gaze.

"I've already wired the governor," Hawk
said. "He'll be expecting us tomorrow."

". . . You must have had *some* night." James
smiled knowingly and some of his anger
faded. He started to speak, but the look on
Hawk's face stopped him.

"Don't push it, James," Hawk warned, not ready to cope with his friend's teasing. He'd never been very good at lying.

"Does Julia know about our change of plans? I didn't want to disturb her until I found you." They moved up the big staircase.

"We'd better tell her," Hawk said. "I've already taken care of the rooms."

Mandy heard a knock at the door. The moment she'd been dreading was at hand. Her bags were packed and she wore her pink muslin, clean and pressed for the occasion.

"Come in," she said, as light-heartedly as she could manage. She could hear a tiny quaver in her voice. The door opened and both men stood in the hall, James looking handsome and refreshed, Hawk back in his buckskins and looking dour as usual.

"I'm ready," she stated flatly, unwilling to meet either man's gaze.

"There's been a change of plans." Hawk moved into the room, picked up her bags, and carried them back over to the bureau. "We aren't leaving today."

"What!" In one moment her fondest wishes and her worst fears were both realized. "But I thought the governor . . . I mean, my father, was expecting us?"

"Now he's expecting us tomorrow," Hawk said dryly.

"Something came up," James added. "Besides, you wanted to see Virginia City, didn't you?"

"Well, yes, but . . ."

"Then it's all worked out for the best," he continued smoothly. "I don't know about you two, but I'm starved. Let's get something to eat."

Mandy gritted her teeth, pasted on a smile, and swept from the room.

At first the conversation was agonizingly stilted. James kept glancing at her and then at Hawk. She straightened her shoulders and held her head high, determined not to let either of them know how disturbing this whole affair really was.

James ordered a bottle of wine with lunch and after a few sips Mandy began to relax. She decided she had come this far, she might as well make the best of it.

After lunch they took in the sights. James pointed out the Mackay Mansion, home of the "Bonanza King," John Mackay, as well as "the castle," built by the Gould and Curry Mining Company. The homes were fashioned in grand Victorian style and ornately trimmed.

The travelers walked several blocks farther, passing more saloons than Mandy had ever seen in one place: the Bucket of Blood, the Delta Queen, the Washoe Club, the Silver Dollar, and others with equally notorious names. They passed the *Territorial Enterprise*, famous as the newly formed state of Nevada's first newspaper, and the first publisher of the already legendary Mark Twain.

"Look over there," James instructed. "Beside that barn at the north end of town."

"What in the world is that?" Mandy asked. A strange, straw-colored beast with a giant hump on its back was being led by a blue-uniformed soldier.

"That's a dromedary," Hawk said with a smile, glad to see some of her spunk returning. "A camel. They're one of the orneriest beasts you'll ever want to meet. Don't get too close," he added with a twinkle in his eye. "They've been known to spit at people they don't like."

"Now you're teasing me," she said.

"He's not kidding," James said. About that time a passerby was unlucky enough to provoke a demonstration of the camel's defense.

Mandy broke into giggles. She tried to stifle her laughter behind her hand, but to no avail.

"I think it's time we head back to the hotel," Hawk said. "Someone's liable to think we're laughing at him instead of the camel. In Virginia City, that could be dangerous." They headed back down the street.

It turned out to be a delightful day for Mandy, even with the cloud of unhappiness hanging over her head. They had an early supper and called it a night. She glanced discretely in Hawk's direction as they headed up the hotel stairs, but his features were inscrutable. Sighing to herself and wondering what he could be thinking, she shut the door to her room.

She undressed with little difficulty, brushed her hair, and readied herself for bed. She climbed beneath the covers but couldn't fall asleep. Her mind kept conjuring heated memories of the night before. She lay tossing and turning for what seemed hours. Then she heard the unmistakable sound of a key turning in the lock. *Surely he wouldn't come back tonight!* Her heart pounded.

He strolled into her room as if he belonged there and, just for a moment, she imagined he did.

"Good evening, little one," he drawled lazily. "You look as though you weren't expecting me."

". . . Ex . . . pecting you!" Mandy stammered. "Of all the conceited . . . ! How dare you come into my room!"

"You didn't think I went to all the trouble of missing the train for nothing, did you?" He casually removed his buckskin shirt, then sat down on the settee and unlaced his moccasins.

"But Hawk, you can't just expect me to . . . to . . ."

"I thought I made myself perfectly clear last night. There is nothing to keep you from me now." He removed his buckskin breeches and strolled immodestly toward her. She glanced away and felt the heat rush to her cheeks.

"Hawk, I know you don't believe me, but I don't do this kind of . . ."

He turned her face with his hand and covered her mouth with his lips before she could finish. She struggled momentarily against his chest, trying to push him away before it was too late. He held her effortlessly, stroking her hair and running his hand down the line of her hip. He cupped her bottom with a wide palm and pulled her firmly the length of him, tugging her cotton garment over her head as he made room for himself on the mattress.

A shiver tingled her blood. She struggled harder, knowing she would soon be in his power, a part of her hoping he would win. As his tongue probed the recesses of her mouth, she moaned softly. *How she wanted him!* He kissed her deeply, and she let him begin his magic, transporting her to unknown worlds.

She lost track of time, their lovemaking at first heated and surging, making her breathless with its passion, rendering her helpless, yet lending the courage to give of herself in return.

Slowly they spiraled down.

Then he took her again. Slowly, languorously, they reached an even higher plane, until at last they lay sated. She drifted to sleep within the curl of his powerful arm.

An incessant pounding awoke them. Hawk checked the time, muttered beneath his breath, and rolled from the bed.

"Julia, wake up," James demanded. "We're

going to make that train today—with or without Hawk!"

Mandy cringed. There was no way around it now. No way to keep James from guessing the truth. Hawk tossed her the thin silk wrapper and pulled on his breeches.

"Julia, can you hear me? I'm coming in."

"Don't bother," Hawk answered gruffly. "We'll be right out." He caught her look of mortification, and cursed himself for a fool. At least James was the kind of friend who would understand—he hoped.

Within the hour they were packed and ready to leave. James barely spoke to Hawk, and Mandy felt herself blushing continually. How had she ever let this happen?

They boarded the stage and rode toward Reno in silence. In just a few hours they would arrive in Sacramento City. Her true identity would be discovered. She wrung her hands nervously. *What would Uncle William do? What would Hawk say? What about the money he and James would lose?* She could just imagine how Hawk would handle being made a fool—especially by a woman. She groaned inwardly and glanced back out the window of the coach.

They arrived in Reno, which turned out to be just a small cluster of wooden buildings established by the Central Pacific Railroad in its mad dash eastward to span the continent. The Union Pacific was rushing westward at an equally breakneck pace, and if all went as planned, the two lines would eventually meet somewhere in the territories. The tracks had only been open over the Sierras for a few months.

The travelers boarded the train in thoughtful silence. The coach was plush and elegant, but it was the scenery that captured her attention.

Mandy thrilled as the train began its long ascent, winding higher and higher into the pine-covered mountains. They crossed spindly trestles over deep gorges and rounded curves overhanging sheer dropoffs thousands of feet deep. It was not a trip for the faint-hearted. Mandy remembered the dime novels she had read. On her perilous journey west, she'd experienced adventure far greater than anything she'd ever read about. She'd never be sorry for that.

Another hour of strained silence passed. Hawk left to speak with an acquaintance in another car.

"Would you like to tell me about it?" James offered as soon as his friend was out of earshot.

Mandy looked out the window, shamefaced. "I'd really rather not discuss it, if you don't mind."

"You know, even if he is a friend, I'd be happy to black his eye if—"

"No!"

"Whatever you say." He sighed resignedly, leaning back against the tapestry seats. He could see the girl was agonizing, but there was probably little he could do for her. He couldn't believe Hawk had broken his word. He was a man of honor, a man you could trust with your life. This woman must mean a great deal to him—even if he wasn't willing to admit it.

Chapter Twenty-one
✦✦✦✦

EVEN THROUGH THE hustle of debarking passengers, clanking luggage carts, and yelling porters, Mandy spotted the governor's sleek black carriage. The driver loaded their baggage, and they rode through town toward the governor's mansion. More nervous every minute, Mandy twisted the kerchief she carried in her lap. A fine sheen of perspiration damped the hair at her temples and the nape of her neck. She wished she had the courage to tell the men the truth before she reached the mansion. She should have done it on the train, but she hadn't the courage, and now was certainly not the time.

Instead she turned her attention toward the hustle of Sacramento City. They passed Dingley's Spice Mill as they traveled the cobblestone streets, and the Central Pacific Western Headquarters Building, which, James mentioned, was occupied by Leland Stanford, C. P. Huntington, Charles Crocker, and Mark Hopkins—the Big Four.

The buildings were mostly brick, and stretched for blocks along the river. The people were an odd mixture of river ruffians in buckskins and broad-brimmed hats, gold seekers in canvas breeches and plaid flannel shirts, and elegantly dressed ladies and gentlemen. Pink parasols and black bowlers passed dun-colored felts and striped stocking caps. Mandy forgot her cares and let her senses soak up the sights and sounds of the city. The horses clip-clopped along, stilling the buzz in her ears.

Making a short detour, they moved down a side street.

"What in the world—" Mandy said, glancing at the hubbub of activity on each side of the road.

"They're still at it," James said. "Bet you thought they'd be finished by now."

"Yes . . . yes I did." Mandy looked around. Most of the buildings had been elevated on jacks, with dirt filling the space beneath. Some three-story buildings were converted to two-story buildings—their first floors packed with dirt. Apparently the town had originally been built at the same level as the river. Flooding had motivated the citizenry to move the whole town up about twelve feet.

The carriage descended to a section of the city that had not yet been raised. Portions of the board sidewalks ended abruptly—ten feet above the ground.

"I'd hate to be walking these streets on a dark night," she commented wryly. "A fall off one of these sidewalks could be deadly."

Hawk smiled for the first time that day. "More than a few drunks have taken that tumble." His dark eyes lingered on her face and Mandy wondered if he would still look at her like that after he found out who she really was.

In short order they reached the mansion. A small stiff-necked Chinese houseboy greeted them formally at the door.

"Good afta'noon Mista' Langley, Mista' Long." He glanced at Mandy and furrowed his brow. "Missy." He seemed slightly confused. "His Hona, the gov'na, was called away on beesness. He sends his aporogies and asks that he receive you in two hours."

He looked at the men. "Dhere is a room upstairs for your convenience, if you weesh to freshen op." He wrinkled his nose at their sooty attire.

"I think we'd prefer to go on over to the hotel. We'll return at six." James spoke for both men.

"May I show you op to your room, Missy?" the Chinese asked. Mandy expected the houseboy to give her away at any moment, but he said nothing.

"Thank you," she answered. She considered telling the men the truth but, seeing Hawk's stern profile, decided to wait. She would put herself in the hands of fate.

"Miss Ashton." Hawk inclined his head slightly, then replaced his broad-brimmed hat and backed from the room, his expression unreadable.

"Julia," James gave her a speculative glance, "we'll see you at six."

"Yes . . ." she whispered. She watched the men depart, then followed the little Chinese up the sweeping staircase.

"What do you intend to do about Julia?" James ventured during the carriage ride to the hotel.

"Nothing much I can do, if it's any of your business," Hawk replied sourly. "If the governor's willing to pay us six months' wages to keep her from marrying some damned Army officer, what do you think he'd pay to keep her away from me?"

James nodded. "Well, at least it isn't as though you were the first." James made the comment flatly, but Hawk knew his friend was seeking some reason for his dishonorable behavior.

Hawk gave James a long, deliberate look as the carriage turned down the main street of town. "Unfortunately . . . I was the first," he said, not wanting James to think badly of the girl and not understanding exactly why he should care.

"What! You seduced . . . ! She was an innocent? How could you break your word?"

"I'm afraid I don't quite understand it myself," Hawk said quietly.

James looked away, deciding not to push the issue. He felt sure his friend must be suffering a tremendous amount of guilt already. He needn't add to the burden.

They reached the hotel and bid the carriage return a little before six. The evening ahead would be a trying one for both of them.

"Your room, Missy Julia," the Chinese said, in a slightly sarcastic voice.

It was obvious he knew she wasn't the real Julia, and Mandy wondered again why he hadn't given her away. She decided he was probably more concerned with keeping his position in the household. He set her baggage down and backed into the hall.

The mansion was similar to those she'd seen in Virginia City, Victorian in style and thoroughly charming.

"Bessy weel be op to he'p you change," the man added before leaving.

Bessy, as it turned out, was Julia's personal maid, a big raw-boned black woman with a wide mouth, hearty grin, and sparkling white teeth.

"Land sakes, chil', yo' ain't Miss Julia!"

Mandy put a finger to her lips.

Bessy howled with laughter, then took in Mandy's appearance. "Do those men think you're my Julia?"

Mandy nodded.

The woman howled again. "Yo' must be her cousin, Samantha. I done heerd her talk 'bout you fo' years. I just knew my little lamb would think o' sometin' to outfox the ol' gov'nuh." Heavy jowls beneath shining eyes shook with mirth and approval as the tale unfolded. At least it appeared Mandy would have one ally in the house.

"Lord a mercy, His Honor's shorly gonna be sore when he finds out what you and Miss Julia gone and done." Bessy smiled ruefully. "Is Miss Julia done married off to her soldier?"

"Well, I can't say for certain, but she should be by now. How did you happen to know so much about all this?"

"In dis household, dey ain't many secrets when it come to Miss Julia. Da gov'nuh was mad as a hornet when he got dat letter from Miss Julia 'bout her beau. But I knowed Miss Julia too long. If'n she done found herse'f a man, he be some kinda' good one. She may 'a been a wild li'l thing, but she weren't never no fool. Seein' you here makes me even more certain. I'm glad yo' stuck by her, Miss Samantha."

"I know she'll be happy with Jason," Mandy reassured her. A tiny ache touched her heart as she thought of Julia and her new husband. The image of a tall man in buckskins surfaced, but she fought it down and returned her attention to Bessy, who was unpacking Mandy's satchel.

"I'm not sure I'll be staying, Bessy. When the governor finds out what I've done . . ." She let the sentence trail off, feeling a little queasy.

"Don't you be silly, chil'. Da gov'nuh he be mad all right, but he won't never turn you out in da streets. You family, honey, and da gov'nuh is one mighty lonely man."

Mandy felt comforted by the woman's words. She really wanted to spend some time with her uncle, try to make him see that she and Julia had done the right thing.

Bessy instructed the kitchen to send up a bath, then had Mandy select one of Julia's many gowns. Bessy set to work on it immediately, making it shorter and a little snugger in the waist. The two-hour wait seemed to fly as Bessy chatted pleasantly, filling her in on the latest gossip, then listening to the rest of Mandy's tale. Of course Mandy was careful to avoid any mention of her involvement with Travis Langley.

All too soon she could hear men in the hallway. Hawk and James had returned. The moment she dreaded was at hand.

Mandy stood at the top of the stairs watching the scene below.

"Governor." James extended his hand. He had bathed, shaved again, and wore a clean black well-tailored suit.

"James, Travis, come in. Come in." The governor shook hands and stood in the foyer with his back to the stairs.

Hawk stood in the entry, looking handsome in his dark brown breeches and fawn-colored coat. He spoke the required niceties, then glanced above.

Mandy could barely meet his gaze.

Hawk felt an instant rush of desire. Descending the staircase in a pink satin gown was the most beautiful woman he'd ever seen. Her thick chestnut hair was swept up fashionably, and the gown displayed a generous amount of her full cleavage. Tiny beads of perspiration formed on his brow.

Following Hawk's gaze, the governor turned to see the woman he assumed would be his daughter descending the staircase. He blinked, then blinked again, wondering if he were focusing correctly. There was no denying the family heritage, but it certainly wasn't his daughter. Who, then? Was there some mistake?

A tiny ray of comprehension worked its way to the back of his mind. *She wouldn't! She wouldn't dare!* He heard a pounding in his ears, his rage in that moment so great he felt his blood might boil. His neck above his collar felt hot and flushed, and his eyes narrowed to tiny slits.

Mandy's heart pounded wildly. The look of fury on Uncle William's face was unmistakable. Maybe he would beat her. One foot touched the bottom step, and she reached out for Hawk's arm to steady herself. She could feel his strength. She used it to meet her uncle's furious gaze.

"Uncle William," she said, breaking what seemed an endless silence.

He did not reply. He just stood there with his face puffed up and turning red. He closed his eyes and looked as though he were trying to calm himself. Then all of a sudden he started to laugh. First, a soft chuckle, then louder and louder, until he was doubled over with guffaws.

Hawk and James stood motionless, trying to comprehend the scene. Neither could understand the governor's strange reaction.

Finally, his color returning to normal, the governor turned to them. "Well, gentlemen." He wiped tears of laughter from his eyes. "I'd like to thank you for escorting my niece to Sacramento. It's been years since we've had a chance to visit. I'm certain we have a lot to talk over." He laughed heartily again, this time at their expense.

"What do you mean . . . your niece?" Hawk asked, his ire building rapidly. His could feel the heat in his neck as he turned his hard look on the girl.

"May I present my niece . . . Miss Samantha Ashton. My brother's daughter. My daughter's cousin." He appeared to take perverse delight in the men's discomfort.

Mandy watched Hawk carefully.

"You are Samantha Ashton." He pronounced each word separately, glowering at her. "Not Julia Ashton." His jaw was set, and she knew he was barely controlling his temper. "You're the girl I met two years ago?"

She nodded weakly.

He drew himself up till he seemed eight feet tall. His eyes were so dark they looked like blackened holes. "You let us drag you across fifteen hundred miles of hostile territory thinking you were Julia. You cost us six months' pay. You—"

"It's all right, gentlemen. You'll receive the full amount. It's not your fault my daughter and her cousin are smarter than the lot of us. Besides, I'll extract retribution from my daughter and my niece later." He gave Mandy a stern look.

James just stood there, the hint of a smile on his lips.

"Sorry, sir," Hawk put in. "We cannot accept the money." His carefully controlled fury made Mandy cringe. James gave him a baleful glance, but Hawk paid no heed.

"You hired us to bring back your daughter," Hawk said, "and we failed. We'll leave for Fort Laramie in the morning. This time we won't let you down." He finally trusted himself to look at the girl. She looked pale and forlorn, no longer haughty and regal. His mind in that moment comprehended for the first time that he hadn't broken his word of honor. A wave of relief washed over him. At least that was some consolation, but the fact was he would have, and all because of her.

He watched as she fought to retain her composure. He should have known—somehow he should have been able to see through the deception. His fury surged even hotter. He'd let a woman—no, a slip of a girl—make a fool of him.

"That won't be necessary, gentlemen," the governor was saying. "From what I know of Samantha, she would not undertake this endeavor lightly." He glanced toward his niece for some reassurance.

"No, Uncle William, I would not. Please, give me a chance to explain." Mandy looked at Hawk, hoping to see some glimmer of compassion. She saw none. What little she ever had of him was lost and her heart felt heavier than ever before in her life.

"I think I'd like to hear what my niece has to say. We'll discuss the matter of your compensation at another time. Now, I think it would be best for all concerned if Samantha and I spent some time alone."

Sullenly, Hawk extended his hand to the governor and glowered in Mandy's direction. James said the necessary good-byes and the men left.

Mandy and the governor retired to his study. She felt sick at heart, yet relieved at the governor's willingness to listen. She already missed the big man and frowned thinking just how much she'd grown used to his presence.

The two men moved toward the waiting carriage, Hawk stomping more than walking, James mulling the past few minutes over in his mind. Unable to stop himself, James began to grin, then chuckle, finally laughing out loud.

"Just what's so damned funny?" Hawk asked. "The girl made a fool of us and cost us six months' pay, and you think it's funny!"

James could just barely make out the next sentence.

"You think you're getting to know someone, then find out you don't know 'em at all." Hawk spoke with a hostility that belied a deeper emotion.

James decided his mirth might better be kept to himself. The girl had guts. He had to give her that. It was too bad the whole affair had turned out so badly for them both. Well, he hoped at least the governor's daughter was happy. Maybe it would turn out well for someone.

Chapter Twenty-two

✦✦✦✦✦

THE FOLLOWING DAY the governor wired Fort Laramie, informing them of Samantha's whereabouts. The telegram he received in return advised that her father was still on duty at Fort Sedgewick.

Mandy's ruse hadn't been discovered, and her father, though upset over her trip to "see Aunt Adelaide," had been convinced of her safety. He never considered she might head for California in Julia's place.

Uncle William listened as Mandy told him of Julia's fiancé—or more probably husband. He wasn't completely convinced, but agreed at least to meet the man and listen to what his daughter had to say before taking any further action.

Uncle William had missed Julia over the past year more than he'd anticipated. Having Samantha in his home, he told her, filled a void. He convinced her to stay with him through the winter, promising her a chance to see some of the surrounding countryside and bribing her with a trip to San Francisco. She agreed enthusiastically, but only on the condition that Uncle William would find something for her to do to help earn her keep. She had come west to make a life for herself. She wanted to start as soon as possible. Mumbling something about amends for all the trouble she'd caused, he agreed.

Even with all the excitement, her thoughts dwelled on Hawk. She kept hoping for a chance to talk to him, or even to James, but so far none had arisen.

By the end of the week, Mandy's nerves were taut. She had to speak to Hawk, try to explain what had happened—why she'd done what she did. She had no idea how to find him, but she knew her uncle did. She resolved to ask Uncle William first thing in the morning. She'd have to make up some sort of pretense, but convinced herself she'd think of something.

The next day Uncle William presented the perfect opportunity.

"Samantha, you look charming this morning," the governor complimented. He'd insisted she alter as many of Julia's dresses as she liked, assuring her Julia was certain to buy more new clothes if she returned to Sacramento City.

"Why, thank you, Uncle William." After all the trouble Mandy had been through on her cousin's behalf, she enjoyed the lovely wardrobe to the fullest. She smoothed the skirt of her soft blue batiste as he sat to breakfast with her. The airy little room was bright and cheerful. Wong Sun, the houseboy, served them rich black coffee, the smell reminding her of an open campfire and a big sandy-haired man.

"I have a surprise for you, my dear," the governor informed her, interrupting her thoughts. "Long before you arrived, I made plans for a welcome-home ball in Julia's honor. It seemed such a shame to cancel it, I've decided to have it in your honor instead. It will give me an opportunity to introduce you into society."

Mandy beamed with delight. A ball! And in the governor's mansion. It sounded wonderful. She felt a flush of happiness as much from her uncle's gesture of forgiveness as his news of the ball. If only she were going with Hawk it would be perfect.

"Oh, Uncle! That sounds wonderful! Do you think we could invite James and . . . Travis?"

"Certainly, dear, if it makes you happy. Now, if you'll excuse me, duty calls." He kissed her cheek lightly and left the room.

Mandy was ecstatic. Not only would she get a chance to speak with Hawk, but she would attend a ball as well. As she finished her breakfast, she practiced what she would say to Hawk, discarding one idea after another. *Hawk, I'm so sorry I lied to you, but I just had to.* She sighed and shook her head. *Hawk, Julia found the man she loves and . . .* That wouldn't do either. Well, she'd think of something.

She pushed back her chair and raced upstairs to her room, intent on finding something of Julia's to wear to the ball. She wanted to look her very best.

* * *

The night of the ball finally arrived. Bessy had helped her select a white organdy gown, with tiny seed pearls its only trim. Bessy said it did wonders for her dark hair and fair complexion. Mandy hoped so. Hawk would be there, and she was determined to speak with him.

The house was filled with sweet-smelling flowers for the occasion—the climate was so mild they were plentiful even this late in the year. In the ballroom, a huge crystal punch bowl shimmered on the center table, and a group of musicians began to play. Mandy could hear the lilting melodies, mingled with the hubbub of voices, drifting up.

She came down the stairs at half past the hour, as the governor insisted was fashionable, and all conversation dropped to a murmur as she appeared on her uncle's arm. He seemed delighted to have her with him, introducing her to so many young men she thought her head would spin. She looked up at him as he led her into a waltz.

The governor was enjoying himself immensely. It was one of the few purely pleasurable occasions he'd allowed himself since his wife died. Seeing how lovely Samantha looked, and thinking of Julia, he felt a pang of regret that he hadn't spent more time with his daughter. It was becoming painfully clear to him that much of Julia's scandalous behavior was caused by his lack of attention. He'd already decided to let her marriage to the young

Army officer stand. He just hoped he would somehow be able to make up for the lost time.

Samantha's evening was going splendidly as well. She was the center of attention for the first time in her life as she whirled around the floor on the arm of one handsome man after another; but her thoughts remained on Hawk. Both he and James had accepted the governor's invitation, but so far neither had arrived. Surely Hawk didn't hate her so much he wouldn't even be in the same room with her.

Another waltz was playing as she glided around the floor on the arm of Mark Denton, a lithe young man whom her uncle seemed especially anxious for her to meet. But her eyes kept straying to the doorway. *Please let him come,* Mandy thought.

Returning her eyes to Mark Denton's soft blue ones, she met instead a penetrating gaze of deepest brown.

"May I cut in?" Hawk stepped up boldly, leaving Denton little chance to reply. The big man whisked her away without a backward glance.

Mandy's heart raced. She suddenly felt flushed, giddy. *How could he affect her so?*

"Enjoying yourself tonight, Sam?" he drawled lazily. The touch of his hand at her back sent tiny shivers dashing through her.

"Yes . . . yes I am." She felt shy all of a sudden. She liked the sound of the name he'd chosen for her. He wore the beautifully tailored black evening clothes he'd worn in Virginia City. Her cheeks flamed as heated memories came flooding back.

"And you?" she asked at last, forcing her eyes to meet his.

"I am now." His soft tone spoke volumes, and a pulse throbbed in her temple.

She could feel the heat of his hand as he guided her lightly through the steps of the waltz. "I've been hoping to see you," she said, hoping he wouldn't think her too bold.

He cocked an eyebrow. "I've missed you, too, little one." His words made her dizzy with delight. He held her so close she could feel the hard muscles of his legs.

They danced through that waltz and into the next. Still feeling light-headed, Mandy suggested they retire to the terrace for a breath of fresh air. It would be the perfect place for the conversation she had in mind.

"My pleasure, milady," he teased as they exited through French doors.

They reached a quiet corner, and she stammered slightly, trying to find a way to broach the subject. "Hawk . . . there is . . . something I've been wanting to say to you—it's about Julia . . . and our trip."

Hawk's face turned ashen. She could see him working a muscle in his jaw and instantly regretted beginning the conversation. *Why hadn't she left things alone?* She stiffened. There was no turning back now.

"I want to explain about—"

"Whatever you have to say about your

treachery and lies does not interest me in the least."

"Please, Hawk, you don't understand. I had to do it. I—"

He cut her off. "There is something you have I am interested in." He held her stunned gaze a moment, then stepped closer, drawing her into his arms. He crushed her possessively against him and covered her lips with his.

Jolting waves of pleasure made her forget his harsh words. She was back in the deep featherbed in Virginia City, her body trembling with desire. It maddened her that he could so easily arouse her passions. She struggled and pulled her lips away.

"What do you think you're doing?" she asked, her voice shaky.

He released her resignedly, in an attempt to maintain some semblance of propriety. His eyes held a hint of regret.

"There is something I've been wanting to talk to you about as well." He paused, his eyes raking her. They remained overly long on the swell of her breasts. "Now that we both know you're not really the governor's daughter, there's no reason for us to deny ourselves."

He sounded so nonchalant, so matter-of-fact.

"It seems the death of my friend Thomas Rutherford has left me a fairly wealthy man. I'll be spending a good deal of time in Sacramento City. I'll set you up in a comfortable

home, keep you in nice clothes, provide anything you need. You just keep me happy
when I'm in town. We'll keep the whole affair
as discreet as possible. Of course, I'll expect
you not to entertain any other men friends—
including Mark Denton."

Mandy was speechless, unable to stop his
humiliating monologue. She stared at him,
flushed and angry, fighting back tears.

"Get away from me this minute," she whispered, her voice barely audible. "Just leave
me alone. Don't ever come near me again."
Her words sounded choked and ragged.

It was Hawk's turn to be stunned. He'd seen
her green eyes snap with anger, or turn dark
with sadness, but he had never seen the look of
pure fury, tinged with bitter disappointment,
that touched her eyes now. For a moment he
regretted his words. *What had she expected?*
She'd lied to him—deceived him in every way
imaginable. Made a laughingstock out of him
in front of the entire city. There was no way he
could ever trust her again. At least this way
they could have enjoyed each other's bodies.

He took a deep breath. Maybe it was better
this way. Even having the woman for his mistress could be asking for trouble. She'd moved
away from him to stare out into the darkness.
A tear trickled from the corner of her eye and
glistened in the moonlight. The urge to comfort her raged strong. He felt a flicker of pain
in the area of his heart as he stalked heavily
from the porch.

Mandy heard the echo of his fading foot-steps. She flew down the steps of the terrace, out into the garden where no one could see her tears. She sobbed until warm, familiar arms encircled her. She held James tightly, as if only he could save her from her drowning, suffocating feelings.

"Don't cry, Jul—I mean, Samantha," he soothed. "This is supposed to be your special night. Don't let him spoil it for you."

"You know?"

"I can pretty well guess. What did he say?"

"He asked me to be his mistress." She broke into renewed sobs.

James smiled and cocked an eyebrow. "Well, I wouldn't have guessed that."

Mandy stopped crying and looked up at the tall handsome man.

"He obviously cares for you, Samantha. He's never even come close to a commitment before. It's just that . . . well, he thinks you made a fool of him."

"I had to, James. It was Julia's only chance. She loves Jason so much. I had to help her. . . . But I won't lie, James; I did it for myself, too. My life at the fort was miserable. There is no way to describe how badly I wanted to leave. This was my chance for free-dom, my chance to make a life for myself."

James patted her shoulder.

"He'll never forgive me . . . will he, James?" She spoke resignedly, her cheeks wet with tears.

James took a deep breath. "Probably not. He's a proud man, Samantha, and not a forgiving one."

"Well, I did what I had to do. I know Julia is happy, and I have no regrets."

"What about you, Samantha? Are you going to be happy?"

"I want to be, James. But I'm not so sure now."

James sighed. He tilted her chin. "You see, you should have fallen in love with me."

Mandy smiled tremulously, straightened her shoulders, and accepted James's handkerchief to wipe her tears. "I'll not let him make me cry again."

They moved inside, where she accepted James's invitation to dance. She could see Hawk lounging carelessly beside the door, a tall willowy brunette hanging on his every word. *Well, she'd show him!* She forced herself to smile, finished dancing with James, then began dancing with others. The men seemed to be standing in line for her. Now, thanks to Julia, she knew how to give them just what they expected.

The balance of the evening passed in a blur. Hawk left with the brunette, and Mandy was eventually able to escape on the pretense of a headache. She thought her nightmare would be over in Sacramento City. Now she realized it was only just beginning.

*   *   *

"Travis, is there someplace we could go?" the wealthy widow, Doreen Simmons, simpered on his arm.

"I think I've had all the fun I can stand for one night," he heard himself say, not believing he was declining her offer. He didn't stop to question himself. Instead, he helped her into his rented carriage and headed the horses toward her home. Doreen's husband had died over a year ago and the attractive widow was on the prowl. He smiled to himself. If he'd made his earlier proposition to Doreen, there would be no doubt as to the outcome. He escorted the brunette to the door of her Georgian mansion, said a hasty good-bye, then returned to the carriage.

Visions of a petite young woman, swirling in a cloud of white organdy, controlled his thoughts.

Chapter Twenty-three

✦✦✦✦

THE NEXT FEW weeks passed in a whirlwind of activity. The governor came up with a job for Mandy, in which she would help him research the various bills before the legislature. Mandy enjoyed the work. She read everything the

governor had available and took lengthy
notes. At parties she listened for information
and gossip that might help her uncle make a
decision. The governor seemed pleased with
her work. When he called her insight *invalu-
able*, she beamed.

Mark Denton was a constant fixture at the
mansion. He was tall, good-looking, and considered quite a catch. Her uncle constantly
praised him, advising her of Mark's socially
prominent family background, as well as his
blossoming law practice, and Mark was always kind and attentive. *Why couldn't she fall
in love with him?* She was afraid he was falling
for her, but all she thought of was Hawk. She
was just beginning to think of him as *Travis*.
Dressed in city clothes instead of his buckskins, it was hard to believe he was the rugged man of the plains.

Saturday arrived, and with it another party,
this one a formal supper at the residence of
Judge Edwin Crocker. Mark was her escort.
They arrived at the stately three-story home
along with several other guests.

Mark helped Mandy from the carriage, making sure her ice-blue satin gown missed the
puddles left from last night's shower. The
weather was brisk, the mottled sky threatening rain. But she remained warm beneath her
burnoose cloak. She snuggled her head
deeper into the hood with its soft beaver trim.

Beneath her wrap the gown exposed her shoulders, and the waist dipped to a point front and back, accentuating the curve of her body. She felt confident and alluring in the beautiful dress as she graciously accepted Mark's arm and swept into the elegant home.

The interior was grand. Mrs. Crocker had chosen the finest brocade wall coverings and deep-cut crystal chandeliers. Mandy felt comfortable in the elegant mansion, comfortable even in her sophisticated role as the governor's niece—something she never would have believed possible. She secretly thanked her mother for her endless patience—and Julia, for inadvertently changing her life.

By now Mandy knew most of the guests: the good Senator Wiggins and his pudgy wife, Irene; handsome Sam Brannan, recently divorced and considered one of Sacramento's most eligible bachelors; and James McClatchy, editor of the *Sacramento Bee*, to name but a few. It was an elite group of the most influential men and women in the city.

Mandy passed the early part of the evening graciously, enjoying conversations much more exciting than the usual social drivel. There were discussions of the farmer's rights over the powerful cattle and mining interests. Talk of the new Capitol building nearing completion, and a heated debate on the merits, or folly, of the current project raising the downtown portion of the city.

"Well, whatever the costs and disruptions,

at least we'll be free of the blasted flooding."
A familiar deep voice added his comment to
the debate. Mandy felt a tiny shiver as she
turned to face Hawk's handsome profile and
saw a corner of his mouth lift.

"Why, Miss Ashton," he said with a hint of
mockery, "what a pleasure to see you again."
His dark eyes raked her as his mouth curved
in a provocative smile. "You're looking lovely,
as usual." His gaze held a taunting caress and
her heartbeat quickened. Hot color rushed to
her cheeks.

"Why, thank you, Mr. Langley," she replied formally, keeping up the charade. Then
she noticed the willowy brunette clinging to
his arm. "Why Doreen, how nice to see you
again," she said sweetly, but she wanted to
scratch out the woman's eyes.

Mark walked up beside her. Mandy smiled
up at him and reached for his arm, pulling
him closer than she'd intended. "Mr. Langley, Miss Simmons, you remember Mr. Denton." She felt a twinge of satisfaction as Hawk
bristled. She gazed into Mark's blue eyes and
gave him a winning smile. The hostess ended
Mandy's performance with a call to dinner.
Mandy laughed playfully at something Mark
said, saw Hawk scowl, and swept from the
room.

She played her part well through dinner.
Mark had never seen her so attentive, and he
beamed with delight. She felt a little guilty for
deceiving him, but she would worry about

that tomorrow. Tonight she would extract whatever revenge she could from the handsome man seated across from her.

The supper was sumptuous. Everything from quail to fresh brook trout and ending with a flambé of delicate cherries jubilee. It all tasted like sawdust to her. Her attention remained fixed on the man who caused her such distress. She could tell she was having a devilish effect on him as well and her determination strengthened.

"Mark, are you still taking me riding tomorrow?" she asked petulantly as they finished dessert.

"But of course, darling," Mark gushed, "if that will make you happy."

Hawk's dark eyes blackened, and a muscle bunched in his jaw. "Maybe Doreen and I could join you?" he put in. "Would you like that, my sweet?"

"Oh yes, Travis," Doreen gushed.

Mandy's eyes flew wide. There was no way she could tolerate an entire day of that simpering, conniving . . . widow! She glanced at Hawk venomously and saw him enjoying her discomfort.

"Actually, I may have to go shopping instead." She hated his look of triumph. She almost wished she'd suffered through the day rather than let him best her again.

"Uncle William's birthday is next week. I want to buy him something nice," she finished lamely.

The meal ended. The men headed for the study for brandy and cigars, and Mandy sighed with relief. Thank God that was over. Hawk was a tough man to get the better of; but still, she felt ahead of the game tonight.

She let Mark kiss her after the party for the first time, hoping it would arouse some feelings. It didn't. They were sitting in the carriage beneath a low-hanging sycamore in front of the mansion.

"Samantha, my dear, we could be so happy together." Mark's blue eyes searched her face. "I hope you don't mind. I've spoken to your uncle. I know we've known each other only a short time, but I sense you may feel as I do. I hope that you . . . may come to love me."

Mandy glanced away. Her conscience smarted sorely for the way she'd led Mark on tonight. Now to discover he had spoken to Uncle William only made matters worse.

"Mark, you know how fond I am of you, but . . ."

"Please, Samantha, don't say any more. Just give it some thought. We could achieve great things together, you and I. My family and yours together could create a powerful alliance—to say nothing of the way I feel about you."

"Mark, please."

"Just say you'll think about it. That's all I ask."

"Of course I'll think about it, Mark. I'm very flattered." He kissed her again with great sincerity. His arm went around her, and he pulled her close, kissing her softly. She let him continue, hoping he would evoke some response. He smelled faintly of jasmine. She thought of musk and champagne—and the taste of masculine kisses far less delicate than these.

She broke away. "Mark, I think it's time I went in. I've had a wonderful time tonight," she lied. "And thank you for . . . everything." She followed him from the carriage and let him escort her to the door, wondering why his kisses only made her miss Hawk all the more.

Behind a corner of the hedge, Max Gutterman adjusted the patch over his eye and curled his lip in smug satisfaction. "Knew I'd find you sooner or later, little lady," he said to himself. "And my guess is, wherever you are, that big white Indian won't be far behind." He brushed damp earth from the knees of his overalls as he rose from the ground. Just like Myra, pretty but treacherous, he thought. He'd taken care of Myra and her Injun half-breed. He'd taken care of plenty of those red devils after that, too. Those heathens figured they could kill old Sergeant Gutterman, but I showed 'em, he thought. The slight breeze picked up the low sound of his hoarse laughter and spread it harmlessly across the broad expanse of lawn. He watched as the dainty woman entered the house, and the tall, well-dressed gentleman returned to his carriage.

An image of himself slicing through the flesh of a squaw at Sand Creek flashed across his mind. The tobacco pouch he'd made of human skin rested in his shirt pocket. *I showed them red devils, and I'll show you, Myra. You and yer big Indian friend.*

He smiled mirthlessly. Revenge would be sweet. Slipping off into the quiet of the night, he melded, as his laughter had, with the chilly evening breeze.

In her room, Mandy mulled over the events of the evening. Thinking of Hawk with Doreen, she wished again, for the hundredth time, she'd agreed to be his mistress. Instead, she'd forced him into the willing arms of the luscious widow. At least if she'd agreed to his proposal, the loneliness would be gone, and she wouldn't have to endure thoughts of him in another woman's bed.

She sighed. Sitting on the small fruitwood stool in front of the bureau, she brushed her hair. As much as she might wish it, she knew she could never agree to such a degrading proposition. Sooner or later, her conscience would come between them.

She'd seen him at several parties lately. It seemed almost every unmarried female in the city had her cap set for him, yet he appeared uninterested. He spent a good deal of time with Doreen, but Mandy didn't think he'd made any proposal to the widow—yet.

At the Showalters' two weeks ago, he'd danced politely with Mandy, then rudely asked if she'd consented to be Denton's mistress instead of his. It had sent her into a two-day fury. She wished she could just forget about him, but Travis Langley appeared to be permanently engrained in her thoughts.

She plaited her hair into a single thick braid, thinking of Mark's proposal—so different from Hawk's. He was offering marriage, a family, children. It all sounded dreadful when she thought of Mark as the head of her household.

She slipped beneath the covers of her bed and pulled the blankets beneath her chin. A pair of dark eyes loomed in her imagination as she drifted into slumber.

Mandy awoke to a fresh week. Celebrations would soon mark the end of harvest. The first, on Saturday, was a gala masquerade ball. She and Mark were going as Romeo and Juliet. She hoped Hawk would be attending. She wanted to see the look on his face when he saw her with Mark, costumed as the lovers. Bessy had been working for weeks on her gown. It was made of the finest emerald green velvet, the bodice cut square in front and exposing a good bit of her décolletage. The

waistline was slightly elevated, as was the
fashion of that day, and the skirt fell in soft
folds to the floor. She would wear her hair in
a snood of spun gold. Mark was wearing gold
trunks and hose, a green brocaded satin tunic
trimmed with yards of gold braid, and a
broad-brimmed plumed hat.

The week flew by. Saturday arrived, and
Mandy dressed carefully. Mark picked her up
a little past the hour, just as they'd planned,
and they headed for the ball.

Gala decorations, tinsel, and colored paper
decorated the elegant ballroom. Mandy felt
elegant as well. Hiding behind her sequined
cat's-eye mask, she surveyed the partygoers:
the Emperor Napoleon and Josephine, the
outlaw Robin Hood and his Lady Marian,
Friar Tuck, Humpty Dumpty, a scarecrow,
several Spanish señoritas, and dozens of other
famous and notorious figures were among the
crowd.

When Mandy spotted a tall man across the
room dressed as a buccaneer, her heart
stopped. With an earring in his ear, tight-
fitting black breeches, and a snowy white shirt
cut open to the waist, he looked every bit the
dashing pirate. The sight of him took her
breath away. She buried the feeling as best
she could and smiled broadly up at Mark,
who suddenly appeared silly in his glittering
gold hose.

Mandy and Mark danced for what seemed
like hours. Mandy took great pains to avoid

letting her gaze wander to the tall buccaneer, who more often than proper danced beside her. She didn't recognize the raven-haired woman dressed as a serving wench Hawk whirled around the floor, but she noticed how the woman's bosom heaved to near overflowing in her tight-waisted dress. To Mandy's secret delight, Hawk paid the woman little heed, and the woman seemed sorely irritated at his lack of attention.

Instead, Hawk's steady scrutiny followed Romeo's Juliet, and Mandy felt her cheeks burning constantly, to say nothing of the frown on Mark's lean profile.

"Mark," she finally said. "I think I need to rest a little."

"Of course, darling." They walked outside onto a broad, shrub-lined terrace.

"Let me get you a cup of punch."

"Thank you, Mark. That would be nice." She dabbed her kerchief against the perspiration on her forehead as she meandered around a corner of the terrace.

"Lost your Romeo, Miss Juliet?" the tall buccaneer asked with a mocking smile. He tugged distractedly at his gold earring and leaned nonchalantly against the wall.

"Hawk!" Mandy gasped. "You startled me. I . . . I didn't think anyone else was here." She twisted her kerchief nervously, worrying Mark would return with the punch. Her eyes kept straying to the mat of sandy hair exposed beneath Hawk's open shirt.

Hawk directed his gaze to the ivory swells of Samantha Ashton's bosom, feeling more than a little distracted. "You make a beautiful Juliet," he said softly, "though your Romeo looks more like a court jester." He'd promised himself he'd act like a gentleman, yet couldn't resist a snide remark when it came to that sniveling fop, Denton. Why she preferred Denton's company to his he could not begin to fathom.

His gaze raked her boldly, then he felt the stirrings of arousal and turned away. Damn the woman! Would he never get her out of his blood? He watched as she bristled defensively at his cutting remark and thought how the sparks in her eyes made her even more attractive.

"Damn you, Travis Langley!" Mandy heard herself say, cursing for the first time in her life. "Can't you ever say anything pleasant? Why must you badger me so?"

"I don't recall you finding me so unpleasant in Virginia City," he said flatly, and she paled at his words.

"Excuse me," she replied haughtily. "I think it's time I went inside." Mandy tried to brush past, but he caught her arm. He pulled her close, holding her furious gaze with a steady dark one of his own. For a moment she thought he might kiss her, then his look became hooded.

"Is there nothing I can say to make you change your mind and accept my proposal?"

he asked. "Denton's not the man for you."

"I'd hardly call your lewd proposition a proposal, Mr. Langley. More a bawdy joke."

"A joke!" He set his jaw, his dark eyes flashing with anger. "Damn you, Sam, for the little witch you are. What more do you expect from me? You've lied to me, deceived me. Have you ever told me the truth about anything?"

"It's not the way you think, Hawk." She looked up at him, willing him to listen. "Almost everything I told you was true. I only lied about being Julia—and about Jason Michaels. I truly wish I'd never had to lie at all."

He seemed to assess her words. "God, I wish I could believe that, Sam." He released her arm just as Mark walked up with the punch.

"Your court jester has arrived," Hawk taunted for her ears alone. His gaze once more unreadable, he excused himself with a curt "Miss Ashton."

"Was he bothering you?" Mark asked solicitously.

"What? Oh, no, Mark. He was just . . . complimenting us on our costumes."

The night dragged on until Mark finally suggested they depart. Throughout the evening she'd caught glimpses of the big man, but he'd made no further moves in her direction. She was relieved the night was finally at an end.

As the carriage pulled away, Mark instructed his driver to stop by his home, explaining to Samantha he had a gift for her he'd forgotten to bring earlier. When they pulled up in front, he asked if she would care to go in for a sherry while he retrieved the gift. She politely declined.

A carriage rolled by. Mandy caught a glimpse of the raven-haired woman from the ball and knew exactly who was driving the coach.

"I've changed my mind about the sherry, Mark," she declared on impulse. If Hawk wanted to think she was Mark's mistress, she'd give him good reason. He certainly wasn't worried about the company he kept!

Mark dashed around the coach and handed her down just as Hawk's carriage rounded the corner. She let Mark lead her up the brick path toward the front door and knew Hawk had seen her. For a moment she beamed in triumph. Then, as the rattle of the wheels faded into the distance, her spirits sagged. *What had she done?* Hawk would think the worst, and she'd have no chance of explaining. She suddenly felt more miserable than ever before.

"Mark," she stammered. "I've changed my mind. I'm beginning to get a headache." It was not a lie. "I'll wait for you in the carriage. You go ahead."

Mark sighed resignedly. "Whatever you say, darling."

The present turned out to be a pair of tiny emerald earrings that perfectly matched her eyes.

"Why, Mark, I couldn't. They're lovely, but they're much too expensive."

"Please, Samantha, accept them as a token of our future betrothal. Say you'll marry me."

Mandy felt close to tears. "No, Mark, I can't. Please. You've got to give me some time. This is all too sudden."

Mark looked hurt. "All right. I won't ask again for a while. But don't make me wait too long."

The carriage rolled away in silence. She feared Mark was thinking of his Juliet while she was thinking of a far different Romeo.

Chapter Twenty-four

✦✦✦✦

IT WAS FAST becoming the Christmas season. The Nutcracker Ballet was being performed in San Francisco and Uncle William had invited her to go.

Mandy was overjoyed to be leaving Sacramento. She wanted to be as far from Hawk as possible. She and her uncle, along with Mark and Bessy, were to board a paddlewheeler, the *Sacramento Queen*, and proceed downriver through the great San Francisco Bay and into the city.

With agonizing slowness, like watching a kettle come to a boil, the time for their departure arrived. Mark had agreed to accompany them at the governor's request. Uncle William would be disembarking from the boat in Vallejo to conduct some business, so Mark would escort Mandy on to the Palace Hotel. The governor would rejoin them there at his earliest opportunity.

The big paddlewheeler was everything Mandy had dreamed. It rose three stories above the water, gleaming white, with bright red trim. Sounds of the calliope lilted whimsically through the air as the party crossed the gangplank. They were quartered on the Texas deck—in staterooms fit for royalty.

Once settled, Mandy moved outside to stand by the rail. She saw several other brightly painted flat-bottomed paddlewheelers, along with myriad other river craft: barges, dinghies, even a canoe. Anything that would carry a load of merchandise or passengers was used along the route to the sea. Mandy could see an ancient river doxy plying her trade to a load of crew members disembarking from the *Daisy Belle*. The beautiful old sternwheeler had seen better days and her rough-looking crew, better years.

Mandy glanced up as the smokestacks bellowed thick black smoke and the horn hooted its good-byes. They were off. Two huge paddles, one on each side of the vessel, churned the water and pushed the boat into the current.

Mandy waved to the crowds lining the dock, and they waved back enthusiastically. Mandy smiled and glanced up to find Mark Denton watching her.

"Allow me to get you some refreshment, Samantha," Mark offered, his manner, even after months, still very proper.

"That would be lovely, Mark."

"Think I'll go along, if you don't mind, my dear," the governor said to Mandy. "I believe I saw an old friend as we came on board."

"Not at all, Uncle William. I'm enjoying the view." Mandy watched the governor's powerful frame depart along with Mark's thinner one.

Suddenly feeling uneasy, Mandy looked up and a little to the right. Deep brown eyes, hard as steel, bored into her.

"Why, Miss Ashton, fancy meeting you here," Hawk drawled arrogantly.

"Mr. Langley," she answered, trying to hide her emotions. She felt a familiar rush of pleasure at seeing him and chided herself for it. She hadn't missed the undercurrent of sarcasm in his voice and wondered, not for the first time, how she could still care about someone who treated her as he did.

"What are you doing here?" she questioned, knowing his presence would do nothing but ruin her trip.

"I'm just doing my job," he answered. If he'd known the governor's party would be on board, he would never have accepted the assignment. He and James were there to guard a gold shipment for Jack Murdock's company. He no longer needed to do this type of work since he'd acquired the Rutherford estate, but James had played on his sympathy. James wanted to buy the Riverfront Saloon in Sacramento City and had saved almost enough cash. James was too stubborn to borrow the money from Hawk—he was too close to his goal.

Now Hawk was forced to come face to face with the woman who plagued his thoughts nightly. He'd bedded no other since their encounter in Virginia City, his mind still unwilling to accept a substitute. His behavior was out of character and he knew it, but he couldn't seem to remedy the situation. Seeing her again would only make matters worse.

"You're looking well," he continued, assessing her boldly. "Sacramento must agree with you." His eyes took in the fullness of her breasts clearly outlined beneath her velvet-trimmed dress. The rich brown tones of the dress matched her hair exactly and accented her full ruby lips. He longed to crush her against him, remind her of their nights together. How could one woman affect him so? The knowledge of her power infuriated him.

"Thank you." She lowered her lashes and watched him covertly. She felt his magnetism and knew no matter how pleasant the trip, from this moment on it would be torture for her.

"I see you brought your friend," he baited her, his eyes dark and mocking.

"Mr. Denton agreed to escort me to San Francisco as a favor to my uncle. Uncle William has business in Vallejo. Mark will be taking me on to the hotel."

"How convenient for you both," he taunted, "though I'm surprised your uncle approved. But then the Denton family's very well respected in these parts. Maybe your uncle is trying to marry you off."

"My uncle is only looking out for my best interests—something I'm sure you wouldn't understand, Mr. Langley." She lifted her chin defiantly. "All you care about is making sure your . . . your pleasures are taken care of!" She blushed hotly, and noticed a lazy smile curve one corner of his mouth.

"Still a lady of delicate sensibilities, I see," he teased.

She could see he was enjoying her discomfort. "You're the most irritating, the most annoying man I've ever met, Travis Langley!"

"And you're the damnedest, most temperamental pain in the neck I've ever met, Miss Ashton. Now, if you'll excuse me, I'd better get back to work." He touched the brim of his hat and departed, leaving her frustrated and furious.

Mark and the governor returned shortly with refreshments. The trip was officially under way. Mandy did her best to keep her mind off Travis Langley, but it was impossible.

She'd watched him walk to the deck below, and her glance kept straying toward the passageway. He was dressed in his buckskins, as usual when he was working, and she remembered all too well the muscular body beneath the snug-fitting leather.

The day rushed past. Sunlight sparkled like crystals on the smooth surface of the water. Willows and oaks lined both banks and cattle grazed in the fields beyond. The boat docked briefly at Vallejo. The governor departed, assuring Mandy he would join her at the hotel as soon as he completed his business.

Mark was attendant to all her needs, escorting her to supper in the elegant dining salon, pulling out her chair, and ordering for her from the sumptuous menu. She had dressed for the evening in red velvet, and Mark looked handsome in his black frock coat. Both ladies and men eyed the couple as they made their way to the floor and began dancing to the soft strains of violin and the crisp clear notes of piano.

Though Mark was a good dancer, Mandy's mind kept wandering. Eventually, feeling a bit of a headache, or at least pretending to, she asked to be excused for the balance of the evening. Mark accompanied her to the upper deck for a stroll and a chance to view San Francisco Bay. It was all very romantic and did nothing to alleviate her lonely mood.

*   *   *

"I'll take the last shift," James suggested to Hawk. "Why don't you get us something to eat?" James had felt the change in the big man's mood from the moment he spotted the tiny girl standing arm in arm with Mark Denton. He wished there were some way he could help his friend, but he knew Hawk had to work the situation out for himself. James didn't envy his friend's position.

"That sounds good. I won't be long." Hawk turned and walked out the door, his moccasins padding softly down the pine deck, then fading as he mounted the stairs to the dining room.

Leaning back in the oak chair, James propped his feet on the desk. The purser's cabin was small but comfortable, a picture of the *Sacramento Queen* hung on the opposite wall, as well as a calendar marking the schedule for the *Queen* through the following month.

James clasped his hands behind his head and gazed out the window to the slowly passing shoreline. The bay stretched ahead of them, and the lights of San Francisco flickered dimly somewhere in the distance. The moon was full, giving him a clear picture of the surroundings even in the dark. He kept a watchful eye. They were getting close to their destination. The trip had been uneventful so far, but they were guarding a shipment of gold, and a few too many people knew of its existence.

Without warning, James hurled against the bulkhead, his head viciously thumping against the wood as a huge explosion rocked the vessel. He blinked once, tried to focus, then his vision dimmed and he slumped to the pine deck in blackness.

Elegantly garbed travelers screamed and raced toward the exits of the wildly listing dining room, knocking each other down in their mad dash to escape. Tables were up-ended, plants and crockery littered the aisles. Even fallen passengers blocked the way.

"Don't panic!" Hawk boomed authoritatively above the din of hysteria. "We'll all get out safely if we just keep calm. Head down the stairs to the lifeboats; there are life vests inside the boats. Take your time and remain calm." The even tone of his voice soothed the group temporarily, and they made their way in an orderly fashion through the doors.

Outside all hell had broken loose. White steam billowed from the smokestacks, then thick black smoke covered the milling crowd with soot and further added to their hysteria. Orange and yellow flames leaped through a huge hole in the middle of the vessel.

"Get over here and open this thing—and make it quick." A burly man with a beard and long stringy hair pushed the purser into the office on the main deck. Henry Jeffers had been finishing some paperwork in his cabin when the men broke in on him. At gunpoint they forced him down the stairs to his office below.

He spotted James Long's body, noticed the rise and fall of the man's chest, and wondered where the other man was. With trembling fingers, he unlocked the safe and slowly withdrew the heavy contents. His spectacles magnified the terror in his eyes.

"Hurry up in there." A second man, thin and pale, his clothes wrinkled and dirty, stuck his head through the door. "Hurry up! This tub's takin' on water like a hairy dog gets fleas in a flea patch."

Henry Jeffers stared at the two men dumb-founded, his first realization that the men had blown the boiler to cover their crime seeping into his fear-drugged brain.

"What do we do with him?" the burly man questioned.

In answer, a gunshot rang out. Henry felt a burning pain in his chest, the room dimmed, and he crumpled to the floor. His eyelids felt heavy.

"Had to be done," the pale man replied. "He could 'ave identified us."

"Let's get the hell outa' here," the burly man said.

The pain in Henry's chest became fierce. He let his eyes close and wondered who would care for his wife and child. Then he drifted into blackness and the pain went away.

The bearded man pushed the purser's short squat body out of the way. He grabbed the heavy strongbox by one end, his partner picked up the other. They fought their way through the screaming pandemonium outside the door. Instead of making for the lifeboats as the others were doing, they headed calmly toward the bow of the sidewheeler.

A small wooden dinghy bobbed patiently beneath the pulpit, a heavy-featured, one-eyed man grinning at its helm. Max Gutterman adjusted the patch over his eye and glanced toward the bearded man and the pale man beside him.

"Maybe I get two dead birds with one big blast." Gutterman laughed heartily at his own joke. "Revenge is sweet, my friends."

The two men joined him, taking their places in the dinghy, and rowed toward the distant shoreline. Gutterman watched in deadly fascination as the rapidly failing vessel—and its terrified passengers—battled the freezing depths of the bay.

Three questions weighed uppermost on Hawk's mind. Was the explosion a diversion to rob the gold shipment? If so, what was happening to James? And most importantly, where was the chestnut-haired girl? James was capable, he knew that. Money could not buy lives, and Sam might need help. He fought his way through the departing throngs, searching madly. She hadn't been in the dining salon. That meant she was either on deck, in the social hall, or in her cabin. By now, unless she was hurt by the blast, she would be swallowed by the hysterical mob. He searched the social hall, moved to the second deck, then headed downstairs. He checked each lifeboat thoroughly. She wasn't among the frightened passengers.

Rounding a corner, he spotted James holding his head and swaying slightly. "They got the shipment," James told him. "Killed poor old Jeffers. You okay?"

Hawk nodded. His eyes scanned the last of the remaining passengers.

"Samantha!" James gasped. "Where is she?"

"I don't know. I've checked the main salons, the second deck, and looked in the lifeboats. She isn't there. But Denton was, the bastard. Couldn't get near enough to talk to him. I'm heading back up to the top deck. You search down here. The lifeboats look like they're full. If you can't get on, make for the closest island. That's what I'll be doing."

"Good luck, my friend." James clapped Hawk on the back and headed toward the stern.

Hawk knew the odds were not in their favor. By staying aboard, they might lose their lives. The icy bay had claimed many others. The boat was listing strongly as Hawk raced up the stairway. If he didn't find Sam soon, it would be too late. The water had reached the second deck, and the lifeboats had all been launched.

Mandy opened her eyes to a swirling world and a throbbing in her head. She rubbed her temples, trying to get oriented. She thought she'd heard screaming earlier, but now it seemed eerily silent. She could only discern distant voices. She tried to sit up, then discovered the deck was slanting crazily beneath her. *My God, we're sinking!* She tried to stand and swayed crazily. Flames flickered and smoke curled. Her eyes burned. Was there no one left on board? Her heart pounding, she glanced around desperately. There must be something, some way to survive.

"Sam!" It was Hawk's deep, resonant voice. Suddenly his powerful arms were around her, his face buried in her hair. "I'd almost given up hope," he breathed in her ear.

She clung to him with every ounce of her strength and felt a surge of joy at being held in his arms, regardless of the circumstances.

"The lifeboats have already left," he told her. "We'll have to make for the island. Can you swim?"

She smiled up at him. He had risked his life for her. Worry etched lines in his face. "I'll race you!" she said.

Hawk felt his heart twist. His chest swelled with pride at her spirit. He ached to set aside their differences, tell her how much he cared.

But now their lives depended upon the next few crucial moments.

"It's a long, cold swim. We'd better lighten up."

He unlaced his moccasins and threw off his leather shirt. Then he turned Sam's back to him and ripped her dress to the waist. She stepped out of her garments quickly and stood facing him in just her chemise and thin pantalets. She looked achingly beautiful. He longed to take her in his arms again.

The ship lurched and shuddered, throwing them to the deck. The rapidly rising water covered all but the upper level.

"It's now or never." Hawk drew her to him, kissed her soundly, then they dove into the freezing water of the bay and began the long, desperate pull toward the island.

Sam's strokes were smaller, but she surprised him with her strength. They seemed to be getting closer to the island, but it was still a fifty-fifty chance at best. The icy water did its deadly work quickly. He could feel his muscles knotting up. He thought of his Indian father and used his Cheyenne training to will himself to feel no pain.

The shore was clearly visible now. He felt a rush of confidence. They might make it. Then Sam went under.

Inky blackness enveloped her, so cold she wondered if she were already in the grave. Her stomach knotted in agony; her arms and legs would not move. She said a prayer for Hawk's safety—she knew it was the end.

Chapter Twenty-five

✦✦✦✦

IT WAS THE shivering that woke her. She knew she was alive—she'd never experienced such all-encompassing pain. Her body trembled violently, her arms and legs ached, her chest burned—just from the sheer effort of breathing. She shook her head, trying to clear it, then glanced around for Hawk. Terror clutched at her, its tentacles threatening to sap her strength again. Had she lived only to find he had not? Her eyes searched the darkness for some sign—then he was there, hugging her to him.

She sobbed softly against his chest and thanked God for his safety. He was alive! Nothing else mattered—not all the hateful words, not the misunderstandings, not the mistrust. He was here, and he had saved her.

"It's all right, Sam. Hush now . . . we're safe. I've built a shelter in the willows." He slipped his arms beneath her legs, lifted her effortlessly, and carried her away from the shore. "We've got to get warm or the cold could kill us yet."

She sniffed, wiped her eyes, and smiled, happy to be back in his arms. He carried her to the shelter and sat her down on a mat of leaves.

He'd constructed a kind of lean-to against a bluff with reeds and branches. Now, patiently and persistently, he spun a dry branch between his palms, the point against a notch in another branch surrounded by shavings and dry leaves. At last he coaxed the tiny pile into a puff of smoke.

"Take off your clothes," he ordered, stripping off his soggy buckskin breeches.

Mandy's eyes flew wide.

He smiled. "We have to get these dry. I'm going to lay them across the top of the lean-to; the fire will dry them in a few hours. Besides, without these wet clothes, our bodies will provide each other with warmth."

She felt the color rush to her cheeks. The muscles of his powerful frame rippled in the flickering firelight.

"But I . . ."

"Take them off now, or I'll take them off for you, Sam," he threatened. "And you know I mean what I say. . . . Our lives are more important than your modesty."

She swallowed hard and slowly discarded her wet garments. He ducked his head through the small opening and placed them above, near the fire. When he returned, she glanced at his solid physique, then turned away, not wanting her eyes to betray her thoughts.

Hawk had every intention of maintaining his distance. The girl had suffered enough already. She didn't need him forcing his attentions on her again. But damn, she was a tempting sight. Seeing her sitting on the soft mat of leaves, the fire highlighting her silken skin and glistening hair, he could not control his desire. He reached out a hand to cup her chin, then gently brushed her lips with a soft kiss as he pushed a strand of damp chestnut hair from her face.

"God, I've missed you, Sam," he murmured against her cheek. He pulled her down beside him and caressed the swell of her breasts, the line of her hip. He ached with wanting her.

Mandy knew, the moment they lay together, she would not stop him. He didn't love her; she knew that. But he wanted her, and she wanted him. Just to be near him again after their weeks apart was pleasure for her. As his tongue parted her lips, she smelled the deep musky scent of him. His hands moved knowingly across her shoulders, rubbing her aching muscles, soothing away her pain. He kissed her neck, cupped her face, and kissed her deeply. She felt his feather-light touch all over her body. When she trembled with need, he entered her slowly, carefully, pleasing her with gentle soothing motions.

She responded, her nipples taut beneath his

hand. She locked her fingers behind his neck and pulled him closer, heartbreakingly aware this might be the last time they would lie together. Her fingers traced the corded muscles of his back and moved along the narrow line of his hip. He kissed her again, fully, longingly, and began to move within her. As always, he stirred delicious sensations.

At first he moved slowly, gently. His lips savored hers, his tongue touched the corners of her mouth, then plundered the depths within. Then he moved faster, urgently, yet gently, careening her forward, her desire mounting along with his. His large hands grasped the roundness of her bottom, pulling her against him with each powerful thrust. His strength, tempered with gentleness, set her aflame. Each thrust carried her to a higher peak than the last.

A tiny gasp escaped as she reached fulfillment. His massive frame shuddered with pleasure just seconds behind her. Afterward, she curled beside him, sharing his warmth, happy for the first time in weeks. The rhythm of his even breathing lulled her into a deep, untroubled sleep.

Hawk awoke to find the fire had died. He cursed himself for his carelessness, then smiled as he thought of his night in the arms of the chestnut-haired girl. The sun was already peeking over the bay, but a light chill tinged the air. He picked up the two small sticks and rekindled the flame, then brought their clothes in from outside. As he glanced toward the sleeping figure, he spied a tiny smile and knew she was awake and watching him. He leaned down and kissed her cheek.

"How are you feeling?" he asked.

"Content," she replied. Then a cloud passed over her face. "Do you know what happened to the others—James, Bessy . . . and Mark?"

The sound of the man's name sent a surge of anger through him. "Bessy boarded one of the lifeboats. I'm not certain about James; he stayed behind to help me look for you. As for your lover, he decided to save himself and left you to fend for yourself."

Anger blazed in her green eyes.

"You're lying! Mark would never do a thing like that!" Furious at his implication that Mark was her lover, Mandy fairly spat the words. "You're just saying that because you're jealous!"

"Jealous! Of you and that . . . that coward? I might think you're a fool to choose his bed over mine, but I'm certainly not jealous." He glowered down at her.

"How dare you accuse me of such things!" she shrieked. "I wouldn't accept such an offer from him any more than I would from you! Besides, for your information, Mark has asked my uncle for permission to marry me." It was obvious Hawk cared nothing for her. How could she have been duped into letting him use her again? What a fool she was! She should accept Mark's proposal and be done with it. But would it be fair to Mark after the way she'd acted last night?

"Then why don't you go ahead and marry him? That's what you want, isn't it? A nice, respectable relationship." He practically snarled at her. He moved closer, his angry eyes boring into her.

"Can Denton make you feel like this?" he ground out. He hauled her against him and held her with an iron grip. His mouth bruised hers savagely, all trace of gentleness gone.

She would not let him best her again. Not this time. She fought like a tigress, scratching and clawing until he forced her down on the mat of leaves. He held her hands above her head and parted her thighs with his knee. Lowering himself, he thrust into her violently, giving no thought to her pleasure.

Even in his unleashed savagery she desired him. She could feel the rippling muscles of his body as he plunged into her time and time again, and her passions mounted against her will. His lips plundered hers, forcefully, brutally, his tongue moving with the same fury as his thrusts. Her body exploded with heat and wanting, and she unwillingly parried each savage thrust. Her blood boiled, the sensations more powerful than ever before. The flames of his passion burned her. Heat seared through her veins. Like wildfire, she flashed upon the horizon of pleasure, the feeling molten, scorching her with its brilliance.

Their coupling, reckless and intense, was

over quickly. Hawk rolled from the mat and stalked away.

She refused to cry this time. He'd proven his power in the most humiliating way, but she would not cry again. With self-loathing, she brushed away the one tiny tear that refused to obey her command.

Picking up what little clothing she had, she headed for the shoreline to bathe and dress. The sun warmed the island, but not her spirits. She hoped the search party would find them soon. Tears threatened again as she thought of the big man. How could she have ever imagined herself in love with such a heartless devil of a man? She decided she would give Mark Denton's proposal further consideration. Mark was kind and attentive. He would never use her cruelly, as Hawk did. She prayed for Mark's safety and that the boats would come soon. She could not tolerate another night in the company of that ruthless monster, even if he had saved her life.

By late afternoon search boats were everywhere, looking for survivors. One launch beached on their island and Mandy spotted James's familiar figure. As she ran to his arms, she felt like sobbing with relief but caught herself and refused to concede to the urge. She'd cried for the last time.

"Thank God you're both safe. I was worried

sick." He grabbed a woollen blanket, covered her scantily clad body, then smiled at his friend.

Hawk would not meet his gaze. James glanced at Sam and read the misery in her eyes. He swore beneath his breath. What had happened last night? The two obviously were not speaking. Surely Hawk hadn't forced his attentions on the girl again. Glancing from one to the other, he wasn't so sure. Damn, what was it about those two that caused such fury between them? He helped them both into the wooden lifeboat, and the crew pulled hard for shore.

During the long ride, Hawk sat sullenly. It had happened again. He couldn't believe she'd made him lose his temper after all the promises he'd made to himself. Aboard the *Sacramento Queen*, when it looked as though they'd not survive the night, it had all become achingly clear. If she wouldn't be his mistress, he'd marry her. Whatever had happened between her and Denton had been partially his fault anyway. James had explained a little about Sam's father and her life at the fort. He understood all too well the longing, the unstoppable urge to find one's place in the world. His Indian family had helped him in every way. If they hadn't, he would have done just what she did—found some way to escape. He knew she felt something for him. If he worked at it, maybe he could make her care for him as deeply as he cared for her. He was willing to settle down. If it took marriage to have her beside him, then so be it.

But what had happened instead? He'd acted like a madman, driven her straight back to Denton's arms. She'd never forgive him for the way he behaved this morning. He could see it in her eyes as she clung to James. Damn! What jealous demons possessed him? Just the thought of her with Denton drove him wild with rage. Well, it was too late now. Nothing he could say could change what he'd done. Maybe it was for the best. He'd probably make a lousy husband anyway.

San Francisco was still the closest place for Mandy to recuperate, so she was taken directly to the Palace Hotel. Her uncle met her in the lobby, his handsome features haggard with worry.

"Samantha, my dear, I'm so relieved you're safe. I would never have forgiven myself if anything had happened to you." He helped her upstairs to their suite of rooms and ordered a hot bath. "We'll talk about it when you're feeling better," he said, patting her hand. She was grateful to have some time to sort through her emotions.

Mark was there and acting solicitous. He said he'd been separated from her during the explosion and thought she was safely aboard one of the lifeboats. She accepted the story without question.

Bessy too was safe and none the worse for the trip. Though terrified for Mandy's safety, Bessy had been herded into the lifeboat with little chance to complain. Now she clucked and fussed over Mandy.

As soon as he was certain of her safety, Uncle William wired Sacramento City to send fresh clothing. Within nine hours after her arrival at the hotel, she had a complete wardrobe at her disposal.

If Virginia City was silver glitter, San Francisco was golden. The Palace Hotel, with its massive gold marble columns and arched glass skylights, reflected pure elegance and grace. Mandy, Mark, and Uncle William attended the ballet as planned, only several days later, after Mandy had time to recover from her ordeal. Uncle William took her to the opera, and there were gala balls to attend in his honor.

San Francisco seemed an episode out of a fairy tale, but the glitter was tarnished by lonely nights and constant thoughts of the sandy-haired man. She relived their night on the island a thousand times, each with the same result—a fiery, burning desire to be back in Hawk's arms. Nothing, no amount of determination, could make her forget him. She knew he'd returned to his ranch near Placerville. The idea of his being so far away saddened her even more.

The night before they were due to return to Sacramento City, Mark invited her to a production of *Romeo and Juliet*. She wore a gown of rich winter-white velvet trimmed with ermine.

"Darling, you look ravishing," Mark complimented. He cut a handsome figure in his black evening clothes and crisp white shirt. Mandy wished, not for the first time, she could fall in love with him.

Outside the theater, after the play was over, a line of hacks waited to carry the sleepy theatergoers away. After a few minutes in the chilly night air, Mark was able to hail one to return them to their hotel.

"I had a wonderful time tonight, Mark," Mandy told him as she snuggled beneath the folds of her cloak.

"We could have many nights like this, Samantha, if you would consent to be my wife." The privacy of the coach encouraged Mark's attentions.

Mandy heard the clopping of the horse's hooves against the street, the bell of a passing streetcar. "I . . . I'm not ready for a commitment, Mark. I told you that before."

"I've tried to be patient, Samantha. But I don't know how much longer I can wait."

"Please, Mark—" The sound of voices outside the carriage interrupted her. The hack came to an abrupt halt, nearly unseating her, and the door flew open.

"Well, now, lookie what we 'ave 'ere." A red-faced man with a bit of a cockney accent stood in the doorway.

"Driver! Driver!" Mark rapped his gold-headed cane on the wall of the carriage. "Move on!"

"Ya done foine, Billie Boy," the Englishman called up to the driver. A tiny derringer gleamed in the moonlight. "If you please, yer lordship." He gestured the couple out of the carriage.

Watching with horror, Mandy clutched her escort's arm. "Mark? Mark, what's happening?" she whispered.

The Englishman heard her and chuckled evilly. "Yer bein' robbed, me lovely."

"But . . . where are we?" Neither she nor Mark had been watching their surroundings as they traveled in the hack. She glanced at a street sign: Pacific and Stockton—not street names with which she was familiar. The distinct odor of decaying wood and rotting fish filled the air.

"Take a good look, milady. You're on the Barbary Coast. Wildest, wickedest den o' thieves this side o' Tortuga!"

They were stopped at the edge of what did indeed appear to be a seedy section of town. She could hear the *plinkity-plink* of a cheap piano and the raucous laughter of men plied with drink. Several disreputable looking characters ambled along the street, curiously eyeing the carriage and the two well-dressed people beside it. A garishly dressed woman ran laughing down the sidewalk, holding up the bodice of her dress and playfully dodging the drunken sailor who was staggering along behind her.

Mandy glanced at Mark. His face was pale, and he looked as though he might faint.

"Empty yer pockets, mate." Spoken softly, but ominously, it was a command not to be ignored.

Mark handed over his pocketbook, his jewelry, and several loose gold pieces, then reached down to unhook the beautiful diamond necklace Mandy wore. The piece belonged to Julia. Her uncle had had it delivered along with the second set of clothes.

"What are you doing, Mark?" Mandy grabbed his hand and pulled away. "These belong to Julia. I can't let anything happen to them. Please"—she turned to the Englishman—"you've done well enough already. These are not mine to give you."

The man snorted his mirth. "Hear that, Billie Boy?" he called as his friend stepped down from the hack. "Her ladyship thinks we ought to leave these little baubles behind." They both hooted with laughter, the second man moving close to finger the necklace.

Mandy stiffened as she felt his rough fingers brush her neck. She tried to step away, but the man's hold on the jewels stopped her.

"These jewels are my responsibility!" she said.

"Samantha, please," Mark pleaded, "for God's sake, do as they say!" His hands trembled.

Mandy suddenly realized Hawk's words were true. Mark Denton was a coward. He had left her on the paddlewheeler to die. Furious at the knowledge, she jerked free, accidentally hitting the Englishman, her movement so swift and unexpected the tiny derringer went flying into the darkness. The Englishman grabbed for it and so did the driver. They collided comically, landing on the ground.

"Run for the carriage, Mark!" Mandy cried, giving him a shove to jolt him from his fear-frozen state. They dashed for the hack and Mark, now forced into action, grabbed the reins and whipped up the horses, careening away from the two men. Mandy watched as the unsavory pair cursed and followed for a distance.

The carriage rounded a few more corners at breakneck speed, Mark unwilling to chance another incident. Finally he slowed. Mandy, relieved and exhausted, refused to look in his direction. *How could she have been so blind?* She had to see Hawk—apologize for doubting him.

They pulled up in front of the hotel in silence. Mark helped her down and escorted her inside without a word.

Christmas arrived with a whirlwind of balls and parties, but Hawk was nowhere to be seen. Maybe it's best, she reasoned. If he cared for her at all, he would have sought her out by now.

On Christmas Eve, the Ashton household opened the gifts piled beneath the huge fir while a warm fire crackled in the hearth. A cap for Wong Sun, a mother-of-pearl comb for Bessy. Mandy gave Uncle William a book of poems and several pairs of socks she'd knitted. He loaded her with gifts: furs, jewelry . . . but the best gift of all was Lady Ann. "I know how much you love her," he said. "She's yours. After you get home and settled in, I'll send her to you."

In the past few weeks it had become painfully clear to Mandy she would have to return to Fort Laramie. Not to her old life; but there were things to be settled before she would be free of her past. Julia and Jason were there now. Besides, she'd had enough adventure to last a lifetime. It hadn't brought her happiness, but it had forced her to grow up. The work she'd done for her uncle assured her she could take care of herself, and there was little left of her relationship with Mark after the accident. It was time for her to go home.

Only one incident made her think about staying. On Christmas morning she found a small package beneath the tree. Her name was on it, but nothing more. She tore off the paper and opened the tiny velvet box. Sitting on a cushion of white satin, a miniature jeweled kitten stared up at her with diamond eyes.

The eyes danced in the firelight, and her own eyes filled with tears. Only one person would give her such a gift. She clutched the kitten fiercely to her breast and wondered at the meaning of the present. She dared not hope for too much. Knowing Hawk as she did, if it were from him, it could be either as an apology for his behavior on the island or just a token of their past friendship. She refused to let herself use any other word to describe their somewhat dubious relationship.

The next day she asked her uncle's permission to use his carriage, then instructed the driver to take her by the Enterprise Hotel. There were several hours remaining before the guests would be arriving for the Christmas festivities. She could be back in plenty of time. She needed to speak to James.

He was just coming down from his room as she entered the lobby. She thanked him for the perfume he'd given her, and he thanked her for the muffler she'd knit him. Then she told him briefly of the tiny jeweled kitten.

James smiled wryly. "It's from Hawk, all right. I'd bet my life on it. He never quite got over that scene you two had with the bobcat cub. He was awfully proud of you that day, even if he wouldn't admit it."

"Where is he, James? I want to thank him."

" 'Fraid you won't be able to do that for some time. He's accepted some sort of high-level government assignment. He'll be gone at least three or four months. It's all very hush-hush. He wouldn't even give *me* the details." He walked her back to the carriage. "I'm keeping an eye on the ranch for him, but he really doesn't need me. Jesus Ramirez, his *segundo*, is an extremely capable man."

Mandy glanced away. "Then I guess the gift was just his way of saying good-bye." She let James help her aboard the carriage. "I'll be leaving for Fort Laramie as soon as the snow clears enough to get over the mountains."

"I'm sorry things worked out the way they did," James said. "I'll see that he gets the present you made him when I see him again."

Mandy could scarcely keep her mind on his words. *Hawk was gone from her life for good.* She thought of his velvet brown eyes, the way one corner of his mouth curved when he smiled, the feel of his strong tanned hands on her body. Somehow, some way, she had to find the strength to forget him.

The next several months dragged by. Mandy waited anxiously for the weather to change so she could plan her trip home. More and more she yearned to be away from Sacramento City and her memories. She wondered if being fifteen hundred miles away would help. She doubted it, but it was worth a try. She was eager to see Julia and Jason and there were matters to settle with her father as well.

Though she'd given up hope of seeing Hawk again, she missed him terribly, as she had ever since they'd been separated. There were times she wished she'd admitted her feelings to him, even wished she'd agreed to become his mistress. But all that was behind her now.

Finally the weather broke. She was scheduled to depart in one week on the train, then continue by stage on the long trip home. In less than three weeks she'd be back at Fort Laramie.

Chapter Twenty-six
✦ ✦ ✦ ✦

"OH, UNCLE WILLIAM, I'll miss you." Mandy's eyes misted as she hugged her uncle goodbye.

He cleared his throat and turned away. "Take care of yourself, my dear. And give Julia my love. Tell her . . . tell her . . ." He patted Mandy's hand. "I know you'll say the right thing."

Mandy nodded.

"Give my suggestion some thought," he added, referring to the job he had offered. "You've spoiled me. I don't know how I'll manage without you."

"I will, Uncle William." She hugged him again and boarded the train with just a few small satchels. She had already said her good-byes to Bessy and Wong Sun at the house. Mandy stashed the satchels beneath the seat and turned to see a lanky, familiar figure strolling toward her down the aisle.

"You didn't think you were going to get out of town without saying good-bye to me, did you?" James grinned broadly, sweeping her up in a big bear hug.

The last of her control dissolved. She felt tears prickling her eyes. "Don't make me cry, James." She took a last look into his mischievous dark eyes. "I'm so glad you came. You know I'm going to miss you." She hugged him again and felt an ache around her heart. "Tell . . . Hawk . . . good-bye for me . . . will you?"

"I'll tell him," he answered, a little gruffly.

He turned, but not before she saw the flash of sadness in his eyes.

"Tell him . . . tell him . . . I'll be thinking of him," she finished in a whisper.

James nodded. "You take care of yourself, now, you hear me?" He hugged her again, then hurried to the exit as the train rumbled slowly from the station.

She watched both James and Uncle William from the window, waved till she could see them no more, then wondered whether she'd made the right decision. She sighed and relaxed against the seat, her small frame already uncomfortable.

*   *   *

The train ride was lengthy but uneventful. The stage was waiting as they pulled into the Elko station. The railroad had pushed even farther east over the past few months, which helped to shorten her trip at least a little. Elko looked a lot like Reno. It was just another railhead built to house the men working on the line. Already Elko was the jumping-off spot for the stagelines—the next town of any size they would come to would be Great Salt Lake City, still hundreds of miles away.

The stagecoach was, as usual, uncomfortable and crowded. Mandy was traveling with a rotund merchant who smelled distinctly of garlic, and a spindly matron who'd accepted a position as schoolteacher in one of the forts along the Platte. Other passengers came and went in a nondescript blur.

Dusty miles of desert passed by her window. Even the animal life seemed to have gone underground. Sagebrush, in tiny dark patches, interrupted the stark landscape. It had all been so exciting when she'd traveled with Hawk and James. Now the scenery appeared as bland as the food in the dirty way stations.

Over the next few days, way stations, tiny towns, and trading posts all ran together. By the time they reached the plains country, she'd come to a decision. As soon as she straightened things out with her father, she

would return to Sacramento City and accept
the job as her uncle's assistant. She would
find Hawk and become his mistress—if he still
wanted her—and her conscience be damned!
Her life was empty without him. At least if
she were with him, she might have a chance
to make him love her as she loved him.

Then she thought of Wishana. She was the
woman Hawk loved. Maybe he was with her
now. Thoughts of the big man in another woman's arms tormented her. How could she go to
him when he clearly loved another? She argued with herself endlessly. If only she'd
never met him.

The coach pulled up briefly at an adobe station. The horses were changed. One passen-
ger departed and another, an arrogant young
cowboy who eyed her much too boldly,
boarded the coach.

"Howdy, ma'am." He tipped his wide felt
hat. "Name's Jeremy Lake." The slim, bow-
legged cowboy introduced himself to her and
shook hands with the merchant. Dusty denim
breeches scratched noisily as he seated himself beside her.

"Peabody's my name," the merchant said.
"Pleased to make your acquaintance, I'm
sure."

"I'm Miss Sarah Farminton," the schoolteacher put in, primly straightening her cuffs.

The coach rolled away in a cloud of dust.

"And your name, ma'am?" the cowboy
asked.

"I'm Samantha Ashton. How do you do, Mr. Lake." After these polite formalities she turned her head to gaze outside, indicating clearly she wished no further conversation.

"Heerd talk back yonder there's been some Injun trouble 'round abouts." The cowboy eyed her, hoping to spark her curiosity.

She ignored him, pulled out a book, and scanned a few pages.

"Could be, we'll be in for some trouble," he continued.

The schoolteacher looked faint.

"I certainly hope not!" Peabody blustered. "And I don't think this kind of talk is good for the ladies."

The cowboy just smiled, enjoying the discomfort his remarks were causing. He leaned his lanky frame back against the seat and pulled his hat low, eyeing Mandy with what he assumed was discretion. An appreciative smile curved his lips as his gaze rested on her bosom.

Mandy continued to ignore him. She decided to take an afternoon nap. Having finally convinced her body to sleep sitting up, she drifted off, dozing fitfully. She didn't fully awake until the first rays of morning crept across the hills. She stretched and yawned, still half asleep. She was just smoothing the wrinkles from her burgundy traveling suit when the Indians came.

Wild shrieking screams jolted Mandy fully awake. Her heart began to pound. Pandemonium broke out in the coach as the driver whipped up the horses and the coach careened madly along the narrow winding road. The slim cowboy helped Mandy keep her seat, pulled his revolver, aimed, and fired a steady stream of bullets at their pursuers.

Miss Farminton sobbed hysterically. "We're all gonna die. I just know it. We're all gonna die. I should never have come to this godforsaken . . ."

"Shut up!" the slim cowboy warned her. "Keep your mouth shut and your head down. Peabody . . . you got a gun?"

The merchant sputtered, then finally found his tongue. "Why yes . . ."

"Then use it!"

Mandy was doing her best just to stay in her seat. She could see the Indians behind them. They were naked, except for breechcloths, and heavily painted with war paint. Some wore feathers in their braids, some carried decorated leather shields.

The coach roared along, gaining a little distance. It looked as though they might make it when fresh cries sounded ahead. Mandy saw more of the dreadful painted warriors in front of them and small groups descending from the surrounding hills.

Soon the coach was surrounded with half-naked savages on horseback, and Mandy had never been more terrified in her life. She saw the driver fall from the coach, an arrow protruding from his back. The team bolted wildly—the guard apparently wounded or dead. Suddenly the din of gunfire quieted inside the coach. Only the hum of churning wheels filled the air. The cowboy slumped heavily across her skirt, blood oozing from a wound in his chest. Peabody just kept firing. His gun was empty, but the hammer kept clicking against the empty chambers, Peabody staring straight ahead as if in some kind of trance.

The coach slowed as the Indians climbed atop the stage and took control of the frightened animals. Mandy and Miss Farminton just looked at each other, then at Peabody, who was still clicking the empty revolver. Terrified, they gripped each other's hands.

"We must be strong, if we are to survive this," Mandy whispered. Then the door of the coach flew open and a broad, sweat-covered savage, his face a mask of red, thrust his head inside. He shrieked gleefully and pulled Mandy out. The opposite door was flung open by another Indian, and Miss Farminton was pulled to the ground. Then the Indians did the same with Peabody, who stared straight ahead with empty eyes.

The Indians ransacked the coach, then searched Peabody. They threw down the strongbox. They were disappointed to discover it contained only mail. With their little success, one brave returned his attention to Peabody, who started to sob. Three warriors beat him viciously. Blow after blow rained on his head; fists and feet punched his stomach. The Indians began shredding his clothes in their struggle to see who would get to wear his houndstooth vest.

The women looked away, as Peabody, now naked and still sobbing, was carried to a patch of dry earth and staked in the sun.

"I can't survive this. I know I can't." Miss Farminton's voice was almost inaudible.

"You can and you will!" Mandy whispered harshly. She knew she must be strong for both of them.

The leader busied himself searching the wagon and the strongbox. Then he stalked boldly up to the women. Grinning gleefully, he grabbed the lapel of Mandy's suit and ripped it down the front. The others joined in, shoving the two women into the dust and tearing at their clothes. The braves stopped only momentarily, to fight over the spoils. Fear gnawed at Mandy like a great vicious beast. One of the braves pulled off her jacket, holding it up triumphantly. The sun glinted off the tiny jeweled cat. She thought of Hawk, and the thought gave her courage. She clutched at what remained of her shredded garments, her hair wildly tangled, her face covered with dirt. She knew they would tear the rest of her clothes away at any moment.

An idea began to take shape in her mind. It was a long shot, but she had nothing to lose. She remembered stories James had told her of Hawk's Cheyenne training. Steeling herself for whatever might follow, she willed herself to be calm.

"Stop this at once," she said brazenly. The leader stopped what he was doing and looked at her incredulously; the others paused.

"You have no right to do this. I'll take that back, right now!" She snatched away her jacket and stuffed her arm back into a sleeve. One of the braves ripped it off again, cursing her in a language she didn't understand. She gritted her teeth, steeled herself, and slapped him hard across the face. In the silence that followed, Mandy heard her heart beating so loudly she was certain they could hear it too. But she stood her ground. She fixed her hands on her hips and stared into the dark eyes of the Indian warrior. If this didn't save her, maybe he would be mad enough to kill her and spare her the horrible suffering.

"Are you out of your mind?" she heard Miss Farminton whisper.

The brave stepped toward her, his eyes narrowed into slits. Sweat gleamed on his paint-smeared skin. He spat guttural words at her, then hooted and struck her a vicious blow across the cheek that knocked her sprawling into the dirt. The salty taste of blood filled her mouth. She thought of all she'd been through since she left her home, then prayed to God for the strength she needed. She took a deep breath and rose to her feet. Blood trickled from the corner of her mouth as she reached for her torn garment.

"That is mine!" she fought back. "You have no right to it!" The Indian struck her again, knocking her back into the dust.

She couldn't let him win. She stood up again, staggered a little, then, gaining her composure, reached for the garment.

"That is mine," she told him, her voice weaker but still determined. He hit her again. She stumbled, then fell. Her head ached, and she felt a wave of nausea, but they made no move to kill her. She had to keep going. She started to rise again, straining with the effort. The Indian towered above, ready to strike.

"*Heyoka!*" the leader shouted, stepping between the two. He glanced at her with a strange light in his eyes. He gave the men more orders; they grumbled, but left her where she lay. Through her hazy vision, she could see Miss Farminton staring at her incredulously.

The Indians readied themselves to leave. One of them jerked her to her feet, bound her hands tightly in front of her, and hoisted her up on one of the stage horses. They did the same to Miss Farminton. With a few last hoots and hollers, they headed into the hills. Mandy could see a dark plume of smoke rising and knew they'd set the coach afire. She rode astride in what remained of her torn traveling suit. The tiny jeweled kitten had been lost in the scuffle, making her feel more alone than ever. With no saddle, and in her weakened and shocked condition, it took ev-

ery ounce of her strength just to stay atop
the horse.

They rode throughout the day, stopping
only briefly to water the animals. The ride was
torturous. The insides of her thighs felt raw
and sore; the side of her face ached where the
Indian had slapped her so brutally. The terrain was so steep she had to wrap her legs
tightly around the animal's sides and twist her
fingers in its mane to stay on its bony back.
Mandy remembered her first week with Hawk
and James. The hardships she'd endured with
them were nothing compared to this, and yet
because of those hardships, her chances for
survival were greater.

She pitied Miss Farminton, who had already
lost consciousness. The Indians had tied her
body across one of the horses. Mandy willed
herself to have courage. Her only hope would
be escape. If she could survive the next few
days, she might have a chance.

By the time they made camp that night, the
leader had to pry her fingers loose from the
horse's mane. He dragged her off, but she
couldn't stand. Instead, she crumpled to the
ground on useless limbs. They left her where
she fell. One of the braves brought her a bowl
of something warm to eat. It tasted slimy and
foul, but it was sustenance, and she knew she
would need it.

As her aching body began to respond, she
looked around for the other woman. Miss Farminton was conscious and whimpering piti-

fully some distance away. Mandy focused her vision on the men around the campfire. The paint on their faces, the sweat on their bodies glistened in the moonlight, making them look like messengers from Satan.

There seemed to be some sort of argument going on. A horrible fear snaked through her as she realized she was the object of their debate. The leader kept shaking his head, moving between her and the rest of the braves. Finally, pulling his knife, he seemed to be challenging his companions. They backed down, grumbling. He spoke a few more words then pointed to the teacher. Mandy gasped. *Please, God, don't let them hurt her.*

The braves swarmed around the woman. Brutally, they ripped the remainder of her clothing away. She sobbed and screamed, but made no move to defend herself. One after another the men satisfied themselves with her frail body, hitting her with their fists as they pawed her. Mandy watched, sickened by the horror but unable to turn away, fully expecting to be their next victim. But the men did not approach her. They seemed satisfied with their debauchery and finally drifted back toward the fire. She closed her eyes. After what seemed hours, she mercifully fell into an exhausted sleep.

The next day they continued the journey, except today when they left the camp, the Indians led an extra mount. The lifeless, bat-

tered body of Miss Farminton lay discarded
beneath a scrubby sage.

They rode hard, and Mandy clung tena-
ciously to her horse. They were entering even
more mountainous terrain. By nightfall, after
cresting a rocky ridge, they reached a small
Indian village that nestled beneath it.

The women rushed from their teepees, followed by barking dogs and smiling children,
to surround the victorious warriors.

After looking her over and pulling at her
tangled mane of hair, the women dragged
Mandy from her horse. They tore the balance
of her clothes away and battled each other for
pieces of the dirty cloth and lacy undergarments. Mandy refused to give in to her mounting hysteria. She knew exactly how she
looked—her hair was filthy and matted, her
face bruised and swollen, her eyes sunken
and hollow—but she was alive.

The women beat her with sticks and forced
her into the center of the village, where finally
she crumpled to her knees. They hauled her
up and bound her to a pole in the middle of a
grassy knoll. She felt ashamed and humiliated, but held her head high, trying to keep as
much of her dignity as possible.

The leader came forward, speaking in a
manner that, she gathered, indicated a certain
possessiveness. Inside she cringed, wishing
they'd killed her that first day after all. Instead, she met his gaze fully and spat in his
face.

With a deep, feral growl, the man slapped her hard across the cheek. The blow made her ears ring. She slumped forward, sinking slowly into blissful oblivion.

When she roused herself, she heard voices around her arguing in bitter debate. Her head lolled against her shoulder. They are planning to torture me, she thought. They're arguing about which horrible means they will use. With a great effort she raised her head.

A huge warrior stood before her. He wore only a loincloth. His torso glistened with beads of sweat. His corded bare legs were tensed as if he were angry. She stared into his eyes: ominous black circles set in a mask of bright yellow paint. Geometric patterns in black and yellow marked his upper body. Mandy shuddered inwardly in fear and revulsion. The ache in her temple thudded violently, but she controlled her terror. She tried to focus on his face, but her head lolled again, and she stared at his broad chest instead. She willed herself to look up, but couldn't quite focus her eyes. Maybe he would kill her. Death would be a welcome alternative to the torture she was certain they had planned.

She wet her cracked lips and forced her voice to respond. It came out in a hoarse whisper. "If I get a chance . . . I'll kill you. If you try to force yourself on me . . . I'll fight you till my death." It was all she could manage before her head slumped forward again.

The big Indian lifted her chin gently, his

deep brown eyes trying to penetrate the curtain of pain veiling her vision.

"You have fought me, little one, but in the end I have always won."

The softly spoken words, delivered in English confused her. ". . . Hawk?"

It was an anguished whisper, and it tore at his heart.

Mandy closed her eyes. She must be delirious. She only imagined she heard Hawk's voice. The strong hand still held her chin, gently but firmly.

"Sam, you must listen to me. You must do exactly as I say."

Her eyes flew open. Her heart pounded. *It was Hawk! He was really here!* She felt a weak surge of strength and stood a little straighter.

"Do you understand me, Sam?" He shook her gently.

"Yes," she whispered.

"Swift Eagle has claimed you as his prize. I have told him you are my woman, and he cannot claim something that already belongs to me. But he says you are his. By Cheyenne custom, the only fair way to settle the matter is to fight for you." He gazed down at her, his eyes unwavering.

She knew he was trying to will her some of his strength. "You're going to fight him?" she questioned, her voice a little stronger now. "But he might kill you!"

"What's the matter, little one? Have you no

faith in me?" He grinned, then gently lowered his mouth in a feather-soft touch to her bruised and bloodied lips.

"Don't go away," he teased. "I'll be right back." Turning away from her, he walked slowly toward his opponent.

Never in his life had he sustained a greater test of self-control. Beneath his surface calm, he seethed with anger. It took every ounce, every tiny particle of his willpower to keep from ripping apart the ropes that bound this small courageous woman. He wanted to destroy Swift Eagle with his bare hands—but to do so might mean the girl's death. If he wanted her to live, he must abide by the rules—the Cheyenne rules.

Chapter Twenty-seven

❖ ❖ ❖ ❖

HAWK STRENGTHENED HIS resolve as he walked toward his opponent.

The story of the raid had traveled swiftly through the mountains. Linked with the victory was the tale of a beautiful woman with gleaming chestnut hair and the courage of a mountain lion—a woman Swift Eagle had claimed. Hawk had gone to the remote village in an attempt to do what he could for the woman. Maybe he could bargain for her release. He hadn't expected to see Samantha Ashton, the woman who haunted his dreams. He and Swift Eagle had argued bitterly, then agreed to settle the dispute as Cheyenne custom required.

Thinking about the events, he shuddered. *What if he hadn't come? What fate would have been hers?* With guilt, he thought of the way they'd parted. He would win this fight, then somehow, some way he'd make it up to her.

Mandy watched in horror as the two men bound their left wrists together with a length of rawhide, leaving a three-foot separation. Each of them clutched a knife in his right hand and began to circle the other warily. Both men were painted and in minutes covered with sweat. Hawk was broader at the shoulder, his waist narrower than Swift Eagle, and there was an animal litheness in his moves as he circled his prey.

Their movements were deft and graceful. The blades swished through the air in deadly anticipation, each man skillful and cunning with a knife. Hawk crouched and sprang toward Swift Eagle, then danced away. Swift Eagle did the same. Mandy felt the prickle of new fear as the silver blade streaked lightly across Hawk's torso and a tiny line of red appeared, spreading in tentacles across the knotted muscles of his chest and stomach. Swift Eagle lunged forward just as Hawk parried and lunged in return. Swift Eagle caught the blade full on, but the knife glanced off a rib, deflecting the blow.

Swift Eagle sliced through the air. Hawk ducked. Only the edge of the blade slashed his cheek. Then he cut Swift Eagle deeply across the arm. Circling away, Hawk pivoted just as his opponent lunged. Swift Eagle missed his target, but gashed Hawk across the shoulder. Blood was everywhere. Both men wore macabre costumes of blood. Even their wrists where bound were ringed with blood.

Mandy's eyes were riveted to the grisly scene. She could barely watch, yet couldn't look away. Her own blood surged through her veins as the men continued their combat. Her fatigue became unimportant. She knew how close to death Hawk was.

Another slicing thrust sent Swift Eagle to his knees. Growling in agony, he rammed Hawk hard in the stomach with his shoulder. They rolled heavily in the dirt—two gladiators, each proud and fearsome, locked in a death grip. The blades flashed again. Mandy's stomach lurched. *Please God, don't let him die*.

Hawk's large frame rolled on top of the tall, fearsome warrior; the muscles in Hawk's neck and arms coiled into tight knots. He pressed his advantage. With a quick thrust of his knife, Hawk buried the blade between his opponent's ribs, lifting and turning it at the same time.

His expression grim, he raised himself off the dead warrior.

Hawk found no joy in his revenge. The once-proud warrior lay silent and bloodied. Swift Eagle had fought against the tide of whites in the only way he knew. Attacking the stage was a symbol of his denial of the death of a way of life. Hawk silently saluted the dead warrior's courage, then cut the thong that bound them together and headed toward the girl.

Mandy sagged against her bonds in relief. The big man's moccasins tramped softly against the damp earth of the mountains as he came toward her, yet there was a grim determination in his stride. Members of the band cleared a path, but the rumble of their discontent could be heard behind him.

"Thank God you're safe," she whispered as he began to slice through her bonds.

"Sam, there is one more thing you must do." He lifted her dirt-streaked face with his bloodied hand. "You must walk behind me of your own accord. You must demonstrate the truth of my words. Can you make it as far as my horse?" It tortured him to have to ask for more courage.

She smiled weakly. "Wanna race?" she croaked in her raspy voice.

He grinned back. His mind replayed the scene on the deck of the *Sacramento Queen*,

and he loved her more than ever. He'd let her
go before. He'd not let it happen again.

He cut the final rawhide strip and steadied
her. "Let's go." He squeezed her hand, then
turned his back on her and began walking
slowly, but proudly, toward his horse.

Mandy's legs felt like willow boughs—they
trembled and swayed beneath her, but they
held her up. She threw back her shoulders
and held her head high. Clinging to the look
of pride she'd seen in Hawk's eyes when he
cut her free, she walked what seemed like
miles toward where he waited with his horse.
She fixed her gaze on him and witnessed his
anguish at not being able to help. She took
one slow, tortured step after another, placing
each foot firmly on the ground in front of her,
not wanting to risk the chance of falling. He
unfurled a soft doeskin blanket as she drew
near. When she reached him, he wrapped her
in its enveloping warmth and lifted her gently
into his arms. He swung her up on the roan
and settled her protectively against his chest.

Her body seemed wracked with an agony of
aches, yet even with the pain to remind her,
none of this seemed real. Hawk guided his big
roan through the hostile, milling tribesmen
and headed into the hills. Mandy slumped
against his broad chest. She wanted to sleep,
but every few minutes she would rouse herself and grasp Hawk's arm or touch his chest
to make sure she wasn't dreaming. Then she
would smile up at him and drift back to sleep.

As they rode in silence toward his own village, Hawk cradled the girl gently. Even dirty, battered, and beaten she looked beautiful. His heart ached for her. He kept the roan at a brisk walk, trying to keep her suffering to a minimum.

He'd returned to his village over two months ago, as the warrior, Black Hawk. The tribe had accepted his presence without question. The Cheyenne were officially at peace with the whites, but Hawk was there at the direct request of President Grant. There were rumors of gold in the Black Hills, an area granted by treaty to the Cheyenne and Sioux nations. Whites had been trickling onto the Indian lands, breaking the provisions of the treaty. The tribes were becoming restless and several small bands had begun to raid and kill. Swift Eagle had been the leader of one such band. Hawk's heart felt heavy at having to kill the courageous warrior, but, looking down at the pale face of the woman sleeping in his arms, he knew he would do it again if he had to.

They rode through a granite pass and his village, a large encampment at the edge of a pine forest, came into view. Steep mountains, notched with craggy peaks, surrounded the camp and teepees dotted the grassy flat. Cooking fires burned brightly, filling the air with the smoky smell and crackle of hot pine logs, and Mandy awoke dreamily.

As they rode into camp, dogs barked and

men, women, and children rushed to greet them. Holding Mandy within the circle of his arms, Hawk raised his leg above the horse's neck and slid easily to the ground. He spoke rapidly in Cheyenne and ducked inside a teepee, closing the flap behind them.

He carried her to a pallet of buffalo robes and laid her down carefully. She wanted to thank him. Tell him all the things she hadn't before. She wanted to tell him she loved him. Instead she felt a wave of dizziness, then slowly swirled into blackness.

Hawk looked down at Samantha, unconscious on the robe, and felt tears sting his eyes. He barked orders like a madman. Indian women fetched water, wood for the fire, broth, clean rags. Anything he asked. He set about the task of healing her, knowing it could be a futile effort.

As the hours passed, he felt more and more despondent. *Had he found her again only to lose her?* Why hadn't he put his jealousy and distrust aside, asked her to be his as he'd wanted to do a thousand times? Why had he let his pride and his fear of rejection stand between them? Since his return to the village, he'd had time to think, to muddle through all the experiences of the past six months. The answer always came up the same. He loved her, but he let her go. What had happened with Mark Denton didn't matter. If she were with him, he might have a chance to win her love. Now it could be too late.

He looked down at the tiny pale figure on the mat and his heart turned. She looked so innocent, so small . . . so vulnerable. He would not let her die. He would will her to live. She must get well so he could tell her all the things he'd planned to say when he saw her again.

He had already decided he was going to find her as soon as his mission was finished. He wasn't sure she would still be in Sacramento City, but he was sure he could find her. He felt certain she'd ended her affair with Mark Denton. He'd rarely seen them together after her trip to San Francisco. At least that was one obstacle no longer between them. He planned to offer her marriage, as he should have in the first place. Then if she denied him again, so be it. At least he would have told her how he felt, how empty his life had been without her. Told her how much he loved her.

As hard as it was to admit, he knew he loved her, had loved her almost from the start. He'd tried to fight it, but all he'd done was make himself miserable.

She stirred on the mat.

"Let me go!" she mumbled, tossing and turning. Beads of perspiration trickled down her brow.

He laid his hand on her forehead. It felt feverish, and she seemed delirious. It was not a good sign.

"My father . . . powerful . . . can't hurt . . . governor's daughter."

Leaning closer, he could just make out her words and knew she was reliving the nightmare of her kidnapping. "It's all right, little one," he soothed. "They can't hurt you anymore. Please, little one, you have to get well. Hush now. Hush." A sob escaped him, and he bowed his head in prayer. He beseeched his god—the god of the forest and the mountains, the god of the trees and the rivers—the god of all things great and small. Please—just let this one small thing be saved.

Mandy dwelled in an evil world where everything glowed blood red. The people were grotesque, their hands and faces were larger than in the other world, and they reached out after her, trying to drag her deeper into their world. Some of them she knew. She remembered the yellow teeth or the patched eye. Some were naked, their bodies glistening with sweat or painted with gleaming red blood. These wore feathers and tried to strip her naked too.

"No! No! . . . fight . . . till I die!" Maybe she was already dead. Maybe she was in hell—payment for her wanton desires for Hawk, the nights she'd spent in his arms. When she thought of those times she saw them in red too—the red fires of passion, the heat of wanting and pleasure. But how could such loving be evil?

She heard vague words of comfort through

her haze of pain. Sometimes the voice was deep, richly timbred. Other times she heard female voices, speaking in a language she did not understand. What? What were they saying? She heard it clearly this time. *Wishana*. It came from one of the Indian women.

She was beginning to remember.

She was in Hawk's village. He had brought her here after the fight with Swift Eagle. She heard it again, *Wishana*, more clearly this time. Oh God, Wishana must be here! That's why Hawk was here—to be with Wishana! The pain became unbearable. She sank deeper into the bloody red world.

Chapter Twenty-eight

✦ ✦ ✦ ✦

FOUR DAYS PASSED before Samantha regained consciousness. Four of the worst days of Travis Langley's life. He'd left the teepee only briefly since Sam fell ill. He bathed her himself and talked to her constantly, fluctuating from whispered words of love to violent commands she get well. The villagers left him alone, buried in his grief. None held much hope for the tiny white woman's recovery.

*   *   *

Mandy smelled the smoky air before she could focus her eyes. As her vision cleared she saw a man bending over her, his eyes closed. At first she didn't recognize him, so gaunt was he. He was dressed as an Indian, but she sensed no fear of him. He felt her slight movement and opened his eyes. There were dark smudges beneath, but she recognized the soft brown velvet gaze. He saw that she knew him, and his face lit up, for a moment banishing the deep lines of fatigue.

"Sam," he whispered, "thank God you're all right."

"Hawk . . . I thought . . . I was . . . in hell. I . . . you saved me from the Indians, and the outlaws and the . . ." It all came flooding back.

He held her close and rocked her, stroking her hair, then pulled back to look at her as if to make certain she were real.

"How . . . long was I sick?" she stammered, trying to get her voice to work.

"Four days. For a while . . . I thought you might leave me again . . ." His voice trailed off. He swallowed and glanced away.

She reached a shaky hand to his cheek, turning his face toward her. "I'll never leave you again," she whispered. As she said the words another memory flashed through her mind and her stomach knotted. *Wishana!* He was here with Wishana! She wanted to cry in agony and despair, but the tears would not come. She dropped her hand and looked away.

He sensed her mood change. "Don't look away from me . . . please." The words sounded strangled and she wondered why.

"Who cared for me?" she asked, refusing to meet his gaze. She felt her strength returning a little but knew she wasn't ready to hear the answers to the questions she must ask.

"I did," he said, "and some of the women."

"You!" She felt her face grow warm with embarrassment as she thought of all it entailed. *Why would he do that unless he cared for me?* But then it would be like him. It would be a matter of honor. She knew some of the Indian women had helped, she could remember hearing their voices. She wanted to ask which was Wishana, but felt her strength ebb and knew the answer would be more than she could handle now. She drank broth from the gourd Hawk held for her, then drifted back to sleep.

Morning found her feeling renewed. She heard Hawk rummaging around the teepee as she yawned and stretched and took comfort from his presence. She watched him from beneath her lashes. He seemed unaware of her scrutiny. He looked clean and fresh today, dressed in buckskin leggings and an open buckskin vest. Heavy bone beads rattled on his chest. His hair, longer now than in Sacramento City, curled against his neck. She longed to finger the soft strands.

She ran her hands through her own hair and noticed for the first time it was clean and shining. She could smell the fresh scent of pine soap and wondered if it was he who had bathed her. She propped herself up as he worked to repair and organize his hunting gear. He pulled a long arrow from its quiver and checked the straightness of the shaft.

Hawk felt Samantha watching him even before he turned to look at her. As she leaned against a lodge pole, he saw that her face looked healthier, glowing just a little even in the dim morning light inside the teepee. Full breasts lay barely concealed beneath the buffalo robe, and for the first time since the ordeal began he felt the familiar twinge of his desire. Her dark hair rested softly against her shoulders.

"I see you're feeling better today. Already the color returns to your cheeks." He walked toward her.

She blushed, making them appear even rosier.

"And you, kind sir," Mandy teased lightly. "I like you much better without your war paint." As Hawk smiled down at her, the knot of despair returned to her stomach. *Where had he spent the night?* She glanced away.

Hawk read the look of pain in the beautiful green eyes. *Was she thinking of what Swift Eagle had done to her? Was she worried about how he would feel?*

He sank down beside her, feeling the heat of

her skin. He put his hands on her smooth shoulders and turned her toward him. "Whatever has passed before now is of no importance. Not Swift Eagle or Mark Denton . . . not anyone. Do you understand me, Sam?"

Mandy looked at Hawk in confusion. *What was he talking about? Did he think Swift Eagle had taken her? Hadn't he believed what she'd told him about Mark? Why should he be concerned, when he spent the night in another woman's arms?* She straightened her spine and lifted her chin defiantly.

"Is Wishana here?" she asked, her voice trembling slightly, her eyes meeting his only by force of will.

He stared at her, his expression confused. "Yes . . . Wishana is here."

Mandy's heart ached. *It was true! It was all true.* For the first time in weeks she felt the sting of tears. Even through her ordeal she'd been able to control them. Now they gathered beneath her lashes and threatened to spill.

"Do you love her?" she asked, her voice barely a whisper.

"Yes. . . ." Hawk's own voice sounded husky, yet resonant. "I love her very much." His brown eyes tried to read the thoughts betrayed by her green ones. "I guess I've loved her all along."

A sob escaped and Mandy pulled away. Tears trickled down her cheeks. She was a fool! And worst of all, now he knew what a fool she was.

"Sam, what is the matter with you?" He'd just told her he loved her, and now she was crying. Surely she didn't think . . . ? This time he would allow no misunderstandings. "Look at me!" he commanded, his tone gruff. He turned her chin with his hand and waited for her eyes to meet his. Her anguish twisted like a knife.

"Wishana is the name of a tiny flower that grows only in the high meadows. It is fragile, yet it can withstand the most bitter storm. The beauty of the Wishana is unsurpassed in the mountains." She looked even more despondent. He paused and kissed her cheek. "You are Wishana," he whispered softly. "It is your Indian name."

She raised her lashes and blinked, trying to make some sense of what he was telling her. "I am Wishana?" Her heart pounded.

"You are Wishana."

"I am Wishana," she repeated, trying to convince herself.

"Yes."

"Then you . . . must . . . love . . . me?"

"Yes . . . I love you." He kissed her cheek again. "I think I have loved you almost from the first." His powerful arms enveloped her, and a surge of joy filled her heart.

He loved her! He had called out to her in his pain at the cabin. He'd thought of her in Virginia City. It was she he had wanted, even from the start.

"Oh, Hawk." The words were a half-choked sob. She threw her arms around his neck and hugged him hard against her. "I love you so much . . . so much." She clutched him tighter, and swallowed the lump in her throat. "You were with me always. After the stage was attacked, you were my will to survive. I would ask myself, what would Hawk do? Or, what would Hawk think of me if I gave up?"

Hawk could scarcely believe the words he was hearing. She loved him! It was all he had hoped for, all he'd dreamed of. "I've been such a fool, Sam. Can you ever forgive me?"

"There is nothing to forgive, my love."

He stroked her hair and held her close. Neither spoke for a time. Finally Hawk tilted her chin and kissed her gently, wanting to explain things he felt were important. He held her a little longer, then said, "We need to talk."

She nodded. "Yes."

He took a deep breath. "I'm here at the request of the president. When Grant sent word asking me to accept this mission, I declined. I refused to come here on false pretenses. But somehow I had to help my people. Eventually, I reconsidered. I came here on the pretense of seeing my family, just a simple family reunion. I hated to lie to them, but it had to be done. I was forced to be deceptive to help the people I love."

He stroked her hair, twisted a finger in one of the soft brown curls. "I came to understand what you did. I should have admired your loyalty to your cousin, the courage it took for you to try and help her."

"Hawk, I want nothing left unsaid between us. I want you to know that as much as I loved Julia, and believed she was doing the right thing, I didn't do it just for her. I did it for myself, too. I had to try and find my own way, try and discover what I really wanted out of life."

Hawk remembered the story James had told him of Samantha's past, the death of her mother, her father's severe restrictions. "And have you?"

"I know my capabilities now—in many ways because of you. I don't have to prove anything to myself or anyone else. I can do or be anything I want."

"And what *do* you want?" he asked, his voice a little raspy, a thread of worry wrapped around his heart.

"I want to be with you, wherever you are, whatever happens. The rest is unimportant— I know that now."

"Sam." He pulled her into his arms, kissing her fiercely, powerfully. He knew she sensed his desire for her, but he wanted to show her his love, make her certain of it, let her feel it with his every touch.

"How I love you, Sam." He pulled the buffalo robe from between them. His eyes roamed over the curves of her body. Her cheeks flamed at the heat of his look, but she didn't glance away. He quickly discarded his buckskins. She watched him, and he enjoyed the look of desire in her eyes.

Mandy wanted him. Her body beckoned him to take her. This time she would enjoy his every caress. He loved her. There was no need to hold back. Her hands stroked the bunched muscles of his back, a firm buttock. She felt the muscles tighten beneath her fingertips. His mouth moved from her lips to her eyes to her cheeks, then down to her shoulders, leaving her burning wherever they touched.

He cupped one of her breasts and the heat of his touch spread through her, making her body ache. Her nipple turned hard and rose against his hand. She heard him groan with desire. Her body arched against his coiled, rippling muscles. He spread her legs with his knee and lowered himself. She felt his hardness and quivered.

The soft mat of his chest hair felt warm against the swell of her breasts. His firm lips tantalized her as he eased himself into her. She held tightly to his lean hips and pulled him closer, wanting to consume him with her love. His massive frame covered her completely. He filled her with every thrust. She was in a world of sensuous torture. She knew he was holding back, being careful not to hurt her, yet wanting her to taste the sweetness of fulfillment. Swiftly it came—a thousand stars exploded in unison. She cried out her happiness, her love.

Afterward, they lay peacefully entwined in each other's arms, their demons at rest—at least for a time.

Chapter Twenty-nine
✦✦✦✦

AT HAWK'S INSISTENCE, and finally at peace, Mandy rested for two more days.

The following spring morning, Bright Feather, one of the women, gave Mandy a fringed leather dress and led her to the stream. The icy water felt wonderfully refreshing after her long confinement. She bathed, washed her hair, then let it hang loose to dry. She returned to the teepee and waited impatiently for Hawk to return.

He entered the lodge wearing clean buckskins and a broad smile.

"You make a fine-looking squaw," he teased. Then he scooped her into his arms and kissed her soundly. "There is something we haven't discussed, little one."

She looked up at him thoughtfully. "And just what might that be?"

"Our forthcoming wedding." His eyes twinkled merrily and a boyish grin appeared.

"Oh, Hawk!" She raised on tiptoes and

threw her arms around his neck in a big hug. "I thought you'd never ask."

"Is that a yes?"

"Of course it's a yes!" Hawk lifted her off the ground and whirled her around the teepee. "I love you," she whispered in his ear.

"Tonight you meet my family. Tomorrow I'll go to the trading post and get a wire off to your father and uncle. I know they'll be relieved to hear you're safe. I would have wired them sooner, but I wasn't quite sure . . ." His voice trailed off and she knew he was thinking of her illness.

"You're fit now," he said, "and nothing's going to spoil our happiness." He nuzzled her neck and buried his face in her hair.

"Are you sure your family will like me?" she asked, frowning a little at the thought.

"Like you? Why, you're practically a legend here in the mountains." The dark image of Swift Eagle pressing himself into her body flashed across his mind. He willed it away, but the fleeting grimace did not go unnoticed.

"What were you thinking just then? I've seen that look before."

"I was only wishing you were already my wife," he lied, determined not to hurt her. "That we didn't have to suffer through the ceremony."

"I don't believe you. You were thinking about Swift Eagle, weren't you?" She knew there must be gossip in the village, speculation about what had happened on her journey through the mountains with the renegade band.

His expression became grim. "I told you it is unimportant." As his temper flared, he slipped into stilted Cheyenne-English. "We will not discuss it again—now or ever!"

"We will discuss it! Right now! You don't own me yet, and even after we marry, I'll have my say!" She glowered at him.

He glowered back, then gave an exasperated sigh. "All right, just this once, but I mean it, Sam, never again."

She knew what it had cost him to concede to her wishes. "Swift Eagle didn't force himself on me," she told him.

"You mean you consented to bed him? You went willingly!" Outrage distorted his features. "Why are you telling me this? I don't want to hear another word!" He pushed her roughly aside and stormed toward the tiny opening. She caught him as he stooped to leave and pulled him back into the teepee, down onto a buffalo robe beside the entrance.

"Will you listen to me! I didn't consent to anything. Swift Eagle never asked. He never . . . nothing ever happened," she finished.

He tilted her face up, searching her eyes for the truth. "Swift Eagle never bedded you?"

"No."

He shook his head, then smiled at her ruefully. "No wonder they speak of you with such awe. Swift Eagle has paid you the highest compliment. He meant to take you to wife. I'm sorry I had to kill him."

"As am I. The other braves wanted to take me, but he wouldn't let them. They took the other woman instead." She saddened at the painful memory.

He hugged her to him. "Then it's done. We'll talk no more of the past."

She wouldn't let it rest. "No. There is one thing more." She held his gaze. She could feel the heat of his hand where it rested possessively on her thigh, even through the thick folds of the leather garment.

"It's about Mark Denton." She saw him wince ever so slightly, but he made no move to silence her. "He and I . . . we never . . ." she stammered, trying to find the words. "That night you passed us in the carriage. I went only as far as the door. I was jealous. I wanted to make you jealous, too. . . . There has never been another . . . only you. I have been your woman in my heart since that first time."

Hawk knew she spoke the truth and his heart soared. He kissed her deeply, intending only to show his love. But the spark of desire ignited between them. As they made love on the buffalo robe his heart was filled with joy.

That night at the campfire, Mandy stood anxiously as Hawk presented her to his family.

"This is my father, Strong Arrow, and my mother, Willow Wind." He introduced Mandy formally, using her Indian name, Wishana. Hawk translated Strong Arrow's response.

A high chief of the Cheyenne nation, Strong Arrow looked every inch the warrior. Tall and proud like his son, he betrayed no emotion. His straight nose and high cheekbones spoke of his heritage, and only the tiny sparkle in his black eyes told of the pride he felt in his son.

"My father says to tell you he has heard the stories of your bravery. He thinks your name, Wishana, is wisely chosen." Hawk squeezed her hand.

"Tell your father I thank him. Tell him I know he must be a fine man to have raised such a wise and courageous son." Hawk colored at her praise and she thought how much she loved him.

He repeated her words to his father, then his mother spoke, handing him a bundle. She was a small woman not much taller than Mandy. Her skin was brittle, veined, and translucent, but her mind was keen and her love for her son obvious in the expression on her withered face. Hawk stroked her leathery cheek affectionately, then turned back to Mandy.

"My mother says she will be proud to call you daughter. She hopes she lives to see many fine grandchildren."

It was Mandy's turn to blush.

Hawk winked at her and continued. "She

gives you this gift with her love." He handed her the bundle.

Mandy unfolded the bundle gently. It was a fringed garment of fine white leather. She held it in front of her. It was straight cut and open at the neck, and Mandy could see it would fit perfectly in the hips and fall gently to about the middle of her calf. Hawk explained to her the garment was made of elkskin tanned with a special mountain clay to give it the light color. In style, it was not unlike the heavy leather garment she wore, but this was much softer, feather-light, and painstakingly beaded in colorful designs of turquoise and white. A pair of matching beaded high-topped moccasins were handed to her next.

Tears touched Mandy's eyes at the old woman's generosity. "Tell Willow Wind my mother died many years ago. Since then, I have had an empty place in my heart. Tell her I am fortunate to find another I can love in her place."

Hawk translated, and the old woman beamed with pleasure.

Mandy, Hawk, Strong Arrow, and Willow Wind ate together that night. Mandy was taken to another teepee after they finished. Cheyenne custom dictated the pair would not see each other again until after the wedding. She was glad Hawk had been discreet in their lovemaking. The Cheyenne were very moral people. Only the fact that she was white and considered a captive allowed him to keep her in his lodge. Now that he had formally declared his intentions, strict Cheyenne codes would apply. Mandy gave Hawk a sorrowful look as she was led away. He appeared none too happy himself, but soon they would be man and wife—at least in the world of the Cheyenne.

Early in the evening two lonely nights later, Mandy bathed carefully at a private place in the stream. Bright Feather and Spotted Buffalo Woman attended her, and though she could not understand more than the few words Hawk taught her, it was easy to grasp the meaning of their embarrassed giggles.

Back in the teepee, Mandy dried her hair, then brushed it until it gleamed. She sat while the two Indian women plaited it into thick braids that hung down each side of her neck almost to her waist. Tiny blue cornflowers, their perfume mild but sweet, were expertly woven into the braids.

Mandy was getting more nervous by the minute. There was an air of anticipation in the camp, and the thudding of the drums matched the pounding of her heart. She took a deep breath to steady herself, slipped into the soft elkskin dress, then allowed the women to rub a tiny trace of red berry juice on her lips. Spotted Buffalo Woman placed a garland of the same pale blue flowers on top of

Mandy's head. She wasn't quite sure how she looked, but she certainly felt pretty.

The rhythm of the drums beat louder. Mandy could feel the vibrations in the ground beneath her feet. She felt a shiver of anticipation as the women lifted the flap of the teepee and beckoned her forward.

Since Mandy had no family in the camp, Spotted Buffalo Woman would do the honors of leading her, mounted on Hawk's big roan, to the lodge of her future father-in-law.

The spring air was brisk but not uncomfortable, and was scented heavily with the smell of pine. A huge fire crackled in the middle of the grassy flat, and warriors pounding skin-covered drums ringed the blaze. Spotted Buffalo Woman helped Mandy up on the horse and led the animal to Strong Arrow's lodge. As custom dictated, Mandy was ceremoniously carried into the lodge on a blanket. Once inside, she was ritually dressed again in another new beaded dress provided by the mother of the groom. Shawls, rings, bracelets, leggings, and moccasins were given to her as gifts.

Afterward, she was led outside. Her gaze searching, Mandy spotted a warrior, taller than the rest and fairer of skin, standing next to Strong Arrow, and recognized the man who would soon be her husband.

Seeing the pride and happiness on Hawk's handsome face, Mandy smiled brightly, her heart near bursting with pleasure. She was led to his side and the ritual was completed.

Strong Arrow provided the feast, though Hawk told her it was usually a gift from the family of the bride.

Finally, she and Hawk were able to escape. Hawk held her hand and looked at her with love in his eyes—and something more. A smile tugged at Mandy's lips as she recognized the heated look and thought of the nights they'd spent apart.

In silent agreement, they headed toward Hawk's lodge. As they got closer, Mandy saw garlands of flowers decorating the entrance. Inside, more flowers greeted them, the pallet of buffalo robes had been widened, and the smell of fresh pine needles rose from beneath. It looked deep and soft, and she blushed at the thought of the pleasures ahead.

Hawk gathered his tiny new wife in his arms and cradled her against him. In his bachelorhood he had never realized how much he longed for this feeling of completeness.

"I've waited all my life for this moment, though I never knew it until now."

"You make me so happy," she whispered.

He pulled something from a small leather pouch that hung at his waist and carefully opened his palm. "Lose this?"

"How did you . . . ?" She picked up the dainty jeweled kitten with its tiny diamond eyes.

"One of Swift Eagle's tribesmen said it belonged to the woman with the courage of a lion. He said Swift Eagle meant for you to have it back.''

She eyed the jeweled cat, then turned her gaze to Hawk. ''You did buy it for me, didn't you?''

''Yes,'' he whispered. ''Merry Christmas.'' All conversation ended as he lifted her chin and covered her mouth with a tender kiss. He could feel her tremble at his touch and groaned inwardly as he remembered a hundred lonely nights and the agony of these past few days, missing her small warm body lying beside him.

She looked beautiful tonight. The elkskin dress gently molded the rounded curves of her figure. Her upturned breasts seemed to heave in rhythm to the sensual beat of the drums. His forehead beaded with perspiration as the physical need for her swept through him. He parted her lips with his tongue and sought the berry-sweet depths of her mouth. He slipped an arm beneath her knees and carried her to the soft nest created for them on this special night.

Mandy felt his tenderness as he set her down. His lips left hers only for a moment as he undressed quickly and returned to her side. He pulled the soft leather dress smoothly over her head. When his lips closed over hers again, she felt the tiny flame of passion burst into a thousand fires. His hands were everywhere, soothing, kneading, stroking her heated flesh. His lips moved like embers from the hollow of her throat to the tips of her breasts, then parted to taste her nipples.

Everything about him aroused her. She loved the smell of him, rich with pine soap, and a smoky hint of the campfire. He tasted of wild gooseberries. His legs felt sinewy and hard as he moved to cover her with his muscular body. She tensed in anticipation as he parted her legs and she felt his male need. He entered her slowly, possessively, as if in this one moment he would brand her as his for all time. She knew theirs was a rare love, as timeless as the winds across the mountains.

Her passion began to build, his thrusts no longer gentle. Her body surged upward, meeting his again and again. Her nerves grew taut, her body rigid. She reached fulfillment, crying out in her happiness and love, and he followed her to release.

Their glistening bodies lay entwined upon the robes and they held each other tightly as if each were afraid to believe such good fortune.

Though the night was late, there were hours before dawn, and Hawk lifted her to the stars again and again.

Finally, just before dawn, they rested. Content in each other's arms at last, neither Mandy nor Hawk was willing to give thought to the problems that might lay ahead.

Chapter Thirty

✦ ✦ ✦ ✦ ✦

HAWK BENT OVER the sleeping figure nestled beside him. After their night of lovemaking, her hair lay softly disheveled across the wolfskin pillow; her lips still carried the blush of his kisses. He reached out a finger to stroke her cheek and saw the fringe of her lashes stir. She opened her eyes and smiled.

"How are you feeling this morning, Mrs. Langley?" he teased, kissing the tip of her nose playfully.

"I feel wonderful, Mr. Langley." She stretched her arms and yawned with great satisfaction, then paused, a tiny furrow creasing her brow. It did not go unnoticed.

He tilted her chin. "What was that for?"

"What was what for?" she said.

"You know very well what I'm talking about." He sat up, his mood darker at her evasive answer.

She sighed and squared her shoulders. "You don't miss a thing, do you?" she said, not expecting an answer. "It's just that, well, after last night, it's easy to think of myself as Black Hawk's squaw. I wasn't certain if you meant me to be Mrs. Langley as well." She glanced away from him, uncertain what she would see in his eyes.

"Is that all!" Hawk felt relieved. He nuzzled her shoulder and kissed the curve of her neck.

"I should be finished here by the end of the month. We can leave for Fort Laramie as soon as I'm through. I fully expect to endure the entire ritual again at the fort." He laughed, lowered his head, and kissed her soundly as proof of his intentions.

She beamed up at him. "In my heart I've been married to you since that first night, but still . . ."

"Still, you want all of Willow Wind's grandchildren to be recognized by your father and uncle as well?"

"Yes . . ." she agreed shyly.

"I would allow it to be no other way." He pulled her into his arms and wiped away her happy tears. "I love you so damn much." He pushed her into the thick robes and kissed her. After their endless hours of lovemaking he was sure he could not be aroused again this morning, but his body, with a will of its own, would not be denied. He cupped a full breast with his hand and teased the rosy crest. As sated as he knew she was, he could feel her body respond and chuckled proudly at his prowess.

They stayed in the wedding lodge for two full days. Food was brought to them—they left the teepee only to bathe and tend to their private needs.

By the third day they were ready, reluctantly, to face the outside world.

"We will be here only two or three more weeks," Hawk explained as they dressed. "Still, you will be expected to do your share of the daily work. It is the Cheyenne way."

"I'm honored to be accepted into your tribe. I look forward to helping."

He smiled at her proudly. "Willow Wind will instruct you. It may be difficult for you to understand without the language. Just do your best."

"What will you be doing?" she asked.

"More of what I came here to do. I have a meeting with Crazy Horse. As with my tribe, both he and Sitting Bull have so far evaded the reservation. Their villages are west of here, farther into the Buffalo Territories."

"But Crazy Horse is Sioux, not Cheyenne. Can you speak his language?"

"I speak several Indian tongues including Sioux, and sign is the language of all the plains." He smiled. "Whether he'll listen to what I have to say is another matter altogether, but I have to try. That's what I was sent here for."

"But I thought when Red Cloud signed the treaty—"

"All the tribes are disgruntled by the broken promises of the whites, especially Crazy Horse and Sitting Bull. The situation's heating up. The raid on the stage was just one example." He laced up his moccasins. "I'm afraid their struggle is futile—there are just too many whites—but I also understand why they have to fight." He sighed, experiencing the feeling of helplessness that had plagued him since he arrived.

"The bloodshed has been far too great already. If there's any way to avert more of it, I have to try."

She looked at him, an expression of worry mingled with pride creasing her brow. "I know you do. It's one of the reasons I love you so much. When will you be leaving?"

"Tomorrow morning. The sooner I go, the sooner I'll be back. Once I'm satisfied I've done all I can, we'll leave for the fort. . . . I hope you don't plan on a long visit."

"Just long enough to clear the air with my father, see Julia and Jason—and of course hold you to your word about the wedding."

He grinned broadly, pleased with her answer. She wove her arm through his, and they moved to the opening. Outside the air was clean and mild. Spring had come to the mountains—lupine bloomed, tiny snowflowers dotted the meadow, and there was a feeling of rebirth in every tree and leaf.

"I'm anxious to get back to Sacramento City," he confessed. "My ranch is in capable hands with Jesus Ramirez, but I'm anxious to take the reins myself. I can't wait for you to see it, Sam. From where the house sits, you can look for miles out across the San Joaquin Valley." He shifted uneasily, suddenly feeling a little shy. "It ought to be just about the perfect place to raise a family."

He looked away and Mandy's heart nearly burst with happiness. "Oh Hawk, I know I'll love it. I guess I've come to think of California as home."

He hugged her briefly, then led her toward his mother's teepee. He wished he didn't have to leave Sam, but the sooner he left, the sooner he would return.

The day passed far too swiftly. Their love-making that night was tender and gentle. They stayed awake late into the evening making plans for their return to Sacramento City and discussing the changes they would make in the ranch. It all seemed a perfect fantasy to Mandy—if only Hawk didn't have to leave at first light.

Inevitably the sun peeped through the stately pines. Its warming rays roused her as she rolled over to snuggle next to her sleeping husband. She found him already up and gone. She sprang to her feet, dressed, and headed outside. She found Hawk with two other braves: Running Wolf, whom she knew to be her husband's closest friend, and Lean Man, a brave of great reputation as a hunter and warrior.

All traces of the gentle man who had held her last night were gone. Dressed only in breechcloth, buckskin leggings and moccasins, and a heavy buffalo bone breastplate, he barked orders, his manner brusque. She could tell by his businesslike movements he had already immersed himself in his role. She watched him in silence as he prepared for his journey.

When he finished, he looked across the camp in her direction. His wide strides carried him swiftly to her side. She noticed the hard set of his jaw. Leaving pleased him no more than it did her. He walked with her back to the teepee, bent, and led her inside.

He looked at her regretfully. "I swore I'd never leave you again, but even as I said it, I knew it was a vow I couldn't keep." He rested his cheek on the top of her head.

"You must do what you can," Mandy said. "There's been too much death already. After being here with your people, I think I can understand about Swift Eagle and the stage. The Indians have been treated unfairly, but more killing won't solve the problem. I understand why you must go."

He lifted her chin and wiped away the tears on her cheeks. "I'll return as quickly as I can. You'll be safe here with my family. Never forget how much I love you."

She lifted a leather pouch on a rawhide thong from around her neck. "Your mother and I made this. She believes it holds powerful medicine and will ensure your safe return." She stood on tiptoe to place the pouch over Hawk's head, then threw her arms around his neck. "I love you so much."

He kissed her deeply, then ducked through the small opening and walked resignedly toward the horses. She watched him until he rode out of sight.

Chapter Thirty-one

✦✦✦✦✦

HAWK, RUNNING WOLF, and Lean Man rode into the Oglala Sioux village followed by dust, children, and barking dogs. A mottled gray sky streaked with wispy tendrils of white promised a spring shower. Crazy Horse was expecting them. He lifted his lodge flap and walked stoically out of his teepee.

Hawk dismounted and handed the braided reins of his tired horse to one of the eagerly awaiting youths. Running Wolf and Lean Man did the same.

"It is good to see you, my brother." Hawk spoke for all three Cheyenne. Each clasped arms with Crazy Horse in the traditional greeting. The chief motioned them toward his lodge and the crowd of curious onlookers parted. Hawk's gaze scanned the camp as he followed the others, taking in the hollow-cheeked women and the scrawny frames of the underfed children.

The winter had been a hard one on the People. After Red Cloud signed the treaty in November, they thought they would have new tools, weapons, blankets. Instead, they were forbidden to go near the trading posts. They were forced to make do with the articles they already had, and any man foolish enough to disobey the rules risked being shot. Game was scarce, and there was trouble with the whites over the horses.

"It has been too long since last we met, Black Hawk of the Cheyenne," Crazy Horse said as the group moved toward the lodge. He was heavily dressed in rawhide leggings, breechcloth, and leather shirt. An eagle feather, a sign of his bravery, hung from one of his thick black braids. A heavy buffalo bone breastplate, another sign of valor, clattered as he bent to enter the lodge. Once inside, Crazy Horse crossed sticks at the entrance, giving notice the men were not to be disturbed.

Brave Bear and Man Afraid, two lesser chiefs, waited within. More formalities were exchanged and the men seated themselves cross-legged around a small fire that warmed the teepee. The camp was high up in the mountains, so the warm spring sun had yet to complete the winter thaw. A teepee liner of soft leather, a means of insulation against the cold, was painted in bright designs that told stories of coup counted, horses stolen, and deeds of valor.

Crazy Horse filled a fine long-stemmed stone pipe and lit it. A long draw filled the room with the smell of red willow bark mixed with a little tobacco. As custom dictated, he passed the pipe to Hawk. In years Crazy Horse was younger than Hawk, but his taut lean features and the fine lines of responsibility around his hard eyes made him look older.

"It is good to be here, my brothers," Hawk began, after the ritual of the pipe was complete. He held the intense gaze of the razor-faced man across from him. "I have come at the request of the white chief, President Grant. He asks that I try to help you adjust to the new peace."

"Peace! What peace?" Man Afraid jumped to his feet and spat into the fire. "The whites have already begun breaking their word and killing our people!" He curled his thick lips and turned away.

Hawk took a deep breath. "The whites are often unfair in their demands, their laws often unjust when it comes to those whose skin is a different color. I did not come here to try to justify the broken promises of the white man." He turned his attention toward Crazy Horse. "I came to show you the folly of trying to win a war against them.

"All of our nations, all of our people together, could not fill one of their great cities. They are like the water that flows from the high mountains in springtime—a vast, never-ending stream. They can defeat us by the sheer force of their numbers."

"Every Indian brother is worth ten of the whites." Crazy Horse spoke the words many believed. His thin face reddened, and his voice rose.

"*Hoye!*" the others cried in the sign of agreement.

"Our brothers are strong. There is no question of that," Hawk said. "But there are a hundred times more whites than Indians."

"Then by our deaths we will win a victory in honor!" Crazy Horse said. "Without honor there is no life!" The firelight flickered across the hard, sharp features, making the lean redman appear even more foreboding than his words.

Hawk glanced from Crazy Horse to Lean Man and Running Wolf. It was easy to see why the Oglala warriors of the Sioux would follow their leader wherever he led. Even Hawk's own tribesmen were entranced with the power of the man's words. It was a difficult argument for any man of honor to counter.

"What you say is true," Hawk said. "But there are other lives we must consider—our women, our children, our children's children."

"Their lives would have no value without honor." Brave Bear spoke and Man Afraid nodded in agreement.

Crazy Horse moved toward the teepee opening. He called to one of the women to bring food and drink. The council was only beginning.

The debate continued for hours; the hours turned to days, and the days became a week. Each man's views were presented, argued against, and new ideas exchanged. By the end of the week, it was becoming apparent Hawk's mission would fail. The pride of the red man was too strong, his sense of honor too precious to concede. Hawk himself was not completely sure Crazy Horse was wrong, not completely convinced there weren't more truths than falsehoods to the chief's words. But the loss of human life was never something to be taken lightly.

It was with a heavy heart that Hawk swung onto the back of the big roan. Lean Man and Running Wolf were already mounted and ready. Hawk wished there was more hope for the Indian way of life. Then he thought of the white families as well as red who would bleed in the coming war and that, too, tore at his heart.

Only time would bring the answer. Time and people like himself who truly understood the red man's world. When he returned to California he would renew his efforts to make the whites—and the government—understand.

"I wish you a safe journey, my brothers," Crazy Horse said as the men departed. "Though our hearts may differ, I am certain I will be able to count on you if all else fails."

Hawk knew Crazy Horse was right. His Cheyenne tribesmen would stand with the Sioux if the whites continued their string of broken promises. He waved good-bye, nudged the big roan forward, and headed back toward his village. Lean Man and Running Wolf followed close behind.

*   *   *

Max Gutterman rubbed his hands together and allowed a crude smile to lift the narrow dry line of his lips. From where he sat behind a granite boulder, high atop the mountain, it was easy to keep an eye on the trail below. He'd been waiting impatiently for his quarry to finish his palaver with Crazy Horse and head back to the Cheyenne village.

As he watched the Indians ride down the path, it was easy to tell which was the man he hunted. He smiled again, pleased his vigil had paid off. He wasn't a man to let a score go unsettled, no matter what the cost. After robbing the gold shipment, he had plenty of money—and little besides revenge to while away his time.

He'd thought for a while the Ashton girl and the big Indian had drowned in the bay—just desserts for a job well done. Then he discovered they still lived.

He shifted his heavy frame on the cold earth, waiting for the men to ride out of sight. It was better this way, he thought—he always enjoyed the personal touch.

The men pushed hard that first day, each eager to return to the village now that the mission, even though unsuccessful, was complete. They crossed range after range of jagged mountains, dipped into deep forested valleys, and emerged again to repeat the cycle. Hawk remembered the hungry villagers he'd left behind. He pressed ahead, his thoughts unusually absent, his mind dwelling on his failure with Crazy Horse, how he could best help them in Sacramento City, and, more and more often, the woman who waited for him back in his teepee.

As they approached the last leg of their journey, the men began to relax. They were close to home; they'd done their best, and there would be a next time.

Feeling lighthearted at last, Hawk called playfully to his companions. "Running Wolf, I'll bet you that new bow of yours and your quiver against my steel knife that I can bag a deer for camp before you can!"

"Not a chance, Black Hawk. It is I who will be the first. My bow and quiver against your white man's knife."

"Done," Hawk agreed.

"What about me?" Lean Man cut in. "It is I who shall be the first! I will wager my horse against you both."

The men laughed heartily and the challenge was laid down. Lean Man circled right; Hawk circled left, and Running Wolf rode straight ahead. They hunted for more than an hour, then all three converged at the river, meaning to ford just above a set of rapids that crashed into a deep ravine. The rifle shot took them by surprise.

Hawk clasped his head as a lightning-sharp

flash of pain knocked him from his horse and into the swiftly moving current.

Lean Man leapt from his mount, grabbed the slender branch of a river willow, and leaned far out into the white water in a frantic effort to save his friend. Hawk, face down in the water, passed by out of reach.

Hawk rolled to his side, fighting to remain conscious as the stream swept him toward the rapids. He caught a glimpse of his two friends running wildly along the shoreline, but the current was moving faster than they. Rocks battered him, and his mind swirled close to darkness. He felt the rawhide tie of the medicine bag pull against his neck as it floated to the surface and lifted just above his head. He remembered Sam's words, "It holds good medicine and will ensure your safe return. I love you so much."

Arms leaden, only a second's breath left in his lungs, he grasped the bag as he crashed over the rocks and into the raging current in the ravine. He imagined Sam's beautiful face, her gold-green eyes, and his fingers tightened on the bag. He clutched the tiny bit of leather to his chest as he slipped into unconsciousness.

Chapter Thirty-two

✦✦✦✦

ANOTHER DAY GONE without news of her husband.

Mandy had mastered some of the Cheyenne ways, but the waiting seemed endless. Willow Wind, Bright Feather, and Spotted Buffalo Woman were her closest companions, but another woman, Dark Moon Rising, who spoke a little English, began to visit her teepee. She wondered why Hawk had not introduced her to one of the few people she could communicate with before he left but presumed he just forgot, his mind preoccupied with his mission.

Dark Moon was one of the most beautiful women Mandy had ever seen. She was several years older than Mandy, but her legs were long, slim, and firm, and her breasts full. But it was her eyes that set her apart: they were blue, pale blue, the color of the sky on a hot day.

"Dark Moon, how is it you happen to have such beautiful blue eyes?" Mandy asked one evening as she and the girl sat doing some beadwork. Mandy wanted to surprise Hawk with a pair of new moccasins. Willow Wind was helping her.

Dark Moon lifted her pale gaze. Her eyes turned icy. "My father was a white man, a dog soldier. That is how I learned to speak your language. My father taught my mother; my mother taught me." She glanced away, then went back to her beading.

Mandy could see she'd picked an unpleasant subject so she tried to lighten the conversation. "Where is your mother? Is she here in the camp?"

"My mother is dead. She was at Sand Creek, as I was. I escaped. She did not." The words came out in a hiss, and Mandy shivered at the memory. The Battle of Sand Creek, infamous throughout the West, had taken place a little over five years ago. The white version described a great victory against hundreds of savage warriors. The Indians told of a different battle—a defenseless village of squaws and children massacred and mutilated.

From their first meeting, Mandy had sensed something in Dark Moon's nature that made Mandy uneasy. Suddenly she wished the girl would leave. She thought about asking, but it seemed an unreasonable request. Instead she decided just to finish the task at hand. Besides, whatever else Dark Moon was thinking was hidden behind her thick dark lashes. Watching her surreptitiously, Mandy decided to make one last effort to communicate with the willowy girl.

"I'm sorry, Dark Moon. I know it must have been horrible for you. But all whites are not like those soldiers. Some care about what happens to the Indians—"

Scowling, Dark Moon leaped to her feet and spat into the coals of the fire. The fringe on her leather dress whooshed through the air with a violent rush. Without a reply she strode from the teepee, her long legs carrying her swiftly away. Stunned, Mandy felt more than a little shaken.

Three more days passed. Mandy was sure each day would bring Hawk's safe return. On the second morning of the third week since he'd left, she awoke to the sound of horses and scuffling people outside her teepee. She dressed quickly, certain that Hawk had returned. But instead of the happy sounds of laughter and welcome she expected, a low keening tortured the air.

The sound was unearthly. It started as a low wail and rose to a baleful moan. At first just the voice of one woman, but soon other women joined in. The first rays of sun brightened the horizon, casting just enough light to make out the frail shape of Willow Wind among the women lying almost prostrate on the ground. Mandy's heart began to pound. Her eyes searched the dawn for any sign of Hawk. Instead she saw Running Wolf walking toward her. He held his head high, but the lines of his face were tense, his eyes dim with fatigue. Just as he reached her, Dark Moon rushed between them.

"This is all your fault!" she said to Mandy. "Wherever the whites go, death follows! You have killed him as surely as if you fired

the bullet." Her pale eyes were hot with un-
shed tears as she turned and raced toward the
women on the ground. She threw herself
among them and took up the keening sound.

Mandy looked up at Running Wolf. Someone was dead? What could Dark Moon mean,
she killed him? Killed who? Her eyes continued
to search for Hawk, but she could not see him
among the others.

"Where is Hawk?" She turned to Running
Wolf in desperation. He might not understand
her language, but he would know she was
trying to find her husband.

He shook his head and spoke in Cheyenne,
trying to make her understand. She refused to
listen. Fear gnawed at her. Her insides coiled
into a knot as she read the sympathy on his
face. She started to run toward Lean Man, but
Running Wolf grabbed her arm and pulled her
up short.

He spoke a few words to Dark Moon, and
the girl rose from the ground.

"He says to tell you Hawk is dead. He
says to tell you he grieves for both of you.
The warrior Black Hawk was shot as he
crossed the river toward home. His body fell
into the current and was carried away. They
could not find him. But they are certain he is
dead."

Mandy closed her eyes. Her mind reeled
and she swayed against Running Wolf, barely
able to stand. What were they saying? Hawk
couldn't be dead. He'd promised to return.

They were going to the fort and then on to Sacramento City.

"It is your fault." Dark Moon was screaming at her. "Your fault. You and all the whites. He should have married me. I would not have let him go. It is all your fault."

Running Wolf stepped between them. He couldn't know what Dark Moon had said, but her tone was clear enough. He shoved her away, and then addressed Mandy, calling her Wishana. He said something in Cheyenne, then left her alone with her grief.

Mandy could barely breathe. How could Hawk leave her again? He said he would return. He never broke his word. Maybe this was all some horrible mistake. She wandered into the teepee and sank down on the buffalo-skin pallet.

A mistake. Please, God, let this be a mistake. But her eyes clouded with tears and an awful ache choked her throat. Running Wolf would never lie to her. No. There was no mistake. Her husband was dead. The ache in her throat became a sob. The thick buffalo robes beneath her dredged painful memories of the pleasures she and Hawk had shared. It had been a place of great happiness. Now it would be a place of great sorrow. She remembered his gentle lovemaking and promises of their future together; the home they would make in California and the family they would raise. Her fingers trembled as she touched the wolfskin pillow and memories of the handsome white warrior flooded her mind. How she would miss him. She closed her eyes and felt the heavy, hot tears roll down her cheeks. I love you. I have always loved you, and I always will, she thought. Her chest burned with great heaving gasps. She drowned in her sorrow as she imagined her husband drowning in the swirling depths of the river. Her grief became a tangible consuming force. She wondered if she could survive the agony of it.

For three days the village remained in mourning. Willow Wind came to her teepee each day, and the two women held each other in silent communication, sobbing out their grief.

For Mandy the tears would not end. Food nauseated her. She was unable to eat more than a few mouthfuls. The endless nights she spent lying awake on her lonely pallet. She felt weak and helpless. Her body was becoming thin and frail.

Finally, after days of grieving and with the help of the others, she began to regain some semblance of control. She decided the sooner she left the mountains, left the bittersweet memories, the sooner she might recover, if she ever recovered at all.

With the reluctant help of Dark Moon, she was able to make Running Wolf understand her wishes. By the middle of the second week after her husband's death, she was headed toward her home at the fort.

Chapter Thirty-three

✦✦✦✦✦

EVEN AFTER WEEKS at the fort, Mandy could not conquer her grief.

She ate little and her face looked sunken and pale. Both Julia and her father worried about her constantly. She tried to erase thoughts of the big man, but nothing could make her forget him. Maybe Dark Moon was right. She should never have let him go. She blamed herself for a while but knew in her heart he would have gone no matter what she said. He had been determined to help the people he loved.

Forcing herself to be thankful for the short but happy time she had had with him, Mandy finally gained some semblance of order in her life. And some good came from her return to the fort. She and her father became closer than they had been since her mother died. They talked for hours about things rarely spoken of before: her mother, his career, the promotion he had received during her absence—he was Major George Ashton now. Mandy could sense his pride in having achieved that rank, and it made her proud too.

Mrs. Evans had begun to play a prominent role in her father's life since Mandy left. Mandy noticed how he fidgeted, seemed just a bit uncomfortable, every time the plump, rosy-cheeked woman arrived at the door. Mandy hoped she would be able to encourage the gentle courtship.

The subject she and her father discussed most often was her future. That was the toughest topic of all. She couldn't seem to think ahead. Her mind would cloud with images of her husband: his boyish grin, his sandy hair, his soft brown eyes. Any plans she tried to make felt hollow without him. She knew she must do something constructive, but couldn't seem to find the will to start. In the back of her mind, Uncle William's job offer loomed the most promising. She loved California, had come to love Sacramento City and to consider it home, but the memories there were strong. Going there might make her feel worse.

Her father would have been happy to have her stay with him, but she was afraid that if she did, she might interfere in the budding romance between him and Mrs. Evans. Besides, after all she'd been through, just caring for her father could never be enough for her. She hoped time would bring the answer.

* * *

Four weeks after her arrival at the fort Mandy began to feel ill.

"Sam, honey, are you sure you're okay?" her father asked, taking up the nickname he had called her as a child. It made her feel closer to Hawk, and she liked it.

"Seems like you've been under the weather a little too much lately, and I don't like it." His gray eyes squinted with concern, the lines deepening in his weathered, suntanned face. She huddled beneath the quilt on her narrow bed. Her stomach rolled, and she closed her eyes, trying to control her nausea. Her father placed a damp cloth over her forehead.

"You look mighty peaked. I'm gonna have the surgeon stop by this afternoon," he said.

"I'm sure it's nothing, Papa, really I'm fine." A knock on the front door interrupted them.

"I'll get it. You just stay put." He crossed the short space to the door and moved into the parlor. Mandy could hear the soft murmur of voices and knew her cousin had arrived for her daily visit.

Julia burst into the room with her usual enthusiasm, and Mandy was always pleased to see her. She and Jason were doing splendidly, both very much in love.

"Are you sick again this morning?" Julia asked as she took the tiny room by storm. Her calico skirts swirled around her. Her chestnut hair swung wildly.

Mandy smiled weakly. "I'm sure it's nothing. I'll be fine by tomorrow."

Julia pursed her lips and scrutinized Mandy oddly.

"Uncle George, would you please excuse us? We women need to talk." She smiled up at him, and Mandy could see that in the past months Julia had softened her uncle's heart.

"Excuse me, ladies. I'll leave you for now. But I'm still sending the surgeon." He pulled the heavy door closed.

Mandy wet her lips and felt another wave of nausea. She swallowed hard, finally able to control it. "What's all this about?" she asked.

Julia sat on the edge of the bed and cradled Mandy's cold hand. "When you came back you told us you'd fallen in love with the man who took you to California. Travis . . . ?"

"Yes."

"You also told us the man had been killed. Neither your father nor I have had the heart to press you further on the subject." Julia held tightly to Mandy's hand and searched her eyes with a pair of the same green shade. "There is no easy way to say this, so I'll just come out with it. Is it possible you're . . . with child?"

Mandy bolted upright in the bed and stared at her cousin, speechless. *Of course! Why hadn't she thought of it?* The monthlies she'd missed she'd contributed to depression. But it wasn't depression at all! A small place in her heart knew she was going to have a child. She felt tears well in her eyes as she thought of the baby's father, but she pushed the sadness away.

"Yes! Oh, yes! I'm going to have a baby!" She threw her arms around Julia and hugged her tightly. For the first time in weeks, Mandy felt something besides numbness. She looked down at her stomach. It was still flat and firm, but soon . . . soon . . . I'll be round with child, and then I'll have some part of him again, she thought.

The look of dismay on her cousin's face brought her back to reality. "But what's the matter? This is the most wonderful news of my life!"

"Mandy, dear," her cousin said gently. "Don't you realize the babe will be a . . . will be a . . ." She couldn't bring herself to say the hateful word.

"But we were married!" Mandy exclaimed, reading her cousin's thoughts. "We were married in the Cheyenne village with Strong Arrow and Willow Wind and—I know I should have said something, and I planned to, but somehow I just couldn't bring myself to talk about it yet."

Julia hugged her, then set her away. "Well, I'm happy for you," she said. "We'll tell the rest of them to go straight to hell, if they don't like it!"

Mandy gasped at her cousin's language. Slowly, comprehension of her predicament dawned. The people at the fort wouldn't believe her story, and even if they did they wouldn't recognize an Indian wedding ceremony as legal. She hadn't even told her father. Maybe he wouldn't believe her either. Maybe he'd throw her—and her unborn child—out of the house. It was a long way back to California, and maybe even Uncle William would be unwilling to help her.

"Oh, Julia!" Mandy felt fresh tears welling. "I don't want our child to be called a bastard. He doesn't deserve it." She realized she had referred to the baby as a *he*, and that same tiny voice told her the child would be a boy.

Julia looked determined. "You once said, 'Don't worry, we'll think of something,' and we did. Jason and I are together because of you. My happiness is a result of your courage. I'll think of something. I promise you."

Mandy stopped crying and looked up at her cousin. There was a familiar set to her chin and something new—a fierce protective gleam in her eyes. Mandy relaxed a little and reached for a handkerchief. Nothing was going to spoil her happiness. She had something to live for again. She refused to let anything stand in the way of that.

"Thank you, Julia. I feel better already." Mandy dried her eyes. "But I think I better tell my father right away." She gave Julia a quick hug, sat up a little straighter on the bed, and cleared her throat.

Julia took a long look at her cousin as she left to retrieve her Uncle George. It was hard to believe the girl on the bed was the same reserved girl who left the fort last summer. This was a woman with a new inner confidence. She was definitely not the mousy little girl Julia had come to visit almost a year ago. Even the death of Mandy's husband—as Julia fully believed him to be—could not daunt her cousin's spirit. Mandy was ready to face life's challenges. Julia hoped her uncle was as ready to face this new crisis as her cousin appeared to be.

George Ashton entered the room quietly, closing the door behind him. He had fully expected to find his daughter prostrate with her illness; instead, she sat up on the bed beaming at him. He liked the way she looked since her return and regretted having made her hide her beauty for all those years. It had been foolish to think he could protect her by preventing her from living a normal life. Thank God she'd gone to California. He would always be indebted to his brother, William, for helping her make the painful transition to womanhood.

"Papa, please. Come sit here beside me." Mandy patted the edge of the bed. "There is something I have to tell you." She looked at her father. He had changed in the months since she left. He looked older and more fragile, yet somehow more content with his lot in life. She called him Papa again, as she'd done as a child before her mother died. She could tell it pleased him. He sat down beside her and kissed her gently on the cheek.

"What is it, honey? You look a little better, but the doc will be here shortly."

She looked up at him imploringly, willing him to understand. "Papa . . . I think I may know what is wrong." She'd spoken to him of her relationship with Hawk—told him of her love for the big man and of his death. Her father had comforted her—something she hadn't expected—and it had been the first step in bringing them together. Now what she was going to say might destroy that fragile bond.

"I know this will be difficult for you," she continued, summoning her courage, "but you have to try to understand."

He just blinked and stared at her with his sad gray eyes.

"I think I may be with child," she whispered softly. Then she raised her head proudly, staring into eyes now wide with surprise. "It's not what you're thinking. Travis and I were married in the Cheyenne village. I know I should have told you, and I planned to, when the time was right. If he'd lived we would have been remarried here as soon as we arrived. As it is," she looked away, blinking at the painful memories, "this child is the most precious gift he could have given me." A tear rolled down her cheek. "If you wish me to leave, I will understand."

His leathery arms surrounded her. He

pulled her close and pressed a tender kiss on the top of her head.

"Samantha, honey, I never knew how much you meant to me until I thought you were dead. Those days after the stage was found burned were agony. I realized how much time I'd wasted building a wall around you. I knew then the only person the wall kept out was me." He lifted her chin, his craggy features displaying his affection. "You've told me how much you loved this man Travis. You told me how he saved your life, not once but several times. I'll always be grateful to him for that. He brought you back to me. . . . I love you, honey, and the rest of 'em be damned!"

It was the most passionate speech he'd ever made, and she loved him for it. She hugged him, wiped away her tears, and smiled.

"Oh, Papa, I do love you. Thank you."

He cleared his throat and rose, not wanting her to see the moisture in his eyes. "I'll want the doc to take a look at you for sure now. We want that baby to be healthy, don't we? 'Bout time I had a grandchild around here." He talked with his back to her and moved toward the door, closing it softly behind him.

The next few days passed in a blur. Mandy's instincts were right. The child would be due in less than seven months. Her figure remained trim and firm, but she knew it would not be long before she would begin to show. She and Julia worked vigorously to come up with a believable story—so far to no avail. If only she'd told everyone when she'd first arrived that she was married. Of course it wasn't in her nature to lie, and if it weren't for the babe, she would do just as her cousin suggested—tell them all to go hang.

Life at the fort remained hectic. Julia and Jason carried on as blissful newlyweds, and Mandy felt content that her hardships had been well rewarded.

Standing inside the door of Washburn's Livery, Max Gutterman eyed the hoopla of activity about the fort. He'd arrived three days ago and spent his time watching the comings and goings of the officers and their ladies—one special lady in particular. He smiled thinly, remembering the gentle sway of her hips as she'd stepped out of Johnson's General Mercantile. He'd watched her all the way to her cottage, alongside a tall graying man. At first he'd felt jealous of the man, but after a few answers from old Ned Washburn he learned the man was the girl's father.

It hadn't taken him long to find her, once he'd set his mind to it. An Indian girl from the Cheyenne village seemed more than eager to point him in this direction. Now he could take his time, savor every moment of his triumph. He adjusted the patch over his eye and smiled through dry lips.

Chapter Thirty-four
✦✦✦✦

THE DAYS WERE getting warmer. Summer was on its way. Her nausea had ended, and Mandy decided if she was ever going to finish the spring cleaning she'd started, she'd better do it today. Her father had left at dawn on an overnight patrol.

Mandy tied an apron over her gingham dress, dragged out her broom, mop, pail, and soap, and readied herself for the work ahead. She began by sweeping out the front closet, thinking her life had fallen into at least a quiet routine. If it weren't for her lingering grief, she would have considered herself happy.

But the fact was Mandy missed Hawk terribly. Not an hour went by in which she didn't think of him. *Oh, Hawk*, she would grieve, *if only you could be here to see our child*. She regretted the misunderstandings that had kept them apart for so long. *If only we could have had more time together. Why did we squander those months so foolishly?*

Though she hid her grief from her friends and family, every minute by herself was an agony of loneliness. Today was no exception. She ached to feel her husband's arms around her, longed for the touch of his lips. Even as she cleaned and scrubbed, her mind replayed their wedding night, the passion she'd known in his arms.

"Well, well, well. Look who we have here."

It was a voice from her past—one that chilled her to the core. She whirled to meet the one-eyed gaze of her nightmares.

"You!" Standing just an arm's length away, the man leered at her and grinned. His overalls were dirty and his shirt stained beneath each arm. Just as she remembered, his features were heavy, his brows bushy and low. She threw down her broom and rushed for the door.

He blocked her way, agile though his frame was bulky. She tried to make a second dash, but his arm locked around her waist, and he hauled her against him, clamping a meaty palm over her mouth, muffling her scream. She struggled, tried to twist free; then, remembering her unborn child, she stilled herself, trying not to tremble against him.

Looking down, she saw a shiny silver blade held against her throat. It was wide and curved and crusted at the base with a rusty brown substance. She wondered fleetingly if it was someone's blood.

"Now that's better, little lady. Yes, sir. You and me is gonna be good friends." He chuckled, and his stale tobacco breath assaulted her.

"What do you want from me? How did you know I was here?" Her eyes searched the room for some means of escape. Her father would not be back until tomorrow night, and Julia had already paid her morning visit.

"Came to the fort just to see you. Been

watchin' you for three days. You're even per-
tier than I remembered." He caressed her
cheek with his rough hand. She shivered, re-
pulsed by his sweaty nearness.

"You and me, we got some unfinished business, as I recall."

"Please," she whispered, "leave me alone."

"I'll leave you alone, all right." No longer
amused, he grinned mirthlessly.

She felt the knife slice ever so slightly across
the line of her throat and a tiny trickle of blood
begin. Fear clutched at her. She was tortured
by a desire to scream, but feared he would kill
her.

"I'll leave you alone," he was saying, "just
like you and that big Indian left me alone out
there in the wilderness. Thought I was dead,
didn't you? But I fooled you. I fooled you
both." He dragged her toward the back of the
house. His fingers bit into the flesh at her
waist, and the bile rose in her throat. She felt
light-headed at his touch.

"I swore I'd get even with you," he said.
"Thought I got rid a both of you in the bay,
but your luck was too good. I followed the
Indian east. Took care a him real fine. Shot
him right in the head." His laughter rang low
and maniacal.

Mandy knew with certainty the man was
insane. Fear for her unborn child consumed
her. She swayed on her feet and only by force
of will remained standing.

Finally, what he was saying began to register. He was the man who killed her husband! She thought of Hawk lying dead, killed by this madman's bullet, and the thought filled her with rage. Now Gutterman was here to finish her—and their child. Her anger gave her courage and she stiffened in his grip. Her mind went over her options. They were limited, but if she was going to die, she would not make it easy for him. She tried to assess his mental stability. She was unsure whether telling him of her condition would stop him or make him worse.

"Please," she pleaded, stalling for time. "You've killed my husband. Isn't that enough?"

"I want what should have been mine before. You ain't no governor's daughter. You tricked me an' the boys. Now it's my turn!" He grabbed the front of her dress, and the fabric ripped as she fought to pull away. Struggling, she tried to scream, but his hand smothered the sound.

"Shut your mouth, you whoring bitch! You're just like Myra. I paid her back. Now it's your turn." He slapped her hard across the face, knocking her to the floor. Then he was on top of her his heavy weight pressing her against the hard pine floors. She could feel the steel blade forced just slightly into the soft flesh beneath her chin.

She struggled and tried to loose herself, deciding to play her final card. "Please . . . I'm with child."

For a moment he faltered, a hint of uncertainty in his eye, as if he were remembering another time, another place. Then he shook his head, bringing his thoughts back to the present.

"So much the better, little lady," he said. He grinned at her, enjoying her distress.

She closed her eyes and swallowed hard, feeling the point of the blade and a new trickle of blood.

"Let her go, Gutterman," instructed a menacing voice, deep and calm.

Mandy would have known that rich timbre anywhere. She couldn't move beneath the sergeant's heavy weight, but her searching gaze found the man she had missed so much. He stood in the doorway, his feet apart, his face a mask of controlled calm. Her heart pounded. A lump formed in her throat and tears touched her eyes. Her chest constricted as a fierce joy wrapped around her heart.

"You!" Gutterman cringed with fear, but kept the knife pressed firmly to her throat. "Stay away from me or I'll kill her."

"Like you tried to kill me?" Hawk circled his quarry, his moccasined feet padding softly. Buckskin fringe rippled as the muscles in his arms bunched.

"Don't come any closer. I'm warning you. I'll cut her deep—clean to the kid. I'll cut the brat right outa her belly." A note of desperation touched his voice.

Hawk looked down at his beautiful wife.

Her dark hair tumbled around her shoulders;
the torn bodice of her dress exposed a glimpse
of smooth skin. There was no swell to her
stomach, but he didn't doubt the truth of Gutterman's words. "Let her go, and you might
live," he threatened, continuing to move
closer.

Gutterman dragged Mandy to her feet. His
thick fingers bruised the soft flesh across her
ribs. He held the knife dangerously close to
her throat.

Mandy saw Hawk tense. "Please, my love,"
she cautioned. "What he said about the babe
is true."

Hawk ignored her, his mind fixed on a sin-
gular purpose. He was almost within reach of
his prey.

"Get back! You hear me!" Gutterman looked
wild-eyed, panic written on his face.

Mandy felt him move the knife away for
just a second. She opened her mouth and sank
her teeth down hard into the wrist that held
the blade. With a shriek of pain, Gutterman
knocked her to the floor. Her head thumped
the table; for a second she thought she might
black out.

Hawk was on top of Gutterman in an instant, wrenching the blade from his grasp and
grappling with the heavy man. They crashed
to the floor, fighting head to head, first one on
top, then the other. Gutterman held the knife
away from his throat, his strength nearly
matching Hawk's own. Twisting to the side

and using his body as a lever, Hawk changed tactics and caught Gutterman by surprise. Hawk rolled on top, pinned Gutterman beneath him, and forced the blade home, driving it deep into his heaving chest. Blood gurgled from the man's mouth as he gasped out a final breath.

Dazed, Mandy's mind blotted out the grisly scene. All she could see was the handsome face of her husband. Hawk rose swiftly and started toward her. Her senses reeled. Though he moved quickly, it was as if in slow motion. She noticed the thick sandy hair falling across his forehead, the soft brown velvet eyes looking at her lovingly just as she imagined each night before she fell asleep. For a moment she feared she might be dreaming. Then his powerful arms were around her, his tanned cheek pressed against hers.

"Oh, Sam . . . Sam. I thought I'd lost you again." Hawk felt a catch in his throat. "God, how I've missed you. It was agony not knowing if you were safe, wanting to get word to you, wanting to be with you again." He kissed her tenderly, trying to express the anguish he had suffered these past weeks. He lifted her gently and carried her into the parlor, cradling her in his arms as he sat down. His hand trembled slightly as he unintentionally brushed a full breast. "I've missed you so much."

There was so much to say, yet no words would come. Mandy clung to Hawk's neck.

She kissed his cheek, his eyes, then his mouth. "I love you," she whispered, the words choked by her tears.

She wrapped her arms tighter around him, and he tightened his hold on her. She forgot the lonely weeks, forgot the painful memories. There were a thousand questions to ask, but there would be time for that later.

Hawk used a piece of torn cloth to wipe the blood from beneath her chin. The wound was only superficial. He pressed his lips against her slim throat, then moved to her cheek. He only meant to show her his love, show her how much he cared, but when he covered her full ruby lips, white-hot flame ignited. He felt the soft warmth. His tongue found its way into her mouth. He stroked her breasts until she moaned, then he lowered his head and encircled a throbbing peak with his lips. He nibbled the hard bud, moved back to her mouth, and kissed her fully again.

Carrying her to her bedroom, he quickly shed his clothes, then undressed her. He sat beside her on the bed, barely able to fit on the narrow mattress, holding her, touching her, still trying to convince himself she was real.

Mandy forgot the carnage in the other room. Forgot the terror of only moments before. He was her world, and he had returned. It was like breathing after holding her breath to the point of suffocation. She couldn't get enough of him.

Suddenly he stopped. "What about the babe?"

She drew him back to her. "The babe is not due for many months yet. I'll not have to give you up for some time." She kissed him deeply, and he moved to cover her with his hard body. His muscular frame surrounded her. She trembled at the pressure of his corded thighs against her legs and the heat of his hard chest against her nipples. She could feel his maleness pressing against her. She reveled in anticipation, wanting him more then ever before. She ran her hands down his back and cupped a firm buttock just as he thrust into her. He groaned in pleasure at her touch.

Their mating was wild and passionate— weeks of anguish and despair released in one reckless coupling. Their passion seemed limitless. Though he'd been long without release, Hawk willed himself to endure until the last possible moment, wringing from their mating every ounce of pleasure for them both.

Mandy soared to mounting peaks of pleasure. When the sweet torture was no longer bearable, a warm rush and a thousand tiny pinpricks of ecstasy assaulted her body. She gasped and moaned her husband's name.

Hawk's body glistened with a fine sheen of sweat. A fever of sensation raced through his blood as he followed his wife to release. His pleasure was doubled by his abstinence and the warm glow of his love.

As they lay sated in each other's arms, reason returned, but neither was willing to move or speak. Hawk knew his wife needed reassurance that all of this was real, but the afternoon was passing swiftly. There would be much explaining ahead, and their time alone together, at least until after the wedding, would be limited.

Tracing the line of her cheek with his hand, he felt a second wave of desire surge through his veins. He smiled to himself at the power his tiny wife held over him.

"If I lie next to you much longer, I won't care who finds us here."

She smiled up at him lovingly. "I haven't the courage to move from your side. The thought of you more than two feet away is more than I can bear."

He kissed her soundly. "I may never let you leave the bedroom once we're in our own home. But right now I think we'd better have our talk. It's time I found the commander and explained what all this is about."

"Yes," she answered resignedly, not really caring about anything but holding her husband in her arms and loving the sound of the word *home* on his lips.

"I believe our late friend told you he shot me?" Hawk said.

"Yes," she replied weakly, feeling suddenly chilled by the thought.

"Well, the bullet just grazed me. It was the ride through the rapids that nearly killed me.

The creek was so rain-swollen, I was washed miles downstream."

He looked at her and smiled boyishly. "It was that little rawhide bag of yours that kept me going. I kept remembering your words. I managed to keep my head above water, though I knew my body was taking a pounding against the rocks. Just when it looked like I would make it, I must have hit my head. That's the last thing I remember until I woke up in a miner's hut two weeks later. Apparently, he dragged me out of the river, but I was pretty badly busted up. I had several broken ribs, some internal injuries, and then came down with pneumonia."

She clutched his hand, and her heart turned. "Are you all right now?" she asked, suddenly worried.

His mouth curved in the devilish smile she loved so well. "Did I seem all right?"

She felt hot blood rush to her cheeks at the memory of their passion and knew she wanted him again. She ran a hand along his hard chest and willed herself to listen.

"I tried to get him to bring you a message," he told her, "but he was working an illegal gold claim in the Black Hills, on the Dakota reservation. He wasn't about to leave." He entwined his fingers in her hair and absently kissed her shoulder.

"I'm just happy to have you safely returned to me," she whispered. As always between them, he sensed a sudden shift in her mood as she took a deep breath and glanced away.

"Is it Dark Moon you're thinking of?" he asked gently, wanting to clear the air.

"Yes."

"When I returned to the village they told me she'd been coming to see you. It's not difficult for me to imagine what she must have said. It's the reason I never took you to meet her."

"She said your death was my fault, that if you'd married her instead of me it wouldn't have happened. . . . Did you intend to marry her before I came along?"

Hawk ran a hand through his hair and sighed. "Before I left the village as a young man, I fancied myself in love with her. I considered marriage, but only when—and if—I returned."

A small cloud darkened Sam's eyes before he went on. "When I did come back, I was older, wiser. I could see the hatred and bitterness she felt for the whites. I realized I never loved her, but she had convinced herself she loved me. I knew by then my future lay not with the Indians, but with the whites. I didn't see her again until I returned to my village this last time."

"And how did you feel when you saw her again?" his wife persisted.

"Just as I had before. She is beautiful, but cold and hollow. By then she'd been married to Red Bear, but he divorced her. Her bitterness has ruined her life. Before I brought you into camp, she came to me, asked me to consider marriage. She offered herself to me—I refused. I knew by then there was only one woman for me. You had already captured my heart."

Mandy smiled with satisfaction. She curled her arms around his neck and ran her fingers through his thick sandy hair. She pulled his head down and kissed him tenderly. Whatever problems they had now, they would face together. After what they had suffered apart, nothing would be insurmountable. As long as they were together, their love gave them strength and courage beyond anything they would need.

She placed her husband's hand on her stomach. Their child grew within—proof of their love. The look of pride on his face was all Mandy needed to confirm the happiness they would share. Tears of gladness welled in her eyes as he covered her lips in a deep, loving kiss.

The End?

The end of a book is never really *the end* for a person who reads. He or she can always open another. And another.

Every page holds possibilities.

But millions of kids don't see them. Don't know they're there. Millions of kids can't read, or won't.

That's why there's RIF. Reading is Fundamental (RIF) is a national nonprofit program that works with thousands of community organizations to help young people discover the fun—and the importance—of reading.

RIF motivates kids so that they *want* to read. And RIF works directly with parents to help them encourage their children's reading. RIF gets books to children and children into books, so they grow up reading and become adults who can read. Adults like you.

For more information on how to start a RIF program in your neighborhood, or help your own child grow up reading, write to:

RIF
Dept. BK-1
Box 23444
Washington, D.C.
20026

Founded in 1966, RIF is a national nonprofit organization with local projects run by volunteers in every state of the union.

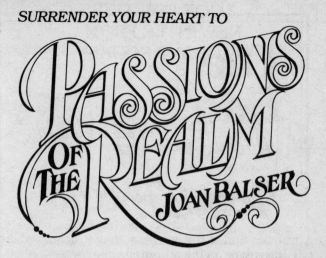

About the Author

Kat Martin, born in California's great central valley to early California pioneers, was raised close to stock and ranching. Her father, a member of the Professional Rodeo Cowboys Association, and her grandmother, whose leather riding skirt and cuff guards are among Kat's prize possessions, quietly influenced her appreciation of all things historical. After graduation from the University of California at Santa Barbara, Kat worked in public relations until travel beckoned. After three years on the East Coast, she returned to Bakersfield, where she resides with her husband, also a writer. Long an aficionado of Western art, Kat owned an art gallery and traveled to showings in the western states, collecting art and historical information from Texas through Montana, and including her home state of California. She and her husband enjoy packing into the High Sierras, hunting, fishing, snow skiing, and studying history. They collect historical memorabilia including firearms, western express company history, and antiques. Their travels have taken them along the trails of the pioneers, to Mexico, the Caribbean, Brazil, and Europe. Kat is a member of the Western Writers of America and the Romance Writers of America. Look for Kat's next novel, *Lady Jay*, to be published by Pageant Books in 1989.